A Small Matter of Importance

CLIVE RIDGWAY

www.cliveridgway.com

Copyright © 2024 Clive Ridgway
All rights reserved.

For my brother and sister.

ACKNOWLEDGEMENTS

My thanks go to those who read and gave me advice, suggestions and encouragement, namely Rémy, Lesley, Katy, Dave, Suzi, Mark, Sarah, Jenny and Phil.

Also, thanks go to my wife for her love, laughter, support, and encouragement — and for discovering little research books on dusty shelves.

Also by the same author

A River of Retribution

Humorous fantasy written under the name of Clive Mullis

Banker's Draft
Scooters Yard
Under Gornstock

www.cliveridgway.com

A dictionary of 18th-century London canting language used in this novel.

Affidavit men – Paid to give false witnesses in a Law Court.
Ark – Boat.
Bawdy house – Brothel.
Bene-cove – A good man.
Blackjack – Leather drinking vessel.
Blind-Harper – A beggar pretending to be blind.
Bottle headed – Without wit.
Bowsing-ken – Rough drinking establishment.
Bung- nippers – Cut purses.
Butter-boxes – Dutch.
By-blow – A bastard.
Captain-hackum – Bully, fighter.
Captain queer nabs – Poor, wretched.
Case – Warehouse, house.
Chink – Money.
Cloyers – Thieves, robbers, rogues.
Clunches – Awkward foolish men.
Clutter – Noisy talk.
Cock-sure – A forward confident character, maybe too big for his boots.
Codsheads – A stupid man.
Cove – A man.
Cracked – To break into a house etc.
Crew – Gang.
Cruisers – Beggars.
Cully – A male fool, whore fodder.

Dambers – Rascals.
Darkman's – Nighttime.
Dew-beaters – Boots.
Ding-boy – A rogue, a bully.
Divers – Pickpockets.
Dock – To copulate.
Downhills – Dice loaded to go low.
Doxy – Low whore.
Drab – Low whore.
Dry-boots – A close cunning sly fellow.
Filching – Stealing.
Filching cove – Thief.
Fire-priggers – Those stealing from buildings damaged by fire.
Foxed – Drunk.
Gages – Clay tobacco pipes supplied by the Inn.
Gentry cove – Rich man.
Green-heads – Innocent, a novice, inexperienced.
Grub-Street news – False information.
Huff – A bully.
Hushed – Murdered.
Jade – Whore.
Ken-miller – House breaker.
Kinchin-coves – Young children.
Lullaby cheats – Very young children.
Madge – A Homosexual.
Molly – A Homosexual.
Mother Abbess – Brothel owner/ manager. A Bawd.
Nanny-house – Brothel.
Nazie-cove – A drunkard.
Nunnery – Brothel.
Nutmegs – Testicles.
Peepers – Eyes.
Pot-valiant – Drunk.
Prigs – Thief, cheat.

Rum – Not good.
Rum-coves – Rogues, thieves etc.
Rum-culls – Rich fools.
Sapphie – A Lesbian
Shabaroon – Waster, poor man.
Shuffler – Sly, sneaky man.
Slubber-degullion – Slovenly, dirty, nasty fellow.
Snitch – Informant.
Squeaker – Young boy.
Stall whimper – A bastard.
Tats – False dice.
Tommie – A Lesbian, a boyish woman.
Tib – Young lass.
Tipping a stoter – Throwing a punch.
Uphills – Dice loaded to go high.
Whipster – A sharp man, clever, quick of mind.
Windy-fellows – Giddy men, men without sense.

CHAPTER 1

I stood on the ground securely, feet shoulder width apart and raised the pistol. Taking a few breaths to steady my arm and slow my heart I sighted along the barrel, finger curled around the trigger. I took another breath, this one slow and I could feel a calmness come upon me as I fixed my target, closing my left eye and concentrating intensely. I squeezed gently, putting a little pressure on the trigger and then the pistol sparked and cracked, spitting out the ball, the noise like a short clap of thunder. My arm jerked with the recoil, smoke billowed, the acrid smell seeping into my nostrils.

'Missed again,' announced Ned, failing to suppress the grin now forming on his face.

Hidden between the shrubs and trees in Upper St James' Park close to the waterworks, my home not far away in Jermyn Street, I aimed my pistol at a target; a small wooden board tied to a branch by two lengths of twine, the mound behind absorbing the shots that missed. Purchased just the day before from a reputable gunsmith, a Mr Freeman of St Martin's Lane, the pistol, a breechloader with a tip-up barrel, used ready-made self-priming cartridges. Three shots a pistol without reloading. I bought a pair, both barrels rifled for increased accuracy, somewhat belying my performance thus far.

'I will move closer, Ned. Mr Freeman said that it would take the head off a rabbit at sixty yards.' Unfortunately, I could not blame the weather as it was a bright day, full of sunshine and warmth.

'That may be so, sir, depending on the skill of the man holding the weapon, of course.' He looked at me again with that smirk still fixed on his face.

'Perhaps if you would care to be my target I might find a little more incentive, Ned,' I replied, only half joking as his observations regarding my ability to shoot the pistol were beginning to grate.

'I would happily oblige, sir, however, I would have to keep walking back to reload the weapon.'

I ignored his sarcasm. 'No, I think I have it now.' I pulled on the trigger guard and released the catch, allowing the barrel to rise so that I could remove the steel cartridges. 'There,' I said, holding out my hand, the three empty containers nestling in my palm.

He snatched them out of my hand petulantly and handed me three fresh charges. I reloaded, snapped the barrel back into position then renewed the priming chamber. I put my hand on the hammer to cock it in readiness then I hesitated, grinned and handed the pistol to Ned. 'You try,' I said, confident that he would have no more success than I had.

'And what will I receive should I be successful?' he asked, taking hold of the weapon and stroking it lovingly.

'I will pay for our refreshment at the Crown and Sceptre.'

'Grapes serves better ale,' he countered.

'Yes and the Anchor serves better food but the Crown is closer and I am already thirsty. Besides, should I prevail then you can have the honour of paying.'

Ned snapped his head around. 'What?'

'I think it a fair wager. We will advance five yards at a time. Two consecutive shots on target wins, removing the chance of a lucky shot.'

He cast me a brief glance of a distrustful nature and then fixed his features into one of determination. We stood about eighty yards from the target having begun at one hundred. So far I had yet to hit, coming close once or twice judging by the little puffs of earth thrown up behind by my errant shots.

I felt a little unease as Ned took aim knowing that he had ability. I watched tentatively as the pressure on the trigger increased. The pistol discharged and I admit to feeling pleased that the target stayed still, the splatter of earth indicating a wider shot than mine.

Pursing his lips, he cast me a glance, then looked at the pistol for a moment before reluctantly handing it back. I grinned as I stood in his former position and took aim again, just as a fit of coughing erupted.

'Sorry, sir. A fly or summat took me in the throat,' he explained, as I lowered my arm.

'Really?' I asked, turning my head towards him.

'Truly, sir,' he replied, clearing the phlegm. 'Won't happen again.'

I turned back and felt a grin on my face as I took aim again, expecting the next intrusion into my concentration. It came with a sniff just a few inches from my ear.

'That will cost you, Ned,' I said, keeping my arm steady as I pulled the trigger.

'Unlucky, sir.' The relief evident in the tone of his voice.

'If it were a big plump bird you would've had it there.'

I did not deign to reply, instead, knowing I had one shot left, I advanced five yards. Ned continued to drone on, pontificating on the art of target shooting and the quirks of the various weapons he had handled. Without thought and with his voice blending into the background noise of birds and beasts I raised my arm, aimed, fired and the target jerked and spun, spitting splinters of tiny pieces of wood into the air.

Suppressing my glee at a successful shot I just unloaded the pistol and put my hand out with the empty cartridges, expecting him to replenish me with new ones. I waited, still staring ahead with my hand out and I waited some more until eventually, and with great reluctance, he delved into the pouch at his waist and produced the fresh ones, grunting and muttering beneath his breath.

'You seem a little melancholy, Ned,' I observed, reloading the weapon.

'Not in the least, sir, just amazed at your good fortune, so much so that I'm at a loss for words.'

'Not good fortune, Ned; skill at arms,' I replied, taking aim.

I fired and the target jumped and jerked again, spinning on its tethers, rubbing salt into his delicate wounds.

He coughed, sniffed loudly then rubbed his nose, his mouth twitching in annoyance. He held out his hand. 'Not done yet, sir. It be my turn now.'

I handed the pistol over with a light heart, already anticipating the repast now due to me. 'Miss with this and you will have to dig deep into your purse.'

'You ain't won yet, sir,' he replied, licking his lips. 'Two shots will make it even.'

His first shot hit, taking a large splinter off the bottom left of the target and he barked a laugh at his success, shooting me a triumphant look. He took his time with the second and I could see his arm begin to waver. He should have lowered the weapon to begin again, holding on for far too long. I saw his arm twitch and the pistol discharged, the puff of soil indicating the errant trajectory — he had indeed missed.

'Well, Ned,' I began, with him frowning in disappointment. 'This is a thirsty endeavour and I must admit that I am fair parched in the throat.'

'I thought you might be, considering it'll be my chink that pays for it.'

I slapped him hard on the back. 'Come on, you can take it all back home and then join me in the Crown to toast my success. I will allow you to clean the pistol later. Now hurry or I might drink the place dry.'

We parted company as we left the park, Ned stepping quickly into Jermyn Street. I did not want to enter the inn with pistol, cartridges and powder in my possession; it would be all too easy for an accident to happen with all the bare flames around, besides the general risk of thievery.

I watched Ned for a moment before heading for the Crown, his short brown hair bobbing as he stepped jauntily along, his wig stuffed into a pocket. We were of the same age, though he lacked an inch or so of my height but made up for that with his solid build and fierce countenance. Despite his outwardly grumpy demeanour I employed him as a footman, he also acting as assistant in my role of apprehending felons, a private endeavour to keep my mind active. He excelled as an assistant though only occasionally reached those heights as a footman. Together with Mary, my housekeeper of about forty years of age, a petite attractive woman, brown-haired with some strands turning to grey and Jane, the maid, a pretty girl of sixteen years who had long hair, the colour of ripened-straw, Ned completed my household.

My fortunate circumstances meant that I had a private means of support, being a Gentleman with an allowance that allowed me to live any kind of life I chose, my father now being one of the richest men in England following the crash of the South Sea Bubble some years before. I would one day inherit being an only child. Once, I studied law with my friend, Barty and quickly became bored with the monotony of it all, so I decided to chase felons for both the reward and the excitement.

I found a table at the back of the inn, most others already occupied, where I could lean against the wall and observe the comings and goings of the customers. Despite the daylight outside, the small grubby windows prevented adequate illumination so the innkeeper had scattered a few candles about. Smoke hung heavy in the air as did the aroma of unwashed bodies and stale beer. A pot-girl took my order and I settled back to wait for Ned to arrive, indulging myself by pressing a little tobacco into my pipe and lighting it with a taper from a candle.

My ale arrived with another for Ned, brought by the pretty pot-girl with a few unruly strands of dark-brown hair peeking out flirtatiously from beneath her cap. At fifteen, she had already become worldly-wise and totally off limits, her chastity fiercely protected by her father, the Innkeeper.

Lily placed the ale upon the table and smiled at me again. 'You eating, Mr Hopgood?' she enquired, straightening up.

'Maybe,' I replied. 'What have you got to tempt me, apart from your good self, that is?'

She laughed and I received the smile again, her eyes creasing up in mirth at my not-so-subtle attempt at wit. 'An' you a gennulman of refinement too, sir. I must be well turned out today to receive such a compliment from the likes of you. However, the only thing warm and moist you're likely to have is a game pie or a bowl of pottage, though there is a cold collation if that takes your fancy.'

'Ah, Lily, you know too well how to wound a man,' I replied, playing along by holding my hand to my chest in dejection and giving her a wink. 'In that case, I'll just have to indulge in the game pie and as Ned will be along shortly, you can bring him one too.'

Another smile and she spun around, coyly looking over her shoulder, her skirts bunching against her ankles before moving away.

I felt myself grin for a moment and then I turned my head and began to indulge in one of my favourite pastimes when alone in an inn. I watched the people, not overtly as if to cause offence, just subtly, speculating as to their purposes and hazard a guess to their personalities.

Some of the people I knew so I turned my attention to those I did not. Just across from me sat three men, all hunched forward, their pots protected by their arms with their elbows on the table. The three passed a pair of dice between them, checking the roll and speaking softly. I could see no coins on the table so surmised that they had tampered with the tats to make them either a downhill or an uphill and wished to confirm that the tampering had worked before partaking of a game at another venue. Next to them, two old men sat in conversation wearing old-fashioned wigs and puffing gages, clay pipes furnished by the inn. They wore good quality clothes, although a little jaded now and I got the impression that they could both be in trade, maybe the owners of a shop or a small business. They jabbed the stems of their pipes into the air as they talked as if making a point on the issue they discussed.

I cast my eyes over to a couple, an old man wearing tired clothes sporting a battered old wide-brimmed beaver hat; he too smoked a gage. A woman sat next to him, matronly in appearance wearing a dress that had seen better days. A dirty cap adorned her head and every now and again she took hold of the man's pipe and put it to her mouth, inhaling deeply and then passing it back. She drank ale from her own pot and the pair sat, neither saying a word to each other. A married couple, I surmised.

Over on the far side a small group of five men, perhaps in their twenties, all looking sullen as if a melancholy had come upon them. Their clothing looked dirty and unkempt; those that wore wigs sported old crude ones, probably from the two-penny dips where you paid your money and took the first one you picked. They did not drink with enthusiasm, taking small sips to prolong the time before ordering another. I took them to be out of work, eking out their pennies for an hour or so of imbibing. Next to these sat another group, these of middling age with the appearance of being Gentlemen of Leisure with wealth enough to indulge without fear to the future. They laughed and ribbed each other, being loud and slightly annoying, especially to the young sullen men at the adjoining table who occasionally cast malicious glares in their direction.

I began to speculate on the next table, possibly a father and son as they looked so alike, when the door opened and Ned came in. He spied me and walked quickly over, pausing briefly when he noticed the sullen young men and briefly conversed with them. He patted the back of one before joining me. He sat down and took a slow drink from the pot in front of him.

'Lost 'is mum yesterday, poor sod. Dad be heartbroken,' he explained, flicking his head in the direction of the young men. 'Bloody flux took 'er. From what I hear his friends wanted to take him out of it for a while, though there's no joy in their drinking.'

'Ah, I didn't know.'

'No reason why you would, sir. Works in the stables down the way; lives in a cottage in Catherine Wheel Yard.'

'I've been to those stables, I cannot remember seeing him,' I said, thinking hard.

'You normally send me fer a horse; you ain't been there for over a year, from my recollection that is.'

'Oh, really? You may be right, Ned. Time seems to go so fast.'

'Indeed, sir.'

He took another pull on his ale then reached into his pocket and passed a note over towards me. 'Mary said this came for you earlier. Lad from the Bear fetched it over.'

He meant the Brown Bear in Bow Street opposite the

magistrates, where those found innocent of the charges made against them celebrated their good fortune with family and friends. Alternatively, the friends and family of those found guilty drowned their sorrows and bemoaned their misfortune. It also catered to those in my trade, thief-takers, and the innkeeper, for a small charge, would forward messages as and when he received them.

I took a sip of my ale and then unfolded the note, smoothing it out with my hand on the table. I raised my eyes to look at Ned as he gazed around the inn and then lowered them again as I picked it up and began to read the neat, balanced and fluid script.

The writer of the note requested my assistance to find the perpetrators of a murder. The victim, a Dutch merchant, had received a wound to his chest. The constable attending appeared dismissive, holding out little hope that he would find a resolution; the victim being of a foreign persuasion. Unfortunately, an all-too-common reaction when it concerned overseas people, unless they had status or a great deal of money to grease the wheels. A Femke van Hoebeek of Basinghall Street had signed the note.

'We may have a task, Ned,' I said, lowering the note and tapping it with my finger.

'Really, sir? About time too, what is it?'

'The note says it is about a murder of a Dutchman.'

I watched as a small grin made its way onto his lips.

'I have some pies coming, so we'll eat up and then make our way.'

CHAPTER 2

We took a hackney, chancing that the jolting would not churn the meal in our stomachs over much. The traffic became a little heavy around St Paul's and Cheapside and for a time I thought to get out and walk the rest of the way, suddenly it all began to move again and shortly after we entered Basinghall Street.

The directions in the note bid us to make our way to the northern end, past Girdlers Hall and to look out for a green-painted door on the right just before Basinghall Court. We found it easily enough, alighted from our conveyance and paid our fare. The driver put a knuckle to his hat, a brief nod and then left us at the side of the road.

I looked up to the end of the street and could see London Wall, the great encirclement of London City, built during the Roman occupation all those centuries ago. Much of it had now been demolished just leaving some sections still intact, like the part I could see running from Cripplegate just to the west along to Moorgate in the east.

The house in front of us with the green door rose to five storeys high with a basement below, the door itself had a porch supported by two Doric columns of stone — a house for the wealthy.

Ned stepped up to rattle the doorknocker and then we

waited, watching a few ladies walking by. I smiled at the women, bidding them all a good day and received a shy smile from one or two in reply. Presently the door opened and a stern-looking woman of middling age, her hair turning grey and wearing a plain grey dress with a white apron, regarded us silently, an inquisitive cast to her eyes.

'Richard Hopgood,' I announced. 'Here at the request of Femke van Hoebeek. This is Mr Edward Tripp, my assistant,' I added, pointing towards Ned.

The woman nodded then opened the door wide to allow us entry; clearly she had been informed of our probable visitation.

We stepped into a comfortable-looking hall, floored with polished wood, a table and a chair to the side, the walls sporting a few paintings of landscapes. Ned and I removed our hats and held them loosely. Ahead, a staircase led up and the woman indicated that we should follow as she began to climb. She led us to a door on the first floor, knocked and waited until the incumbent called out.

'Yes?'

'Mr Hopgood to see you, ma'am,' replied the maid beside me.

'Show him in,' I heard in response.

The maid opened the door and ushered us inside.

'Mr Hopgood, thank you for calling,' said the woman, already standing and waiting to receive me.

I gave a polite bow of my head. 'Femke van Hoebeek?' I asked, remembering not to smile, considering the circumstances.

She nodded and showed me to a chair, indicating that Ned

should sit too.

I took a moment to glance about the room: a comfortable drawing room with a turkey rug upon the floor, several upholstered chairs, two highly polished tables, a case with several books upon the shelves and an ornate clock sitting on a small side-table. The lady herself stood a little over five feet tall, slim build with light auburn hair piled upon her head. She had soft features, faintly lined and beneath her small nose, thin unsmiling lips. Her blue eyes seemed intelligent, shrewd and intense. I judged her to be in her early forties, a handsome-looking woman despite her downcast demeanour, dressed in a plain gown of dark green trimmed with white silk.

'Thank you for coming to see me, Mr Hopgood,' she began, sitting down herself. 'You have read my note so you have some idea of the task I wish you to undertake.'

'I do, er...Mrs?' I replied, tentatively.

'Miss, I am unmarried, Mr Hopgood.'

Her status surprised me as I certainly would not think she lacked suitors in the past. 'Then perhaps, Miss Van Hoebeek, you would be good enough to explain the circumstances in more detail so that I may judge how best I can help you.'

She nodded slowly and then looked at me intently. 'My brother, Pieter, was found two nights ago in his warehouse. He had been attacked and killed. The night guard found him when he returned.'

'Returned?'

'Yes. Pieter had sent him out, told him to get some food and ale, suggesting he took an hour or so as he wanted to do some work on his own.'

'What time was this?'

'An hour before midnight I believe.'

I nodded. 'Was that unusual, I mean to send the guard away?'

'It had happened occasionally, once or twice recently. Pieter liked a little solitude.'

I would save my questions regarding that for a little later, deciding not to interrupt her discourse by enquiring further. 'How was he found?' I asked instead.

'The guard came back and found the door ajar. He said that he had locked it as he left. When he returned he went in and saw Pieter sitting on some crates, in shadow, as the only lantern was on the desk. He thought Pieter was just resting there for a moment until he called out and got no reply. He stepped closer and found that my brother had been attacked; blood was all over his chest and breeches with drops on the floor beneath him. The guard ran out and called for assistance and several men came to his aid. A man called for the constable and the guard sent someone here, to me. I arrived to find Pieter as I described, dead, with a wound to his chest, the incision appearing to be from a knife. The constable came a little later, made a few enquiries in the vicinity, then said he did not hold out any hope of finding the perpetrator.

'I spoke yesterday to the alderman, William Baker of Winchester Street, who though sympathetic to my situation, said that without witnesses he could do little. One of the staff spoke to me as I left and gave me your name as one whom might be of assistance.' She looked at me, a grim smile on her lips.

'Where is this warehouse?' I asked.

'Not far, in Basinghall Court, just a short distance away.'

'Miss Van Hoebeek,' I began. 'You said in your note that you are Dutch but you speak English like a native.'

She nodded. 'I was born here; our family came with William when he took the throne. I speak both languages fluently. Does the fact that I am Dutch cause you a problem, Mr Hopgood?'

I shook my head. 'Not at all, it makes no difference where you come from; I am only curious as to your circumstances.'

'Then I hope your curiosity is now satisfied, sir.'

'As to your lineage, then yes I am, as to your brother's demise, then no. Tell me, you say he sometimes wished for solitude at the warehouse; what is his domestic situation, you have mentioned no wife?'

'Pieter lived here with me; he too was unmarried.'

'His age?'

'Forty-one; a year younger than me.'

'And the solitude?'

She sighed. 'Pieter put all his energy into his work. He took no wife as he did not wish for distractions.'

'And the work kept both of you?'

'Yes; I deal with the accounts, Pieter deals…no, dealt with everything else.' She sniffed and looked away suddenly towards the wall, wiping a tear from her eye. She turned back after a moment's reflection. 'He sometimes wished for time on his own, just an hour or so, so that he could gather his thoughts.'

I nodded as if to understand. 'What about enemies?' I asked, looking at her closely. 'Were there people who wished

Pieter harm?'

She shook her head. 'No, not as far as I know. Oh, there was the normal rancour that occurred between fellow merchants but nothing that would indicate this extreme recourse to action.'

I did not notice any of the signs of falsehood in that; I hoped Ned had been keeping a close eye on her too, in case I missed something. 'And the goods you deal with at the warehouse?'

'It is mostly cloth and pottery, a few other things too if we can get a good price and feel we could get a good return.'

'Like?'

'Like wine and spirits, occasionally coffee and tea, furniture; even tulip bulbs, though the price for them is now not much above other flowering plants.'

I gave a laconic smile as even I had heard that in the early part of the last century a madness descended where the simple tulip bulb demanded a price higher than gold. Unsurprisingly that market collapsed, since then, the Dutch always hoped that the high price would one day return.

Beside me, Ned coughed and straightened himself up. 'Please excuse me, Miss Van Hoebeek, did your brother frequent any places, I mean coffee houses, taverns and the like? Did he gamble at all? How about the company of ladies?'

'Mr Tripp,' she began, shooting him a fierce glance. 'My brother was abstemious in all those respects. A good man of impeccable virtue, a member of our church and concerned only with his work and helping the needy of our community. A stalwart, Mr Tripp, a righteous man with high morals,' she replied, indignantly.

'I apologise,' returned Ned, holding up his hands.

'I am sorry you take offence,' I said, interjecting. 'But we have to ask these questions if we are to come to a satisfactory conclusion,' I added, trying to be reassuring.

'I understand, Mr Hopgood,' she replied, sighing heavily. 'It does pain me greatly to be discussing my brother in this way. However, I do now recall that he occasionally visited a coffee house in Birchin Lane; Cole's, I do believe.'

I smiled. 'Thank you, that is most useful.'

She nodded as if to herself, indicating that we had come to the end of the interview. 'Would you be prepared to look into the circumstances of my brother's death, Mr Hopgood?'

I did not need to think too long, elements about it I found interesting. 'Of course I will, but first we need to discuss the monetary arrangements.'

'And they are?'

'Fifty guineas for a successful outcome, twenty if I fail to find those responsible, plus any disbursements I may have to make. Should there be any large costs involved then I would seek your approval first.'

'Very good, that would be acceptable,' she said, without a pause.

I found that a little odd as most people took a few moments to think it through first before agreeing. 'I would need ten guineas to begin, in advance of course.'

'Very well,' she said, standing up and moving over to a cupboard. She opened a drawer and rummaged inside, bringing out the required sum and handing it over.

'Thank you,' I said, as I accepted the money. 'Tell me, this church; I take it you mean the Dutch Church in Austin Fryers?'

'I do, Mr Hopgood. The Church of the Temple of the Lord Jesus, if you please.'

'I apologise,' I replied, giving a slight bow of the head. Like many others, I knew the place only as "The Dutch Church" and always will do. 'And that is where I will find Pieter? I do need to see him, to view his injuries.'

'It is; do you really need to disturb his rest?'

'I am afraid it is necessary.'

She sighed and thought for a moment. 'Very well. In that case you may proceed. I will give you a note indicating my permission.'

'And the warehouse, would you allow us access to that as well?'

She nodded. 'Indeed, I will give you a note for that too.'

She took a few moments to write the notes and then handed them over. 'I will expect swift progress. Pieter will rest much easier with his assailant found and punished.'

'I promise I will do my best, and of course, I will keep you informed as and when I can.'

She nodded, holding her hands tightly clasped in front of her and I could see the knuckles whiten.

'We will set to the task right away,' I said, giving her a nod.

'Thank you, my maid will show you out. Good day to you.'

I did not expect the perfunctory dismissal; it gave me a strange feeling as if I had missed something. Had she told me everything?

CHAPTER 3

We stepped out of the house onto the street and I glanced up as we began to walk. I saw her outline framed at the window where we spoke, just watching and when she saw me looking she stepped back away from sight. I gave a rueful grin to the air.

'What do you think, Ned?' I asked, as we headed up towards Basinghall Court.

'Bit strange, sir. It were like she didn't want us to be there.'

'Yes, I had that feeling too, at the end. She seemed to change when you asked about her brother's interests outside of his work. I'm wondering if Pieter van Hoebeek had a secret side to his life.'

'You think she's keeping something from us?'

'Possibly; she would not be the first to keep things hidden. It will be up to us to find out.'

'You can always refuse to help her.'

'I could but I am puzzled and I do not like to be puzzled, if truth be told. Let us find out what we can, she has engaged our services so we will proceed as we would with any other client.'

'As you will, sir,' replied Ned, a disheartening tone to his voice, as though he had already lost interest.

'You can always return home and assist Mary in the house,

you know, Ned. I can just as well investigate this on my own,' I said, knowing how he loathed being at Mary's beck and call.

'No, no need for that; mind those pistols still need to be cleaned.' I saw his eyes widen as he realised his mistake. 'Thought I'd do them later when we return, no haste needed there. Besides, you would not go as far or so fast without me to assist.'

He had a point there. I relied on his street sense and he knew he had the advantage over me when it came to digging around in the rougher parts of London, having been brought up in the slums. I relied on him to provide me with alternative opinions too or even confirming my own. One thing he did not do was pander to me; he would tell me straight what he thought, even if it went against my own judgement. I grinned and stared straight ahead, letting him think that I may be pondering upon the decision.

We turned right into the Court and walked along. In this part houses lined the road; although not as fine as those in Basinghall Street they were still of a standard to house people of means. We passed a baker's and a shop selling everyday necessities, then just before the corner where the Court turned left to go towards the London Wall, a lane led between two storehouses into a cobbled yard. We took the turn and saw a small stable to the left and more storehouses of wooden construction in front of us and to the right, two storeys high with big wide doors leading into them.

'I believe this to be the warehouse, Ned. It seems to be a little lacking in activity.'

'It does, sir, you would've thought it would be bustling.'

'You would, however, maybe the demise of the master has

rendered the business stagnant.'

As I said that I heard a noise to my left and then the stable door opened. A man came out pushing a handcart full of horse-muck and straw, saw us standing there, hesitated a little and then continued to push the cart over to the far side. Once he had placed it to his satisfaction he walked towards us.

'You wishing to place an order for goods, sirs?' he asked, brushing his hands on his breeches.

I shook my head. 'No, we are here at the request of Femke van Hoebeek. This is the family warehouse?'

'It is, sir; though presently we are without a master.'

'So I understand which is why we are here. Miss Van Hoebeek has requested we look into the circumstances regarding the death of her brother.'

He nodded solemnly. 'It is indeed a sad time for us all.'

'It must be, and you are?'

'Martijn Thyssen. Overseer.'

I regarded the man, probably in his late twenties, fair-haired with blue eyes. He dressed in rough working clothes of torn breeches with an old shirt under a leather waistcoat, wearing battered leather boots on his feet. He scratched his wig-less head.

'I am Richard Hopgood and this is Edward Tripp. I have a note here allowing us access and to speak to the workers.'

He took the note, regarded it then shot me a look and handed it back. 'What do you wish to know?' he asked, looking me in the eye — a little cock-sure I thought.

'Firstly, I would like to see where your guard found your master.'

He nodded. 'Then follow me, sirs,' he said, turning and walking back towards the cart. A single door just to the right of the cart gave access into the warehouse; he opened it, and then led us inside into a large open space with boxes and crates stacked here and there, bales of tea and small packets of tobacco. I could see a desk with a chair positioned against the left-hand wall next to an opening leading into another part of the warehouse.

'He found him there, sir,' he said, pointing to some crates next to the far wall over on the right. 'Sitting on that bottom crate and leaning slumped against those next to it.'

'You were the one that found him?'

'No, he hadn't been moved when I came in that morning.'

I walked over to look more keenly and noticed bloodstains on the box and on the floor beside it. I saw a bloody handprint on the side of the box he sat on, as if he had gripped in order to push himself up. 'Were there any signs of a struggle?' I asked.

He shook his head. 'None that I could see. Everything appeared normal when I arrived, apart from our master, of course.'

'Look at the floor, Ned, see if you can see anything amiss,' I said, stepping back and looking around. 'What of Pieter van Hoebeek, what was he like as a master?' I asked Martijn, turning my head to look at him.

He shrugged his shoulders. 'Good enough, fair enough, I suppose — considering.'

'Considering what?'

'Just that he expected me to run the business when he went away, without any extra pay for the work.'

I inwardly shrugged my shoulders; that did not sound unreasonable. 'Did he go away often?'

'Often enough.'

'Where did he go?'

'I don't know, he just said that he would be away for a time. A day or so sometimes.'

I suspected that Martijn resented having to shoulder the responsibility, even for a short time. 'Did his sister not take charge?'

'No, she would leave it all to me.'

'She must trust you then,'

'I know the business so, yes—'

'Sir,' said Ned from behind me, interrupting. I turned and saw him on his haunches, looking at the floor. 'There's a little blood here, or what could be blood and another spot there.' He pointed to a spot directly in line from where he crouched to the crate where the body had been found.

I stepped over to Ned and looked. 'It certainly appears to be blood,' I agreed. 'Could it be that he was attacked here and then staggered over to the crate?'

'That would be my assumption,' said Ned, standing up, his knees creaking with the effort.

I turned back to Martijn. 'Did anyone find anything, do you know, something that should not be here?'

Martijn shook his head. 'Nothing as far as I know; you would have to speak with Lars to be certain.'

'Lars?'

'The night guard who found him.'

'And where will I find him?'

'He'll be here later, around eight of the clock.'

'Where does he lodge?'

Martijn hesitated and then shrugged his shoulders, meaning he had no wish to tell me.

'It is of no matter; I will call here later to speak with him. Be sure to tell him that.'

'I will, Mr Hopgood,' replied Martijn, with a nod of his head.

I walked around the warehouse, looking at the stored goods; a lot of pottery, bowls and plates, the new tea sets that had lately become fashionable made of porcelain. I could see glassware displayed, reams of cloth, bottles of beer, wine, brandy and geneva, tobacco, tea, coffee and more reams of cloth. Other goods, contained in boxes and crates scattered about gave no clue to their contents; seemingly, there appeared to be no lack of products to sell. I looked at the desk: paperwork, invoices, customs notes, writing quills, ink and a lantern.

I returned to Martijn. 'Did you notice any sign that the assailant forced an entry?'

'I...I don't know if anyone checked.'

'In that case we will now. Ned, if you could, please.'

Ned ambled over to the doors, the ideal man for the task as he had expertise in getting into supposedly secure places, the expertise honed as a youth on the streets and reinforced through his association with me.

'Martijn, tell me more about Pieter,' I asked, as Ned began his scrutiny.

'In what way?'

'You must have known him some while if he entrusted you with the business. Did you not have conversation about things other than work?'

He made a face. 'In truth, very little. Our church community mainly. Sometimes he met other merchants in a coffee house or a tavern. Other times he would just go off for an hour or so and not say where; I suspect he had a woman somewhere, maybe even kept one, he had wealth enough and a man cannot live on work alone, can he?'

'A woman, you say? Do you know where?'

'I only suspect from his demeanour when he came back. He always seemed in a better mood.'

'Would his sister know?'

He laughed. 'I doubt it. Would you tell your sister something like that?'

'Maybe not,' I conceded.

Ned announced that he could discern no sign of any fresh damage that would indicate a forced entry just as a cart trundled into the yard.

'Back from the delivery; if there is nothing else, Mr Hopgood, we have more goods to get out,' said Martijn, walking over to the desk and picking up a sheet of paper.

'No, thank you and do not forget to tell this Lars that I intend to speak to him. Oh, yes, there is something else,' I said, touching my head as if I had forgotten something. 'The other question I have, forgive me; where were you on that night?'

'Me? In my room, asleep.'

'Any witness?'

He shook his head. 'No, just me. Why?'

'Just asking. Thank you, Martijn; I'm sure we will speak again.'

Ned and I took our leave, Martijn watching us as we left the warehouse.

'Where to now, sir?' asked Ned, as we left the yard.

'The church, I think. Let us take a look at our victim.'

We turned left and walked up towards the Wall and then down into Moorgate, discussing our observations.

'What did you think of Thyssen?' I asked, stepping around a noxious puddle.

'Full of himself, I reckon,' he replied, taking a large step to get over the fluid. 'Thinks he's better than he is. A dry-boots if ever I saw one.'

'We can agree on that,' I said, pleased that we shared the same impression.

Ned batted away the hand of a beggar clawing at his ankle. 'Blind-harper,' explained Ned, kicking out with his boot. 'Saw him looking at us on the sly.'

I grinned; I admit I missed that being deep in thought. All I saw was a beggar staring vacantly, unable to see. 'So, no forced entry and he sent out this Lars beforehand,' I said, dismissing the beggar and going over it again.

'You think in order to meet with someone?' he replied, as the blind-harper spat an expletive.

'I do; whom then?'

'A jade? One of them would perform anywhere.'

'Unlikely, he had money, it would have been easier and more private should he go to her. More likely a prior arrangement with someone, someone he knew. He wanted the meeting to be unobserved so he sends this Lars out whilst it takes place.'

'Would his sister have known?'

I shook my head. 'If she had known whom, then there would be no need for us, she would already know the likely murderer.'

'True but Pieter obviously knew the murderer as he allowed him into the premises.'

'A late-night meeting and what type of meetings are normally held at that hour?'

'Ones where something illegal is to be discussed.'

I nodded. 'It is just an assumption going from what little we know. We cannot rule out anything, we will have to dig a little deeper.'

We continued walking and then turned right down Winchester Street, where ironically, Alderman Baker lived, heading towards Austin Fryers where we would find the Dutch Church.

We came to the door of the church and entered into a brightly lit nave, or what I took to be a nave, as it seemed as if the congregation sat or stood facing widthways with the pulpit against the long side of the church. Stone columns supported the roof and large arched windows gave illumination like any other church; the peculiarity of the layout momentarily confused me as I had not been here before.

'Goedemiddag heren,' said a smiling man dressed in black, apart from a white neckband.

Ned and I looked at each other, both of us wearing frowns of question.

'I do beg your pardon, sir,' I said, returning the smile he offered us. 'We are seeking the minister here.'

'Ya? Then you have found him, sirs. I apologise; I took

you for Dutch. I am Henricas van Haemstede; how may I help you?'

I took the man to be in his forties, of average height with his hair hidden beneath a wig. Despite his crow-like appearance he had bright smiling eyes, a cheerful demeanour and a pronounced Dutch accent. 'My name is Richard Hopgood and I have been tasked by Femke van Hoebeek to look into the circumstances relating to the death of her brother, Pieter. I have a note here from her regarding that and I wish for your assistance.'

'What do you wish, Mr Hopgood?' he replied, after reading the note and handing it back.

'To view the body in order to establish the means of death and to ask one or two questions regarding him.'

'View him? He has already been prepared and is resting before God.'

'That I understand, sir. I just ask that you consider the circumstances as it would help greatly and we have been granted permission.'

'You have,' he conceded and he turned away, tapping his lips in thought. 'Very well,' he said, turning back. 'I wish for you to be respectful and to disturb him little as possible, he was an elder of this church and held in high esteem.'

'Thank you, Minister; of course you may observe us so that you can be sure we do only what is necessary.'

He nodded. 'Then follow me, Mr Hopgood.'

The minister took us down the nave to the far end of the church, through a door and into a small room. A wooden coffin lay on a table, light from the window bathing the room with a warm glow.

'When is he to be buried?' I asked, as I indicated to Ned to open the coffin.

'Tomorrow morning,' replied Van Haemstede. 'At ten of the clock. Many mourners should be paying their respects.'

Ned took the lid off to show a shrouded body lying within; an intense smell of putrefaction wafted over us taking a little while to dissipate. We stood back a little until the smell eased.

We worked as quickly as we could, unwrapping the body to get our first glimpse of our victim. He lay in repose with half-lidded eyes, his jaw slack and partly open. Death had given him a mottled complexion, his light auburn hair giving a stark contrast.

'The wound is to the front of his chest,' informed the minister, from a good few steps away, covering his nose with his hand.

'Thank you,' I replied. 'These clothes, are they the ones he wore when he was killed?'

'No.' He shook his head. 'Femke provided us with the clothes he wear now.'

I watched as Ned untied the garments until he had exposed the chest and I could see a wound, a slit-like incision below the heart. I locked eyes with Ned and gave a slight nod of my head and he pulled out a small knife with a thin blade to probe the wound.

'An upthrust,' he said, sensitively showing me the sharp angle. 'The assailant twisted the knife as he pulled it out as you can see the tears in the flesh.' He pointed with his knife to show the cuts above and below the initial injury. 'Not a short blade as it had a way to travel to reach the heart.'

I cast my eyes over the rest of the exposed torso, just pale unbroken skin and prominent ribs. 'Very well,' I said. 'I think we are done here.'

Ned retied the clothes and then I assisted in rewrapping the shroud, a difficult procedure with the body contained within the coffin. We eventually managed to present the body in a suitable condition to satisfy the minister and closed the lid with some relief, covering up the odour.

We hastily left the room and thankfully shut the door.

'Have you seen enough, Mr Hopgood?' asked the minister.

'Yes, thank you,' and I gave a grin of fellow feeling over the ordeal of the noxious smell. 'Only that I have a question or two to ask. The clothes he wore; you still have them?'

'I do; Femke did not want them back so I mean to give to the poor.'

'Can I see them?'

He shrugged. 'By all means; follow me.'

He took us to another room close by and pointed to a pile of clothes folded upon a chest. 'There, Pieter's clothes.'

Ned and I began to pick through everything, noting the slits and blood stains on the shirt and waistcoat, both of good-quality silk.

'Confirms the size of the blade,' observed Ned. 'Thin.'

'But it did the job,' I remarked, picking up his jacket. Inside, a pocket had been sewn and I felt something rustle as I put my finger inside. I withdrew the item, a folded piece of paper. "I will come," it said simply.

'Has anyone been through these?' I asked the minister.

He shook his head. 'Nee,' he replied. 'Just left there.'

I showed Ned what I had found. 'Could be useful,' he

said.

'Mr Van Haemstede, is this writing familiar?' I asked, showing him the note.

He shook his head. 'Sorry, I not recognise the hand.'

'Are you certain?'

'Ya,' he replied, 'Not one I know.'

I placed the note in my own pocket and patted it down. 'Now, Minister, tell me, did you know Pieter well?'

He shook his head. 'Not well as I have only been here a year; he was an elder before I arrived. I know his sister better as she frequently attends here,' he said, as we walked back down the nave.

'So even as an Elder he did not attend regularly?'

'No, not lately.'

'Why would that be? I mean, him not attending.'

'I believe his work kept him away. He was a good man, would always employ men needing work.'

'You mean Dutchmen?'

'Ya, always Dutch.'

That did not surprise me; he would probably prefer his own countrymen to be his workforce. 'Tell me, did he have any particular friends here, someone to whom he would confide?'

He rocked his head, thinking. 'He would always speak to Ruud Janssen. I believe Ruud and he did business together.'

'Where would I find this Ruud?'

'Wapping, I think. He not a local man.'

'Will he attend the funeral?'

'Ya, would think so,' he replied, nodding.

'Thank you, Minister, you have been most helpful. I may

make an attendance, if you do not think I would be interfering.'

'That would be for Femke to answer, Mr Hopgood; er, perhaps if you are discreet?'

'Of course, I understand. I will not take up any more of your time, Minister.'

'You are very welcome, Mr Hopgood. I pray to God that you find whoever did this to Pieter.'

'That is my intention, sir. If anything occurs to you or someone tells you something of interest then please would you let me know; you can always get a message to me through the Brown Bear in Bow Street.'

CHAPTER 4

We sat in the Crown off Broad Street, just behind the Dutch Church, discussing what we had learned so far. Ned and I lit our pipes, our smoke adding to the thick fug through which everyone there viewed the world. Shouts and good-humoured comments followed the pot-girl as she went from table to table, expertly dodging the groping hands.

'Then we both agree that he likely knew his assailant,' I said, leaning back and taking another draw on the pipe.

Ned nodded. 'He let them in and they talked together, standing in the middle of the floor.'

'Maybe they had a disagreement, maybe an old grudge. Then the assailant stepped up close to him, produced a knife and then thrust it up between his ribs. It did not kill him immediately, he staggered back, hand clutching his chest to stem the flow of blood and then as the back of his legs touched the crate he fell back, putting his hand down for support.'

'And then he died. The assailant then left, leaving the door ajar and escaped before this night guard returned,' Ned concluded.

I took a drink. 'He allowed the person to get close to him; with that acute angle the knife must have come from low down, then they twisted the knife to remove it — accident or design?'

'You mean did they know what they were doing or by desperately trying to pull it out, twisted it?'

'Yes, we both know that a twist makes it easier to remove as the body is loath to let go when something has penetrated the flesh; it clamps like a vice.'

He nodded. 'Don't help us though; someone who knew what they were doing or someone who didn't.'

I shrugged. 'True, but not a random act, thought had gone into it. This note; I'm wondering if it could have come from the killer agreeing to meet him, or had he kept it in his pocket from another liaison? I'm thinking you should listen to what the streets are saying around Moorgate and Bassishaw wards; perhaps you will learn something to our advantage.'

I saw a grin appear on his face at the prospect of having free range in all the alehouses and taverns within that area. 'Might take a while, sir, lots of places to go and ask questions in,' he remarked.

I gave a long drawn-out sigh. 'Yes, I thought you might say something like that.' I took another sip of ale. 'So be it, Ned. Just do not get drunk,' I warned. 'You need to keep your wits about you.'

'Never fear, sir. I will be the very example of restraint.'

'That's what I am afraid of.'

He grinned again and took up his ale. 'And what will you be doing while I'm hard at work?'

'I, Ned,' and I took out my pocket watch to check the time, 'will need to speak to Alderman Baker and then this Lars at the merchants. After that I may have an hour or so to spare and I intend to make full use of it.'

He gave a knowing grin. 'Very good, sir. I'm sure you'll enjoy that.'

'I fully intend to, Ned. Anyway, you're a fine one to make comment, considering your liaisons of late.'

'What about them? Nothing wrong with a little dalliance every now and again.'

I took a deep breath and began to count on my fingers. 'One, pot-girl at the Cheshire Cheese; two, that woman from the market; Three, scullery maid from that house in Dover Street; four—'

He held up his hand. 'Yes, yes. I know.' He grinned. 'Jealous, sir?'

'Not in the least, Ned,' I replied, though I would not tell him even if I was. 'I am just pointing out that there are some elements of your life where you should show a little... what is the word... consideration? No, you said it yourself, restraint. You will end up stoking a fire and getting seriously burned.'

'Only commerce; they was earning a little chink on the side. You could pay me a little more and then I would be able to visit some of those places you go to.'

'Heaven forbid, Ned. I pay you too much as it is.'

He grimaced. 'I wish, sir.'

I gave a curt nod, ending the conversation before it got out of hand. 'It is past six, so I suggest you finish that,' and I pointed to his ale, 'then begin.'

'Right you are, sir,' he replied, raising his pot and grinning again.

The Aldermen of the City of London governed under the office of The Lord Mayor, dealing with political issues on a local level: street lighting, building and road repairs, sanitation and the like. They had also recently taken on the mantle of Justices of the Peace, empowered to investigate crimes, for which, an elected constable acted under the alderman. As a Justice of the Peace, the alderman could also judge minor crimes and hold inquests; presumably, in the case of our corpse, he had already done so as someone had cleared the body for burial.

I rang the bell outside William Baker's house and waited, adding a knock on the door for added emphasis in the hope that I would not have to wait too long. Unfortunately, my hopes of an audience with that august official evaporated like the mist on a sunny morning.

'I am here to see the Alderman regarding the demise of Pieter van Hoebeek,' I said to the liveried footman standing erect in the aperture of the door, looking down at me with his nose in the attitude of superiority. 'Late of Basinghall Street.'

'The Alderman has repaired to the country, sir,' replied the man. 'For several days,' he added, as he saw me frown.

'Then who would now be dealing with this unfortunate situation?'

He coughed. 'I believe, sir, that all the documentation has been forwarded to Colonel Thomas De Veil at Bow Street. I myself conveyed it this very morning.'

'You are at liberty to discuss the alderman's business?' I asked, sliding a knife into his bubble of superiority.

'Er…I merely wish to assist a Gentleman in his enquiry.'

'Then please assist me more; the name of the constable who attended the murder.'

'Um, that would be Ben Thomas.'

'And where will I find him?'

'He sells fruit and vegetables in a shop near the Wall, opposite the hospital.'

I gave him a smile. 'Thank you. I will be sure to mention your assistance when I next see the alderman.'

'Er…' He swallowed nervously. 'Er…'

'Or perhaps I will not,' I said, after a second or so.

I turned on my heels and left the footman standing there. My intention being to keep his lack of discretion to myself as, in my business, I benefit from it more often than not; it is just that sometimes I cannot resist the temptation to deflate the ego a little bit.

Instead of speaking to the alderman I went in search for this constable, Ben Thomas, whom I hoped would furnish me with a little information; though from what Femke van Hoebeek said, I had little hope.

I walked up towards the Bethlem Hospital for the deranged, where you could pay your money and take a tour to be entertained or conversely, shocked by the inmates' behaviour. I found the constable easily enough in the little shop selling fruit, vegetables and other commodities; I could buy little bags of sugar, tea, coffee, bottles of ointments, honey; he sold clothes and wigs, bottles of wine, soap, candles and everything else in between. How he crammed so much into such a small space, I did not know.

'Good day, sir,' said a man, just rising from his stool at the back of the shop.

'Good day to you too, sir.' I replied, stopping at a bench and looking at several small bags. I picked one up and sniffed. 'Tea, is it?'

'It is, sir. That has come all the way from the east, has that, the distant fabled land of China. A merchant of my acquaintance allows me a little supply now and then.'

'Costly?' I asked, innocently.

'Indeed, sir, more through the tax than the commodity; Best Bohea is that, leaf not dust. Just three shillings a quarter pound bag, sir and you won't find finer in all London.'

I smiled. 'Maybe not finer but certainly cheaper.'

'Ah, yes, sir. You always take a risk if you buy from the inns and taverns or from hawkers on the street; you never know what you're getting. Maybe as good as that,' and he indicated the bag in my hand, 'more often than not you'd be getting the scrapings, the leftovers with dirt and droppings to make up the weight.'

'That is true; so your merchant friend only sells you the best?'

'Well, he did. Murdered, sir, just the other day and as the constable hereabouts I made an attendance. Dead as a stone he was and sad to see.'

'You knew him well?'

'That I did, done business with him for a long time.'

I nodded. 'Sad to lose a friend; I suppose as a friend and a constable you'll be seeking whoever did this?'

'Acquaintance, sir, acquaintance more than friend; mind you, it would not surprise me to learn he had bitten off more than he could chew.'

'Meaning?'

'He were a Dutchman and I know he often went to Canvey.'

'Canvey, eh?' I pretended ignorance.

'Yes, Canvey Island. I reckon whoever did it is long gone now.'

'What makes you think that; I mean, why Canvey?' I could tell he knew something, I just did not know what and how much.

He looked around as if to make certain no one else could hear him, even though I was the only person in the shop. He leant forward and tapped his nose.

'Ah,' I said, already aware of his inference — smuggling.

He did not elaborate further, so I left the shop with the constable still unaware of my interest in the murder, also with a small bag of tea I did not need as I already had plenty at home. I wondered if he would have confessed to facts if I had pressed him, or did he just repeat rumour? I suspected gossip as someone involved in the smuggling trade would be unlikely to advertise it to a Constable of the Ward; he was too free with his mouth to be a party to it all. I decided to bide my time with Ben Thomas, he had told me enough for the moment and I could always return another time to question him further.

As I walked along in the late evening sunshine, I mused upon the Dutch and the Canvey Island connection. I knew very little except that the Dutch helped build dykes and ditches in the last century and many stayed on to live there. A desolate place of marshland I had heard, though there must be land enough to sustain a population. I had never been there but I knew that smuggling was a large part of the local trade, like many other isolated coastal regions.

If Van Hoebeek had his finger in that particular pie then it could well be a reason for his demise in such a way.

I turned into Basinghall Court and followed the lane down and around the corner to the yard. Three carts stood idle, parked by the stables, presumably having finished deliveries for the day. I could hear horses moving, a whicker here and there, a bang as one of them kicked a partition. I headed over to the already open door of the warehouse, called out and entered.

A large-built man with dark shoulder-length hair sat at the desk, wearing a waistcoat with breeches and stout leather boots. He had a plate in front of him of cold meats and bread, a jug and drinking pot beside that. 'Are you Lars?' I asked, as he looked up.

'I am. You this Hopgood?'

I nodded. 'So Martijn informed you of why I wish to speak with you?'

'He did; though can't see how I can help you much.' He bit off a chunk of bread and chewed slowly, looking expectant.

'I just want you to tell me what happened.'

He finished chewing and took up his pot, taking a long drink. 'Easy. I were here with Mr Van Hoebeek and then he tells me to go out for an hour or so, told me to take a drink, so I did.'

'Where did you go?'

'The Anchor, down the road a bit; had a quart, chatted with a few men I know then came back.'

'What did you find when you got back?'

'Well, the door was open to start with and I knew I had locked it as I left, as instructed by the master. When I went inside I found him dead, over there on that crate,' and he pointed appropriately.

'You thought him resting, I heard?'

He nodded. 'I did, he were sort of slouched over, as you do, then I walked over to him and noticed the blood and that he weren't breathing.'

'You called the hue and cry?'

'I did, went to the street and yelled and a couple of the neighbours came out to help. It were too late then, I couldn't see anyone around and I didn't see no one when I came back.'

'What time was this?'

'Around midnight, I reckon.'

'And you saw no one leaving here?'

He shook his head. 'Nope.'

'Would he often send you out of the warehouse?'

'Every now and then, he would. Send me out to have a drink for an hour, always around the same time and when I gets back he's sitting at his desk, then a short while later he gets up and goes home. I ain't gonna complain when I gets to have a drink when I'm at work, am I? He were always good like that.'

'You think these were meetings?'

He shrugged his shoulders. 'Didn't know, didn't care.'

'He would work here quite late?'

'Yeah, most of the time.'

'He did not want to go home?'

He grinned. 'Would you, with that sister of his waiting?'

I felt my forehead furrow. 'What do you mean?'

'She's a bit; well, you know?'

'No, I do not.'

He sighed. 'Strict she is, apparently even with her brother. Won't suffer fools; you know what I mean?'

'Martijn did not mention that.'

'He wouldn't as he's been getting right friendly with her recently.' He took another bite of the bread. 'He used to moan about her; not now he don't.'

'Maybe he has seen another side to her.'

Lars laughed. 'Mebbee he thinks he can dock with her.'

I felt my eyes widen. 'Really?'

'Who knows,' replied Lars, still laughing. He shook his head as the laughter petered out. 'Just a bit of fun, you know.'

That's how gossip begins, I thought, so I decided to change the subject. 'Are all the goods here legal?'

'What?' he asked, now wide-eyed at my change of tack.

'I mean has everything been cleared by the customs men?'

'Course it has, that old bitch of a sister wouldn't allow it otherwise.'

'Your mistress, you mean?'

'Yeah, well, her anyway. Didn't mean no disrespect, but…'

I gave a slight shrug; Lars certainly did not find Femke to his liking. 'So, if I came here with the customs and they checked everything they would find nothing amiss?'

He hesitated. 'Er, not as far as I know.'

'Nothing?'

'Er…'

'Lars, I am aware of what goes on, you know.'

The grin he tried to put on came out more of a grimace. If I did come back with the customs then probably all the contraband would have disappeared, everything in order and no one the wiser.

I changed tack again. 'Did you find anything when you came back from the Anchor; a knife, the murder weapon?'

'No, there were nothing, just himself, dead.'

'And you know of no one who would want him removed?'

He shook his head then ate the last of his bread before lifting the pot and draining it dry.

I came away thinking that there was more to know, much more to know about the business dealings of Pieter van Hoebeek. Lars could not hide his signs of dissembling and I wondered whether Martijn had told him what to say, apart from Lars' opinion on Femke. Most merchants in the city would not shy away from a little extra profit should the opportunity arise to deal with the illegal trade of goods — I got the impression that Van Hoebeek dealt less in opportunity and more in design.

The evening had begun to draw in with the light fading fast, the warm and sultry air giving a pungent odour of waste and decay. I negotiated the people still out and about in the street, those picking over the remains of the stalls and haggling for bargains. The inns and taverns seemed full to bursting with the hot weather bringing on a raging thirst, quenched only by ale or gin. The street-girls touted for early business, more in hope than expectation, as they might have to wait until later to pick up custom. Close to Cripplegate I found an idle hackney waiting for a fare. Even though my journey would only be a mile or so, my weary legs gave notice that I had already walked enough, besides, the warmth had begun to sap my energy. I climbed aboard, giving my destination and sat back, hoping the broken windows would allow a little draught of cooling air.

I alighted at The White Hart, Drury Lane and paid my fare. I did not intend to visit that hostelry right now, stepping towards the tenement next door instead. I hoped that my lateness in the appointment would not be held against me as I knocked upon the door of the upstairs lodging. I brushed the dust from my clothes trying to make myself more presentable as I waited for my knock to be answered.

Kitty Marham opened the door and gave me a big smile in greeting. 'Richard,' she exclaimed, drawing me inside and then wrapping her arms around my neck, kissing me, a warm kiss, gentle and unhurried. I held her about her slim waist and we pressed our bodies close, savouring the initial moment of intimacy, like we had done many times before. After a little time, we broke apart and I looked down into two vibrant green eyes, sparkling with a joyous energy. Twenty years of age, Kitty's wide full lips now opened in a smile, her tongue darting out to moisten those lips before slipping back into her mouth. She had long unbound light-auburn hair hanging down to her waist, a pretty nose and a clear, fresh, unblemished face.

No one could tell that Kitty once plied her trade on the streets, offering herself for just a few shillings a time, a jade, a whore but never a doxy or a drab. She could have had the rich men of London in the palm of her hand had she the opportunity and the desire. Instead, she suffers me, with my admittedly many and varied faults. Kitty tells me I am a handsome man, having shoulder-length dark hair tied with a ribbon at the back of my neck, my deep dark eyes and a smile to break a woman's heart. She likes that I am tall, just over six feet and keep my body fit and healthy — so who am I to argue with such an astute woman as she?

She took my hand and drew me across to the upholstered sofa, room enough for two, and sat me down. She turned and went over to the table, picked up the bottle of wine and poured a measure into two glasses. She handed me one and sat down, laying her head briefly against my shoulder.

The room had rugs on the floor, four chairs by the table, two more upholstered chairs, painted countryside views adorning the walls and some cooking equipment by the hearth; a very comfortable home for a woman of her standing. The only other room had a large comfortable bed. Despite my wealth, I contribute nothing to the cost of her lodging, although I did insist on helping her furnish it.

We sat leaning against each other, my arm around her shoulders as we drank our wine. I spoke about my day and then she spoke about hers.

Kitty now made her living in Covent Garden, taking a stall where she sold anything she could procure at a price low enough to return a healthy profit. She started by selling just a few candles from a tray around her neck, quickly building on her success and taking the stall, selling bespoke items made by local artisans who copied the styles of the rich to sell to those who wished to emulate them. She keeps her stock in a storehouse near to the Garden where she rents a space and has a local lad to help her.

'So, you have no idea why someone wished this Dutchman dead?' she said, once she had spoken about her toils of the day.

'Not really; possibly smuggling, possibly an argument gone

wrong. I'm hoping Ned might come up with something so I cannot stay overnight.'

'Then we are wasting time, Richard,' she said, standing up. 'You have a duty to perform, Mr Hopgood,' she added, heading towards the bedroom, her hips moving seductively and giving me a certain smile.

I sighed and then grinned. 'I am always dutiful, Miss Marham,' I said, as I stood up to follow her.

CHAPTER 5

'You were both late last night, sir,' said Mary, as I entered the kitchen then sat down at the table to eat my breakfast.

Ned had arrived home even later than I had. Thankfully, he had not imbibed too much being reasonably sober for a change. He had little to report; speculation as to smuggling being involved, retribution from a cheated customer, a woman wronged, a cuckolded husband, all gossip with no basis in facts, so we retired to our respective beds and slept the night through.

'We were,' I admitted. 'I hope we did not disturb you.'

'No more than normal, sir,' and I detected a slight admonition in her choice of words.

She bustled about arranging my food whilst Jane supervised the water boiling in the kettle in readiness to make my morning tea. I liked to take my breakfast in the kitchen; being full of chatter it amused me to hear them go on about this or that. I could have sat in my dining room and stared at the walls, missing all this entertainment.

Ned, already up and sitting on a stool with a bowl of coffee in front of him, grinned as Mary spoke to me.

'You can wipe that smile off your face, Mr Tripp,' said Mary, turning and brandishing a knife in his direction. 'I have plenty of tasks for you today.'

Ned shot me a wide-eyed look, the grin having quickly disappeared.

'Alas, Mary, Ned is required for my own purposes today and will not be at your disposal,' I said, before she could begin the list, wishing in part to see Ned squirm under the onslaught.

'Oh,' she replied, her plans disappearing like smoke.

Jane poured the water into the teapot then gave a shy smile in my direction before carrying it over to set before me, next to the porcelain cup and saucer, the recent addition to our dining pleasures and similar to what I saw at Van Hoebeek's warehouse. I would quite happily drink my tea out of anything really, but Mary had insisted on a proper tea set, bought from the small grocer nearby; Mr Fortnum and Mr Mason seemed to be expanding their business quite well.

Ned sat up straighter and the grin reappeared on his face.

'No need to be triumphant,' said Mary, still with the knife in her hand. 'There is always tomorrow.'

Thankfully, she put down the knife to carry my plate over, consisting of eggs, cold meats and cheese with fresh bread and butter, a repast to set me up nicely for the day ahead.

Ned chuckled to himself as we sat in the hackney. 'Tomorrow is another day,' he observed, relating to Mary's last words with him.

'You know she will have her way, do you not?'

'Aye, sir. But it fair tickles me to see you thwart her like that.'

'It is not done for your benefit, you know. Anyway, I have already said that you are free to leave to live on your own.

You do not have to stay as my footman, though I would wish you to stay as my assistant.'

'No, I'm happy enough as I am, sir. If I lived on my own what would I get up to? Taverns and jades would be most likely and I've no wish to become a nazie-cove or be poxed to me eyeballs. Anyways, what would Mary do if I weren't there to irk her?'

'Irk me probably.'

'Then I'm doing you a favour, sir. Besides, someone has to keep you in check.'

'Keep me in check? I thought it was me keeping *you* in check.'

'A delusion is that, sir.'

I laughed; we had a strange relationship, Ned and I, one that transcended the simple employer and employee.

We arrived at the church with plenty of time to spare. A few people had already begun to gather, so I waited outside so as not to disturb the mourners. Ned stayed out of sight along with Kitty, who had come at my request because I hoped someone would appear who may be able to shed a little light on the personal habits of Pieter van Hoebeek.

Femke arrived accompanied by another woman of similar age, dark-haired and quite striking in appearance, both dressed in mourning clothes. Behind them, I saw the maid who showed Ned and I into the house in Basinghall Street, accompanied by two more maids and three young men whom I took to be servants.

Miss Van Hoebeek saw me and acknowledged my presence with a slight nod of her head then brushed past me and went into the church grounds to approach those already there, the woman accompanying her glancing briefly in my direction. Martijn and Lars then came along with six more men whom I took to be the workers from the warehouse and they walked by me without acknowledgment. More folk arrived, most in couples, though some single men of varying ages.

The mourning bell sounded its last note and those assembled then headed into the church. I followed at the rear, being as unobtrusive as I could by taking a place at the back and to the side.

I kept my eyes on the congregation as the minister, Van Haemstede, began to speak, in Dutch, meaning that I could not understand a word. Apart from myself, I could see no one who looked out of place. Watching closely, I saw various emotions play on the faces of the people: sadness, indifference, even one or two who looked amused. Femke van Hoebeek sat at the front with the woman she arrived with and I noticed that they appeared very easy in each other's company. I could not see their faces nor judge their emotions as they conversed. The coffin rested upon a trestle in front of the pulpit, covered by a plain orange drape with some cut flowers adorning it. At a nod from the minister, four men stood up and made their way to the front, taking up position at the four corners of the coffin.

The bearers shouldered the coffin and then slowly began to make their way to the burial ground, the congregation following closely behind.

Again, I brought up the rear and stood at a discreet distance as the four men lowered the coffin into the grave. The minister spoke again for a few minutes, closing his bible as he finished. A few moments of respectful silence followed before the mourners began to drift away, allowing the gravedigger to approach, ready to shovel the earth back in. I caught the eye of the minister who after speaking to Femke and her companion, made his way towards me.

'Good morning, Mr Hopgood. I am unsurprised to see you here,' he said.

I smiled at him. 'I think I had to be; tell me, who is the lady with Miss Van Hoebeek?' I asked, watching as the pair walked away.

'Ah, that is Cornelia Visser, a friend of hers from childhood,' he replied. 'Married to a gentleman in Walbrook, an Englishman.'

'Is he present?'

He shook his head. 'Nee, to my knowledge I have never met or seen him.'

I nodded. 'What about this Ruud Janssen, is he here?'

'He is.' He turned around and pointed to a man speaking to Martijn Thyssen.

Janssen looked to be in his forties, well-dressed in a dark blue embroidered jacket, a wine-coloured waistcoat, dark breeches with white stockings, a jabot about his neck. He wore a dark wig and had a chiselled angular pale face with sunken eyes; a walking skeleton came to my mind. He held his hat in his hands, gripping it tightly as he spoke to the overseer. 'Thank you, Minister,' I replied.

Martijn had noticed the minister pointing and said something to Janssen before moving away. Janssen turned his head and looked at me, quickly wiping away the frown on his face as he saw me regarding him. He stepped towards another man, spoke quickly and then began to move away again, just as I began to walk towards him.

'Ruud Janssen, may I speak with you for a moment?' I called.

He stopped, turned towards me and I could tell he was reluctant to engage me in conversation. 'What you want?' he said, a little irritably.

'Pieter van Hoebeek. I hear you and he were friends. I just wondered if you know of a reason why someone would wish him ill?'

He shook his head. 'Nee.'

'He did not speak about any troubles he had?'

'Er, sorry. My English not so good.'

'Oh, I apologise. I would just like to know a little more about Pieter.'

He shrugged, rattled off a string of Dutch and then shrugged again. 'I sorry, not to say much. He not tell me anything.'

'Nothing?'

He shook his head. 'Ya, nothin'. Excuse, please. I go now.'

He gave me a fleeting grin and then moved away quickly, not giving me the chance to ask anything else. I stood for a moment in exasperation and then relaxed, looking around. I saw Cornelia Visser approach Martijn, touching him on the arm with a stroke of her hand, tipping her face up to speak a few words as he leant down. She gave his arm a gentle pat and then moved away to rejoin Femke. All the mourners seemed to be leaving now and I realised I would not have the chance to speak with anyone else. I headed towards the gate when the minister, Van Haemstede, approached me.

'You speak with Ruud?' he asked.

I gave him a grim smile. 'Sort of; you did not tell me he had poor English.'

He looked confused. 'Ruud? He has excellent English, better than mine.'

'What?'

'Ya, very good, like yours.'

I felt stunned for a moment and then I turned around as the mourners disappeared. I could try to catch him up and confront him with what Van Haemstede had just told me but he had every right not to answer my questions, so why did he pretend not to understand me?

'Thank you again, Minister, you have been most helpful,' I said as I nodded absently, my mind still thinking.

I left the churchyard and began to walk up Austin Fryers when I spotted Ned walking towards me with a grin on his face.

'You were right, sir,' he said, when he joined me. 'Stood at the wall looking over; didn't want to go in and cause a scene.'

I let out a long breath of relief that at least something seemed to be going my way. 'Where is she?'

'Kitty has taken her to the White Lion in Throgmorton Street. She didn't want to wait around with all of them here.'

'Does she have a name?'

'She does. Emily Cooper, been with him nigh on two years.'

'Two years?' I exclaimed.

'Aye, a long time to keep a girl, that.'

'It is; what is she like?'

'You'll find out; she ain't a bad one.'

We walked into the White Lion and spotted Kitty sitting in the corner with a slim curvy young woman. She could be of Greek or Turkish heritage with her complexion, long dark hair, full-lipped mouth and sharp cheekbones. Sultry and eminently desirable, she, along with Kitty, was on the receiving end of a bit of unwanted attention from the men in the tavern.

Ned ordered us ales then we walked over and sat down, both of us taking a few moments to lock eyes with the more forward of the commentators, casting them into guarded silence. I turned my head back and smiled at Emily, hoping to put her at ease as Kitty made the introduction; I then noticed a small posy of flowers on her lap.

She saw me looking and gave a thin smile. 'I were going to put them on 'is grave when they all went. I'll go back when I leave 'ere.'

I nodded and Kitty patted the back of her hand. 'He meant that much to you?' I asked, interested in how deep the relationship had been.

She smiled ruefully. 'Best I've known. Didn't want much, just a bit of company, a bit of…well, you know, and a friendly ear.'

'He kept you?'

She nodded. 'Paid fer everything. All I 'ad to do was to be there for 'im, whenever 'e wanted.'

Our ale appeared and we went silent for a few moments until the pot-girl had gone; Kitty and Emily still had wine in front of them.

'You could not stay at home all the time, so did you make arrangements?' I asked.

'Sometimes,' she replied, nodding. 'A boy would come with a note, other times 'e'd just show up; 'e were always good about it if I weren't there. Other times 'e would say 'e'd come at such an' such a time on such an' such a day as 'e left my lodging.'

Ned pulled out his pipe and began to fill it with tobacco, dropping a few strands on the table. He brushed the bits up, not wishing to waste any, and put them back into his pouch. 'How did you meet him?' he asked, reaching for a taper.

'I were working fer Mother Reynolds off The Strand; 'e were always asking fer me after that first time. I never worked the streets, you know, I always had me standards.'

I shot Kitty a look to see how she would react as *she* worked the streets until just a few months ago, but she did not bat an eyelid as Emily besmirched her character.

'So he took you out of there and set you up in your own rooms?' asked Ned.

'Yes, 'e did. It's all gone now. I'll have to go back to that 'ouse if she'll 'ave me.'

I thought that maybe she might be a bit too old now for a bawdy house, at least one of reasonable repute. She might well have to lower her standards in order to live.

'Tell Richard what you told me,' said Kitty, touching her arm and smiling at her.

Emily looked at Kitty and then at me. 'Wot, about 'is troubles?'

'Yes, he would talk to you, wouldn't he?' she added, encouragingly.

'Most don't when they've got what they wanted, you know. Pieter were different, 'e would talk to me as if we were more than what we were; told me everything, 'e did.'

'Like what?' I asked, taking a sip of ale.

'Told me about 'is sister which 'e shared an 'ouse with. Prefers women to men, apparently, if you know what I mean. A sapphie, a tommie; can't unnerstand that, can you?' she asked, turning her head towards Kitty.

'Sometimes I can,' replied Kitty, a rueful tone in her voice. 'Considering some of the men in the city,' she added, pointedly not looking at me.

Emily nodded. 'That's true,' she agreed. 'You know, 'e walked in on 'er once, 'e told me, and to make matters worse the other woman 'ad been a lover of 'is. They were doing it on the sofa. The sister didn't notice 'im, 'e said, just saw the face of 'is lover an' she just smiled at him.'

'Who was the lover, do you know?' I asked, leaning forward.

'It were someone called Cornelia, 'e said. Loved 'er, 'e said, wanted to marry 'er, 'e said. Spoke about seeing 'er before that; I think 'e thought there were still a chance; men, eh?'

'Sapphism is not illegal,' I said. 'Not like a Molly or a Madge.' The revelation did not shock me as Molly houses were common enough; it only stood to reason that some women would have similar inclinations.

'What else did he tell you?' encouraged Kitty.

She took a breath. 'Said 'e had somefing on his mind, wouldn't talk about it, just said that it were a problem 'e 'ad to sort.'

'He didn't say what kind of problem, when did it happen?'

She shook her head. 'No, 'e didn't. Were recent; that's all.'

Kitty looked a little disappointed. 'Never mind; you said

something about his business.'

She nodded. 'I did. Another merchant were causing 'im a bit o' trouble, 'e said. Thought it might come to blows one of these days.'

'What kind of trouble?' I asked.

She looked keenly at me. 'Wot's it worth? I got to learn to live now 'e's gone, you know,' she said, reaching for her wine and casting me a glance.

'You don't want to help me find the man who killed him?' I asked.

'I do but you know 'ow it is.' She looked down at the flowers in her lap and sighed. 'Ten shillings, just enough to see me through a day or so,' she said, sadly.

I fished out a few coins from my purse and put them on the table. She did not catch my eye as she scooped them up and placed them in her own purse.

'Jaggers. Tom Jaggers. A merchant down Rood Lane off Fenchurch Street. Started trying to take Pieter's customers. I unnerstan' some 'eated words passed between them.'

'When was this?'

'Last few weeks it's been 'appening; 'e said 'e used to like going to that coffee 'ouse.'

'The one in Birchin Lane, Cole's?'

She nodded. 'Yeah, that one. Said 'e'd 'ave to find another now that Jaggers seemed to be there all the time.'

'This business, Emily, did he engage in any illegal trade at all?'

'You mean smuggling?'

I gave a grim smile. 'I do. I have heard some rumours to the effect.'

'Who doesn't if they gets the opportunity? I got the impression that 'e did, don't know where and who with.'

'Impression? This could be important, Emily. If you know anything it could help greatly.'

She hesitated a little and looked at me, studying, wondering if I should have her trust. I could see her wrestle with her conscience as her face screwed up in thought. She seemed to come to a decision and nodded to herself. 'Alright; 'e did receive goods, mainly tea, I think. In truth, 'e wouldn't turn 'is nose up at other stuff too.'

'Where did he get it from?'

She took a deep breath. 'I don't know; 'e did talk about Wapping and Canvey a lot. Went to those places a bit, 'e did.'

'Did he mention any names?' asked Ned, blowing a great cloud of smoke out of his mouth.

'No; you think that's the reason 'e were 'ushed?'

'I don't know,' I replied. 'It seems the most likely explanation. I will have to make a few more enquiries to be sure. Where do you live at the moment, Emily, just in case I need to ask some more questions?'

'Won't be there much longer,' she said sadly, lowering her head and taking a breath. 'The other side of the Wall, Little Moorfields.'

She told me precisely where she lived and quickly finished her wine then left, taking her flowers back to the church in Austin Fryers where she could say her farewells in private. I felt a little sorry for her as although she had not loved Pieter van Hoebeek, she did have some affection for him, despite the purpose of their relationship. I moved over to sit with Kitty on the bench and pulled my pipe out from my pocket.

'What now?' asked Ned.

'We have one or two choices,' I said, thinking aloud, once I got my pipe going. 'This Tom Jaggers for one and then there is Wapping. I—' I hesitated for a moment as my mind signalled a recollection. 'Ruud Janssen,' I said, as I looked at the ceiling. 'The minister told me a Ruud Janssen has a place at Wapping, a friend of the family who did not want to talk to me.'

'And Canvey?' asked Kitty.

'Yes and Canvey too, we know the Dutch use that island to smuggle contraband into London. It is a long way unless we really need to go, so we will start a bit closer to home, I think.'

'What about the problem she said he had?' asked Kitty.

I shrugged. 'Could be anything, perhaps with this Jaggers.'

'Do you not think that Femke van Hoebeek should receive a little of our attention?' asked Ned. 'I mean, considering what Emily just said about her inclinations and what that worker at the merchant's told you.'

'She is the one who has given us this task; she is hardly likely to have killed her brother and then requested me to investigate,' I replied, reasoning it out.

'Maybe,' said Kitty. 'What if her brother walked in on her again and saw her with someone else? That someone might have taken exception, someone who didn't want her proclivities to be known.'

'You can't discount that Martijn neither,' said Ned. 'He resented being put in charge of the business when the master went away.'

'Valid points, both of you. All we know for certain is that

Pieter van Hoebeek allowed his assailant into the warehouse, therefore, he knew them.'

The three of us lapsed into silence, deep in thought until the pot-girl came past and Ned ordered us some more drinks. 'May as well lubricate the mind whilst we think about it,' he said, grinning.

CHAPTER 6

Sitting in the White Lion thinking about things did not help get things done, so I sent Ned down to Wapping to discover what he could about Ruud Janssen; fortunately, Ned had seen me trying to talk to Janssen at the funeral so he could at least recognise him. Kitty wished to lend assistance. so I asked her to look into the secret world of the sapphists, cautioning her not to probe too deeply lest she discover a latent interest in the subject, hitherto unknown. I said the last as a jest and she gave me a wistful knowing look in reply, confounding me for a moment until she winked and squeezed my thigh.

I pulled out the note I found on the corpse and looked at it again; just a simple message and I wondered who had written it. I refolded it and put it back, thinking of the tasks I had given myself; Tom Jaggers, the merchant who had dispute with Van Hoebeek and to delve a little into the smuggling trade. I did not know much, except that the trade proliferated in the city due to the government's high taxes on certain goods, to fund the war against the Spanish in the West Indies. A war precipitated, I believe, by the callous amputation of an ear of a ship's captain named Jenkins some years before. You could find these goods on the street corners and on market stalls, in inns, taverns and alehouses;

people who knew people would ply the trade and many in authority would turn a blind eye.

I decided to begin with Jaggers, first wishing to view his establishment in Rood Lane.

The early afternoon sunshine made the walk quite pleasant, the little breeze helping to disperse the odour of the city. Carts and coaches rattled by, the horses dropping their muck in piles. People scampered across the roads, mindful of where they trod. Handcarts carried goods stacked high for sale in a market or for delivery to either a shop or home. I heard shouts from vendors selling wares, their cries competing for attention. Musicians piped and banged drums, adding to the cacophony. I saw a small crowd gathering as a man proclaimed the latest news, reading from newssheets and papers, informing the illiterate and hoping for a few pennies for his trouble. I passed chophouses, taverns, coffee houses and shops, announcing what goods they sold by their swinging signs above. I passed Halls for Guilds next to pawnbrokers and lending houses. London life was out in all its forms.

I turned into Rood Lane, thankfully unmolested and began to search out Tom Jaggers' establishment, walking down, casting my eyes to the left and right, the affluent and well-built buildings comprising a mixture of residential and trade. The church of St Margaret's Pattens lay at the bottom on the left and about halfway down I spied an opening between a shop selling ironmongery and a draper's, wide enough for a horse and cart to enter. I hesitated, then decided to take a look.

I came into a yard surrounded by sheds and barns, the

cobbles covered with horse muck and straw. Three men attended a horse and cart, two loading whilst the third held the horse steady. All three turned to look at me as the loaders ceased their labour.

'I am looking for Tom Jaggers,' I said, by way of opening the conversation. 'I am hoping this is the correct establishment.'

'He ain't here,' said the horse holder, sharply. 'Not today.'

'That is a shame; I hoped to speak with him. Do you know where he might be?'

The man shrugged his shoulders. 'Could be anywhere; you'd best come back another time.'

I nodded, smiled and then waited a moment to see if he would add anything more, but he did not, just continued to stare at me as if I had two heads. 'No matter, I am sure I will find him soon enough,' I said, in the end.

I bid the three a good day and then left, leaving me with the distinct impression that my appearance had been unwelcome to say the least. I found surly and uncommunicative workers, distrustful, wary, not like any merchant's I had been to before. Feeling somewhat frustrated, I retraced my steps, deciding to take a break when I arrived in Birchin Lane and visit Cole's to see if Jaggers happened to be there, or to listen to whatever might be said regarding him or Van Hoebeek. I did not regret going first to Rood Lane as I now had a taste of Jaggers' business, an unsavoury taste, leaving my mouth dry and bitter. I would be very surprised if my initial impression did not bear out the truth.

Cole's lay at the lower end of Birchin Lane, between a

barber's and a baker's, one of the many coffee houses in the lane amidst the other small businesses from cabinet makers to stationers. I approached from Lombard Street and received a heady aroma as I passed the cheesemonger, enough that my stomach growled in protest, reminding me that I had not eaten since morning. I resolved to correct that omission as soon as I left Cole's, unless they served something that agreed with my palate.

On pushing open the door, I encountered a raucous noise of dissent and argument coming from a table over to the right; the other men in the house laughed and pointed, urging the opposing sides to greater heights of discourse. I could not discern the reason for the row as I made my way over to a place on a bench with three other men, laughing uproariously at the antics of the argumentative group.

'What's the clutter about?' I asked as I sat down, indicating the source with my head.

The man I sat next to had tears in his eyes and had to wipe them before he could reply. 'Walpole; who else? Our friend over there,' and he pointed to the top end of the table, 'proclaimed a poem. "Fearless of danger, steadfast as a rock, great Walpole stood the senatorial shock, malice of merit is the best defence, impeachment the best proof of innocence." They are arguing as to the truth and also the rhyme.'

'It rhymes,' I said and left it at that, not wanting to get into a spat of a political nature as I knew not the view of my companion and his friends.

'Yes but is it a *good* rhyme?'

'Ah, that's a different question. Far be it for me to argue literary matters,' I replied. 'I will leave that to those more *versed* in the subject.'

'Hear him! Hear him!' cried my companion. 'My friend here just announced that he leaves his opinion on rhyme to those more *versed* on the subject! Ha ha ha!'

A great guffaw of laughter greeted my witticism, hands slapped on the tables and some raised their bowls in my direction as if I had proclaimed I could turn lead into gold.

'Bernard Cotespill,' introduced the man, wiping his eyes again as he regained his seat.

'Richard Hopgood,' I replied, grinning and giving a slight bow of my head.

A mature young man, Cotespill had an open face and smiled easily; he wore an expensive horsehair powdered wig and dressed in the latest fashion.

'Well, Hopgood, you have quite made my day with your sharp retort. I don't think I've had that much enjoyment for many a month.'

'I'm only pleased to have done so, Cotespill.' I replied, with a slight nod of acknowledgement. 'Mind, it would seem their argument has run its course,' I added, indicating the table now returning to a state of equilibrium.

'Ah, yes, pity that; we'll give it a few minutes and then maybe we can relight the fire.'

I grinned and then the proprietor came over to take my order and I asked for refills for my table as well. Cotespill introduced me to the two other men, George Bryant and Arthur James, attired similarly to my new friend. All three said that they invested in various enterprises and dabbled in the stock markets. I just admitted to being a Gentleman, living off my means.

'You should listen to our advice, Hopgood, you would put penury to history,' said Cotespill, leaning back and puffing out his chest. 'Live life to the full as we do and watch the guineas come rolling in.'

'I might well do that, Cotespill,' I replied, taking a drink of my coffee. 'I put a little money in The East India Company and that gives me a reasonable return.'

'Pish!' exclaimed Cotespill. 'Stagnant, is old John Company. Take my advice and invest your money somewhere else.'

'Like where?'

'Obviously slave ships, unless you find that notion unpalatable. There is coal, everyone needs that, armaments too, we are at war after all. You could also help to set up as a merchant, that's always worth considering as with the right man in charge it can give a good and steady income. There is also the lottery.'

I shook my head at that. 'Tickets are expensive.'

'They are, but…' and he tapped his nose. 'There are ways and there are ways.'

'You mean the trade in tickets?'

'I do; you can get eleven percent by trading, far more than you get from John Company.'

'That sounds interesting, Cotespill, I'll give it some serious consideration.'

'You could do far worse than come to Cole's, Hopgood. We have finance experts here, with knowledge guaranteed to make us more wealthy.'

As I sat talking to Cotespill and the others I tried to picture Van Hoebeek amongst this raucous and boisterous crowd and I admit that I found it difficult to reconcile his presence here with these people, from what little I had heard of him. Then, I thought, maybe the man might well have yearned for the cut and thrust of lively discussion in total contrast to what I expected he endured at home with his sister. Then something occurred to me, something Cotespill had told me earlier, something about the merchant business returning a healthy amount of money and I wondered how Jaggers had come to the business.

I wanted to turn the conversation back to the subject I had come here to learn about and wondered how best to do that, when fortuitously, a man walked in and joined the table next to Cotespill.

'Who's dead?' asked Cotespill, overhearing the conversation.

'The Dutchman,' replied the man. 'Struck down in his own warehouse, from what I heard.'

'Van Hoebeek?' asked Cotespill.

'Yes.' The man nodded. 'Him.'

'Oh, shame. He was quite good company, for a foreigner, that is.'

'What's this?' I asked, as innocently as I could.

Cotespill turned his attention back to me. 'Dutchman who used to come in here, a merchant.' He leant forward conspiratorially. 'There are some here who will certainly not mourn his passing.'

'Trouble, was he?'

Cotespill shook his head. 'Oh no, not he.' He shot a look around the coffee house. 'Others might have been, though I cannot see them here today. Six fellows set up a merchant house, competing with him, resulting in a good deal of rancour between them all; it nearly came to blows more than once until the Dutchman absented himself. Shame about that, I certainly preferred his company to the man who now runs this new merchant's. Jaggers is his name and he now comes here to report on the business to his masters.'

'Who are the masters?'

'Oh, Cannard, Ransom, De Griese, Sommerville and Balton. As I say, they're not here today; probably still sleeping off their debouch. I saw them go into The Hoop tavern in The Strand last night, where they spend their money, you know.'

I knew The Hoop; only the serious gamblers went there. It would not be unusual to go in flush with money and come out a pauper, vast sums changed hands on a regular basis. I keep well clear of the place.

Cotespill changed the subject as if Van Hoebeek only merited minor interest, to the gambling house he and his friends had been to. I feigned my enthusiasm long enough to give distance between talking about Jaggers and the merchants, consuming more coffee in order to be able to leave without suspicion as to my motives.

I rose to my feet to bid Cotespill and his friends a good day, promising that I would think hard on their suggestions and advice and call in at Cole's soon, when a man walked in, took a quick look around, sniffed then pulled a face and then began to walk back outside.

'That's Jaggers,' said Cotespill, tugging my arm.

I looked and saw a man of similar size to me, maybe stockier and broader of shoulder; he had a ruddy complexion with unruly long dark hair. I noticed he had hands like shovels, fingers thick as sausages, perhaps in his forties; he seemed more like a pugilist than a merchant. His eyes were dark with thick eyebrows, a misaligned nose, indicating it may have been broken in the past, and what I would term a mean mouth, as I could not see him smiling much. I could not believe my luck. I smiled and nodded to Cotespill as if Jaggers held no importance to me.

I followed Jaggers out of the door into the crowded street and stood a few moments, trying to see where he had gone. For a second or so I thought I had already lost him, then I saw his dark hair moving amongst the throng of people heading down towards Lombard Street.

I caught up with him just after he turned the corner. 'Mr Jaggers?' I asked, coming alongside him.

Jaggers immediately stopped walking and turned to face me, forcing me to stop too. 'Who wants to know?' His voice sounded harsh and unpleasant as if speaking through a mouthful of gravel.

'My name is Richard Hopgood and I hope you can spare me a moment of your time.'

He looked me up and down. 'You were in Cole's, were you not?'

'I was,' I admitted.

'Then why not speak to me there?'

It struck me that he must be very observant because at best he could only have given me a passing glance. 'I could not catch you in time.'

He began to walk again at a brisker pace than before. 'What do you want then, Hopgood?' he barked, as we strode along.

'I have been engaged to investigate the demise of Pieter van Hoebeek and I understand that he and you had several disagreements,' I explained, as I hurried to keep up.

He stopped again abruptly and turned to me. 'Are you making an accusation?'

'Not at all,' I responded, as pleasantly as I could. People passed by on either side of us, cursing as we blocked their path. 'All I wish to know is the reason for the rancour.'

'Businessmen fall out occasionally, Hopgood,' he said, jabbing his thick pudgy finger into my chest. 'We sell to the same market, sometimes he won, sometimes I did. That's all there was to it. As he's dead now, it's of little consequence.'

'To you, maybe; others may think differently.'

'That is no concern of mine so I will thank you not to bother me with this again.'

'I may well need to, Mr Jaggers,' I replied, taking a step back. 'My enquiries will continue.'

Jaggers shot me a look of venom, his eyes narrowed and his lips turned up in a silent snarl. I saw his hands squeeze momentarily into fists before he regained his composure. 'If you know what's good for you, Hopgood, then stay away from me,' he said, storming off down the street.

I moved to the side of the pavement, next to a broker's and watched as Jaggers walked away, pondering on his strange aggressive reaction to my simple question. The man unquestionably had a hostile nature, lacking the charm and tact needed with his standing as a merchant. He seemed at odds with that perception, behaving more like a gang member, threatening violence to curb any dissent. I wondered if he had the good business acumen needed to consolidate and grow, and then I wondered what view his customers had of him; did he intimidate them into buying?

I thought pursuing him again would be a waste of time and I felt hungry anyway, so I resolved to find a reasonable chophouse where I could address the problem of my complaining stomach. Food had been available at Cole's but I felt the raucous atmosphere would have prevented adequate digestion.

I found a suitable place off Cornhill and ordered roasted chicken with vegetables. The plate did not stint on content, though the vegetables had been overlong in the pot, judging by the soggy green mess. As I ate, I turned my mind back to the conversation with Cotespill and the names of those who own Jaggers' warehouse; I had five more people to add to my ever-growing list and hoped that I would not have to add many more. I would have to put faces to those names; maybe I would have to go to The Hoop to find these men — Jaggers certainly did not want to talk with me.

I pushed my plate away, finished my watered lemon drink, paid my bill and then left. I had one more place to visit before I could catch up with Ned and Kitty a little later and I hoped they had been more successful than I had been.

The hackney bore me away to Westminster where I hoped to find some information regarding the trade that seemed to be at the heart of the investigation.

Alighting in New Palace Yard, I paid my fare and walked through the bustling place full of traders and stallholders, booths and ramshackle shops built up against the walls of the buildings. It might well be the seat of government but commerce reigned out in the Yard. I ambled into Old Palace Yard and headed to the little inconspicuous door that led down to a basement. I had been given a key only a few weeks ago and this would be just the second time I had used it; the first only to familiarise myself with what could be discovered down there. The office, the centre of the intelligence network of His Grace the Duke of Newcastle, Thomas Pelham-Holles, Secretary of State for the Southern Department, had just a few little rooms. Newcastle's writ encompassed foreign and colonial policy together with some homeland responsibilities. I became involved when I uncovered a group of Jacobite agitators a few months ago.

The Duke of Newcastle himself had given me the key as well as permission to use the information, though that came with a price that had yet to be charged; the price being that sooner or later I would become involved in something "secret."

My boots clattered on the flagstone floor of the corridor and then down some steps, along another corridor until I came to the door that led into the inner sanctum. I found the room devoid of occupation, the table showing the remnants of a meal, a pack of well-used cards, and a battered lantern giving off a little light.

I heard voices coming from beyond the door to the next room and called out, not wishing to enter whilst they discussed certain things. After a few moments, the door opened and a face appeared, nodded to me briefly, then the door closed again and the discussion continued. I sat down at the table and looked at the walls, studying the array of maps pinned upon wooden boards: intricate and finely detailed maps of London, the provinces and the coastline of the south and east. Larger maps of England, Scotland, Wales and Ireland showed the major cities and towns; maps of the coastlines of Spain, Portugal, France and up to Sweden and beyond, with lines indicating the trading routes of ships. Hard up against the walls stood cupboards and benches, strewn with pamphlets, newssheets and gazettes.

I picked up a publication to peruse when Fulton and Monk exited the inner room, both of whom I had worked with only a few months ago, bringing to justice the group of Jacobites as well as a murderer. The taciturn Fulton just held up a hand acknowledging my presence; a large-built man, John Fulton had a quiet introverted demeanour, until roused. He would never shirk from using rough tactics to get the result required. He had light brown hair topping a grizzled face and was of similar age to me.

Monk grinned. 'You joining us in our little enterprise, Richard?' he asked, walking towards me as I replaced the pamphlet. Philip Monk would pass unremarked in the street, an unassuming young man with dark wavy hair, quick to humour and an open friendly face.

'Monk!' yelled a warning voice from the room he had just left.

Monk twisted his head and grimaced. 'Not in the best of moods today,' he said, quietly.

'No discussions, no utterances of any description will leave your lips,' continued the voice. 'I made that clear.'

'Yes, sir,' replied Monk. He sighed and then sat down opposite me. 'Thought you were joining us,' he added, picking up the stale end of a loaf.

'No, I am looking into something—'

'Richard, do you want to see me or not?' said the forceful voice from within.

I grinned at Monk. 'Seems like I have no time to explain.'

Jarmin looked up at me from his desk as I entered and I could see there had been some recent alterations.

'That is new,' I remarked, looking at a door in the far wall that had not been there before. Then I turned my attention back to Jarmin. 'Good day, to you,' I said, sitting down on the proffered chair.

Jarmin had short light-brown hair, hazel eyes and wore a perpetual stubble on his face, about forty years of age and I had yet to discover whether he had a forename or not. 'Good day to you too, Richard, what brings you here?' he asked, without preamble.

'I wish to cast my eyes upon a file you might have. Smuggling, to be precise,' I replied, getting straight to the point as well.

'You intend to expand your interests?' he asked, a slight smile playing on his face.

'Maybe I should, it's quite a lucrative enterprise, I understand.'

'Not one without a certain amount of risk; however, grease the palm of a friendly magistrate and you have the freedom of the beaches. Does your interest have any bearing on our work here?'

'Not that I am aware of,' I answered, guardedly. 'I am looking into the death of a Dutch merchant and I'm getting whispers that smuggling may be involved.'

'Dutch? What name do you have?'

'Pieter van Hoebeek of Basinghall Street.'

Jarmin shook his head. 'I'm not familiar with the man, though the Dutch are involved with smuggling.'

'Yes; Canvey Island, I believe.'

'You are correct,' said Jarmin, sitting back in his chair. 'The customs go there now and again to search but find little evidence of it.'

I smiled. 'You do surprise me.'

Jarmin returned the smile. 'Canvey is a wild place full of marshland and it's all too easy to hide a few crates and bales of contraband there.'

'May I look at what information you have?'

'Be my guest,' he said, pointing to the new door in the wall. 'I requested another room, so the duke just took over that one and knocked through. At least we have a little more space now.'

Jarmin gave me a lantern and I stepped into the new room, full of files of information and someone had been diligent enough to put them into some sort of order. I found the section on smuggling, then sat down at the table to read in more comfort.

As I read, I became staggeringly aware of how much the illegal trade impacted on the legal trade and how the proportions between the two narrowed significantly. The high taxes on luxury imported goods created the demand for cheaper alternatives and the smugglers stepped in, only too happy to provide a ready supply. It seemed, from what I read, that those involved ranged from small coastal communities at the hard end of the business to inland villages and communities. Many respectable people of money and standing in society like the aristocracy, the gentry and officials, including magistrates, supplied the finances to fund the business, and of course, to take their share of the profits.

'Jarmin,' I called through the door. 'Why are these men financing the smuggling not being taken before a judge? You know who many of them are.'

'Ah,' he replied. 'There are two reasons really; one, we have to catch them in the act and most of them use diverse means to hide their involvement. Knowing they are involved is one thing, proving it, another. Second, now that is influence; who you know plays a large part in it and few men would not turn a blind eye to the prospect of having a cellar full of wine and brandy for their trouble. Let's be honest here, how many of us here in London have not occasionally bought goods knowing that they have bypassed the customs? I know I have.'

'Hmm,' I mused. 'I have too. So, we are all complicit in some form or other in that case.'

'Where there is a demand then there will be a supply. Unfortunately, those upstairs in government raise the taxes so high that many cannot afford to buy what they want. The customs do catch some of the free-traders, mainly just the small operators, unless serious violence is involved. Most are not even troubled.'

I turned over another file, this one having some details about the Dutch and I stared hard at the page as a name suddenly leapt out at me — I felt a grin come to my face.

CHAPTER 7

We had agreed, or rather I insisted, that we all meet at The White Hart, next to Kitty's lodging, at dusk. Communication between Ned and I had always been a problem when we were out and about following separate strands during an investigation; we would generally agree to meet up at a certain time or return home to Jermyn Street to leave a message. With Kitty being involved, I decided we should all meet at the tavern as I did not wish for Kitty to undertake the journey to my home.

I alighted from the hackney into the melee of people on their way to the theatre. I pushed through the crowd and walked into the tavern where I struggled to see anything other than a sea of anonymous faces, the noise intruding into my ears from all the shouted conversations. I nudged a few people out of my path as I headed towards the back, being as friendly as I could, giving a smile and an apology every now and again. Fortunately, a space opened and I could see Ned and Kitty sitting at a table full of discarded containers.

Kitty noticed me and beckoned, smiling warmly as I eased onto the bench and shoved her up against the wall. Ned, sitting opposite, greeted me with a nod.

'Glad you've arrived, sir. Been struggling to hold on to these seats these past twenty minutes or so.'

'What's on at the theatre,' I asked, scrutinising the table, seeking a pot for myself.

'Othello,' answered Kitty, pushing a full tankard in my direction. 'Most of these have been left,' she added, indicating all the empty pots and clay wine cups. 'Poor girl can't get through to clear them.'

The hubbub of noise made talking quietly impossible and I had no wish to shout out our business to all and sundry, so we talked of banalities as we waited for the tavern to empty as the time of the performance neared. After about ten minutes an exodus of souls occurred, discarded pots, bowls and cups were left upon any available surface, with some just dropped to the floor to be crushed and ground underfoot.

It seemed as if the tavern itself emitted a sigh as the theatregoers left, leaving the rest of us in a momentary state of peace and tranquillity, lasting all of a few seconds until the noise ascended from those of us who remained. The two pot-girls dashed about clearing up the mess with the enticing prospect of knowing that there would be a repeat, once the performance had ended and the theatregoers poured out into the streets and back into the inns and taverns.

Once the girl cleared our table and brought replenishments, I thought it time we related what we had learned since dispersing at the White Lion.

I turned to Kitty and patted her arm. 'Did you learn anything of Femke van Hoebeek, her friends and society?' I asked, attempting a wry smile.

Ned gave a grunt, indicating a mild contempt and I surmised Kitty had already told him what she had found out.

'A little,' she replied, shooting Ned a sharp look. 'I spoke to some of the girls working the area; as you know they tend to hear all the gossip and rumours, who pays well, who doesn't, whom to avoid. When I mentioned her name, one of the girls pointed me in the direction of a girl working down the road, saying that she would be able to tell me all about the Dutchwoman.

'I offered to pay the girl, Philippa, for her time if she talked to me. A poor wretch of a girl not suited to that type of work but she had no other choice. She worked as a maid in the household until they threw her out when she became unwell and unable to work. She had no money, no work and no food. Being innocent of life, she didn't realise what she would have to pay when she accepted an offer of a room; her innocence departed that same night.'

'You sound sad for her, but *you* once led that sort of life,' I said, seeing the look on her face.

'Yes, but I wasn't innocent. I grew up with the business; my mother, her sisters, they all sold themselves when work became short. I knew that I would be expected to earn my keep, a natural progression if you like, until recently, thanks largely to you. I did not expect my life to change, Richard,' and she gave me a shy smile. 'You gave me the chance to put it all behind me. Philippa had that way of life forced on her, not knowing anything about it, by Femke van Hoebeek, with the help and advice of her friend, Cornelia Visser.'

'Callous bitches,' opined Ned, taking a drink.

'Maybe,' I said. 'Perhaps they didn't realise what would happen to the girl.'

'You think so?' asked Kitty, her eyes widening.

'I do not know,' I replied. 'What I do know is that we

cannot be hypercritical here. You know Ned and I have both paid for services, have we not, Ned?'

'We have,' he admitted. 'Don't reckon it's the same though, the jades I use go into the trade willingly.'

'How do you know?' asked Kitty, sharply.

'Well, it stands to reason, don't it?'

'Does it? You mean they laugh at your jokes and tell you how much they enjoy your company and attention?'

'Well, yes.'

Kitty slowly shook her head. 'They want the money you pay them, and the better they pretend, the more they're likely to get; given the choice, most would not lie on their backs and invite a procession of men in for the love of it. It's a way to earn, that's all. I hated it, despite knowing all about it, was brought up to it.'

I had to think carefully before I responded to that. I could see in my mind someone handing me a shovel and telling me to dig a hole, refraining from telling me how deep or shallow I should go. I decided to hand the shovel back. 'I'm sorry, Kitty. I did not realise that. Naive of me, I grant you—'

She held up her hand to stop me from saying more. 'Please, let us leave it there. I felt angry on behalf of Philippa and you two are here on the receiving end. I just feel sorry for the girls who are forced into the trade.'

I nodded and cast Ned a warning glance before he could say anything else, considering his last few encounters. 'What did Philippa say about the household?' I asked, trying to get the conversation back to where it should be.

Kitty took a sip of her wine and put the cup down gently. 'Femke and Cornelia are lovers,' she replied. 'All the household staff know of the relationship. From what Philippa heard, they have been since they were young. Femke has no desire to know a man; Cornelia, however, flits between both men and women.'

'Really? What about other sapphists?' I asked. 'Do they meet others?'

'Sometimes; Philippa said that they had gatherings occasionally in the house, women only and the staff were not allowed to enter the rooms. Philippa said they all speculated on what went on.'

'What about clubs and societies?'

Kitty shook her head. 'Nothing like that; there is no equivalent to the Molly houses, if that's what you mean.'

I thought as much; I would have certainly heard about them if they existed and I had not. 'Then it must be through word of mouth, connections and the like.'

Kitty nodded again. 'It would not be difficult, a hint here, a comment there. Many would be married and have children just to appease their society; secretly, their desires would go in another direction.'

'I hope you paid Philippa well for all this information,' I said, once she had finished.

'Ten shillings, I told her I might return and she seemed keen for me to do so.'

I nodded. 'Good. Now this Cornelia; I think we should look at her. If Pieter did disturb her and Femke then maybe an act of revenge has occurred.'

'Unlikely,' replied Kitty. 'Pieter probably knew his sister had those inclinations and perhaps he knew Cornelia had them too; it would hardly be surprising if at some point he observed them together.'

'His sister, and from what Emily said, his former lover?'

She shrugged. 'Many things go on behind closed doors, Richard, that are considered normal by those involved.'

'Perhaps, but we don't know what occurred, if someone had said something, a threat, blackmail, a warning?' I held my hand up. 'We do not know the *whole* story.' I could tell from her countenance that she did not wholly agree with me. 'I have learned through experience, Kitty, that nothing can be discounted until proof is received, however unlikely that possibility seems to be.'

'A lecture?' she responded, a slight narrowing of her eyes.

'No, hardly that, just the grim reality.'

'Most already live in the grim reality, Richard, especially us at the lower end of the scale.'

A heavy silence intruded into our discussion and I felt the barb quite keenly. I should have realised, as Kitty had only recently risen out of the mire, the memory of that existence giving her clarity of thought. Although I did not intend my comment to apply directly to her circumstances or to those of the poorer classes, I could see how the phrase could touch a nerve.

Ned leant across the table and stabbed the stem of his pipe in my direction whilst giving a sly wink towards Kitty. 'Take no heed of 'im, lass, he tries hard, for Gentry, that is. Occasionally he forgets where the rest of us comes from.'

I saw Kitty smile as I screwed up my brow in thought; Ned had decided to disparage both me and my class. I opened my mouth to give a suitable riposte, then realised that whatever I said would be disparaging to both of them. Ned and I regularly poked fun at each other concerning our respective situations in life, knowing that sometimes we should just hold our tongues; Ned, in his wisdom, was telling me that this *was* one of those times. I could easily upset Kitty and be the poorer for it.

'I concede defeat,' I said, holding up a hand, attempting to snub out the discontent. 'I agree that my reality is somewhat different to yours, as you have so kindly reminded me. That does not change my premise with regard to Cornelia Visser. She remains a suspect. Now, Ned, what of your endeavours, did you learn anything of Ruud Janssen?'

I felt Kitty's hand rest on my arm and she tightened her grip momentarily and I knew then that she did not bear me any malice. Ned's tobacco smoke wafted beneath my nose and I delved into my pocket for my own. Kitty took it from my hand, then my tobacco pouch and began to fill it for me. I saw Ned's mouth twitch in a grin as he watched on.

'Janssen,' I said, bringing him out of his contemplation.

'Ah, yes,' he began, his eyes momentarily resting on Kitty before looking my way. 'I took a wherry downriver to Wapping, landed at Pelican Stairs, you know, by The Devil's Tavern.'

'Why there?' I asked, as Kitty lit my pipe with a taper by the candle. I watched mesmerised as the smoke curled out from between her lips.

'Best place to get a bit of information, is the Devil. Nothing gets by that rough old place; anything to do with Wapping they'll know it first, on the river or off.'

'I do not believe I have been there,' I said, wracking my mind for a memory.

'Not with me, anyway. Did a brewhouse in Shadwell Lane once, we did, but had no cause to go in the Devil. I've been a few times, had a friend that worked in the timber yard nearby; dead now, stack of logs fell on 'im a few months back, otherwise I'd be having a word with him.'

'Unfortunate.'

'For him or us?'

'Him, I am not that callous, Ned.'

He grinned. 'Are you not? Maybe I be mixing you up with someone else, sir.'

Kitty passed me my pipe whilst stifling a laugh. I feigned umbrage at Ned's remark and then placed the stem in my mouth and drew in the smoke. 'Carry on, Ned. The Devil,' I said, deciding not to bite back.

He grinned again. 'As it happens, there were a friend of my friend in there and we got to talking about the perils of working in the timber yard, as you would when talking about an old friend who got hushed by a bunch of logs. He were already pot-valiant when I got there so it were easy as you like to get on the subject of the butter-boxes down that way. Janssen has a case down on the front between Frying Pan stairs and King Edward stairs.'

'Did you go there?' I asked, leaning forward.

He held up a hand. 'Wait a while; I'll get there in a moment. Now, as you know, the Devil ain't exactly the most law-abiding establishment; a visit from the revenue were always good for a laugh as they never found anything. Even so, the coves in there are knee-deep in the smuggling trade, whether they be runners or boatmen or just simple buyers. Deals are done there and our friend Janssen, or one of his men, is a frequent visitor.'

'Does he talk to anyone in particular?'

Ned shook his head. 'Didn't say, just tipped me a wink as he said it, just before he fell asleep. Didn't want to waste any more time, so I left 'im a full pot and went to take a look at the warehouse. Rum sort of place, it is, has a jetty next to it and a couple more sheds to the side; enough room to store a fair bit of cargo. Busy sort of place around there, a lot of comings and goings, except for Janssen's, no movement there at all. Couldn't risk having a look inside, not in broad daylight so I just found a place for a bit of a rest for an hour or so. I were just getting to the point of leaving when guess who turned up.'

'Janssen?'

'No, that Martijn Thyssen. Had a key an' all he did. Came with his horse and cart, spent about thirty minutes inside and then came out with a load and off he went. Couldn't follow as he were going at a fair lick.'

'Probably no need to follow,' I said. 'Most likely just getting stock; though it is interesting that he had a key.'

'That's what I thought. You said he were speaking to Janssen at the funeral.'

'I did. Maybe he just sought permission to get some goods. Maybe he's deep in with Janssen, whether legal or not.'

'Illegal, is my guess.'

'Well, it's of a certainty that Janssen is involved in smuggling. I confirmed that earlier.'

'How?'

I smiled. 'Jarmin. I went to Westminster to find out what

they had on Dutch smugglers and Janssen's name came up within the documents. His business is a legal one as he imports from the Low Countries and that hides his illegal trade. As we thought, he has contacts on Canvey Island where the smuggled goods come in and then brought down to London by boat.'

'If that is known,' said Kitty, 'then why hasn't he been taken by the customs?'

'Simple really,' I replied. 'From what I understand he hides it in plain sight amongst the legal goods he imports. I imagine that he's adept at falsifying the paperwork. I said before that knowing is one thing, proving another. Besides, he may be paying people to look the other way.'

'In truth, a bit of smuggling don't do anyone any harm,' contributed Ned. 'We'd all be worse off if there weren't any. Do you think all those sitting in Parliament are paying the full price for all the wine and brandy they put away? Reckon they're as bad as the rest of us.'

'You mean worse than the rest of us,' remarked Kitty.

'You are both probably right; it is in our nature to hunt for a bargain, be we rich or poor.'

I took a draw on my pipe and then caught the eye of the girl to replenish our drinks and I ordered a plate of bread and cheese to ease our hunger pains.

'What else did you learn, sir?' asked Ned, breaking off a chunk of bread. 'Jaggers?'

I smiled ruefully. 'I went to his warehouse first to find him absent, so I decided to spend a little time at Cole's coffee house. As I got up to leave, Jaggers came in briefly and I followed him as he left. When I caught up with him he would not talk, just told me to leave him alone; gave a not-so-subtle threat. A nasty man, more of a huff really. The owners are five men, supposedly Gentlemen like myself, who want to make some money without doing any work. They invested their money in the merchants and chose Jaggers to manage the place.'

'Do you know them at all?'

I shook my head. 'I know of their names, that's all. Cannard, Ransom, De Griese, Sommerville and Balton, all frequent Cole's and by all accounts are partial to a bit of gambling. They went to The Hoop last night, from what I heard.'

'Then they're likely to be a few pounds lighter this morning,' replied Ned. 'That's a house that doesn't lose.'

'Quite,' I said. 'At least it gives us a little indication as to the manner of men they are.'

'Green-heads, you mean,' said Kitty.

'Precisely; more money than sense.'

CHAPTER 8

Ned and I returned to Jermyn Street a little before midnight, Kitty having retired to her lodging and eschewing my company for want of sleep. It had been a very long day for all of us and I admit that I did not feel up to the exertions required, grateful that she had made the excuse before I did.

'You must have hollow legs, Ned,' I said, as he rummaged in the kitchen, looking for something to eat.

'Can't help it if I need to eat more than the next man, sir,' he said, patting his expanding waistline.

'That's because you are a fat greedy oaf,' said Mary, standing at the door. Our entrance into the house had disturbed her slumber and she came down thinking that only Ned caused it.

'I am sorry we awakened you, Mary,' I said, deciding to get the apology in early. 'Ned is feeling faint through lack of sustenance.'

'Though not through lack of drink,' she replied, sniffing the air.'

'Ah, I admit that we have both indulged a little, maybe moderately but certainly not to excess,' I countered, more for my benefit than Ned's.

'What you do, sir, is your own affair; as the housekeeper, footmen come under mine.'

'Yeah, when I'm a footman; today I were assisting the master so your point is mute,' responded Ned.

Mary glared at Ned for a moment and then seemed to relent. 'Besides, what you eat now you will not have in the morning, so it is your choice,' she replied, her arms crossed beneath her breasts, a determined expression upon her face. Unfortunately, her nightcap and night-attire, buttoned up to the neck, leant a comical look to her and both Ned and I began to laugh.

'Oh, Mary,' I said, once my mirth had ceased. 'You have a look that would freeze Hades, if only you could see yourself.'

She pursed her lips, narrowed her eyes and then spun around, holding her head high in dignity before walking purposefully to the stairs and up to her room, not saying another word.

'We're in for it now,' said Ned, staring at the door. 'So, I ain't gonna suffer on an empty stomach,' he added, turning to the bread he had found, taking a bite and grinning before beginning to chew.

True to her word, Mary displayed a frosty countenance in the morning, less so with me, taking aim more at Ned. Young Jane thought it highly amusing, bustling about the kitchen and hiding her wry grins from Mary.

As promised, Ned received a frugal breakfast. I cast him a warning glance as I knew that she just wanted an excuse to continue the tirade from last night. I deemed his scant first meal of the day to be of little importance as a visit to the nearest chophouse would soon put things right.

'You still want me to return to Janssen's, sir?' asked Ned,

finishing the last mouthful of coffee.

'I do, speak to the scavengers, see what they have to say, the casual workers, the vagrants; nothing much gets past these people and for a coin or two they may well give us what we need.'

'With Kitty looking into Cornelia Visser that just leaves you.'

'It does; I wish to find those five owners so I will pay another visit to Cole's to start with and then go from there.'

'Where and when will we meet up?'

'The White Hart again, I think, late afternoon, around five of the clock. If you encounter any trouble at all then back away, I suspect Janssen would not be concerned about flexing a little muscle if need be.'

He nodded. 'Right you are; would you object if I find Little Alex and take him with me?'

A young lad, Little Alex had certain talents of the illegal kind and sometimes we utilised those talents. Residing in Covent Garden, I had him keep a wary eye on Kitty and her stall when she first set up in business and he still helped her now. 'That would not be a bad idea,' I replied, thinking it through. 'Just do not let him fleece you.'

Ned just grinned.

Alex would fleece anyone if he thought he could get away with it.

Once Ned had set off to find Little Alex, I left Jermyn Street and took a hackney down to Cornhill. Mary's expression did not waver as I left the house and I must admit I felt a little sorry for Jane, who would have to suffer for the next few hours.

The day promised to be another warm one, so I just wore my light jacket over my waistcoat. The little breeze did little to dispel the aroma of the city; with the lack of rain, the sewage system struggled to deal with what the thousands of people and animals produced.

I walked into Cornhill to find it already busy with folk going about their businesses; beggars also littered the street seeking a few coins from anyone generous enough to bestow their largess. I ignored them all, easing my way through, then turned into Birchin Lane and walked down towards Cole's.

Most of the coffee houses were already doing a brisk early trade and Cole's was no exception. I opened the door to find it a little more subdued than yesterday. Cotespill sat in the same seat that I had left him and as soon as I entered he stood up and waved me over, a big grin on his face.

'Hopgood, good to see you again, and so soon.'

'Cotespill,' I acknowledged, raising my arm.

'What brings you back here; after some more advice?'

'I am still pondering what you have already told me,' I replied, easing myself behind the table. 'I thought to have a coffee to stimulate my mind and wake me up.'

'Ah, an indulgent night you had then?'

'Well, I certainly indulged,' I replied, giving him a grin.

He laughed, a great big belly laugh and a few people turned their heads to look. He slapped the table and wiped his eyes to recover his composure.

'Hopgood, you have such a sharp wit that I am at a loss to keep up.'

I did not think my wit that pronounced but if Cotespill thought otherwise, then I certainly would not gainsay him.

Instead, I inclined my head in acknowledgement of his observation. 'You are on your own, this morning Cotespill, Bryant and James have other business?'

'Their absence is down to them indulging too, I believe. I would have joined them if I had not a family engagement of music and cards; most excruciating really, but you have to oblige now and again.'

We chatted as we drank our coffee and when someone came in, Cotespill would always raise a hand and utter a greeting. After perhaps thirty minutes, the door opened and Cotespill held his hand up again. 'De Griese, good morning to you,' he said.

De Griese looked his way and then nodded before moving over to a table by the window. He removed his hat as he sat down and picked up a newssheet.

'De Griese? Is that not the name you gave me yesterday?' I asked, keeping a wary eye on the fellow.

He screwed up his brow for a moment until recollection came. 'Yes, yes indeed. One of those merchants I told you about. The others aren't here yet, I suppose they will probably arrive shortly.'

De Griese sat at the table alone, reading the newssheet and I got the impression that he did not wish to be disturbed. He appeared to be older than I, of average build and height with a swarthy complexion, dark intense eyes and a thin pensive mouth. He wore no wig to cover his dark wavy hair. A brooding presence and I could see him sucking the joy from any room he inhabited. I resolved to keep him in sight as Cotespill continued to talk.

Several minutes later, the door opened again and four

young men came in, totally ignoring Cotespill as he called out a greeting, just hurrying over to De Griese's table and sitting down.

'I take it they are the other four owners of the merchants?' I said, watching them as they settled.

'Indeed, they are,' replied Cotespill, sombrely, as if the rebuttal had hit him hard. 'Unfortunately, they are not the most mannerly of men.'

I would hardly have called them men. All four looked to be about eighteen years old or so, all sallow complexioned with the air of immaturity. Kitty had them right without even seeing them; green-heads. The cut and style of their clothes indicated that they had money, though it was unlikely that they had earned it in any way. I would ordinarily dismiss these types of men as unremarkable, the difference in manner and bearing between the four windy-headed youths, as I decided to view them, and De Griese, contrasted widely. De Griese appeared assured, confident and mature, whereas the four others twittered excitedly as if young girls, the total opposite of the elder's demeanour.

My interest increased significantly as I viewed the table. Cotespill kept up a constant stream of observations and opinions as I tried to eavesdrop on their conversation. Eventually, he took a breath, creating a lull and I heard them say something about burning and the river. Cotespill renewed his discourse and between his sentences, I snatched talk from the five that "things should be clear now." Then they all laughed, all except for De Griese, who kept his features neutral. The noise level in the coffee house rose and eavesdropping became impossible, frustrating me immensely.

The neighbouring table then drew Cotespill into a discussion, allowing me a little respite so I surreptitiously resumed my study.

I sipped my coffee, now harsh and bitter as I got to the dregs of the bowl and decided that I should leave. I fished out a few coins and left them on the table, nudged Cotespill and bid him a good day.

'Oh, right, Hopgood,' said Cotespill, distractedly. 'You must think me poor company alas, for my good fellows here caught my attention.'

'Never in life, Cotespill,' I replied, giving him a cheerful smile. 'I look forward to seeing you again soon. Enjoy your discussion.'

I had the measure of Jaggers from yesterday, so I thought it now prudent to do the same with De Griese. The four others I could not entirely dismiss from my reckoning, even though I had the impression that they just supplied the money and that De Griese and Jaggers held the reins and controlled it all. I wanted a bit of space from Cotespill so that I could concentrate on what I wished to achieve.

I left Cole's and moved up the lane a little, stopping by the Swordblade Coffee House. I looked into the window and saw an available seat from where I could view the lane and the entrance to Cole's; it seemed a perfect solution to my predicament.

CHAPTER 9

De Griese finally exited Cole's a good hour or so after I had taken my seat in the Swordblade. I indulged in two further bowls of hot bitter coffee and some sweet pastries. I had looked at three newssheets, positioning myself at an angle to view the lane, holding the sheets appropriately as I perused the articles, the majority hardly registering in my mind. A few drew my notice like the continued funding of the bridge at Westminster by taking two pounds from every lottery ticket bought came to my attention, having spoken with Cotespill on the matter; an article about Sweden declaring war on Russia because of territorial loss; another war, between the Dutch and Chinese in Java out in the east. All very depressing and it seemed to me the whole world was in conflict. A child pulled out from the Thames in a decomposed state by some watermen, another to add to the many already dragged out over the last few months; a short list of absconded negroes with rewards for capture; another list of felons due to hang at Tyburn, none of whom were the result of my work. I felt a wry grin come to my face, then I quickly finished my bowl, dropped a few coins on the table, inclined my head to the proprietor in thanks and left the establishment.

I knew nothing of De Griese's background or station in life, where he came from, nor anything else for that matter. I would have to discover that for myself. I followed him down to Lombard Street where he turned left, I thought him to be heading towards his merchant's warehouse in Rood Lane, so I eased off a little and allowed a discreet distance to open up. De Griese did not seem to be in a hurry, keeping his pace slow and steady. I kept stopping and looking into windows to stay behind him, then suddenly he increased his pace, allowing an even bigger distance to develop. I wondered if this amounted to a tactic but he did not turn around to check if someone was paying him undue attention. I decided it must be his awkward way of walking and besides, he could have no reason to suppose that I or anyone else would be interested in where he went or what he did when he got there. The afternoon became hot with sunshine brightening the streets, the sky decorated by a few wispy white clouds amongst the expanse of blue. De Griese stopped at a booth and bought a pie, then carried on walking, eating some, discarding the rest as if he did not like the taste, the remnants quickly picked up by a young, emaciated boy calling to passers-by for a coin or two.

Surprising me, he turned right down Gracechurch Street, the road leading to Fish Street and then London Bridge. The crowds had thinned a little, so I hung back even further, giving a little more distance between us. De Griese kept up with his pacing, slow and then speeding up as the mood seemed to take him. On the left-hand side of the road, the coaches and carts moved slowly as the queue to cross the bridge began to form; it did not bode well for them as it would take an age to move down from this position. The traffic coming up from the bridge began to gather a little pace as if the enforced crawl they had endured to cross over gave them the impetus to catch up for lost time.

As we got to Fish Street Hill, De Griese saw a gap and immediately stepped into the traffic between two oncoming carts and then slipped between two others waiting in the queue. I stayed on my side of the road for a moment or two as I could still see him easily enough. I increased my pace so that I could keep a closer eye on him until the crowd of people began to bunch and it became hard to keep to any sort of rhythm in my walking. As I came abreast of the church of St Magnus, I decided to cross over. The traffic going onto the bridge was still static in the queue, that coming off, slow moving, so I took my chance and reached the other side without mishap, even avoiding the piles of horse manure that covered the road.

The noise of the people and the rattle and shouts from the carts and carters rose significantly, as if the closely packed buildings upon the bridge reflected the sound back to those of us waiting to cross. I could see De Griese, about twenty feet in front of me amongst the press of the crowd, waiting to pay the toll, many managing to avoid paying, being dextrous of foot.

Once upon the bridge, the narrow footway made progression even harder, with those coming out of the shops and chophouses adding to the struggle to retain the flow. Frequent accidents occurred as the wheeled traffic passed just inches from where people walked, you took your life in your hands should you be unfortunate enough to step off the walkway.

I could still see De Griese up ahead, his hat jigging as he

attempted to push his way through the crush, occasionally movement became easier as I passed a choke point, until the next point came and then progression stifled yet again. I wondered why De Griese had not taken a wherry to cross to Southwark; far quicker and for the money you did not have to contend with the crowds.

After several minutes, with the wheeled traffic either slow or unmoving, the southern end came in sight, passing beneath Nonsuch House and then the Gate House, displaying the rotting heads of traitors. Here the crowds began to thin out and walking became easier, allowing De Griese to pick up his pace. The traffic to my right began to move more quickly now and I eased over to my left as a careless driver sent a wheel onto the walkway before it crashed back down onto the road. I looked up as I recovered my step and found De Griese no longer in sight; he seemed to have just disappeared. Perplexed, I continued to walk, looking to see if he had entered a shop without my observing him. Suddenly, I felt a press of people upon my back and it seemed as if the crowd had once more formed and propelled me forward. My short steps became rushed and then I felt a fierce nudge in my back, pushing me towards the side, out into the roadway. I heard women scream and men shouting and got the fleeting impression of a large dark shape looming to my right. I stumbled, desperate to control my errant limbs as I crashed against the wooden shaft of a cart, my face sinking into soft sweaty horseflesh, the odour striking my nostrils. My hand reached forward to grab the girth strap and as I held on, I heard the shout of a man telling me to get off, hearing the crack of a whip above my head. I stumbled, then managed to get my legs working, running to keep up for a few paces until I stumbled again and could sense the wheel behind me. I pushed away, tripped over my legs and then fell, the wheels running just an inch or so from my head. I heard the gasp of the crowd as they recognised my imminent departure from this world, another shout and then the cart rumbled away, leaving me thankfully unscathed apart from a bruise or two and my hat, crushed beneath the wheels. I rolled onto my back and sat up, looking ahead into the crowd, seeing De Griese, a smile splitting his features. He turned quickly and walked away.

'Are you alright, sir?' asked a male voice close to me. 'Gone under those wheels and you would've been food fer the maggots.'

'Thank you, yes,' I replied, testing and moving my limbs, thankful they still worked. 'I have been very fortunate.'

'Someone should do something, 'appens all the time, does this,' said a woman close by.

'They won't do nuffink, not until someone important gets smeared across the road,' said someone else.

'And you ain't gonna get someone important walking down this way, is you?'

'Never a chance, the devil take them.'

I moved over onto my knees and then a helpful hand aided me to my feet.

'Up you get, sir, before another one 'as its go,' said the man with a smile.

I thanked him profusely and all the others around who offered aid and advice for a poor unfortunate man very nearly crushed to death beneath the wheels of a cart.

De Griese had disappeared and I gave up hope of continuing to follow him. The cynical smile I saw, and the fact that he had gone from my view just prior to being shoved into the roadway, led me to believe that I had just survived a deliberate attempt on my life.

I had no desire to force my way back across the bridge so I wiped the grime from my clothes as best I could, reshaped my battered hat and continued to walk to the end of the bridge; I intended to take a wherry in comfort and safety to the north side of the river. I felt an urge for a drink having survived the ordeal and had little appetite for an inn in Southwark just now.

Sitting in the Red Bull, I quickly downed a good half of my pot of ale before remembering that I had to keep a clear head in order to think rationally. De Griese knew that I followed him and for the life of me, I do not know how he had done so. Had he conversed with Jaggers and expected me to do something? He certainly had expertise in the craft, so where did he learn it? I took care to keep myself hidden and I did not once see him look behind, in my naivety I believed I had the advantage. I must have been careless, I must have given myself away. I wracked my memory for the when and how. Whichever way I looked at it, De Griese was a dangerous adversary, posing the question of why had he joined league with those four lackwitted youths? I could readily picture Jaggers and De Griese together — but not as merchants. Something did not sit right. Pure luck allowed me to sit and think about it all; I could be lying in a dead-house. I resolved to find out the truth. De Griese must have hoped that by pushing me under a cart my interest would wane and be at an end. If he knew for what reason I followed him, then that information must have come from Jaggers.

I needed to find the answers to plenty of questions, only knowing from the recent proof that De Griese and Jaggers would not baulk at committing murder.

I concluded my ruminations by finishing my pot of ale, hardly even tasting it but it enabled me to gather my thoughts and to calm me down after my misadventure on the bridge. I became determined to find out what lay behind it and decided that the four youths might well be a weak spot for De Griese and Jaggers. My task for the rest of the day came to me; I would find one of them and ask a few pertinent questions.

Leaving the tavern, I headed back to Cole's to see if the four were still there, or if not, hoped for some indication of where I might find them. When I arrived, Cotespill still sat at the same table, accompanied by a gentleman I had not seen before. I turned my head to the table where De Griese had sat finding a new group now sitting there. My face must have shown my frustration because Cotespill called over to me.

'Hopgood, over here,' he said, waving his hand. 'You do not appear quite as sanguine as you did earlier and you seem to have had an accident; what on earth has happened to your hat?'

I forced a smile. 'That is so, Cotespill,' I answered, walking over to his table. 'An accident occurred where I unfortunately fell into the road. My fault as I was not looking where I was going, hence my bedraggled appearance, my damaged hat and my sour face.' I held out my hands as if in explanation.

'Then you need a tonic to set you to rights once again.'

'Thank you for your concern. Fortunately, I am quite recovered now. I was thinking, which happened to be why I stumbled and only returned here to see if those merchant men were still here, as I wished to discuss a thought I had with them.'

'You mean Sommerville, Cannard, Balton, De Griese and Ransom?'

'I do indeed, Cotespill. Have you any notion of where I might find them?'

'Ah, you have me there. I'm afraid I do not.'

'Those rakes are more trouble than they're worth,' interjected a man from the next table. 'You'd do best to avoid having any interaction with them.'

'You think so?' I said, turning to face him.

'I do. Gamblers and drunkards are what they are. I heard them talking about a cockfight tonight in Southwark at a brewhouse off Counter Lane, I ask you, a brewhouse! Any man of worth would only attend the Royal Cock Pit in Old Queen Street, where at least there is good company and ladies of refinement.'

'Then maybe I will rethink if they are not to be trusted.'

'Wise, sir, in my humble opinion.'

I nodded my thanks to the man who returned to his companions, not realising that he had given me the information I required. I knew Counter Lane, a disreputable area full of cheap whores and cheap drink, both of a dubious and risky quality. Industry proliferated with its tanneries and dyers, timber and coal yards, millers and metalworkers, indicated by the rank odour that always seemed to hang over the place. The several prisons in the area, amongst them the

Marshalsea and the Kings Bench, housed all manner of felon from debtors to murderers. Southwark had a different flavour to that of the north side of the river, with its legacy of blood sports, dog-fighting and bear-baiting, much of those sports having now been removed to Hackney in the Hole. Pugilism still proved popular where men fought for large purses and larger reputations.

I think I might approach the evening with a degree of wariness.

CHAPTER 10

I had a few hours of idleness before meeting up with Ned and Kitty, so decided it would be a good use of my time to inform Femke van Hoebeek of my progress to date, first detouring home to change my clothes so I could at least look presentable. When I arrived in Basinghall Street I found that she had gone out, giving no indication of when she would return. In some respects I felt relieved as I had made no real progress apart from a suspicion that smuggling may be indicated; as to the murderer, I had made no steps forward. I thought not to waste any more time so began to walk up to her warehouse to see if I could speak again to the workers, hoping to garner something there to take me forward.

As I walked, I again mulled over my near miss on the bridge, rankling me further. How did De Griese get behind me and use the crowd as cover to force me into the road — and why? I came up with the answer that something needed protecting, something important that he did not want me to discover. He knew I followed him and without doubt, this expertise indicated professionalism, someone trained in the art.

The more I thought about it, the more convinced I became; De Griese had a history in work of a clandestine nature.

I approached the warehouse still in deep contemplation when a cart drove out of the yard and headed away to the corner and then around. I stopped, momentarily thinking that the driver seemed familiar; I could not at that instance recollect him nor where I had seen him before. I shook off the feeling and picked up my step again, entering the yard to see several men carrying boxes and crates into the warehouse. One of the men noticed me and nodded to Martijn Thyssen to indicate my presence.

Martijn turned abruptly my way, frowning at first and then replacing it with a look of recognition. 'Mr Hopgood,' he said, walking towards me.

'Good afternoon to you, Martijn. I see business is going on as usual.'

'It is, sir. We have stock to procure and deliveries to make; we work, doing so with a heavy heart.'

'No doubt, Martijn,' I replied, convinced that though he said the words, he did not mean the sentiment.

'Have you discovered the master's assailant yet?' he asked.

'Progressing, I would say,' I ventured, after a moment's pause. 'Like many things in life, time and perseverance will lead to a satisfactory conclusion.'

'Then I wish you well in your endeavours, Mr Hopgood. Now, if there is anything you need from me?'

'Ah, yes, I wish the opportunity to ask your men some questions. Are these all your workers?'

'Pretty much; Lars is not here as he works overnight.'

'That is splendid, Martijn. It seems I have judged my arrival appropriately, call them over, please,' I replied.

He gave a slight hesitation and then began to call the

workers over and soon a small gathering of men stood in front of me, most looking keenly at their feet to avoid any contact with my eye. It seemed as if I were about to address a small group of unruly children, awaiting a punishment from an earlier transgression.

'For those of you who are unaware,' I began. 'My name is Richard Hopgood and I have been engaged by your mistress to look into the murder of your master, Pieter. I need to know if any of you have any information or suspicions regarding the demise of Pieter, then needless to say, it is imperative that you make me aware of it.' I waited a few moments to see if anyone would respond, hoping that at least one of them would meet my eye. None did. 'Did Pieter say anything to any of you? Did you see or notice anything unusual?' Still no response. I looked at each of them in turn and they all stood with their heads down, lips firmly closed. 'Very well,' I said in the end. 'I can always be contacted at The Brown Bear, Bow Street should any of you recollect something that may be of interest to me. If no one has anything to say then I will leave you to your work; you seem to have a delivery of tea, if I am not mistaken.'

'Is that it now, Mr Hopgood?' asked Martijn, eager for me to be on my way.

'For now, it is,' I replied. 'No doubt I will speak to you again,' I added, as I turned to walk out of the yard.

As I got to the street, I looked towards the corner where the cart earlier had headed and thought again that I had seen the driver before. I walked away with my mind whirling as I desperately tried to place him.

When I got to Cripplegate I managed to hail a hackney to

take me to Drury Lane and settled onto the badly repaired wooden bench seat; I had to be careful of splinters as it had yet to be polished smooth by the rears of many travellers.

My mind dwelt on my interaction with Jaggers yesterday and the aggressive stance he took when my mind suddenly cleared and I knew where I had seen that driver before; Jaggers' warehouse, he held a horse whilst the other two men loaded.

What, I wondered, was a man working for Jaggers doing at the warehouse of Pieter van Hoebeek?

I arrived at the White Hart a little before our agreed time, not surprised to find that neither of them had arrived. I quickly claimed the booth where we normally sat, spreading myself out as best I could with my jacket and hat to indicate occupation. I began conversing with the pot-girl about the food on offer when Kitty and Ned, with Little Alex in tow, came in.

'Hungry?' I asked Little Alex when he settled on his seat next to Ned.

The boy nodded. 'Ain't I always?'

Yes, I thought, the Little Alexs' of the city were always hungry. A scrag of a boy a little below five feet tall, skinny as a wand with a mop of dark dirty hair. His clothes, third-hand at best, hung off him. His lack of nourishment had stunted his growth, making him look about ten years old; I knew him to be at least thirteen and wise beyond his years. 'Then you may have your fill, young man. I understand from our hostess here that there is a choice of either fish cooked in a pan, chicken with potatoes and vegetables, a stew of mutton and finally, veal. Which would you prefer?'

'What do you get most of?'

I smiled at the girl. 'The young gentleman seems to favour quantity over quality; what would you suggest?'

'Mutton,' she replied, giving the boy a wink.

'Then make it so. I will have some veal and you two?' I asked, turning my attention to Kitty and Ned.

Kitty decided fish and Ned the mutton and as we awaited our fare, frothing tankards of ale and a bottle of Portuguese wine arrived and then chunks of bread with a lump of freshly churned butter. Little Alex's eyes widened and then he set to eagerly.

'Now,' I began. 'I suspect the fact that you have arrived together is significant, is it not?'

'Not,' replied Ned, grinning. 'We saw each other on the way here. Simple as that.'

'Oh, erm...how did you get on?'

'Burnt to a cinder,' said Little Alex before Ned could answer. 'The place you were interested in, burnt, it were.'

'What?'

'The lad's right, sir,' said Ned, shooting Alex a look. 'It were just ash and burnt timber. Someone set fire to it last night by all accounts.'

'Not an accident?' I asked, surprised and a little shocked.

Ned shook his head. 'No, the few people I spoke to claimed they knew nothing. Me and Alex took a walk along the wharf and found a crew of youngsters living on the shore in an old boatshed. They were a bit wary of me at first, until Alex put them to rights. They scavenge the shore and the sewers, selling what they find, poor buggers, so I gave them a little chink so that they could get a decent bit of grub; the mites were half-starved, they were. Anyways, they saw what happened.'

He stopped talking and took up his pot for a drink as Kitty and I waited for him to continue. Alex looked at Ned and then shrugged his shoulders before taking up the story.

'They's all kinchin-coves, they is but they's have sharp peepers. They sees an ark come by wiv three coves in it. It were dark but there were just enough light to see and they saw it going by and wondered wot it were up to as it didn't 'ave no stern light. A pair o'them upped and followed, reckoning that if they were up to a bit of filching, then there might be some leftovers. Anyway, three rum-coves went straight to the butter-boxes case, tied up and cracked it. Next thing, they's go running back to the ark, jumped in and off they goes, just as the case went up in flames. It were done quick like, no messing.'

'Where did the boat come from?' I asked, feeling my brow furrowing.

'Upriver,' said Ned. 'From the city; went back that way too.'

'No idea who they were?'

Ned shook his head. 'The boys didn't get close to 'em and who could blame 'em.'

I thought about what I heard in Cole's, those four and De Griese talking about a burning on the river and that things should be clear now. I wondered whether they had heard something that morning or could it be that they had a hand in it? I could only speculate and that would not be proof. 'Shame,' I replied. 'No, we cannot blame them; they did well to notice anything. Any word about Janssen?'

Ned shook his head again. 'No one has seen him. Strange that; his warehouse goes up in flames and he's not come down to see the damage; I believe he were sent for first thing from what I were told.'

'What about the watchman?'

'He took a walk as he had several businesses to look after. He didn't see a thing 'til the fire took hold and then it were too late.'

'Not a good watchman then.'

'Seems not, unless he was paid not to be a good watchman.'

'Ah, yes, that is a possibility.'

'You think someone paid him to look the other way?' asked Kitty.

I shrugged my shoulders.

'He only had six or seven places, none of them big. You'd have thought he'd see a boat and three men tie up, fire the place and then leave, wouldn't you?' said Ned.

'But does this have anything to do with Pieter van Hoebeek?' asked Kitty.

'That's a good question,' I replied. 'Is it just coincidence that a Dutch merchant is murdered, whom we suspect, sold smuggled goods and his supplier, who we know smuggles goods, has his premises burnt down just a few days later?'

'Unlikely,' answered Ned.

'My thoughts also,' I said, pondering the situation. 'I saw one of Jaggers' men at the Van Hoebeek place earlier. I wonder…?' I said, tapping my chin.

'What happened?' asked Kitty, her eyes widening.

'Later, let me hear what you have to say about Cornelia Visser first.'

The food arrived and a hiatus entered the conversation to allow the girl to serve and for us to begin to eat. I noticed Little Alex's plate had a somewhat larger quantity upon it than did Ned's and I saw the girl smile at the boy as Ned looked askance.

'Leave it,' I warned Ned, nipping the comment in the bud.

He shut his mouth then pursed his lips in umbrage.

'I suspect our fair maid has taken pity on Alex,' I said quietly when she had left our table.

'Pity?' replied Ned and nudged the boy with his elbow. 'You ain't going to manage all that, are you?'

'Too right I will. Watch me,' replied Alex, picking up his spoon.

After a few moments of contemplative chewing, or slurping, in Alex's case, we returned to the business at hand.

Kitty finished her mouthful and then began. 'Cornelia Visser is married to a wealthy man, a Roger Tewksley. Despite that, it seems she regards marriage as just a convenience, indulging her pleasures where she will.'

'Even though she's married?'

'You sound surprised, Richard. We know she has sapphist tendencies.'

'Yes, but she *was* Van Hoebeek's lover.'

'*Both* Van Hoebeeks' lover,' replied Kitty, a slight smile on her face.

'Ah, yes.'

'I thought you understood these things, Richard.'

'I thought so too.'

'I told you last night how things can be, that a woman's inclinations may not reflect her marital situation. I know that some men too take a wife, just to show respectability to their social and professional circles, allowing them to indulge their preferences in private; the Molly houses are proof of that.'

I held my hand up for her to cease the flow. 'You accused me of lecturing to you last night, now you're doing the same.'

'Not lecturing, Richard, explaining,' she defended, with a spark in her eye. 'Last night, I believe you called it the "grim reality."'

Ned barked a laugh. 'She has you there, sir. How did the man Shakespeare put it? Oh, yes. "Hoisted by your own petard."'

'Alright,' I replied after a moment's thought. 'I concede,' I acknowledged, smiling and shaking my head slowly in defeat.

'The marriage may be just a sham,' she added.

'There are no children?' I asked.'

'No, just a small dog, does that count?'

'From all accounts, she's a bit of a bitch,' quipped Ned.

'Enough,' I said, placing my eating implements upon the plate. 'In truth, we cannot malign the woman, at least not until we know more. What of this husband?'

'An Englishman,' replied Kitty. 'He is known to visit bawdy houses and he likes his whores young — and I mean *very* young. So, feel free to malign *him*.'

'Interesting,' I said. 'It would seem that both of them are not as clean as they appear.'

'No, they're not. This Roger Tewksley is meant to be respectable in all other ways. A church elder and a philanthropist. Like you, he has a private income and some business interests.'

'Someone who cloaks his vices in good deeds, perhaps?'

'Or someone who uses his good deeds to enjoy his vices.'

'Meaning?'

'Word on the streets says he funds a small establishment for orphaned children.'

'Like Thomas Coram's foundling hospital?'

'Maybe *not* like Thomas Coram's foundling hospital.'

'Ah, I get your meaning,' I replied, thoughtfully. 'And if Pieter van Hoebeek knew something, er, sordid…'

Kitty nodded. 'The husband of his sister's friend. Maybe he heard something he should not have heard.'

I sighed and leant back in my seat; my appetite had suddenly deserted me.

'What's more, a girl saw him have a blazing row in the street with a Dutchman.'

I looked up. 'A Dutchman? How did she know?' I asked.

'Because Tewksley called him a butter-box.'

CHAPTER 11

My anger had abated some while ago as I related my events without emotion, just giving the details in a calm and precise manner. I could feel the anger emanating from Kitty and Ned regarding De Griese, with Ned squeezing his hands into tight fists as if wringing a neck. Kitty stroked my arm at first, then I felt her grip tighten and I saw her eyes narrow before she regained her composure.

Little Alex appeared disinterested, concentrating on wiping the plates of our leftovers so that nothing would go to waste. As soon as I mentioned the cockfight in Southwark Ned's anger dissipated and I could see an eagerness come to his features.

'A cockfight? Haven't been to one of them for months,' he said, draining his pot.

'Neither have I, thankfully,' I said, as I picked up my drink. 'Doubt the standard will be very high.'

'Maybe, but it's still a cockfight.'

'I'll come too,' said Kitty. 'There is safety in numbers. I might wager a shilling or two even though the sport is not to my liking.'

Little Alex looked up expectantly having now polished the plates clean, apart from the fish bones.

'No,' I said to his unasked question. 'You are not joining

us.'

The boy's shoulders slumped in dejection at the rebuff, though I expect his full belly compensated for his disappointment.

We left Alex outside the White Hart, watching for a while as his laboured legs carried him towards Covent Garden, then hailed a hackney to take us to Southwark. The driver vociferously refused the bridge, dropping us instead on Thames Street by Old Swan Lane, leaving us to either walk or take a wherry.

Ned voiced his opinion on the driver's complaining nature and reluctance to cross the bridge. 'Picked a right one there,' said Ned, as the truculent driver snapped the reins to drive off. 'Hope you lose a wheel!' he yelled and received a single raised finger in reply.

Kitty and I shared a grin as Ned gesticulated wildly, the pedestrians in the street stopping to watch.

'Have you finished?' I asked Ned, who still stared at the departing hackney.

'Bastard hackney drivers, they're all the same. Think they know everything.'

'Ned, he is driving off and we are standing here, so in this case, he does.'

'Alright, point taken, sir.' He held up his hands.

'Come on, let's make for the stairs,' I said, trying not to laugh.

We walked down Old Swan Lane towards the stairs, joining several people already waiting for a crossing. They shouted and waved arms towards the river attempting to draw attention from one of the watermen. Two wherries eventually answered, leaving us three for the next. Ned bellowed and shortly a boat appeared. The men behind us tried to push their way past, discovering their mistake after a short remonstration, with Ned giving them a detailed account of their immediate futures. They changed their minds and allowed us to take the boat.

'St Mary Ovarie,' I said, as I settled next to Kitty.

The two men shoved off and we scudded across the river, the looming monstrous bridge to our left. The men plying the oars bent their backs to it, picking up the pace and swearing copiously at the other traffic; a false move, a missed stroke could cause a collision resulting in a ducking for all of us.

Accidents occurred frequently on the river, caused mainly by inebriation or lack of experience and it pleased me that our conveyance showed no sign of either. We traversed the river at a rapid speed and within a few short minutes, we glided towards our destination. I paid our fare and as we stepped off, two couples eager for the race to replace us in the boat rudely pushed us aside. Remarkably, Ned did not complain, instead just stared hard at them, garnering no response whatsoever.

'Come on,' I said, as we stepped off the jetty and onto the wharf, entering the Liberty of the Clink, under the authority of the Bishop of Winchester; his old palace, now converted into tenements, lay just ahead. The Clink Prison, to our left, suffered through lack of maintenance, a building in decay, now hardly used because of its condition. 'Or I'll claim you are a heretic, Ned, and have the bishop incarcerate you.'

'Ha ha, sir. That wasn't even nearly funny.'

'Best I could do at the moment,' I replied, chastened.

'Mind, I wouldn't say no to all the money the bishop gets from all the brothels, taverns and businesses hereabouts, that is for certain,' said Ned, casting his eyes at the crowds of people.

'Can hardly blame him for that, he owns the area.'

'He don't show his face here now, does he? Those days have long gone.'

'And so should we,' I said, moving away from the wharf and into Storey Street. 'We have a cockfight to find, don't forget.'

'More money for the bishop, no doubt,' observed Ned, wryly, turning to follow.

Stalls and traders began to pack up for the day as we negotiated the detritus that the market produced. Some sellers still called out their wares hoping for last-minute sales before heading to a nearby tavern to quench their thirsts. The buildings here being three and four storeys high cast the street in shadow as the evening drew in. The shops still open, placed lanterns in the windows, hoping to pull in some late customers.

Gaming houses, brothels and taverns proliferated in Southwark, as did all forms of entertainment, including theatres and fairs. People from the northern side of London crossed for the evening to partake, swelling the numbers.

We traversed Storey Street and just past Dirty Lane, we came into Counter Lane. The three of us stuck close together and kept our purses even closer as the drawing in of the evening allowed rich pickings for the myriad thieves that stalked the area. We progressed without hindrance, the presence of Kitty keeping the jades from pestering us —

mostly.

A cockfight attracts all manner of people from the poorest to the richest and I could see gentlemen of standing, finely-dressed, with equally well-dressed women, entering a disreputable-looking alley, one they would never normally consider entering.

I nudged Kitty, who nudged Ned. 'That looks likely,' I said, indicating with my head. 'I think we have found our brewhouse.'

The alley ran between a small grocer's and a merchant dealing in brewing grain and equipment; at first narrow, it opened up into a large yard. Ahead of us, a building that could once have been a stable now had additional buildings built against it, turning the establishment into a proper bowsing-ken. Men and a few painted women milled about outside the entrance, some drinking, others just talking and we eased between them to access the door.

Once inside we took a moment to look around, seeing a large open space filled with tables and benches, all taken, with many people just standing between the tables hoping for a space to develop. Ahead of us on the back wall ran a counter, acting as the bar. To both sides I could see further rooms, these appearing less populated. The loud noise rang in my ears, the language course and the atmosphere, while not exactly convivial, did not appear threatening — expectant would be a more appropriate word.

We pushed our way through to the counter where after a few minutes of trying to catch an eye I managed to procure three pots of ale.

'Here for the fight, are you?' asked the man behind the

bar.

'We are,' I admitted.

'I'll get you some tokens; a shilling apiece is the fee.'

I paid up and received three copper discs in return.

'That door there,' he said, pointing to a door at the end of the counter. 'It's already filling up, so I wouldn't leave it long if you wants a good view.'

'Thank you,' I said, handing a token each to Ned and Kitty.

We moved away and took up a position near the door leading to the cockfight, taking sips of surprisingly rather good ale. I looked around, gauging the relative wealth of the customers, hoping to spot the four young rakes.

Candles and lanterns illuminated the taproom, placed around the walls in niches and on tables, risking fire with the boisterous nature of the patrons. Ned became twitchy, wanting a chance to look over the combatants in the hope of discovering the most likely winner.

In the end, I relented and we headed for the door. Once opened, a man waited with his hand outstretched ready to receive the tokens, after palming them he allowed us through into another yard, smaller this time, then over to a large outbuilding where another man stood sentry. He noted our approach and as we came towards him, he stepped forward, opening the door and bidding us welcome.

We passed into a cavernous building decked out with circular tiers of wooden stands, each tier with a railing and benches, surrounding a central pit of perhaps twenty feet across. I could see a great gathering of people on the far side and as we made our way over, I could see another area set aside for the purchase of drink and tobacco. A roped-off area to the side allowed men and women to study the gamecocks, all separated in small enclosures.

Ned wasted no time and hurried across to look at the birds and to read the sheets of information that detailed name and previous fighting history. Upon the wall, near to the cocks, several sheets of paper gave the draw of the paired cocks and the round they fought, picked by lots earlier on. There were twenty-four birds and the winners of each round would fight again until the last round determined the winner and champion; a bloody and brutal sport where fortunes could be won or lost. The rich wagered high, the poor wagered what they could not afford.

As Ned studied the cocks, Kitty and I studied the customers through the heavy fug of tobacco. A vent here and there allowed some of the air to clear, but the smell stayed and blood sports had a special smell. I recognised a few men, some titled, some merely wealthy and at least two men who served in parliament. Any cockfight, even in a rude establishment like this, gathered the great and the not-so-good and not a few of them were accompanied by ladies who would not be their wives.

Women made up perhaps a third of those assembled, most of them allied to a certain trade, though not all; others enjoyed the sport for sport's sake with plenty of money burning in their purses.

Kitty and I talked and looked around, then I noticed she moved her head to the side to look around me.

'There are four young men behind you, Richard; perhaps they are the ones you seek.'

I turned my head slowly, trying to see, and then someone bumped into Kitty, who had to take a step or two to the side, allowing me to turn with her, unobtrusively.

'Well spotted, Kitty. That is them,' I said, as I took another sip of my ale and turned my face away, having no wish to be caught staring.

Kitty and I talked and I kept the youths in my peripheral vision, concentrating on them and not on the words I spoke. I could not say what we talked about, just that I said words and I dreaded to think what I might have agreed upon.

The four had obviously imbibed a *good* quantity of drink already, acting boisterously and arrogantly with it, insulting the lower classes and groping the women who wandered too close.

'Gives the quality a bad reputation, does that,' observed Ned, rejoining us and giving a nod in the direction of the four.

'They happen to be the ones we are here to see,' said Kitty. 'Richard is concentrating,' she added, raising a hand in warning.

'Oh,' I heard him reply, just as the four began to move away.

'Not anymore,' I said as I returned my attention to Kitty and Ned. 'Did you find your likely winners?' I asked.

He held out his hand and gave it a twist. 'There are a couple worth a try. I've put some money on for us, got better odds doing it now.'

'Then I hope I'm not going to lose too much.'

'Lose? No chance. Dead certainty we'll win.'

Kitty gave a resigned sigh.

'What?' exclaimed Ned, regarding her with disdain.

'I think Kitty doubts your wisdom in this, Ned,' I said, smiling.

'You'll see when we're counting our winnings.'

A bell sounded, indicating that the first battle was about to begin and people began to hurry to get a good view of the entertainment about to be played out in the pit. A guinea a battle and fifty guineas for the winner of the Main, the champion.

The viewing galleries filled quickly and the rising raucous noise indicated the high level of excitement and expectancy. Men walked amongst the crowd taking wagers, flanked by burly protectors. The sound reached a crescendo as two men entered the pit, each carrying a cock bird, the birds squawking and pecking at the hands of the handlers. Attached to the legs of each bird were sharp spurs of about two inches in length, made of silver or metal, some just sharpened bone. These two appeared to have metal spurs; dangerous, even for the handlers. A third man stood at a safe distance by the edge of the pit as the two handlers approached each other in the centre, pushing the birds towards each other, goading them into hate-filled action.

At a signal from the third man, the two handlers stepped back a pace and released the birds, each pushing them towards their adversary, both men beating a hasty retreat, scurrying to safety outside the pit as the two cocks sprang forwards.

Squawking and screeching, wings flapping wildly, the two cocks attacked, beaks pecking, legs flailing with the deadly spurs. The noise in the galleries rose accordingly as the two cocks danced around the pit, tearing into each other as feathers flew and blood began to spurt. The two cocks matched each other in size, the red seemingly to be quicker in its action, its raking legs delivering serious injury to the grey bird. The rapid speed of the first attacks could not continue, slowing as both injury and tiredness began to tell. Both birds now had lacerations and the red bird had somehow lost an eye. The serious wound did not stop the fight, if anything it seemed to make the bird angrier and although the injury restricted its sight, it seemed to have gathered strength as the two cocks scrambled around the pit.

Beside me, Kitty averted her gaze from the pit and began to look around the galleries. 'Poor things,' she said, sombrely. 'All this bloodshed just for entertainment.'

'Unfortunately, where there are people there will always be sports of this nature,' I replied, touching her arm.

The people around us shouted their encouragement for their chosen bird, hands raised, arms waving, their faces a mixture of pleasure, excitement, anger and disappointment. Fists pumped in joyous exaltation as the two birds fought like demons, defending territory and drawing blood.

It seemed as if the red bird had now badly damaged a leg, possibly even broken it, as it moved lopsidedly, unable to bear its weight; couple that with the missing eye and it had a major disadvantage. The grey sensed the red's weakness and the next attack came full and intense.

The third man, acting as the judge, waved and bid the two handlers into the pit to separate the birds; he had made his decision. I could now see the red bird's leg at a strange angle, unable to defend itself.

The carnage of blood and feathers littered the pit and this was just the first battle of many.

Jeers and cheers of derision erupted as the handlers had trouble seizing their charges at first but after a few tense moments their expertise counted and each had their birds under control. The referee pointed to the grey as the winner and the smiling handler held the bird aloft, showing it to all and sundry. The losing handler stalked off with his bird to assess the damage before deciding its fate, more than likely to have its neck wrung in the next few minutes.

'First blood to us,' yelled Ned, into my ear. 'Told you, didn't I?'

'You bet on the grey?'

'Of course; close for a time and I'd be a liar if I said I weren't worried for a bit.'

'A lot of money?'

He shook his head. 'No, only three shillings. The red was favourite, you know. Will get nine shillings back,' he said, punching the air in triumph.

Nine shillings? A paltry amount to some of the men here, they would be betting in pounds and guineas and without doubt, some would go home having won or lost hundreds; even in a low brewhouse such as this, extraordinary amounts of money flew from one hand to another.

From our position I could see the four youths down near the front, having secured a good vantage point to see the battles; the short corpulent one detached himself from the group and wandered a little unsteadily away. I thought it a good opportunity to confront him and perhaps ask a question or two.

CHAPTER 12

I told Kitty and Ned to stay and keep watch on the remaining three, then made my way down from the high tier through the crush of people to the lower levels. The young man thankfully did not proceed quickly, the many trying to access a better view of the pit for the next battle hampered his movement, allowing me to catch up with him.

He headed towards the back, through an open door into a pungent aroma of stale urine. I deduced that the young man had some breeding as he wished to use the rude facilities. Many of the patrons just pulled out their members and relieved themselves against the nearest wall, with some just doing the deed where they stood, sprinkling those in front with a warm stream on their breeches, stockings and the occasional dress.

A wall at the far end of the courtyard had a ditch running in front of it to take the steaming fluid away. An open-fronted shed with a three-holed bench catered for those wishing to defecate; a quick look showed some had even missed that. The women had a little privacy, a wall acting as segregation.

The young man took up his position facing the wall and fiddled with his breeches to expose his implement. I went and stood next to him, doing the same.

'A good battle to begin with,' I ventured, concentrating on missing my boots. 'Let us hope the rest are just as entertaining. I know you, do I not?' I said. 'Cole's, if I am not mistaken, you are part of a merchant group.'

He turned his head towards me, his dark wig askew, his eyes vacant and bleary, a small thin mouth beneath a small pointed nose. His chin seemed to have gone missing. 'What of it, sir?' he said, a touch of arrogance in his voice. 'I do not recall you.'

I gave things a shake down below and replaced it back into my breeches. I gave him a sharp pat on the back and laughed. 'My mind seems to have gone blank, sir, and I cannot remember whether you are Sommerville, Cannard, Ransom or Balton?'

'Cannard, sir, Ralph Cannard,' he replied, warily.

'Ah, Cannard, well met, sir. I am interested in your particular trade; you own Jaggers?'

'We do,' he said, proudly.

Cannard struggled to return his member back into his breeches and when he turned, I noticed a dark patch where he had mistimed the operation. He staggered a little as I guided him away from the wall.

'I congratulate you, sir; must be quite the money-maker. You have a ship of your own?'

'No, we are just the investors. De Griese and Jaggers supply the goods we sell.'

'Do they now; I wonder where they procure these goods?'

'What's it to you, sir?' asked Cannard.

'Just curious,' I replied, smiling at him and realising he may not be as drunk as I thought. 'No harm in that.'

'Indeed not, though impertinent, sir.'

Several people still stood around the yard, relieving themselves or conversing, with some men being loud and close to violence. I eased Cannard further away as three men began to push and shove each other, shouting into faces, spittle flying.

'I hear a merchant had his warehouse burnt down last night. Janssen; do you know him?'

Cannard snapped his head around. 'J... J... Janssen?'

'Yes, Janssen.'

A worried frown came upon his face and he tried to push me away. 'Nothing to do with me,' he said, an edge of panic in his actions.

'You know about it,' I accused, catching hold of his arm. 'What do you know?'

'Ah, Mr Cannard, there you are,' said a voice behind me. 'I believe your companions are searching for you.'

Cannard looked behind me and I saw relief cross his features. I turned to follow his gaze and viewed a rough-looking large-built man of my height; a captain-hackum if ever I saw one as his scarred and battered features testified. He rested a hand upon my shoulder. 'Run along, Mr Cannard, there's a good boy,' he said, condescendingly.

Cannard hurried away saying nothing more, just giving his saviour a brief nod of relief.

'Now, sir,' said the man, turning his attention to me. Only his lips smiled, his eyes holding no humour at all. 'What I would like to know is why a gentleman such as you, Mr Hopgood, would be interested in talking to my young friend there?' He patted my shoulder with a hand the size of a shovel.

'I think that is between Mr Cannard and me,' I replied, returning the humourless smile. It then struck me that I had not mentioned my name to Cannard, so how did this man know it?

'I thought you might say that,' he said, with a sorrowful shake of his head. 'You see, Mr Cannard and his friends hold some importance to me; they are, how shall I say it, under my charge. I protect them from the likes of you, Mr Hopgood. My… er, associates would not look kindly upon me should anything untoward happen to them.'

'I do not believe I gave any threat,' I replied. 'I merely asked some questions.'

'Then you have received answers to alleviate your curiosity.'

'Hardly, I have only just begun.'

'No, I think you have finished.'

More people came into the yard, most to urinate against the wall; others still shouted and remonstrated with each other, making this man and me anonymous.

'You threaten me, sir?' I said, my hackles rising. 'Your master threatens me? Would that be De Griese or Jaggers, or perhaps even both?'

The man smirked. 'De Griese and Jaggers are not my masters, they are colleagues, Mr Hopgood and you are stepping on the wrong toes; shame that you have done so.'

I saw a glint of steel appear in his hand, the light reflecting from a rushlight. His other hand, dropped from my shoulder to grip my upper arm.

'Move, Hopgood,' he said, the point of the knife poking

into my stomach.

'So that you can kill me in the corner?'

He grinned. 'Precisely, and as we move you can have hope that you will escape.' He gave a small chuckle. 'That would be a wrong assumption. You can shout all you want, all here will ignore you.'

'I do not need to shout,' I replied, more calmly than I felt. I stepped back and spun on my heels, away from the knife at my stomach.

He did not expect me to react so and instinctively jabbed the blade forward as I moved; as I turned sideways, it passed harmlessly just in front of me. I grabbed his knife hand around the wrist with my left and forced it away then stepped into him, punching my right shoulder into his chest, breaking his grip on my upper arm. I jabbed my head forward to butt him, giving just a light blow as he realised my intention and avoided it. I brought my arm up, intending to jab him in the face with my elbow and again he avoided the blow. I kept my left hand on his wrist, gripping it hard as he tried to angle the blade into me; the thought of that blade entering my body gave me the extra power I needed to resist. We moved around as if in a dance, bumping into folk who gave warnings that we intruded into their space and privacy. Disgruntled men pushed us this way and that as we moved about, me straining to keep the knife away whilst at the same time trying to entangle legs so that he would trip and fall over. We both used our free hands to punch and push, neither of us getting enough impetus to get in a telling blow.

He grunted as did I with the exertion and I felt beads of sweat break out on my forehead. Somehow, we had traversed the yard to its furthermost point where the stench of human deposits was at its most pungent and I could feel the man's stale breath on my face. Then I heard a shout from behind and then I felt a blow glance off my shoulder; a fist, and after the touch on my shoulder it connected with the man's cheek, snapping his head back. I felt the relief in the pressure of the hand holding the knife, just as another blow came arcing over and I managed to get my leg between his, pushing the knife further away and twisting it. He tripped, barked an expletive and fell, his head entering the urine-filled ditch. I heard a gurgle as his mouth tried to draw in a breath and I saw him twitch, a knee moved as if to raise himself and then another gurgle, then the knee relaxed and all movement stopped.

I turned my head to see Ned standing there, looking businesslike, devoid of emotion, Kitty just behind him looking horrified. He looked down at the man and tapped him with his boot. 'Reckon he'll drown in piss unless we pull him out,' he said, indifferently.

'Are you hurt, Richard?' asked Kitty, taking a step forward; at least one of them seemed concerned for my welfare.

I shook my head. 'No, I am unhurt, thank you, Kitty.' I then looked down at the man. 'He still hasn't moved, Ned. Pull him up.'

Ned grunted in disapproval, sniffed and then leant forward, grabbing the man's collar and pulling, dragging him away; he still did not move his limbs.

'How hard did you hit him?' I asked.

'Not hard enough, that's for sure. Shouldn't be knocked out.'

'Turn him,' I ordered.

Ned warily grabbed the man's arm and tugged, using the arm as a lever to pull him over onto his back and then I could see why he had not moved; the knife was embedded into his chest, right to the hilt.

'Bugger,' exclaimed Ned. 'Must have fallen onto it,' he added, stating the obvious.

I looked over my shoulder, relieved to see that no one took any notice of us or the body lying on the ground, too concerned with their own business to worry about a minor fracas in a brewhouse on cockfight night. I knelt down and quickly searched the man, finding a purse containing a few coins, replacing it entire. I patted his waistcoat and discovered a bulky object that turned out to be a small pistol, one usually used by a woman, lethal despite its size; that I retained. I stood up, having found nothing else.

'What are we to do?' asked Kitty, her voice edged with concern.

'Nothing,' I said, thinking quickly. I looked over my shoulder and saw people leaving the yard. 'We leave him. No one will own up to seeing anything and besides, I do not feel like being at the beck and call of a magistrate for the next few days.'

We walked away, slowly, leaving my assailant to be found later, returning to the pit where the second battle had come to a conclusion. I gazed around at the crowd, looking for the four youths.

'They've gone,' said Ned. 'Which is why we came to find you. The one you went after came back and spoke to the others; he kept looking behind him nervously as if expecting someone to appear. Whatever he told them made them wary too, so they upped and left.'

'When you didn't return we got worried and came to find you,' said Kitty.

'We couldn't see you at first but then we noticed something happening at the back of the yard, heard some grunting noises and it didn't seem like it were the throes of passion. Kitty has keener eyes than me and saw you — then she saw the blade. That's when I stepped up and tipped him a stoter. Didn't mean for him to fall on the thing; that's how luck goes I suppose.'

'Who was he?' asked Kitty.

I shook my head. 'I don't know, an associate of De Griese and Jaggers he said. He had the task of protecting those youths.'

'Why?'

'Good question and one we need to find out. I think it might be time for us to leave too.'

'Not without me winnings,' said Ned, immediately stalking off to collect his nine shillings.

We left the raucous noise, the stench of blood and the reek of human sweat that pervaded the brewhouse and headed towards the bridge. My thoughts tumbled in my mind as we walked, convinced that Cannard knew more than mere gossip about the fire at Janssen's; by extension that implicated De Griese and Jaggers — and how did that man know my name? What did it all mean? Could the murder of Pieter van Hoebeek just be the tip of something else, something hiding beneath the surface? According to my assailant, I had stepped on toes, got too close, so I had to go. What were they up to? What exactly are we beginning to unearth?

CHAPTER 13

The hackney's jolting and shaking certainly curtailed any hope of a few extra minutes dozing as it traversed the streets of London. I had a restless night's sleep having suffered two attempts on my life in two days and wondered whether there would be a third. I had declined to lodge with Kitty for the night and now I regretted that, for if I could not sleep then at least I would have been able to talk it over with her.

After a brief morning meal, Ned had gone to meet Kitty to delve a little deeper into the activities of the husband of Cornelia Visser, Roger Tewksley, and of the argument he supposedly had with a Dutchman. Mary and Jane had been left with the accumulated laundry, much to Ned's satisfaction that he had avoided that unpleasant task. He had walked out with a smug expression on his face, plainly riling Mary.

I wished to speak again to my employer, so made my way to Basinghall Street where I alighted and knocked on the door. I waited only a scant minute or two before the same maid opened the door, her expression still stern as she showed me into a small room off the hall. I was struck by the silence in the house, with even the maid's footsteps being as if muffled. It engendered the feeling of oppression, as if no one could dare to intrude into the peace and quiet, in stark contrast to my own home with its bustling ways and bursts of laughter.

After a few minutes of idleness, the maid returned and guided me upstairs to the drawing room; I somehow suppressed the urge to step heavily and noisily upon the treads of the stairs.

'Mr Hopgood,' acknowledged Femke van Hoebeek. 'Have you resolved my brother's demise?' she asked, as I entered the room.

'Not as yet,' I replied. 'I would say I am progressing.'

She grimaced slightly and then indicated the chair. 'Then how does this progress manifest?'

I sat down, adjusting my jacket for comfort. 'I would rather not go into details at the moment,' I said. 'Suffice it to say that I have an avenue to travel, more than one if truth be told, so I would be reluctant to give details at the moment.'

'You fear to tell me in case you are wrong?'

'Precisely that.'

She nodded as if understanding, though her face showed a sign of frustration. 'So be it,' she said after a moment. 'So, why are you here?' she asked, sitting up straight in her chair.

'It is really quite simple. I spoke briefly to Ruud Janssen at the church on the day of your brother's internment, now I have further questions to ask and seek his place of residence.' I decided not to tell her of the warehouse fire, she would learn of it soon enough, if she had not already.

'What questions?' she asked, a little defensively.

'About his business dealings with your brother, Pieter.' I held my hands out to placate her. 'I believe in being thorough, that is all. The more information I can gather, the quicker I can progress.'

She thought for a moment, pondering, looking at me. 'Wapping. He has a storehouse there,' she said, in the end.

'I know that; I ask because he has not been seen there.'

'Then he will have gone away for a few days, Mr Hopgood,' she returned.

'Where? To Canvey?'

'Ruud is his own man, he will go where he pleases,' she replied, quickly.

I sighed. 'Miss Van Hoebeek, do you wish me to find your brother's murderer or not?'

'Of course I wish you to find the person responsible,' she said, indignantly.

'Then please help me. I need to speak to Ruud Janssen.'

She pursed her lips and then made a thin line of them. 'He has a house in White Chappel, just outside Aldersgate, opposite The White Bear,' she answered, in the end.

I nodded my head slowly. 'Thank you, that was what I wished to know.' For someone wanting to find her brother's murderer she seemed remarkably reticent in providing me with information.

She stood up and brushed her dress smooth from the creases. 'Is that all you wished to know, Mr Hopgood?'

I stood up too, aware of the dismissal. 'One thing more, Cornelia Visser. I understand she and your brother were once, er… close?'

I saw a narrowing of her eyes and a twitch of her lip. 'That was some time ago, Mr Hopgood. She is married now,' she replied.

'So I understand,' I said, thinking from what I have been hearing, marriage made little difference to her with her varied carnal pleasures.

'You must not bother Cornelia, Mr Hopgood. She is my closest friend and has nothing to do with this.'

'If you say so,' I replied, outwardly agreeing, resolving to probe a little deeper; *her* lover too, so would she be protective? 'Then I have nothing more to ask at the moment so I will take my leave of you.'

She nodded perfunctorily and took a step forward, guiding me towards the door.

'Tell me,' I said, just before she showed me out. 'Who is now managing your business?'

'I am, of course.'

'Including orders of stock and the disbursement of the goods to your customers?'

She shook her head. 'No; Martijn Thyssen has taken on that responsibility.'

I put a smile on my face. 'Then I hope he proves to be adept.'

'I have no reason to think otherwise, Mr Hopgood, but that is my business.'

'Indeed it is, my apologies for asking. Good day to you, Miss Van Hoebeek, I will keep you apprised as things move on.'

As I stepped back onto the street I wondered again why she did not seem willing to freely provide me with any information; it proved an arduous task to draw even the simplest thing from her. She certainly felt unease when I mentioned Cornelia; scared perhaps that I would ask about their relationship? It all seemed very odd.

A hail from behind made me turn as a chair hastened

down the street, its chairmen swerving, tipping the contraption precariously. The leading man kept changing direction and I surmised that the two must be either new to the business or unaccustomed to each other. I used that type of conveyance only rarely and as I watched the thing swerve it just reinforced my loathing of the contraption. I heard a bang come from inside the sedan as it leant over at an acute angle and I pictured the passenger sliding upon the seat and hitting the wooden frame. The chair managed to right itself and then disappeared into the many pedestrians ahead. I decided four wheels and a horse would always be the better option and I cast my eyes around looking for one to take me to Wapping, for I had to see the burnt remains of Janssen's warehouse before visiting the man himself.

A sight of charred timbers greeted me on the wharf, set at haphazard angles amongst a jumble of untouched struts and fallen beams of wood. An acrid stench of burning still emanated from the remains, mixed with the salty tang of the river and the effluent that flowed within it. I could see open crates that once contained a blackened leaf-like substance, presumably tea, broken bottles, remnants of burnt cloth and other boxes containing unknown goods littering the small area. Already the remains had undergone salvage by the opportunists, the fire-priggers, who must have flooded the area, compounding the financial loss that Janssen must have suffered; whoever had set the fire had done a thorough job of it.

Four men sifted through the wreckage as I looked on, disinterested at my presence. Men from other warehouses went about their businesses normally, giving the impression that the four had legitimate cause to be there.

'What happened?' I asked, as one of the four noticed me; a rough-looking man in working clothes.

'What's it to you?' he replied, not pleasantly.

'I am seeking Ruud Janssen, I believe this is his warehouse.'

The man dusted his hands of muck and black powder then took a few steps towards me. 'It was, but as you see, there is not much left.'

'How did this happen?' I asked, casting my eyes over the remains.

He shrugged his shoulders. 'Perhaps you could tell me,' he replied, a hint of menace in his voice.

'I wish I could,' I replied. 'Alas, I have no knowledge in this regard. Accident or design?'

The man barked a condescending laugh. 'Accident? You really think so?'

'Then who and why?'

'You're asking a lot of questions, my friend. Perhaps it'd be best if you leave us.'

'I apologise; I just hoped to do some business with Mr Janssen, hence my presence here. Seeing all this is a bit of a shock. You work for him?'

His arrogance suddenly disappeared. 'You assume correctly, sir. I'm the overseer.'

'You are looking for undamaged goods?'

Another laugh. 'The river scum have picked the place clean of anything useful, sir. We will continue searching, there may be something that they missed.'

'Then I wish you luck. Do you know where I might find Mr Janssen?'

'Drowning his sorrows, I would have thought. He was sorely angered by this, as we all are.'

I nodded, feigning sympathy. 'It is certainly unfortunate when a man's livelihood is in ruin.'

'Not ruined, just a setback. Mr Janssen is a resourceful man.'

'I am sure he is, but if this was caused by design,' I said, indicating the destruction. 'Then it would indicate animosity; perhaps I would be wise to seek out another man of business, perhaps even the one you alluded to?'

'I'm alluding to nothing, sir. Mr Janssen will put this to rights soon enough, you'll see. He won't let them win.'

'Who is "them"?' I asked.

He opened his mouth to say something more, then thought better of it, quickly shutting it again. I suppose he had already told me things that he perhaps should not have done and so turned his back, dismissing me, and resumed rummaging in the debris. I continued to watch for a moment, then turned away and began to walk; at least he had given me something to ponder in his unguarded moment.

I intended to go next to Janssen's house in White Chappell to see him but now I had another idea that may prove more profitable. I walked to the nearest stairs to take a wherry back upriver as I wished to speak to an old man who once plied his trade upon the river.

The Old Swan sat in Old Swan Lane just off the wharf close to Waterman's Hall. Retired watermen and those now too bent to ply an oar frequented the inn, wishing to continue being part of the river family.

Llewellyn Owen had a Welsh father and an Irish mother; born in the slum of St Giles he had a hard upbringing. As soon as he could he left the family home and took to the river, acquiring the name Lew the Boat, now just Old Lew, spending his idle retired days in the Swan.

I came to know him through Ned. He had furnished me with Lew's history as he had been friendly with the man's now-dead son for several years and had kept on friendly terms with him.

I entered the inn to be greeted with the customary fug of tobacco, stale sweat and ale; thankfully, the hearth fire stayed unlit, adding no extra smoke to the atmosphere. As usual, most of the tables already had occupants and I was pleased to see that one of them had Lew as a resident.

In his early sixties, Lew still looked sprightly having only lately given up his oars, his wiry frame hiding sinewy muscles and the strength of long years out on the river. He held court to a small group of men and I could hear the loud, raucous and course chatter coming from the table. I caught his eye and he raised a hand to beckon me over.

'Dickie, me boy,' he called out and I inwardly winced, he being the only man to have shortened my name to the one that I loathed the most. 'You standin' or sittin' and are yer going to be buyin' for us poor men of the river?'

They all supped out of blackjacks, so I touched the arm of the passing pot-girl to get them all a refill and one for myself.

'Sitting, if you'll have me, Lew,' and I gave a grin.

'Shove up, boys,' he said to his companions. 'We got a bit of the Gentry amongst us now. Be on yer best behaviour and mind yer language.'

The men laughed as did Lew and I. We gave and received a little bit of banter for a while and then I spoke into Lew's ear. 'I need to speak to you quietly, as it were. I have something serious to discuss.'

'Serious, eh? That sounds serious,' he said, laughing at his own witticism. 'Lads. Lads,' he said, continuing. 'Lord Dickie here needs a bit o' advice of a delicate nature an' 'as come to the one man in all London who can help 'im. So, give us a bit o' room, will yer, just fer a bit.'

With a few comments regarding the pox and pregnant girls and their commiseration on my supposed predicament, Lew's friends left us on our own, their pots full with the promise of more to come.

'Now, my boy. What's amiss?' said Lew, leaning close.

I took a breath and then let it out slowly, as if in great thought. 'What's the word on the river, Lew?'

''Bout what?'

'Down Wapping way, a butter-boxes case was set afire two nights ago. In and out in an ark, I heard.'

Old Lew nodded. 'I 'eard that too. I also 'eard that it were free-traders that did it.'

'Smugglers? What else did you hear?'

He grinned and then took a measure of ale. 'I 'ear an outside crew want the whole business, and I mean all of it.'

'I felt my eyes widen. 'All of London?'

He nodded. 'You 'ave the right of it. Free-trading is lucrative and there's a crew meaning to be sole suppliers. They don't just want a slice, they want the whole pie.'

'You reckon?'

He nodded again. 'That's the word. Big business ain't it. Don't matter to the likes of us who does it, just that someone does.'

'Presumably, they would control the prices in that case, push them up?'

He shook his head this time. 'I 'eard they want to push the prices down and you ain't gonna hear many complaints about that.'

'Down? That doesn't make sense.'

Then I thought about it.

The Lower prices would allow more people to buy more of it, so if a monopoly controlled it, more goods would come onto the market creating more profit. That would mean that someone had access to a vast amount of goods to supply the market. Even less tax for the government. So where would these goods come from? Could my corpse be a casualty of this?

'Lew, would you have heard of the murder of a Dutchman, a Van Hoebeek?'

'On the river?'

I shook my head. 'No, he was a merchant up near Moorfields.'

'Then no, the name don't mean anything to me.'

'Shame, I just hoped you had.' We lapsed into a moment of silence as we each took a drink. 'This new crew coming in, do they have a name?' I asked, more in hope than expectation.

'No, I don't, though…?'

'Yes?' I asked, eagerly.

'Dinal,' he called towards his friends. 'Come 'ere a bit, will yer.'

Dinal came over and took a seat.

'You said summat the other day, a name to do with this new free-trading crew?'

Dinal nodded. 'It were just a whisper, name of Dagry, or summat like it. I 'eard a fare talking about it.'

'Dagry? You sure?'

'It were summat like it.'

I ran the name over my tongue and then my mind took hold. 'It wasn't something like De Griese, was it?'

'Yeah, that were it,' answered Dinal, slapping his hand on the table. 'De Griese. They said this De Griese 'as the contacts. That's what they said,' he finished, triumphantly.

De Griese, why did that name not surprise me. 'Do you know where they hale from?'

Dinal shook his head. 'There be a rumour, only a rumour mind, that they come from down south. Rye were mentioned.'

'Rye? Where is Rye?'

He shrugged his shoulders. 'I dunno.'

'Sussex,' interjected Lew. 'Notorious it is, for the smuggling,' he added, grinning.

CHAPTER 14

I alighted at Aldersgate as a queue of traffic had formed and the driver loudly complained, his diatribe intruding into my thoughts. I walked through the gate leaving the city behind me into a melting pot of diverse nationalities. All manner of people lived here; Germans, the Danes, Italians, the Jews and many others so it would be natural that the Dutch resided there too.

Around me, the street market did a bustling business selling all manner of goods on stalls and barrows, with some goods just simply laid out on the pavement. I walked through all of this to St Botolph's church where building work had just begun after the authorities demolished the old one for being unsafe. Janssen lived in a house just further up the street. Most of the properties had three storeys, built of brick and of reasonable quality, just one or two of timber construction from an earlier time.

Janssen lived opposite The White Bear Tavern and I had to choose one of the five houses to call at first. I walked up to the one at the end of the row and knocked. The servant appeared after a short time and directed me to the other end of the row, then closed the door firmly in my face; my intrusion had obviously disturbed him for no good reason. I walked the few paces down and knocked again, this time waiting for an inordinately long time. I tried knocking again and noticed a window-covering twitch to my right, catching the eye of the individual watching me. A few moments later the door opened tentatively and the face of a middle-aged man appeared.

'Yes?' he asked, a snap to his voice.

'Good day, I wish to speak to Ruud Janssen if you please,' I replied, keeping my voice even and pleasant.

'Mr Janssen is not at home, sir.'

'Ah, that is unfortunate as I thought I saw him through the window just now.'

He hesitated a little before giving a more exact answer. 'Mr Janssen is not at home to callers at this juncture, sir.'

'Then perhaps you might enquire if he would make an exception in my case. You see, I met him briefly at Pieter van Hoebeek's funeral and I wish to discuss a few things with him. My name is Richard Hopgood.'

'Let him in, Michael,' said a voice in the background. 'I will see Mr Hopgood.'

The door opened wider and I stepped inside. Ruud Janssen stood by a door in the hall looking downcast, as if supporting a great weight upon his shoulders.

'Please, Mr Hopgood,' he said, indicating with his hand that I should follow as he turned and walked into a room.

I refrained from giving the servant, Michael, a triumphant grin, instead just brushing past him to follow Janssen.

'Thank you for seeing me, Mr Janssen.'

He did not deign to reply, just indicating a chair in front of a large oak desk situated side-on to the window. Paintings, presumably of his homeland, hung above the cupboards and chests lining the wall. It appeared to be a compact study.

'What brings you 'ere, Mr Hopgood?' he asked, taking his seat so that he could look through the drapes of the window to the front door.

'You, Mr Janssen. Someone murdered your friend Pieter and you did not want to talk to me. You feigned lack of English and made that as an excuse; it is not the case, is it? I am curious as to why you pretended lack of understanding when you may have been of help; still may be. Your warehouse is no more, destroyed by fire, so I am wondering what all this means.'

'Buildings burn down all the time, Mr Hopgood. There is nothing strange about that. My business will recover.'

'That is true, but I am thinking that Pieter's murder and your business in ruin are somehow connected. Two Dutch merchants have suffered catastrophes in a short period of time. You see why I wonder. I perceive you as a confident man and now I find you in your house instead of down in Wapping. You appear to be frightened; are you being threatened?'

A tight smile briefly flashed on his face and he leant forward to pick up a weight that kept his papers secure. He played with the weight and I let the silence fill the room, giving him time to think. I noticed he had ignored my question regarding his ability to speak English.

'Pieter has died, Mr Hopgood; I have no wish to follow him.'

'Then you are being threatened; by whom?'

'That is no concern of yours; business is business.'

'I know the business you are in, Mr Janssen; apart from your legal trade you have another, supplied I believe from

Canvey Island. I think your troubles stem from your dealings with the free-traders. Smuggled goods are no concern of mine, though from what I understand something is happening in a wider context. I hear someone wants to create a monopoly and I think that has something to do with this death. Pieter took goods from you to sell on, it is possible that these people put pressure on him to take their goods instead of yours and killed him when he refused? Did he confide in you at all?'

He shook his head. 'Nee, not confide.'

'Then what?'

'Discuss. I already say, business is business.'

'Then could it have been a warning to other merchants? What might happen, what could happen? The fire at your warehouse; another warning?'

He shrugged his shoulders. 'I suggest, Mr Hopgood that you cease in your task. Keep your money and I will speak to Femke. It will be better this way.'

'I do not understand, Mr Janssen; why would you not want me to find Pieter's murderer?'

'I feel I have spoken enough. Leave it, Mr Hopgood, that is my advice.'

I felt frustrated and a certain degree of anger at his refusal to be open about such a serious matter and I let out a long sigh. He stood up, signalling that our discussion had come to an end. 'Does the name De Griese mean anything to you,' I asked, trying one more time.

He recovered quite quickly after I mentioned the name. He gave a slight hesitation and the look in his eyes told me he had fear of it.

'Good day, Mr Hopgood,' he said, ushering me to the door.

Janssen, I reflected as I walked towards Aldersgate, was a very frightened man. I suspected that he did not frighten easily and I felt certain De Griese had a hand in that. De Griese appeared to be the man at the centre of things, around whom everything revolved. It would also seem that smuggling was at the heart of it; should I continue to look for the murderer of Pieter independent of the smuggling or concentrate on the smuggling to solve the murder? Both matters seemed connected somehow. What path should I follow? I could see an abstract pattern begin to develop, all these little snippets of information and suspicion made me wonder if I had stumbled upon something inadvertently, something that would prove too big for just Ned and I to deal with. De Griese pushed me on the bridge so he certainly would not flinch from murder; had he killed Van Hoebeek or ordered his death? Maybe I needed to take a step back and look at things again — perhaps I had missed something. Ned and Kitty may have discovered that something, maybe they knew what I needed to know. Tewksley, the cuckolded man — could he be the assailant?

I passed through the postern of the gate and re-entered the city, immediately beginning a search for a hackney. I could do little more at the moment so I may as well spend my time profitably in learning more about Rye and the activities associated with the town.

Fortunately, the conveyance I hailed was in a far better condition than the previous one, the bench smooth and the floor relatively clean with two windows complete. I relaxed and stared out, watching the diverse sights of the city; traders selling their wares from stalls, barrows and trays hanging from straps about their necks. Entertainers: jugglers, comic turns, those using sleight of hand to thrill the public with their tricks; musicians on every street with pipes and fiddles. Jades aplenty rubbed shoulders with the titled, wealthy women out perusing the shops for goods and services. Cruisers begged, dambers annoyed, divers and bung-nippers moving quickly between people, feral dogs barking and snatching anything they could. Speakers railed against the government and the distant war against Spain. Others spoke of religion, of injustice and calls for reform, most of whom were largely ignored, only one or two speakers managing to draw a small crowd. The warm day brought out the people looking for diversion from their predictable lives.

My driver pulled up in New Palace Yard where I alighted and immediately headed for a pie stall. I had been informed that it sold proper beef pies, hot and succulent, lean meat and no gristle; you may have to pay a premium but rumour had it that it was money well spent. I moved to the periphery, away from the crowded centre and sat on a low wall, watching the people about their business or pleasure. My first mouthful proved the wisdom of purchasing it, finding it one of the best pies I had ever eaten from a stall, the gravy leaking onto my fingers so that I had to lean forward to prevent splattering my jacket and breeches. I finished the pie and licked my fingers clean, thinking I might have another, then I decided to leave that pleasure for another day. I got up from my wall and made my way, walking past St Margaret's towards Old Palace

Yard and my final destination, the little door that led down to the basement.

'Back again, Hopgood?' said Jarmin as I entered the room, his face relaxed and wearing an easy smile.

'I am afraid so; here to pick your brain and scrutinise your files.'

'Really? What is it this time?'

'The same; smuggling.'

His smile widened. 'Then you *are* looking for an alternative income.'

I returned the smile. 'Maybe not at the moment; from what I've heard, I would be pushed out of the market.'

Fulton and Monk looked up from scrutinising some documents lying before them. Jarmin had his feet up on the table, seemingly at ease. 'Your Dutch friends would take exception?'

'For the time being they have largely been removed from the picture.'

'Really? Do tell, Richard.'

I took a spare chair and sat down, explaining how Janssen's warehouse had been destroyed, the rumours surrounding it and of a smuggling gang's ambitions. Needless to say, this piqued Jarmin's interest and I noticed that both Fulton and Monk had ceased their reading to listen as well.

'And you believe that this is connected to your murdered Dutchman?' asked Jarmin, once I had finished.

'It is certainly possible. In truth, I'm wondering if I have stumbled upon something, a separate issue from the murder, rather like the Jacobites of a few months ago.' I referred to a young man murdered by a jealous clerk, both of whom belonged to a secret Jacobite group plotting insurrection against the government which came to light during my investigation; the murder and the insurrection being separate issues.

'You seem to be in the habit, Richard,' said Monk, 'of searching for one thing only to find something bigger and possibly more dangerous.'

I grinned and held up my hands in innocence. 'It would seem I am fated to do so.'

'Have you two heard anything of this?' asked Jarmin, turning to Fulton and Monk.

Both shook their heads and answered in the negative.

'The southern smugglers, whom you are alluding to, I suspect are the Hawkhurst Gang. Notorious and violent, they control most of the south coast,' said Jarmin, holding his hand up to his brow as if it would help his memory. 'Only last year it is believed a man from that gang shot dead a customs official; as of this moment, we are still searching for the perpetrator.'

'They have their base in Rye?' I asked.

Jarmin shook his head. 'No, Hawkhurst in Kent. They frequently use Rye to land goods, as they do other towns and villages all along the coast.'

'You seem to know a lot about them.'

'I wish I did not, in truth. One day in the future we will break the gang; at least we know of them so that will have to suffice for now. If you wish to know more there is a file through there,' and he pointed to the door that led into his office. 'Most of our knowledge is unattributable, rumour, hearsay and anonymous information, passed in secret. You do not treat this gang lightly; they would kill you as soon as look at you.'

'You did not mention this gang earlier.'

'No, you were more interested in the Dutch side of things. You will find the Hawkhurst Gang have a file all to themselves.'

'Why not just round them all up and put them to the question?'

'When one ruthless gang disappears another will take its place. There will always be smugglers, sometimes it's best just to know who is doing the smuggling. One day we will find the man who murdered the official, until then...'

I went through Jarmin's office to the new files room, picking up a lantern as I went and immediately headed to the table. I removed the requisite files and sat down to go over them again, to find the references to the Hawkhurst Gang. I did not deem them pertinent before, now I looked at it in a different light. With the general file open and the file of the gang in front of me, I looked at the dates and references of both and found that the smaller operators of the free-traders along that coast appeared subservient to the Hawkhurst Gang; a vast business enterprise, controlled by violence and intimidation.

CHAPTER 15

'You will do no such thing,' I exclaimed, as Ned made his suggestion. 'I cannot sanction risking him for such a ruse.'

'He's keen and he's already said he'd do it.'

'No, under no circumstances. Kitty, tell me you did not agree to all this?'

'I did not, Richard,' she replied, shooting Ned a look.

'And this came about after you had gained entrance; when Kitty gained entrance?'

'Well, yes. I 'ad a bit of time after we got back so I went and looked for him.'

'You did not discuss it first with Kitty, or indeed, me?'

'No, I thought you would approve.'

'I do not, Ned,' I replied, shaking my head vehemently. 'That is something I will not have on my conscience; what would you have done if he could not get out?'

'Er…?'

'Exactly, Ned. I dare not dwell on what the consequences could be; to put a child into a nest of paederasts and predators? Really? Your mind must be scrambled.'

'It were just an idea,' defended Ned, forlornly.

'A bad one,' I countered, leaning back, sighing.

Failing Ned's suggestion, he and Kitty had had a productive day. They could not discover the reason for the argument between Tewksley and the Dutchman but they could confirm that the man shouted in a foreign language and that he matched Van Hoebeek's description, confirming too the butter-box reference. This man had apparently visited the house occasionally, so it gave credence to the probable identity of the man. They also discovered the whereabouts of the children's hospital funded by Tewksley, in Southwark, on Maid Lane. The information had been provided by the innkeeper of The Bell Inn, who still felt well disposed towards Tewksley, despite the rumours circulating about him.

'Tell me again,' I said, shaking my head to clear my mind of Ned's suggestion. 'You went to this house in Maid Lane and what then?'

Kitty nodded. 'A big dirty unwelcoming building, three storeys and timber built with the daub falling off, it doesn't seem the most robust of places. We walked about a little and saw plenty of girls, traders and the like about, so we asked some questions. They all said the same thing really, that it took the kids in off the streets. Some said that the older ones were moved on to another place nearer the river, thinking that it might be a nanny-house.'

'You went to this other place?'

'We did,' answered Ned. 'After Kitty came up with the idea of asking if her little brother had been taken in. I kept watch down the way a bit, while she,' and he nodded Kitty's way, 'knocked at the door.'

'What then?'

'I asked the woman who opened the door if my brother had been taken in by them. She said that plenty had and they were well looked after, same as the girls, so I should be thankful if he had been taken in. When I asked if I could look for him amongst the children she refused, saying she did not want to upset the young ones. I started to sniff and cry saying how desperate I was to find him when a man's voice behind her said to let me in.'

'Not Tewksley?'

'No, another man; well-dressed, portly, grey under his wig. Took me down a corridor to a room at the back. He opened the door to let me see inside. A woman sat in the room along with about twenty little kinchins, some just lullaby-cheats; others were older, ten or so. Both girls and boys. The man let me put my nose in and asked if I could see my brother and I shook my head. I so wanted to say they were all my brothers and sisters as they all looked so sad. He then ushered me straight to the front door and showed me out, saying he wished me luck in my search. It were dismal in there, Richard, really dismal.'

'You indicated that the local people were not troubled by the place?'

'Some were,' said Ned, shaking his head. 'Most weren't.'

I shook my head ruefully at that. 'This other house; what did you find?'

Ned took a breath. 'Down Tooley Street way, Joyners Street, near the bridge. Another big place, though this one in good condition. When I tried to get in a couple of captain-hackums barred me way, said members only and I had to be recommended to the place first. I glimpsed inside and it were done up like a gentry-cove's ken, it were, saw a tib and a squeaker walk by, both done up, dressed like, you know, a man and a woman; they could only have been nine or ten.'

I felt a twinge of nausea rise in my stomach at the depravity of my fellow men; to subject a mere child to that sort of degradation, of abuse. The likes of Tewksley and his ilk were beneath contempt and not only did they partake in these foul practices, they profited from them too. Girls of ten could legally consent to lie with a man and they could marry at twelve, but they were still only children.

'What of the locals there?' I asked. 'Do they know what they have for a neighbour?'

'Again, some do, some don't, from what some said they reckon the constables and the Watch got paid to look away.'

'What of the Justices, the Alderman, Sir John Eyles I think it is?'

'Probably unaware,' ventured Ned. 'It don't take too much to keep that sort of thing quiet.'

'Maybe I should speak to him, or at least get someone to speak to him.'

I knew houses like that existed in London though most get closed down with rapidity, as soon as the authorities became aware of them. Tewksley must think that Southwark, with its lawlessness, could sustain such a place. Whatever happened, I was determined that this one would be closed down too and those involved be brought before a judge and suffer the ignominy of having the details printed in the newssheets for all to see and hear about.

'Do you think Van Hoebeek became aware of what Tewksley is doing?' asked Kitty. 'Perhaps they argued about it.'

'That's possible and would be a good reason to keep him quiet, prevent him from repeating it abroad,' I replied, finally taking a sip of my ale, 'Now, however, it puts me in a quandary. Up until just now I've been convinced that the man died because he stood against this smuggling; now I am not quite so sure.'

I explained what I had learned that day and how this Hawkhurst gang intended to gain a monopoly in the London smuggling trade. How, I reasoned, that perhaps Van Hoebeek had spurned the approach and had been murdered to threaten other merchants along with the destruction of Janssen's warehouse, that the two were connected to De Griese, Jaggers and this violent gang. One thing I did come to realise; this investigation appeared to be far more complicated than I first thought.

'What do we do now?' asked Ned, draining his pot and smacking his lips.

'I am not sure,' I responded, my head in a spin.

Kitty took my mind away from deliberating once we had adjourned to her lodging and now I eased myself up and adjusted the pillow behind my head for comfort, my thoughts returning to trying to decide what my next move should be before going to sleep. Kitty's head lay against my chest so I traced with my fingers a line on her skin, from her shoulder down over her ribs to her waist and then on to her hip. She gave a pleasing murmur and snuggled closer, her breath hot against my skin. Our bout had been vigorous and the conclusion mutually satisfying, our perspiration now beginning to cool as we lay in repose beneath the coverlet. Outside, in Drury Lane, the noise of the revellers and the theatregoers continued unabated, whilst in bed we were cocooned in our own little space of quiet and intimacy, too wrapped up in each other to notice the outside intrusion.

'You're thinking again, Richard. I can tell from the way you breathe,' said Kitty, softly.

'I am,' I admitted. 'Though I'm reticent to consider anything other than what we are doing at this minute, I know I must.'

'I can distract you again,' she said, a certainty in her voice as her hand slid down beneath the cover.

'I think you may have to give me a few minutes grace; I'm only flesh and blood, you know,' I answered, closing my eyes and smiling.

'Then you had better tell me what you're thinking whilst I wait,' she replied, continuing with her play.

'You're not being fair, Kitty. It is difficult to concentrate.'

'I said I could distract you.'

I forced my mind just to prove her wrong. 'I am certain that De Griese and Jaggers are the ones trying to monopolise the smuggling trade. They must have powerful financial backers to do so. This gang from Hawkhurst would not have the money needed, but from what I learned, they could very well have enough resources to get the goods into the country. I am also sure that De Griese burnt Janssen's warehouse and we know De Griese is not averse to violence, so I think he is the man behind this murder.'

'What about Tewksley?' she asked, sighing.

'An unsavoury character to be sure,' I answered quickly, not daring to shift my mind to her activity beneath the blanket. 'He appears to be exploiting children for his own and others' gratification. You say a girl saw him having an argument with someone who could well have been Van Hoebeek? If this man knew of Tewksley's predilections and had threatened to expose him, then that would be reason enough to commit murder.'

'So what are you going to do?'

'That is the problem; what do you think?'

'I think I might have to change my strategy.'

'Meaning? Oh, er, I see…'

De Griese, Van Hoebeek and Tewksley now totally forgotten.

I awoke to have a shaft of light from a gap in the window curtain lance into my eyes. I turned my head and saw Kitty slipping on her robe as she walked through to the other room. I heard a rattle of pots and I gave a jaw-cracking yawn.

'You awake, Richard?' she asked softly, poking her head back around the door.

'Just about,' I replied when I finished the yawn'

'Won't be long; just getting the fire back to life.'

She came back through with a plate of some two-day-old bread and a little cheese and set the feast down on my side of the bed, she smiled, then slipped off her robe before climbing back into the bed beside me. 'Tea will be a will be a while yet, fire is low,' she explained 'So, have you decided?' she asked, reaching across me to pick up a piece of bread. I took advantage and quickly kissed what she presented. 'Not yet, Richard, I'm hungry,' she scolded.

'So am I,' I replied, kissing it again.

'Stop it, Richard,' she said, moving out of my reach.

I sighed and relaxed my head. 'In truth, I'm still

considering the options; what do you think?'

She lay back and chewed. 'Tewksley,' she said, once she had swallowed. 'Van Hoebeek is dead and nothing can bring him back. We have to think about those children and I dread to think what might have happened overnight whilst we enjoyed ourselves.'

'The same as every other night, I suppose,' I replied, my ardour dampening. 'You know as well as I that there will always be people who prey on the vulnerable.'

'But you *can* do something about Tewksley. If you cannot stop them all, you can at least stop one.'

I breathed out slowly and put my arm behind my head. 'Perhaps he did kill Van Hoebeek, it certainly seems like he had the motive.'

'Then you must turn your attention away from De Griese for a time.'

I nodded. 'You may be right. I told Jarmin about De Griese and Jaggers and he's taken an interest in their activities. He will make inquiries into it, leaving me free to follow the path to Tewksley.' I turned my head to look at Kitty and smiled. 'We will do as you suggest and see where it takes us.'

She smiled back just as I heard the water in the pot begin to bubble.

We sat in a chophouse just around the corner from Kitty's eating a large breakfast to add to the bread and cheese we had earlier. Ned arrived complaining that Mary had provided him with only scant sustenance, being, as he described her, short of temper.

'It's your fault again, sir. She said that it's impossible to run a house when the master don't give direction. You been back late and out early so she's hardly seen you and she's moaning about your absences — again,' explained Ned, grinning.

'This is your housekeeper, Richard, not your mother?' asked Kitty, whimsically.

'Yes, my housekeeper,' I replied, feeling my shoulders sag. 'I know,' and I held up a hand. 'I have told you about Mary, how she likes to keep things organised. In truth, she has a heart of gold most of the time, until she thinks of me as being just a small boy. I will sort things out with her later, should I go home.'

Ned laughed and I admit I found some element of humour in the circumstances. I gave them a few moments and then brought our gathering to order.

'In the meantime, before I am ejected from my own house, we have work to do.'

'Yes, sir,' replied Ned, sitting up straight. 'And what would you wish me to do?'

I chose to ignore his inane grin. 'You are to go back to Southwark, Ned, and Kitty too, if you are willing,' I said, turning my head to look at her.

'Of course I am,' she answered.

'Good; I also want you to find Little Alex again and take him with you, for a consideration, of course. You are to find anyone, man, woman or child who has had experience of any of those two houses; preferably, someone prepared to speak in front of a magistrate, if not, then at least get a testimony from them.'

'You mean a written one?' asked Ned.

'Yes, if possible. My lawyer friend, Barty, could visit them or you could take them to him. I intend to visit Tewksley's house whilst you are south of the river, to speak to either him or his wife and I am looking forward to what they have to say.'

CHAPTER 16

I had not been down Walbrook way for quite a while, despite it being off The Poultry and the street where builders worked on the new town residence of The Lord Mayor of London. The weather had turned cloudy with a few spots of rain and I hoped it did not presage a downpour as the temperature still felt mild. Much of The Mansion House had still to be completed, promising to be a fine edifice once fully finished; judging by the lacklustre display of those purporting to be working on it, that could still be some time away. St Stephen's Church stood close by, perhaps a bit too close, the planner or the architect making the church look diminished as a result.

I began to walk down, seeking the house of the Tewksleys. Walbrook, named after the river that flows out to the Thames on the western side, is now largely covered to allow for the houses, offices and shops to be built along its length. Thankfully, the odour of the river had been suppressed, as I would hardly think the mayor would have been too happy to have his nostrils twitch as he sat down to his future dinner.

I would call the residences of this street affluent as opposed to wealthy; the buildings mostly lacked grandeur, with only a few being substantial, like Tewksley's house, being four storeys high, double-fronted and close to Cannon Street. A few people walked about and a couple of carts trundled by, a drayman unloaded barrels at the tavern and I passed a shop selling leather items, harking back to the days when tanneries were in the area.

I knocked upon the door and waited for only a short time before a young man opened it and enquired as to my business. I gave my name and requested to speak to the Lady or Gentleman of the house and he bid me to wait whilst he conveyed my request.

A short while later he allowed me entry to a marble-tiled hall and then he took me up a highly polished mahogany staircase to a drawing room that looked out over the street, very much like the layout of the Van Hoebeek residence. This opulent drawing room had a high ceiling with ornate decorations, a large candelabrum hanging from the centre. Several plush couches littered the room with small tables and bureaus. The floor was carpeted fully and I pitied the poor servant who would have to brush and clean it, presumably quite regularly to keep it in its present state. The windows were adorned with heavy drapes that dropped from ceiling to floor and I looked at them through my housekeeper's eyes and calculated their worth — very expensive.

The servant stood sentry-like by the door, keeping me company, staying, I suspected, to see that none of the costly items found a way into my pockets.

Cornelia Visser entered the room in a way that I could only describe as languid, dismissing the servant with a flick of her hand. When the door closed, she glided over, appraising me at the same time. She wore an exquisite day dress in cream silk adorned with gold and silver thread embroidery, quite low-cut at the front showing perhaps a little too much of what lay beneath; of a certainty, it caught my eye. She noticed my interest. She stood a little over five feet tall and had dark lustrous hair teased into ringlets, framing a quite beautiful face with her blue eyes, small nose and full sensuous mouth. She looked a lot younger than her years; a woman with an alluring figure; a slim waist and rounded hips to compliment her full bosom. At the funeral I thought her striking, close up, she far exceeded that initial impression. She stopped in front of me and offered her hand. I took it gently and keeping my eyes upon her, brushed it against my lips, feeling her fingers gently squeezing mine.

'Mr Hopgood,' she began. 'Miss Van Hoebeek has spoken to me regarding your enquiries into Pieter's death. Let me thank you for taking on that task and I am hopeful that you will be successful. I remember seeing you at Pieter's funeral though I regret we did not speak.'

I gave a slight bow of the head in acknowledgement. 'I too regret that. I hope you will rest assured that I will do what I can to find Pieter's killer, Miss Visser, or should that be Mrs Tewksley?'

'You know my dual identity then, Mr Hopgood,' she replied, with the warmest of smiles. 'Miss Visser will suffice, thank you. Mrs Tewksley sounds so old and, in truth, I am still not used to it, even after all this time.'

'Your husband does not object?'

'Not in the least. I am Mrs Tewksley when it is required, otherwise I keep to my family name. Now, may I get you some refreshment?'

I shook my head. 'No, thank you for your kind offer but I have no need. I take it you were born here, like Miss Van

Hoebeek, as your accent is flawless?'

'You are correct, Mr Hopgood,' she replied, taking a half-turn away from me and brushing her hand against my jacket. 'Come and sit down as you obviously wish to discuss something with me.'

The gesture took me aback a little as the touch of her hand indicated a flirtatious nature. 'Thank you,' I replied, following.

She sat on a couch, patted the empty space beside her and smiled up at me again. I hesitated for a moment and then she patted the space again.

'I would not take you for a shy man, Mr Hopgood. We can keep our voices low instead of shouting across the divide.'

'I only hesitate for proprieties sake, madam,' I replied. 'And I am sure our voices will still stay low if I sit here, across from you,' I added, as I diverted my step to another couch and sat down before she could say more.

An amused expression passed across her face and she looked down briefly, hiding a smile before raising her head again and adjusting the folds of her dress. 'As you will, Mr Hopgood. I certainly do not wish you to feel uncomfortable.'

'I am very comfortable, I assure you, madam.'

'Then how may I help you?' she replied, a slight tilt to her head, bordering on coy.

'I hope not to take up too much of your time; I just wish to know whether you can shed a little light on the untimely death of Pieter van Hoebeek. Do you know of any reason he should be attacked?'

She shook her head and I noticed that her eyes lost some vibrancy and the corners of her mouth dropped slightly as if in sadness. 'I do not, sir; I would happily tell you if I did.'

'Only I understand that you and he were very close at one time.'

'Very close?' she replied, a twitch of a smile returning. 'I think that you can say we were once, that was some time ago.'

'Before your marriage?'

'I knew Pieter for most of my life, sir. Let us say a flame kindled now and again which then diminished. We were not destined to be anything other than what we were.'

'What about after your marriage?'

She looked me full in the eye and licked her lip. 'Once or twice. Are you shocked, Mr Hopgood?'

I shook my head. 'Why would I be so?'

'Because people expect people to act in a certain way.'

'Not I,' I said, honestly. 'I have learned not to judge and people should live their lives in the manner they wish to.'

'That is quite refreshing to hear, Mr Hopgood. Even some of my own fair sex would not countenance my outlook; I believe in a certain freedom to enjoy the more pleasurable side of life and I do not wish to be constrained.'

'Have you and Pieter, er…met recently?'

She shook her head. 'Not in the way you infer. I visit the house so we do cross paths.'

'What of your husband, is he aware of your wish not to be constrained? I assume then that Pieter was not the only flame to kindle.'

She smiled and then laughed, bringing brightness to her eyes. 'My husband? If only you knew then you would not need to ask. Mr Tewksley goes his own way too; he does not interfere in my life as I do not interfere in his.'

'Then it is a marriage of convenience?'

'It is. He required a wife and I required security.'

'Then why did you not marry Pieter?'

'Ah, you see, Pieter loved me but I could not love him as he wished or deserved; I would have felt suffocated. However, we continued to have the occasional intimacy,' she said, smiling slightly, as if at the memory. 'He did keep hoping that I might change; in the end, I believe he came to accept that I would not.'

'I would have thought your marriage would have made him accept it.'

'Not so; he knew why I married Roger.'

'Ah, yes; convenience.'

She sighed and looked me straight in the eye again. 'You are a thief-taker, I believe, one who investigates. Would you not have gathered some information prior to coming to see me?'

I took a few moments to think before I spoke. Should I be candid with what I have heard? Undoubtedly, Cornelia Visser was an intelligent woman and she appeared immune from embarrassment, being open about her circumstances. I decided to test the water a little more. 'You are correct,' I began. 'I must admit that I have delved a little. You have said that you enjoy the attention of men; is that exclusively to men?'

That smile appeared on her face again and I noticed her eyebrows rise. 'Meaning?'

'Just that, er...forgive me if I am wrong; it is my understanding that you have a tendency towards sapphism.' I expected my reply to shock her but she hardly gave it thought.

'I wonder where you have heard that, Mr Hopgood? No matter; would it shock you if I said there may be a little truth in that?'

I shook my head. 'No, I have already told you that people should be free to live their lives as they wish.'

She inclined her head in acknowledgement. 'Then I admit my pleasures come in more than one form, Mr Hopgood.'

'With Femke van Hoebeek?'

Her mouth opened a little for a second and then closed. 'My, my; you have been a busy man.'

'It is no business of mine whom you take your pleasures with, Miss Visser, unless of course, it has a bearing on my investigation. Was Pieter aware of that side of you?'

'Did I tell him, you mean? Then no, I did not.'

'So he did not expect to find you in that, er... delicate circumstance, when he disturbed you and his sister at his house?'

'Ah, you have learned that. From whom?'

'It does not matter, only that I have.'

'That is hardly fair, Mr Hopgood,' she said, giving me an amused look. 'It happened a few weeks ago,' she admitted. 'Up until then he had no idea about me, though I suspected he knew his sister's preferment. Femke does not know that he saw us so please do not tell her. She would die of embarrassment.'

'You spoke to him about it?'

'I did, before I left his house that day and he promised not to confront Femke, just asking to speak further with me regarding it.'

'And did he, I mean, speak further with you?'

'No, I believe he decided not to, in the end.'

'And he never mentioned it to his sister?'

'Not as far as I know; she would have told me otherwise.'

'It would seem that you lead a very complicated life, Miss Visser.'

'No more than many others.'

I gave a tilt of my head in acknowledgement. 'You are keeping Miss Van Hoebeek company during her process of grieving?' I asked, as I stood up to leave.

'I am; we have known each other for many years. Did you know that her life is becoming complicated too, Mr Hopgood?' she said, standing up as well.

'How so?' I asked.

'She is being pursued by a man,' she replied and then she laughed. 'Little does he know, of course.'

'Who is it?'

'I have your interest now then, Mr Hopgood.' She grinned and spun away to walk a few steps and then returned, close to me. 'Ruud Janssen has decided he wants a wife before he gets too old and has set his sight on Femke.'

That name did not surprise me. 'Does he not know about her?'

'If he does then it does not worry him.'

Then I remembered something, something Lars the night guard had said in jest. 'Her overseer, Martijn Thyssen, is he not interested in her?'

'Martijn Thyssen?' She asked, her eyes momentarily widening. 'Why would he be interested in her?

'No matter, just a bit of gossip I heard.'

'Then gossip is all it is.' She put on a wistful look. 'I admit I can see the advantage of a younger man for an older woman, especially where the bedroom is concerned. Don't you agree, Mr Hopgood? I'm sure you understand my meaning.'

I opened my mouth to say something then saw Cornelia Visser give me a knowing smile and then a coy bite of her bottom lip. She moved very close to me and patted my chest with her hand. Her eyes looked up into mine and I felt her breasts press against me, her warm breath touching my face.

I decided it safer not to remark further, instead, just giving her a small smile and then moving apart before my resolve crumbled; I admit she stirred a certain feeling. I began to walk towards the door and then I stopped and turned. She looked a little disappointed that I had not succumbed to her wiles, my resistance utilised only by a great deal of willpower. 'Your husband,' I said, as we looked at each other. 'You say he goes his way as you go yours; what is his way, may I ask? Only, I understand he had an argument with Pieter in the street; was that about *his* way?'

'You may ask, Mr Hopgood but that does not mean I will tell you. If he argued with Pieter, I do not know of it. I am sure you know what my husband prefers, you having delved a little. Even though my husband does not claim his marital rights, I am happy to give him the loyalty he would expect from a wife.'

'Is that part of your marriage contract?'

'It is part of every marriage contract, Mr Hopgood.'

'The same as to forsake all others?'

'Maybe not that one,' she said, dismissing it and giving me

that smile again. 'Do please call again, Mr Hopgood,' she added, walking over to me and patting my chest again. 'When you are at leisure, of course. I can assure you a warm welcome — very warm indeed.'

I gave her a little bow of the head and then departed, taking a long slow breath as I made my way down the stairs to the front door; I hardly noticed the servant accompanying me.

I walked down to Cannon Street and then along, passing the London Stone opposite St Swithin's. Some say the stone measured the distances from London in old times past, others that it was an altar stone where the ancient people made sacrifices; now it sat in its own little house and we, oblivious to its true history, protected and cherished it. I carried on until I came to the Bell, deciding to take a drink and think on my encounter with Cornelia Visser before going down to the river, where I intended to take a wherry across to Southwark.

Sitting in a quiet corner I lit my pipe and inhaled, deeply, breathing the grey cloud of smoke out slowly and thoughtfully. I took a drink and cast my eyes around, taking note of the dozen or so customers, chatting amiably in their little groups scattered around the tavern. Cornelia Visser had certainly left an impression upon me, unfortunately, not entirely positive. Physically attractive and alluring undoubtedly, and part of me wished to take her up on her offer. If I had seen her at a social engagement I would have sought an introduction, as would any man with blood running through his veins: beautiful, flirtatious, confident and seductive. For me, the jarring note came when I gazed into her blue eyes, making me feel disconcerted; they of all things seemed cold, unwelcoming, distant, with a hard edge. They say that the eyes are a window into the soul, if so, then what should I make of what I saw there?

Two things made me feel uncomfortable: the blatant invitation of the intimate and her reluctance to provide any information concerning her husband's activities. The former because I had the distinct impression that she solely craved and desired physical gratification, whether it came from another man, a woman or me, it did not matter. Ordinarily, like many a man, an offer like that from a very attractive woman would be hard to resist, but I saw a coldness there. The latter, because I believe she must be aware of her husband's inclinations and that she was complicit in protecting him. Would any moral person protect a man like that, would condone those abhorrent practices?

I took another draw of my pipe and then felt a cold tingling feeling run down my spine and I shivered a little, feeling unclean having been in the presence of Cornelia Visser.

CHAPTER 17

I stepped off the wherry at St Mary Overie, sidestepping the immediate rush to take my place and made my way towards the crowded market at Borough. I barely noticed the market traders, being still deep in thought. I continued across into Tooley Street and then down to St Olave's church where I hoped to meet up with either Ned or Kitty.

The church fronted the street, the entrance straight off the pavement, an iron gate to the side led to the burial grounds behind. I opened the unlocked gate and entered as I had no wish to stand around being conspicuous with my immobility. The church had recently been rebuilt after parts of it fell into decay, though the grounds had been unaffected. Two other people, a man and a woman of similar age to me, presumably a couple judging by their ease with one another, stood a short distance away, paying their respects to a grave. We briefly acknowledged each other with a nod of the head and then they returned to their devotions, bowing their heads in prayer and then laying a small posy of flowers upon a grave of bare earth, yet to have a covering of grass and vegetation; a recent burial then of someone close to them.

I sat down upon a bench a few yards from the gate and continued to look thoughtful. I had no wish to seem disrespectful while the couple stood at the grave showing their grief. Occasionally I glanced to the street hoping to see either Ned or Kitty, but so far I had not caught sight of them. Although the street's noise and bustle were only a few yards away, it seemed as if I sat in an oasis of calm and peace, the bars of the gate acting as a barrier to the tempest beyond.

The couple finished their devotions and then made their slow way towards me, arms interlocked for support. The man caught my eye and I smiled wanly, he recognised my sympathy and gave a slight tip of the head before he pulled the gate open and they walked outside into the throng and disappeared.

I sat there for perhaps twenty minutes or so, reluctant to remove myself from our agreed rendezvous for fear that our paths would never cross. I did not want to walk aimlessly around Southwark for the next few hours. No one entered the church grounds to relieve my tedium and without distraction, my mind kept returning to my interview with Cornelia Visser, both her words and seduction still having an unnerving effect upon me.

The screech of metal rubbing against metal disturbed my contemplation, a rip through the hubbub of the street's noise as the gate opened. I looked up and saw Little Alex with a grin on his face enter the church grounds and come towards me.

'These ol' dew-beaters are fair killing me, what wiv all this standing around. Shove up a bit an' let me give 'em a rest,' he said by way of greeting.

I shuffled along the bench to allow him a bit of room and he sat down, sighing in relief, holding his legs out straight and wiggling his feet. His boots, battered, split and about two sizes too big, seemed near to falling apart. 'Better you get some new ones,' I said, nodding towards his feet.

'Nah, don't want new. Some cove would take 'em first night I got 'em.'

'Let us say new to you, a pair already worn in.'

He grinned. 'You paying?'

'Of course. Kitty can take you to Monmouth Street, fix you up.'

'Yeah?'

'Yes, next few days.'

He nodded, sniffed then wiped his nose with his sleeve. 'Got you a snitch, we 'ave.'

'Really?' I replied, an alert feeling rippling through my body.

'Yeah. Washerwoman from the 'ouse in Maid Lane. Knows about the 'ouse over there too,' he said, cocking his head towards Joyners Street. His feet stopped twitching and he bent his legs to sit properly. 'Ain't right wot they be doing,' he said, after a moment's reflection.

'I agree, and that is why I intend to put a stop to it, one way or another,' I said as I stood up and stretched my back, easing a tension that had just appeared. 'Take me to Ned and Kitty, Alex, and hopefully we can bring this Tewksley before a justice.'

We left St Olave's and headed back to Borough market, this time I took more notice as we threaded our way through the crush of people and traders: the costermongers, the pie-men, the criers, the hapless and the hopeless all hoping to strike a bargain or a benefit. Alex, bless him, thought to guide an old man like me and took it upon himself to keep me safe from predators and vociferously bawled out to anyone coming too close. I guess he thought that I would be marked as a victim. Unscathed, we headed into the alleys and lanes beyond the market, lined by dank and rotting timber buildings where the smell of ordure and the river hung heavy in the air. We emerged behind St Saviour's Church and took Winchester Street at the rear of the old palace, then through more alleys, close to a timber yard and out into Dead Man's Place, the burial site of the plague dead from near a century ago.

As we walked, Alex told me that Tewksley's hospital scared the children of the area, hearing rumours of unnatural acts and even of some children disappearing, with monsters dwelling in the place, ready to eat up any who ventured inside.

We turned left into Maid Lane and like most of Southwark, the buildings had seen better days, all seemingly leaning into one another as if propping each other up. People moved about on their business with the traffic being more of the commercial variety with drays and carts moving stock and supplies, either horse-drawn or by hand. A few private dwellings, tenements housing the poor, cheek by jowl with the tanneries, the dyers, the metalsmiths and the brewers, the timber yards and the bawdy houses. The area had a thick and cloying aroma with the smoke from the chimneys adding to the rich miasma, hanging like a dirty shroud. Alehouses and bowsing-kens littered the streets and alleys, with a few slightly more respectable taverns and inns scattered amongst it all.

We found Kitty near the coal yard by the glass-blowing house that made bottles and glasses for industry and retailers;

it had once been the old bear garden which used to have bear-baiting in a round arena until it was pulled down.

'Where's Ned,' I snapped, aware of her vulnerability on her own, standing on a street with all manner of felon about.

'Don't worry, Richard, he's down there a bit,' she replied, indicating with her head. 'He was with me up until a few minutes ago. Someone came out of the home and we wanted to find out where he went. One of us had to wait here in case you arrived.'

I held up a placating hand. 'You are right, of course, Kitty. Take no heed of me; I saw that you were on your own and felt just a little concerned.'

She smiled. 'Thank you for being concerned. As you see, there is nothing to worry about.'

I placed my hands on her shoulders and smiled back. 'I do see, so will say no more on it. Now, where is this hospital?'

She indicated with her head again. 'Do you see the man with the barrow walking away from us?'

I nodded as I turned my head and looked down the street. 'He's just by the house now, on the left.'

I could see an old building with many small windows poking out between its tired wooden frames. It had three floors and a garret. A large door led straight onto the street; a substantial building, about sixty feet in width. 'Do you know what it was before it became a hospital?'

'Yes, a manufactory for cloth, the local people say; a Huguenot used to own it. There is a yard out back where they dyed the cloth and beyond is the whitening ground where they bleach the linen. A bit further down is an alley that leads to the back where the carts would go.'

'Have you been around the back?'

She shook her head. 'Not me, Ned took a quick look and found a solid locked gate to the house.'

'When Ned returns we should take a look ourselves. Alex says that you have found someone willing to talk?'

Kitty nodded. 'Yes, a laundry worker. She worked there for a few weeks until she walked away when she found out what went on.'

'Where is she now?'

'Works at the skin market a bit further down.'

'How did you find her?'

'Luck, really. We walked down there and just asked as we looked at the skins, one of the workers pointed us towards this Belle and she said she'd be happy to talk when she's done for the day. What's the time now?'

I took out my pocket watch. 'It lacks ten minutes to three o'clock.'

'Then she'll be finished in ten minutes; said she'll meet us in the alehouse opposite.'

'Then we will speak to her before doing anything else.'

Ned returned a few minutes later with a frown on his face. 'Sir,' he acknowledged, as he arrived. 'Lost the bastard,' he announced, none too pleased. 'Dipped into the alleys down there aways; would never find him in that lot.'

'Who is this?'

'Cove came out the house, a bit of a shuffler, I reckon,' he replied. 'Thought to see where he went but those alleys are as bad as St Giles and I don't know me way.'

'Just as well you stopped then,' I said, knowing that Ned would risk all should the need arise. 'We have lost nothing and besides, with this woman, we might have something to gain; let us hear what she has to say.'

The raw and powerful singular smell from the skin market and the tanneries close by assaulted my senses; where we had stood it had been diluted but being this close, the rank concentrated effluence came close to making my eyes water. Ned, Kitty and Alex did not seem to notice the stench; they had already suffered it, so maybe they now had partial immunity from its effect.

The alehouse had no airs nor graces, a rough and ready type of establishment, matching the customers. We received a less than fulsome welcome, though cordial enough to persuade me we would not find any trouble. I ordered the ales and we took up a table to the side, near the entrance so that Kitty and Ned could see this Belle when she came in.

As we waited, I briefly outlined my experience with Cornelia Visser, amusing Ned no end for some unaccountable reason. Kitty did not share Ned's humour; whether it was the woman's audacity in flagrantly making the offer or thinking that I might well accept it, I did not know.

A few minutes later Kitty nudged my arm. 'This is Belle, just coming through the door.'

I gave an inward sigh of relief as I had half expected the woman would not keep her appointment. Ned stood up and beckoned her over.

'One of those for me?' she asked, eyeing the pots on the table.

'Indeed, madam,' I replied, tapping a full pot with my finger.

Belle sat down, immediately picked up her blackjack and

drained it in one continuous swallow.

'You have a thirst on,' I remarked when she lowered the empty pot. 'Another?'

She nodded and I waved the boy over to give a refill. A large, big-boned woman sat before me with wild hair streaked with grey. Her pudgy face had small piercing dark eyes. I found her quite intimidating and not one I would wish to cross.

'This is the gentleman I told you about,' said Ned, turning towards her. 'Mr Hopgood.'

She fixed me with her eyes and I felt her glare penetrate within me, as if seeking a reason not to just get up and walk away. She held me in her gaze for several seconds before blinking and turning her attention back to the pot.

Evidently, I had just passed a test as I saw her lips press together, musing. 'What do yer want to know?' she said, in the end.

'I am certain my friends here have already explained that it's our desire to rectify the wrongs that go on in those places for children. With your help we may find the means to do so. I would like you to tell me what you have seen and heard.'

'It won't make no difference, they're protected, you know. The high and mighty.'

'What do you mean?' I asked, leaning forward.

'Ain't no captain queer-nabs in there, they're all gentry-coves. I seen a churchman, a Lord and the law; a magistrate, if yer like. They were pointed out to me and I had to keep away from 'em. There's others too, come in every now and again; I don't know about them, except one were a judge, I were told; goes from sending a cove to Tyburn to doing what should be sending *him* to Tyburn,' she said, grimacing.

'That is this place here,' I asked, jabbing a finger down the road, my head reeling.

'Yeah, the hospital. All fine gennulmen, supposedly; some of 'em must have wives at home.'

'Do you know who they are?'

She hesitated. 'Some,' she shook her head. 'Don't ask who they are 'cause I won't say, not yet.'

'Why not?'

Her gaze darted towards Ned and then back to me. 'Don't know you yet.'

I held up my hand. 'Then stay silent on that for a time, instead you can tell me how many men run the place?'

'There's maybe eight or nine of 'em.'

'No women?'

'Women? Of course there's women. Most do the looking after, hard bitches too, not local; reckon they were once jades until they got too old fer it. The men tell them what to do and they do it. Pays well enough I suppose.'

'How did you come to work there?'

'Gin 'ouse, down the road. One of the women got foxed with me sitting next to her. She started complaining about the laundry and that she 'ad no one to do it. I said that I'd do it and that's how I came to be there. Don't mind a bit of hard work and laundering is bloody hard work. Paid well, it did, but…' She looked at the table and shook her head, '…not under those circumstances. I 'ad to get out.'

'What happened?'

'I found out what went on. Those men; they're evil, depraved bastards. Reckon they think their class will protect them. They would take a poor mite and instruct them, usually with the help of gin. I saw a bit of what they done once and that were enough.'

'What did you see?'

'Young girl, about eight she were and that Tewksley 'ad is 'ands all over her. She just giggled and I reckon she were foxed. I heard someone approaching so I walked away before I got caught. I told one of the women what I saw and she told me to keep my mouth shut and not to look anymore. She said that the gennulmen will have their recreation and she left it at that. I 'eard all manner of things went on in there.'

'Like what?'

Belle looked up at me, a frown on her brow. 'When the girls get to ten or so they're moved on to that other place, boys are sent too, you know. I 'eard that they sold some girls as a cure for the pox; you know, some poxed man docks with an untouched girl and 'e passes it onto 'er and 'e gets cured.'

I nodded; that was a widely held belief.

'Boys got instructed too. I believe they thought the earlier and younger they got to 'em, both boys and girls, the better it would be. I suppose the kinchins would think it normal to do those sorts of things if they were brought up to do them. Tewksley and the magistrate had their pick of 'em. The clergyman taught the boys, if you know what I mean, and the others…does it matter? They're all in it.'

I looked at Kitty and then Ned and then Alex and I could see their faces lose colour as we listened to Belle.

'This other place,' I asked. 'In Joyners Street, did you ever go there?'

She nodded. 'Once, took some fresh bedding there. The

place is just a nunnery. The girls are all of an age, all around ten, so that it's just about legal. The boys are a similar age; wot they do ain't legal, buggery is buggery and that ain't right.'

'Did you not think to say something to the authorities?' asked Kitty. 'To get them to help the children?'

'Wish that I could've; who do I tell? There were a magistrate in the place, a judge; maybe they're all in it. Anyways, who's going to listen to an old crone like me, eh?'

Belle's testament left us feeling hollow. She had agreed to speak in front of the authorities providing it was not that of Southwark, fearing repercussions. It made no difference assuring her that the alderman would not countenance that sort of thing, she remained adamant.

We talked little as we stood in the whitening fields behind the home and contemplated the rear gate. A boundary wall ran behind the row with the large double gate opening out to the fields. The cloth makers nearby had put out a few linen sheets attached to timber frames to be bleached by the rays of the sun, from the raw grey to a whiter sheen; behind them stood windmills as if sentinels keeping watch, their sails unmoving.

A closer examination of the gates showed that they were sturdy, made of heavy solid wood; a look at the hinges showed that they swung outwards with no handle or means to open from the side we stood.

'Barred from the inside,' opined Ned, having seen it earlier.

Alex scrambled on the ground in front of the gate to try to

see beneath, poking with a stick to clear some mud, shaking his head as he stood up. 'Can't see nuffink,' he said.

'Overgrown, I should imagine,' I replied. 'Doesn't look like these gates have been opened for a good long time.'

'What do we do?' asked Kitty.

'Nothing we can do, at the moment. At least now we have the lie of the land here, so show me this other place and then we will work out what to do.'

Further up, another alley led down to Maid Lane and soon we hurried along the street, retracing the route that Alex had taken me, stopping briefly in the market for something to eat from a stall selling hot pies. The three of us sat on a low wall eating as people milled around, our conversation still muted, each lost in our own thoughts. We did not dally in the market, as soon as we had finished eating we moved quickly away, towards the house in Joyners Street.

'This is it,' said Kitty, as we walked down the street. 'On the left with the blue door. The alley down the side leads to a more discreet entrance.'

Four storeys high, the timber-framed building showed no sign of the depravity that carried on inside. Slightly narrower than the place in Maid Lane, it nevertheless had ample room for the business conducted inside. Belle had briefly described the layout of the building. The top storey had two large rooms, one for girls, the other for boys to sleep in, the floor beneath having smaller rooms where the children entertained the customers. The first floor had storerooms and some sleeping accommodation for the adults working there. The ground floor had lounges and gaming rooms where the gentlemen could relax.

Looking at the building from the outside would give no clue as to its purpose and merged innocently with those next to and nearby it.

'You say there is a discreet entrance down the alley,' I said to Kitty. 'Surely there is access to the rear; a yard?'

'That's where I mean,' she replied. 'You go down the side and then into a yard at the back. A carriage can come from the other end of the alley where it is wider, turn in and drop off the passenger. There is enough room there to turn a coach.'

'Show me,' I said, changing direction and heading down the alley.

At the end of the house, a large high wall continued for several yards and where it stopped, the alley did indeed widen. To my left, I could see the gated entrance, at the moment standing open. I bid Ned, Kitty and Alex to stay out of sight and then walked in.

A heavily built man stood up from his seat on a bench as I came into the yard. 'This 'ere's private property,' warned the man, as I approached.

'Is it?' I feigned surprise. 'I heard it is a place of entertainment.'

'Only for select gentlemen, and you is not one of them.'

'Then how do I become a select gentleman?'

'You don't. You gets invited to become a select gentleman.'

'Oh, I see. Could you not make an exception at all? I mean, I realise a little recompense for you might be in order.'

I could see him hesitate for just a moment at the prospect of a little chink, then he shook his head. 'Sorry, my friend.

Invitation by a gentleman only. Now, be off with you.'

I nodded, turned and walked back out. At least I had seen what I wished to see, a closer look of the door and the locks.

'Come on, I said as I returned to the others. 'Let us go somewhere quiet to talk this all through.'

CHAPTER 18

After having a quick sombre ale in The Boar's Head, the wherry took us west along the river. Following our talk in the inn, I had begun to formulate an idea that may or may not come to fruition. A breeze came from the east, making the waters a little choppy, coupled with the disturbance from the wakes of the myriad traffic, wherries, lighters, barges and the rest, all intent on their own businesses, ploughing through the wavelets to their destinations. Our oarsman showered us with a tirade of chatter and opinions as he rowed along the river, amazing me that he had the breath to row and talk at the same time, his energy appearing inexhaustible.

Alighting at Surrey Stairs, we made our way to The Strand and The Talbot Inn where we managed to grab a booth to allow us some privacy. We ordered a little more restorative and continued our discussion.

'What's to do, then?' asked Ned, as he lit his pipe.

'I am thinking to speak to The Lord Mayor, Daniel Lambert,' I said, leaning back to get my pipe from my pocket.

Kitty looked at me sharply. 'The Lord Mayor? Does he have jurisdiction in Southwark?'

'I believe so,' I replied. 'Southwark is a ward of the city, The Ward of the Bridge Without. I can remind him, as Chief Magistrate, that he has a responsibility to oversee the judiciary of a ward within the city. I would request that the means be found to organise a raid on the two places. I will suggest De Veil takes charge; you know how that man likes to suck the fruit of power to get every last drop of juice. It would suit him to exercise his might in a ward other than his own.'

'Lambert is only mayor because Parsons died,' said Ned, surprising me with his knowledge.

'That is true,' I replied. 'It does not mean he has any less responsibility.'

'Do you know Lambert?' asked Kitty, interjecting.

'I have met him though I doubt whether he would remember it. He works out of the Vintners Livery Hall.'

'Hang on,' said Ned. 'Vintners Hall is in Thames Street, ain't it, so why is we here?'

'De Veil,' I replied, finally lighting my pipe. 'He would be able to get easy access to Lambert, besides, I have another point to discuss with De Veil; it's only just occurred to me that he has a sinecure as Inspector of Imports and Exports, so he may be interested in De Griese and Jaggers.'

'You said that Jarmin would be looking into that,' said Kitty.

'He is,' I replied. 'I'm thinking it wouldn't do any harm for De Veil to be aware of it,' and I grinned, knowing that De Veil would be hard-pressed not to at least get someone to look into it.

'Is that not a little devious?' asked Kitty. 'Getting both De Veil *and* Jarmin looking into the circumstances of this murder.'

I smiled. 'Not in the least. I will, of course, mention it to De Veil so that he's apprised of the situation. However, we could benefit in two areas Firstly, The Duke of Newcastle is Secretary of State for the Southern Department, involved in foreign affairs concerning France and the countries south of there. I think we can now discount the Dutch at the moment because that would involve Lord Stanhope and the Northern Department and I would rather not confuse things. I suspect the smuggled goods are coming from somewhere other than France, probably Spain or Portugal and those countries come under Newcastle's remit. I'm hoping he will look into that and use his contacts overseas. He will also look at the smuggling along the south coast, maybe bolstering the customs men down there whilst De Veil, in his role as Inspector, would look at the goods coming into London, Secondly, Newcastle also has responsibility for the Southern Home Department, including Law and Justice. I might suggest to De Veil and the mayor that should they both prove to be indifferent to what's going on in Southwark, then I might well speak to Newcastle himself about those two homes. De Veil knows I have the ear of The Duke and I would hope he would remind the mayor that I too have connections.'

'That's clever,' opined Little Alex. 'Can I come wiv you to the mayor? Never met him before.'

'Nor will you now, Alex. No, you cannot come with me; you would just pilfer from his office and that would not help me at all.'

'I wouldn't,' he exclaimed, indignantly.

I laughed. 'No, I know you would not; you would just look, digest and then go back later,' I said, giving him a wink.

'Wouldn't be worth it,' said Ned, laughing. 'How can you

get cases and barrels of wine out of there?'

Alex sniffed, pulled a face then sat back in his chair, arms crossed and frowning petulantly until Ned dug his elbow into his ribs and then he laughed too.

'Stop teasing him, you two,' defended Kitty. 'He's been more than helpful.'

'He has at that,' I said, still smiling. 'And that is why we *are* teasing him.' I took out my purse and picked out a few coins. 'Wages,' I said, pushing them across to him. 'Well-earned too.'

Alex's face brightened and the coins quickly disappeared.

'When are you going to De Veil?' asked Kitty. 'The quicker you see him, the quicker those foul places can be closed down.'

'Let me finish this,' I said, tapping my pot with a finger. 'Then I'll go. Ned, I wish you to go to Van Hoebeek's and see Thyssen, ask him what he knows about the influx of smuggled goods and what it may mean to the merchant's business. Perhaps drop into the conversation that Ruud Janssen has designs on Femke, see how he reacts. The night guard, Lars, said that Martijn had changed his tune regarding Femke; dig a little, see what he says about her. I'm still not sure about him.'

Ned nodded. 'You mean be subtle? I think I can do that.'

'Good, I will see you back at the house later.'

'You're not coming to Drury Lane, Richard?' asked Kitty, a frown on her face.

'Not tonight, Kitty, sorry. I do not know how the meeting with the mayor will go and what might follow. Be ready first thing in the morning, you and Alex are done for today, I think.'

She nodded, a little pout about her lips that disappeared quickly, just a fleeting moment of disappointment.

I finished my ale, pocketed my pipe and left the inn. My destination being Bow Street Magistrates Court where I hoped to find De Veil.

I walked up The Strand, mingling with the shoppers and stallholders, dodging the numerous girls looking to pull likely men into their nearby bawdy houses. I ignored the entreaty from an attractive fair-haired young jade to join her for an evening of carousing, giving her a polite refusal. She voiced her disappointment at my rebuff, the disappointment not lasting long as she immediately homed in on a man coming up behind me.

I turned into Catherine's Street and then Bridge Street, heading toward Covent Garden and Bow Street. De Veil's Magistrates Court stood opposite The Brown Bear Tavern where I meet with my fellow thief-takers, to catch up on the latest news and deeds of my colleagues.

The Magistrates Court still seemed to be busy with comings and goings, even though the end of the day approached. I went through the door and stood in the large hallway, taking a moment to look around. Several small groups talked to each other, then one group moved and I could see Digby, a court official, talking to another. I caught his eye and he made his excuses to come over to me.

'Mr Hopgood, a pleasure to see you, sir,' he greeted, giving a little nod of the head.

Digby may have been an average man, of average height, with average build and average looks; but his ability looked down on the average from afar. Born in the slums, he had learned his letters and made his way up in the world, reaching his current exalted position as a court official, working directly under De Veil.

'And to you too, Digby,' I replied. 'Busy as ever, I see.'

'Unfortunately, there are always people requiring our services, Mr Hopgood, as well you know. If only people would refrain from going against the law; I'm sure we would all be in a better place for it.'

'Too true, Digby, though it would be the likes of us who would be out of work, would it not?'

'Indeed, sir, though I doubt I would complain. Now, may I be of assistance to you?'

'The Colonel, is he free at the moment?'

The Colonel being Thomas De Veil, Chief Magistrate of Bow Street and I stood not only in his home but the functioning Court as well.

'He will be shortly, sir. He is just sending a ken-miller to the Old Bailey for trial; goods of over seventeen pounds had gone, so it will likely be the hempen rope for him.'

I nodded sagely, anything over five pounds stolen would often lead to a trip to Tyburn; the best he could hope for would be transportation to the Americas. A rolling noise of anger, resentment and disagreement came down the corridor leading to the court and then I saw De Veil come stomping through, dressed in all his finery with an expression that could freeze the very sun. All the people milling around the hall turned to look as he swept past, some of them even grinning. Ignoring those trying to speak to him, the colonel just waved them away before hurrying up the stairs.

'Sounds like that went well,' I remarked, finding a grin come to my mouth.

'I heard a little of the felon's defence and he claimed that the goods were only worth three pounds and that the householder had inflated the worth for his own purposes. The goods have already been sold on, so who's to say.'

'Did anyone see him?'

'Apparently, someone did. A witness saw him come out through the window and recognised him as a rogue; I am wondering if this witness wanted to get even for some reason, he might even have been paid to say that; fortunately, it is not my problem.' He looked up the stairs. 'Maybe now might not be the right time unless it is urgent. You can come back another time, perhaps tomorrow as he does not seem in the best of temper.'

'Unfortunately, it cannot wait,' I said, a little ruefully. 'So, I had better steel myself for a harsh reception.'

I gave a little bow of the head and then with Digby indicating to the burly helpers to allow me through, followed De Veil up the stairs. From his demeanour as he walked past me, I imagine that even in that short time De Veil would have poured himself a very large restorative.

I knocked on his door and received an annoyed shout from inside. 'What in the blazes is it now?'

I took his question as permission to enter. 'It is just me, Colonel,' I said.

'Oh, it's you Hopgood,' he replied, as I closed the door behind me.

He had his side towards me and I noticed that I had guessed correctly, he had a glass half-full of what I presumed to be brandy, partway heading towards his lips.

'I cannot help noticing that you seem somewhat perturbed this afternoon, Colonel,' I said, inwardly smiling.

'Perturbed? Is that what you call it?' His glass finished the journey to his mouth and he upended it, draining it in one. He reached for the decanter and poured another and I noticed he did not pour one for me. 'That rabble of wasters, scoundrels and good-for-nothings have sorely tested my patience today, Hopgood. That last felon packing my court with his shaberoons and affidavit-men, prigs and cloyers, all to put pressure on the court and the witnesses. The man's a thief, sir, an habitual one at that, brought before the court before now; I'll wager that this time he's bitten off more than he can chew. The villain will pay dearly for his temerity; the rope will be his reward.'

De Veil's speech, being littered with cant, indicated that he had reached the end of his tether. Normally one who used language to indicate his superiority in status, he used street talk out of pure frustration. I found it amusing, even considering the serious nature of my visit.

His brows narrowed as he suddenly rounded on me. 'Why are you here, Hopgood? My memory may be waning a little, but I do not recall seeking your company.'

'No, you did not, Colonel. It is I seeking yours,' I replied.

'For what purposes?' he asked, studying the amber liquid in the glass as though worthy of benediction.

'I have need to speak to the mayor in his role as Chief Magistrate of the City and thought that it may be to your advantage, should what I request come to pass.'

He made a face of passing interest and then walked over

to his chair and sat down. I followed and sat opposite without invitation. A wry expression passed across his face as my class as Gentry precluded his opposition to my sitting down without his permission. 'Then perhaps you should explain, Hopgood,' he said, imbibing once more.

'It is quite simple,' I began and then explained what I had discovered and suspected in Southwark at the house in Maid Lane and that of Joyners Street.

'This woman, Belle, is she reliable?'

'I believe so,' I replied.

He toyed with his glass, turning it this way and that. 'If what you say is true then there may be repercussions should these be men of influence.'

'There may be, I grant you that. Do not forget that these are men indulging in their sordid peccadilloes and the children have no say in the matter. To me, if they suffer any repercussions, then it will be well deserved.'

'A magistrate, a peer of the realm, a judge and a clergyman, you say?'

I nodded. 'Perhaps there are more and who knows whom the members of this private bordello are. I am sure the Mayor and the City would look favourably on the man who cut out this canker from society, Colonel.'

This time he nodded and then looked at me. 'I will accompany you to the mayor,' he said, checking his clock. 'We have time to do so today, Hopgood, so I suggest we do it now. There will be much to organise should I receive a favourable response. Digby,' he yelled, aiming his voice towards the door.

I heard a repeating voice summoning Digby from

downstairs and then a few minutes later, his head appeared at the door. 'Sir?' he asked.

De Veil flashed a grin on his face. 'My carriage, if you please, as soon as possible.'

'Sir,' acknowledged Digby, with a curt nod.

'Thank you, Colonel,' I said, as he drained his glass and placed it on the side-table.

'I just hope you are correct in your assumption, if not, then be sure that *you* will be the one to suffer repercussions, Hopgood,' he warned, glancing at me.

He knew as well as I that a raid risked disappointment; that what we thought would be occurring might not be occurring at the time of the raid. In this instance, I did not think to be overly concerned — perhaps I should be, I thought, as we waited for the carriage. If it proved that I am wrong, then my time as a thief-taker would probably be at an end, as I would be the laughingstock of the City and of my fellow thief-takers. Commissions would dry up as my reputation became tatters. The money I earned meant little, I just enjoyed pitting my wits against the rogues committing crimes; I would be lost without the stimulus and then I had to consider my new involvement with Jarmin and the intelligencers — would that come to an end as well?

I must have pondered for several minutes because now De Veil urged me out of the door as Digby announced that the carriage had been made ready. I hesitated to discuss the matter of De Griese and Jaggers at the moment, thinking that it may be better to raise the subject in the presence of the mayor, as I had a suspicion that De Veil would just point me in the direction of the customs. If the mayor took an active interest, then De Veil's hand would be forced.

Pushing my thoughts to the side, we descended the stairs where decorum had broken out once again, all seemed relatively peaceful with only a few quiet people waiting in an orderly fashion. De Veil and I breezed past and out of the door to enter the carriage waiting there.

'Vintners Hall,' ordered De Veil, as he stepped into the vehicle.

I followed behind and had only just pulled the door closed when we set off with a jolt and I practically fell into my seat opposite the colonel, who grinned widely at my discomfiture. De Veil's eyes gleamed as he had me repeat my suspicions as we journeyed to Thames Street. I could tell the prospect of usurping the authority of the Southwark magistrates excited him, certainly something to gain him a reputation of notoriety south of the river, furthering his ambitions to receive official recognition of his abilities and dedication in the fight against lawlessness. I was pleased that my idea had begun to bear fruit.

CHAPTER 19

Vintners Hall sat behind a courtyard fronting onto Thames Street near Queenhithe dock, a large stone and brick-built edifice, the Hall had two wings on either side of the main building and was the centre of the wine trade in London. A gate between two pillars, each supporting a statue of Bacchus, the Roman god of wine, gave entrance into the courtyard.

We pulled up outside the Hall and immediately alighted, with De Veil leading the way. A porter at the gate allowed us through once he had established our business, guiding us over to the offices in the left wing. Another man then led us up the backstairs to the floor above, then along a corridor to a plain-looking room with few adornments where he bid us wait while he enquired as to the mayor's availability.

De Veil harrumphed and stood impatiently gazing out of the window, his hands behind his back, his fingers twitching. 'One would have thought a little refreshment would be provided as we wait; it is not as if they lack for any wine, Hopgood,' he said to the window.

'Maybe they have to ration it for deserving causes,' I replied, feeling whimsical.

His head spun on his neck. 'Am I not a deserving cause; a Magistrate of this City?'

'Indeed you are, Colonel; the guild may have a powerful voice but I understand their funds are somewhat diminished.'

'Pah,' he exclaimed.

I smiled to his back wondering whether I should prick his self-importance a little more; then I considered why we had come here and I bit my tongue, I had no wish to rile him and scupper any chance of assistance. Instead, I sat down on an upholstered bench and stretched out my legs, taking my ease, waiting as patiently as I could.

Several minutes elapsed, then the door opened and the man once more appeared. 'Follow me, sirs,' he said, opening the door wide and indicating politely with his hand.

'About time,' remarked De Veil with an impatient sigh, as he brushed past me and into the corridor.

The man looked sharply at De Veil before turning his head to catch my eye. I grinned at him and received a quick tight smile in reply before his face returned to his serious demeanour.

We travelled along the corridor once again and were then shown into a more opulent room with The Lord Mayor already in residence behind a large oak desk. Two chairs were placed in front and our man indicated we should take them, just as The Lord Mayor stood up.

'Sit down, gentlemen, please; Colonel De Veil, Mr Hopgood,' he greeted, as he too indicated the chairs.

In his fifties, Daniel Lambert wore a full wig with a dark coat and breeches, his chain of office hanging from his neck, the medallion sitting against his chest; a man of florid complexion with shrewd inquisitive eyes.

'Thank you, Lord Mayor,' I said, giving a formal bow. De

Veil gave a cursory nod and then sat down.

The man who showed us in went over to a cabinet and took out three goblets, placing them on the desk in front of us. He returned to the cabinet and brought over a large glass jug of deep-ruby red wine which he proceeded to pour. I saw De Veil's lips twitch in anticipation of imbibing a quality wine free of charge, as undoubtedly it would be.

'Bordeaux,' explained the mayor as I made pleasing sounds of appreciation. 'A little-known vineyard in this country.'

'Perhaps you would be kind enough to furnish me with the name,' I replied, taking another welcome sip.

'Certainly, Mr Hopgood. You have a good nose for wine, I see.' De Veil upended the goblet, gulped the wine down and then licked his lips. 'One that has to be savoured to be appreciated,' he added pointedly, looking at De Veil.

'Though sometimes the quality surprises you so much that you cannot wait to experience it once more,' I replied, giving a little defence to De Veil.

I saw a smile appear on the mayor's lips just before he took a sip himself. He put the goblet down and replenished De Veil's. 'Now, gentlemen, please explain why you wish to see me.'

De Veil jumped in before I could even open my mouth. 'Hopgood, during his investigation into a murder, has discovered a cesspit of foulness in the heart of Southwark. A so-called gentleman is procuring young girls and boys for the sexual gratification of men. One house purports to be a hospital for orphaned children and another house, attached to the first, he believes is doing business where unnatural acts are being paid for and committed. He has a witness who is prepared to speak, but not to the Southwark magistrates, as this person believes that a magistrate and a judge are involved. Hopgood came to me regarding this issue as he is unsure how to progress. I am willing, should this witness be true of course, to act accordingly. I would obviously need permission to enter Southwark in my capacity of Magistrate to close these places down and to bring the perpetrators to the attention of the law.'

'How young are these children?' asked the mayor.

'Under ten, some infants, I believe,' I replied, getting in ahead of De Veil. 'From what I understand, these waifs and strays are taken in and housed from a very young age and are then given instruction in the, er… ways to please. Once they get to an age where they would pass as ten, the girls that is, are moved to this other house, a member's only establishment. The boys are sent too, though I do not know how old they need to be. I have been unable to gain entry to both these places to corroborate the witness testament.'

'Sounds a vile practice,' returned the mayor. 'Unfortunately, not unheard of.'

'Indeed, my Lord Mayor, a practice that should be punished accordingly, I believe.'

'This magistrate and judge involved; who are they?'

'I do not know as yet. That is partly why I cannot go to the Southwark magistrates.'

'Sir John Eyles is not in Southwark as you may have guessed; his office is taking care of everything. I know that Sir John, should he hear of this, would be most distraught. I can understand why you have come to me.' He sat back in his chair and sipped at his wine. 'You believe these men involved have influence?'

I nodded. 'So I believe.'

'Then it could become political? I only ask, as you may realise, that I have only a week or so left as Lord Mayor.'

I detected a little reticence in his reply. 'In truth,' I began. 'There is the possibility, depending on whom is involved. My way of looking at it is this: one, you can do nothing; if I am mistaken then no harm would be done, if I am right, and you do nothing, it will surely come out that you failed to act. Secondly, if I am mistaken and you act, then you acted upon information supplied by me, if that is the case, you can place the blame firmly on my shoulders. Thirdly, if I am right and you act, then you can take all the plaudits in your final days of office, enhancing your reputation for your future business.'

Lambert looked down his nose at me. 'Succinctly put, Mr Hopgood.'

'I try to be helpful where I can, Lord Mayor.'

De Veil sniffed and looked into his empty goblet, twitching it and the mayor, getting the hint, filled first mine and then DeVeil's, whom, I noted, did not slow his rate of drinking.

'You are happy to proceed in this, De Veil?' asked Lambert.

'Indeed, Lord Mayor. As Hopgood just said, the blame for anything going wrong can be placed on him.'

The mayor nodded. 'And how would you make this happen?'

'Er…' began De Veil.

'If you would allow me,' I interjected. 'We would need to raid the two places at the same time to prevent word getting back from one to the other. Ideally, we would want to establish whether I am right or wrong by taking someone leaving both the bawdy house and the hospital in Maid Lane and question them. Failing that, I believe we should proceed anyway, as I am convinced I am correct in my suspicion and the sooner we do this the better, to prevent any further harm being done to these children.'

'When?' asked the mayor, nodding.

'I can get things organised for tomorrow night,' said De Veil. 'If you approve, of course.'

The mayor let out a slow breath, studying me intently. 'Before we do anything, I would like to hear from this witness. In the meantime, I will allow you to put things into motion,' he said after a few moments thought.

'I fear I will not be able to get her here this evening,' I said. 'Perhaps tomorrow?'

Lambert nodded. 'Then do so. Bring her here and I would like you to be here as well, De Veil.'

'Certainly, Lord Mayor,' replied De Veil. 'I too would like to hear this witness.'

'Very well, if that is all…?'

'Er, not quite,' I replied. 'There is one other matter I need to speak to you about; it may concern Colonel De Veil as well.'

De Veil shot me a fierce look. 'What is this, Hopgood?'

'It is merely one more thing that came to light during this investigation; it may have an impact on both of you.'

'And that is?' asked De Veil, guardedly.

'Smuggling,' I replied. 'You, Colonel, as the Inspector of Imports and Exports, may wish to conduct an investigation, and you Lord Mayor, in your capacity of Vintner, should be aware that there is a gang of smugglers who wish to flood London with contraband, including wine and spirits. This gang also wants to put an end to all the other smugglers bringing contraband to the city, creating a monopoly. That is what I hear.'

Lambert looked up sharply. 'That would be very detrimental to the wine trade.'

'Exactly, so I thought it prudent to bring it to your attention. The names that I suspect are a De Griese and a Tom Jaggers, merchants.'

The mayor looked at De Veil, his eyes intense. 'You will look into this?'

'Um... certainly, Lord Mayor,' replied De Veil, shooting another look my way. 'It would be my pleasure,' he added, giving the lie.

'No doubt,' said the mayor, aware of De Veil's *displeasure*. 'Notwithstanding my own trade, De Veil, I am thinking that there could be a severe reduction in income from taxes and duty. You know the government relies on that money to prosecute the war in the Americas; if we are inundated with these illicit goods, then what impact will it have?'

'As I say, Lord Mayor, I will take steps to look into it,' said De Veil.

'Make sure you do. I will look forward to seeing your report at your earliest convenience.'

'Of course, Lord Mayor,' said a downhearted colonel.

I kept my face devoid of emotion or expression as I listened to the exchange between them. In truth, De Veil would have little to do, he would just issue an order and an officer of the customs would be detailed to investigate. He could hardly complain of any extra work being heaped upon his shoulders.

Even up to only a few minutes ago, I still wondered whether I should mention it and get De Veil involved with the smuggling. With Jarmin also taking an interest, I just hoped that he and De Veil's paths would not cross, though that was now out of my control. I would let Jarmin know that De Veil has been sent sniffing around, just in case.

I took my time eating at a chophouse and so by the time I got home, night had arrived. Mary had made sure that the hearth had a healthy fire burning, the coal, now shimmering like golden jewels, crackled and snapped sharply. The candelabra gave off a good light, the reflection from the mirrors and the silver ornaments, all helping to illuminate the room, allowing me to read easily without straining my eyes.

Ned had yet to return; I knew he would take any opportunity, especially in the evening when I let him free of the leash, to take time to visit a favourite tavern or inn.

Mary provided me with a bottle of claret from my cellar, not as good as the mayors, but enjoyable enough, along with my pipe and newspaper. She took the opportunity to relax by the kitchen fire, catching up on her sewing and drinking a bowl of chocolate, with an additional something extra for fortification, I suspected. Jane had gone to her room with a book, ready for an early start to revive the fire and to get the water on the boil.

A restful peace permeated throughout the house with the ticking of the clock being the only noise intruding, until I heard a shriek of surprise coming from the kitchen, quickly followed by a shout of outrage. I then heard a crash as something metallic came into contact with something solid. More shouting ensued and then a manly laugh, a cackling of glee before I heard a door opening and then the same door slammed quickly shut.

I folded my newspaper and put it on the table beside me, then picked up my glass and took a drink as I listened to the cackle getting louder. 'Come in, Ned,' I called into the disturbed peace. 'Whatever you did to Mary, you'll pay for it a dozen times over.'

The door to my drawing room opened and Ned came in, his face round and pink and with a grin on from ear to ear. 'Small price to pay for a little fun, sir. It were well worth it.'

'What did you do?'

'Well, as it was getting late, I thought I'd be considerate and come in quietly, 'round the back. Took advantage of the privy and then, coming up to the door, saw through the window that Mary were having a bit of a doze. So, I eased open the door and tiptoed in.' He began to chuckle to himself. 'She didn't hear me, so I crept up close, leant forward and blew on her nose, just a gentle puff of wind; as soon as she opened her eyes I planted a great big soggy kiss right on the end of it. Called me all manner of names, she did, some I didn't think she knew. Oh, you might need a new ladle, sir. I think that one has now got a large dent in it.'

'She hit you?'

'No, missed, but not by much.'

'Unlike Mary, perhaps her aim needs more practice,' I replied, wryly.

'With respect, sir. I have learned avoidance; my reactions are getting quicker.'

'When you are sober, you mean. Sit down, Ned,' I continued. 'Tell me about Martijn Thyssen. Ordinarily, I would have you fetch some ale from the kitchen; maybe you wish to refrain considering the circumstances?'

'Thank you, sir,' he said, sniffing and then looking at the door, a thoughtful expression coming onto his face as if gauging the risk to life and limb. 'If you would allow me a moment, I will take the risk.'

I nodded, a grin on my face, reasoning that Mary might well anticipate Ned's return and so would be waiting for him to give a swift retribution.

He returned shortly, with a tankard of ale and totally unscathed.

'I heard nothing untoward, Ned. What happened?' I asked, as he sat down.

He just shook his head. 'Nothing, Mary just sat there, smiling at me.'

'Just smiled?'

He nodded. 'Yes, and do you know what?'

I waved my hand for him to continue.

'It may just be the scariest thing I've seen fer days,' said Ned, giving a shudder as he sat down, managing not to spill a drop of ale. 'I reckon I'm for it soon.'

'She will bide her time, allow you to ponder your misdeed. I'm sure she will catch you unaware and her revenge will be brutal.'

'Thank you, sir. I'm already looking forward to it.'

I grinned; Mary and Ned had a relationship based more on

affection rather than malice. They both love to rile each other, Mary most often coming out the victor. 'We are going off subject, Ned,' I said. 'Martijn Thyssen; what happened?'

Ned sighed. 'He weren't there. Spoke instead to a couple of the workers and all is not happy at that place.'

'Why?'

'Martijn Thyssen. According to them I spoke to, Thyssen is coming over as the lord and master, telling everyone how he plans to grow the business. You told me that Lars said that he had changed his opinion towards Femke van Hoebeek, that he once shared his fellow workers' view of her as a hard mistress; well, now she's his perfect woman, according to these men, can't do no wrong. He spends a lot of time with her, apparently, and the workers don't like it one bit. They reckon he might be after a bit more than just running the warehouse, just like that Lars said to you.'

'Interesting.' I said, picking up on another of his sentences. 'What about his growing the business, how does he plan to do that?'

'By looking at suppliers. They only used Janssen up until Pieter's murder; Thyssen now reckons he can do better than him.'

'I wonder what Femke has said about that? Janssen is a friend of the family and apparently, as I told you, he has set his sights on Femke as a potential wife; now his business is in jeopardy, his warehouse burnt, what effect has that had on his amorous intentions? I saw one of Jaggers' men delivering at the Van Hoebeek's; I am wondering whether Thyssen has already made an arrangement with De Griese and Jaggers. This monopoly I talked about; I think it's starting to happen, the flooding of the market with cheap contraband, supplied by this gang on the south coast.'

'How would they store enough in just Jaggers' warehouse?' asked Ned. 'How could they move all that stock?'

'Good question,' I answered. 'Jaggers has a legitimate business running alongside the illegal one. I would assume he has bought some stock legally from the importers down by the port on Thames Street and that would create paperwork for customs purposes. It's not difficult to supplement his stock with smuggled goods using the legal paperwork as cover, moving goods quickly so that they are never overloaded with stock. They just use the same paperwork time and time again. Customs inspects and everything is in order.'

'Surely the customs are not that stupid?'

'A few bribes here and there, and yes, some of the customs men are that stupid. In any case, maybe having got the mayor to set De Veil into inspecting everything, that might change and suddenly they become competent.'

'Ah, I bet De Veil did not thank you for that.'

'Strangely, no, he did not,' I said, grinning. 'Though if he turns something up, he will take the praise.'

'I take it you got what you wanted from the mayor?'

'I did. De Veil will raid those two houses; before so, both the mayor and he wish to hear from Belle. You and Kitty can go to Southwark in the morning and take her to The Chequers, the one near Vintners Hall, and then we'll go to see the mayor.'

He nodded. 'And you, sir?'

'I think I will pay yet another visit to Westminster; I'm

hoping Jarmin may have unearthed something. You know, Ned. I am liking this Martijn Thyssen less and less as time goes by.'

Jarmin sat in his chair taking notes as I related recent developments. He had told me numerous times that he could never get enough information and that all information could prove useful, whether within his remit or not. His quill scratched across the surface quick as a fly, with only the occasional pause as he dipped the nib into the jar.

'This house in Joyners Street; you can provide no names?'

I shook my head. 'No, I could not even get through the door. I saw no one going in or coming out, but I have only recently discovered it, not time enough to set a watch.'

'Maybe that won't be required. If it is a private establishment where they pay a fee to belong then there should be records; who's paid, who hasn't; they might even have details of attendance, as I suspect they would have to pay extra for er… services. This would indicate that only the wealthy could afford the fees and be trusted enough to keep it a secret.'

'You envisage names you are familiar with?'

'Quite probably,' he said, nodding. 'A good enough reason to have a presence when both these houses are raided.'

'You do not trust De Veil?'

'Oh, he is corruptible in certain circumstances as you well know, but not, I think, in this. He will do what needs to be done.'

I had to agree with Jarmin; De Veil certainly had weaknesses, attractive women being one of them, wealth another and on occasions, he would not dismiss the chance to bed one or receive the other when it would not impact greatly on justice; a pragmatist when it came to certain areas of the law. 'You are not going to take ownership?' I asked.

He shook his head. 'No, I feel political expediency may have an influence, so I would just wish to have someone there.'

'Depending on the names?'

He gave me a grim smile and a little shrug of the shoulders. 'Oh, I'm sure there will be enough fodder for the courts on the whole, I'm thinking that maybe one or two will be given a chance to redeem themselves.'

'You are hypothesising, are you not? There may be no names worth anything.'

'True; we will just have to see when the time comes. Like you, I feel that it will be well worth the effort.'

I nodded then sat back in my chair, a coffee had been provided and I took a sip from the bowl. 'You're not aggrieved that I have De Veil looking into this issue with the smuggling?'

'No,' he replied with a grin. 'I've more interest in where the stuff is coming from than where it's going. I'm happy for the magistrate to poke his nose into that nest. This De Griese gentleman; now, he might be an interesting character.'

'In what way?'

'You mean apart from the fact that you believe he tried to kill you?'

I laughed a little mirthlessly. 'Yes, other than that.'

'Well, from what we can so far ascertain, De Griese does not exist.'

'What?' I exclaimed, leaning forward.

'After your last visit, I sent out a few men to poke their noses into things; by the way, you are correct that a smuggling gang is trying to establish a monopoly over London. Only conjecture at the moment but I think you know where it is heading.'

'Jaggers and De Griese.'

'Yes, so it would seem. Tom Jaggers and those four young men; Ransom, Sommerville, Cannard and Balton are named as proprietors of Jaggers' merchants. De Griese is not. So far, we have found no reference to the man; so who is he and where does he come from? I sent Monk to sit in Cole's Coffee House and he met your friend, Cotespill, who apparently, did not stop talking when he mentioned your name as an acquaintance.'

I could not help rolling my eyes at the mention of Cotespill; nice enough man but lacking in wit. 'Did Monk learn anything?'

'He did. Those four rum-culls were there for a time and this De Griese made a very short visit. Thankfully, Monk managed to stop Cotespill from saying something to him; not very bright is that one, is he?'

'No.' I shook my head, feeling the hairs on the back of my neck standing up.

'Anyway, Monk followed De Griese all the way into Southwark where, unfortunately, he lost him, up near the Marshalsea. Surprising really, as Monk is normally good.'

'De Griese spotted me easily enough,' I replied, feeling a little better about it now.

'That's as maybe; Monk has been trained, you haven't.'

I had to concede that point. 'What now?'

'Good question. If we pulled those four and Jaggers in to speak to them, that would just alert De Griese and I suspect everything would then stop. The four young idiots would undoubtedly speak all they know, which is probably very little, so we would gain nothing of substance from them. Jaggers, on the other hand, would be a harder nut to crack and by the time we had got him to talk, De Griese would have vanished. To me, this De Griese is the one we need along with the proof, and that has yet to be found. I think we need to go to the source. In the meantime, De Veil can make his enquiries here, freeing up men for me; I can send some to the coast to see what can be discovered. A little sea air may do you some good; what do you think, Richard?'

'What?'

He grinned. 'I know you wish to stay and track down this Tewksley, Richard, but I am looking at the bigger picture. Your Dutchman is a small matter of importance when set against this attempt at undermining our economy. I have thought long on this and feel an ideal opportunity has presented itself to introduce you to our ways of working. Anyway, don't worry; you won't be going on your own.'

CHAPTER 20

Despite my protestations, Jarmin would have none of it. I had to agree to carry out his orders, a first step into the murky world that he and the others inhabited. My own fault for unearthing the smuggling connection and I reluctantly agreed that the task was not unrelated to my investigation of the murder. I could not refuse. I had agreed to join his department a few months before and he took joy in reminding me of it, that I knew a reckoning would one day come where my services would be required despite any commitments I might already have. I felt a test of where my loyalties lay had arrived, so tomorrow would see me off to the coast regardless of how the raids in Southwark turned out.

I left Westminster feeling frustrated and anxious about this trip, nervous even. Annoyingly, I could see Jarmin's logic in sending me, even though I thought deploying more experienced men would be the better option, leaving me to concentrate on things pertaining to van Hoebeek here in London. Jarmin had seized the moment to blood me into this intelligencer's world and if I wanted to continue to be part of it, I had to do his bidding — I wondered who he intended to accompany me?

Philip Monk and George Blake sat in the wherry with me as we ploughed our way through the slate-grey waters of the river, the benign surface showing just a few ripples from the wakes of passing boats. Blake had now recovered from his gunshot wound, received from the man Cummings, when we tried to apprehend him some months previously when I first came across Jarmin and his secret basement. Blake had acted too soon and had suffered the consequence of his action; he told me that the incident had taught him much.

Blake was a little older than me, dark-haired with a hard determined face and a muscular physique. He had a habit now of rubbing his shoulder where he had been injured.

We disembarked by Dowgate Wharf, where small boats unloaded their cargo from upriver, then walked up from the stairs between the dank buildings and warehouses that lined the narrow alley, heading towards the Chequers to meet up with Kitty and Ned, and hopefully, Belle.

As I hoped, Ned and Kitty waited with Belle and Little Alex and with him a boy whom I had never seen before. I eased in next to Kitty and gave her hand a gentle squeeze. 'All well?' I asked as I settled down.

Kitty nodded. 'Yes, no problem, apart from Belle being a little nervous about speaking to the mayor.'

'He will soon put her at ease; who is this lad here?'

'Our prime witness. His name is Toby and he spent a few months in the hospital in Maid Lane, until he escaped. Belle found him last night.'

I felt my eyes widen in surprise as I looked at the lad talking with Alex, their heads close together as if planning a conspiracy. 'He has spoken to you?' I asked.

'A little and it didn't make for easy listening. He'd all but removed it from his memory until Belle spoke to him.'

'How did she find him?'

'He's been living on the streets. Belle remembers him from when they were both in the home. She saw him a few weeks ago begging and since then she has kept an eye on him.'

'She didn't mention him yesterday.'

'No, she wanted to speak to him first.'

Monk and Blake pulled up chairs to sit down; Belle and the boy, Toby, gave wary looks, so I hastily introduced them as associates of mine. Toby still looked a little worried, a slight boy, ten or eleven years old with a mop of greasy light-brown hair, narrow-faced with sharp features; his eyes seemed to carry a lifetime of woes and I sensed his nature would be to err on the side of distrust.

Ned caught the eye of the pot-girl and soon ale, lamprey stew, oysters and chunks of fresh crusty bread appeared on our table and Toby certainly lost a little of his reticence, as with Alex's encouragement, he began to eat his fill.

The innkeeper, for a consideration, would send one of his boys to Bow Street with a message to summon De Veil to the inn at his earliest convenience, should he still wish to hear from the witness. I gave the time of two of the clock as the latest I would wait before proceeding to the mayor's office, reasoning that it would give him ample time to get here so the only thing to do now was to wait.

With gentle probing from Kitty, Belle and strangely Monk, Toby gave his harrowing account of his time in Tewksley's hospital for children.

'How did you come to be there?' asked Philip, passing him the last of the bread.

'Ma died,' replied Toby. 'Don't 'ave a pa so I'd nowhere to go. It were cold on the streets an' I just tried to live on the scraps. Then a man saw me and asked if I wanted to live in a nice warm home and have all the food I wanted. I couldn't say no to that, could I?'

'Where were you,' probed Kitty. 'In Southwark?'

He shook his head. 'I remember a river, Fleet it were called, does that help?'

Kitty nodded. 'Yes, it does. So this man took you across the river to that house?'

'Yeah,'

'When was this?' asked Monk. 'How old were you?'

'Reckon a year or so ago. I were about nine or ten.'

'So what happened when you got to this place?'

'Nothing to start with,' replied Toby. 'They put me in a room with the other new boys and I stayed there.'

'Did anything happen to you then?'

He shook his head. 'No. Got food and drink and a bed as they promised. Saw all the other kids there but us lot weren't allowed to talk to them; not then, anyways.'

'When were you allowed to talk to them?' asked Monk.

Toby looked at Belle for reassurance and she nodded for him to continue. 'After we had shown we could be good boys to the gentlemen.'

'And how could you show that?' asked Kitty.

Toby looked at Belle again, his eyes now had a pleading look in them and the woman put her arm around his shoulder and drew him closer.

'They plied 'em with gin,' said Belle, taking over the narrative. 'Toby told me all about it. They got them drunk and then forced them to stand and undress to be examined. This clergyman said that if they did as he said then they would be good boys and God would smile on them, Toby said that he wanted to be good as he didn't want to go hungry again. So he did what he was told. He can't remember much of what happened as he had a woozy head; he only knew that he hurt afterwards.'

'Did this clergyman disrobe?' asked Monk, the anger in his voice apparent.

Toby nodded and then reburied his head into Belle's chest.

'I think he's said enough at the moment,' said Belle. 'Give him a bit o'time.'

I looked around the table at all of the faces and I think they mirrored my own expression of horror and disgust at what we had heard.

'Did the girls suffer the same?' asked Kitty.

Belle nodded. 'So I understand. Both girls and boys got "taught" early, so early that they wouldn't know right nor wrong.'

I took a deep breath in and then let it out slowly. 'The mayor will want to hear this, he will probably ask for more details; do you think Toby will be able to tell him?' I asked Belle.

Belle whispered into Toby's ear and the boy nodded. 'He will,' she said, raising her head to look at me.

'Though in truth,' said Blake. 'A child's testimony does not hold much weight, even when it's obvious he isn't lying.'

Little Alex regarded his new friend, his face still full of anger; a few minutes earlier the two boys had been talking and giggling together, now despair had taken over. 'It ain't right, all that,' he announced. 'I know some boys who do it fer the money in the parks, behind the bushes at night but they knows what they're about. It ain't like all this forcing kinchins to do things they don't want to do.'

A little gloom of despondency lay over the table as all around us I could hear laughter and loud chatter, shouts and screams of mirth, excepting for our small space, with us in what I would term as a period of introspection. All our thoughts stayed inside our heads, scared to let them out should an anger at society take hold.

De Veil arrived at the inn shortly before two of the clock. As he came up to our table both Blake and Monk drew his gaze. 'What is this, Hopgood?' he asked, looking at the two men, his brow furrowed.

'I believe, Colonel, that you have met my friends before. Mr Jarmin sends his regards and he would be pleased should you respect their knowledge and experience should the mayor give his authority for this evening's work.'

I could see that De Veil wanted to reply, his mouth opened a little before he slammed it shut again. I should imagine that he reasoned that should he make a complaint then word would not only go back to Jarmin, but also beyond him to The Duke of Newcastle, a man that no one in his right mind would want to get on the wrong side of. 'So be it,' he replied, a touch grudgingly. He turned his head towards Belle. 'Is this our witness?'

'It is,' I replied. 'We also have young Toby here; they have both agreed to speak in front of the mayor.'

'Good, good; then I suggest we get about it, there is still much to do, should the mayor agree.'

De Veil turned around and headed for the door; he looked over his shoulder and then beckoned with his hand impatiently.

'In a hurry,' observed Ned, as he stood up.

'You should know him by now,' I replied. 'The prospect of mounting a major raid into another ward excites him.'

'Then let's hope he don't go off prematurely,' said Ned, a glint in his eye.

I smiled back; he might not be too far off the mark, as far as De Veil is concerned.

We took the short walk down Thames Street to Vintners Hall where the same porter from yesterday was in attendance at the gate and duly allowed us in, guiding us to the same room as before. No one asked our business, just showed us into the room and asked for us to wait a short while.

Straight away, De Veil took up his position looking out of the window, hands behind his back, fingers twitching. Ned and I stayed standing, as did Monk and Blake allowing the others to sit on the benches. I did not think our wait would be long.

Within a few minutes the door opened and we were guided down the corridor to the mayor's room. Lambert rose to his feet as we entered, then walked around his desk to welcome us all, his gaze quickly resting on Belle, surmising correctly that she was our witness. He looked at me and raised his hand, gesturing for me to begin.

'My Lord Mayor,' I began, as everyone moved towards the chairs. I noticed that he had provided one each for us, so I gathered our wait was because he had to bring in seats from other rooms to accommodate us all. 'Colonel De Veil you already know, sir, so I will make known the others. Mr Edward Tripp, Miss Kitty Marham,' I said, indicating appropriately. 'My associates, or colleagues, if you will. This young lad is called Little Alex and he aids me sometimes, as in this case.' Alex immediately offered a formal bow to the mayor. Lambert smiled at the boy and returned the bow just as formally. 'And these two gentlemen are Philip Monk and George Blake, who are associates of His Grace, The Duke of Newcastle and have been detailed to offer their expertise should the need arise. This lady is Belle Lummen,' I said with a nod. 'She worked in the so-called children's hospital in Maid Lane and this young man is Toby, formally a resident in that same hospital.'

'Thank you, Mr Hopgood. Please, sit down all of you. I'm sure the young men would like a little lemonade, the rest of us can partake of a little wine, I think.' He gave a nod to the man who showed us in and he set to the task, soon we all had refreshments in our hands.

Another man entered the room and went to sit at a small table by the side of the mayor's desk, adorned with writing equipment.

'Mr Cooper here will take notes during this discussion, full notes, you understand, of what our witnesses reveal. I will tell you that I am now acting as Chief Magistrate of The City of London, so what is said in this room can be used in a court of law. Now,' and he looked directly at Belle. 'Mistress Lummen, could you state your name, age and residence so that we can begin.'

I tried to remind Belle of what she said to me the day before until the mayor held up his hand to stop me, accompanying it with a fierce stare, leaving me in no doubt that he did not welcome my interjection as Belle spoke. I clamped my mouth shut as he continued to ask his questions, listening attentively to the replies. Hesitant, at first, Belle soon found her confidence as it became clear that the mayor would in no way dismiss her testament, even when she gave the names of those men she knew were involved.

'There were a rector by the name of Oswald Frammingham, don't know what church he's from; A Lord Pannod, I think he's something to do with the government; a magistrate in Southwark by the name of Silas McCreedy; Roger Tewksley, who funds the place. There may be more but they's the ones I know about.'

She listed the names and I watched as the mayor's expression changed, all obviously known to him in some capacity. I knew Lord Pannod and had heard of the magistrate, not, I suspect, as well as Lambert and De Veil.

'Well.' said the mayor. 'This is most illuminating, I must say.' He sat back, rubbed his eyes with both hands and then drew his fingers down his face. 'You put that all down, Mr Cooper?'

'Yes, Lord Mayor, every word.'

'Good, very good — I think,' he added. 'I can understand, Mistress Lummen, why you did not go to the Southwark magistrates.'

I could tell by the mayor's demeanour that he found Belle's testament distressing, I now wondered how he would feel listening to Toby's; if the lad could find the courage to speak, then that might perhaps take him to the brink.

The mayor made sure we still had drinks and that the

boys' lemonade was topped up and then he smiled at Toby.

'Well, young man. Please take your time and tell me what has happened to you in that hospital.'

Toby began to speak, like Belle, hesitant at first. Belle moved her chair closer to him and took his small hand in hers, squeezing it to reassure him. The mayor's face had now drained of colour and I thought that he probably wished the prospective election for the new Mayor had already taken place. Toby's courage, I think, was bolstered by talking to us in the inn before coming here, because now he gave details that he omitted then and his confidence had definitely grown. The mayor's questions were gently probing, eliciting every detail that Toby could remember.

Kitty had taken my hand in hers as the boy talked; she may have been hardened by her former trade but I could feel her shaking from both distress and disgust. What we heard now could only be the worst kind of hell. I felt a rage grip me as I listened to the ordeal that this boy had endured and judging by the atmosphere within the room, so did everyone else.

'You say that those children who cried a lot after this "instruction" went away; where to?' asked the mayor.

Toby shook his head. 'Dunno. They were there crying and then they were gone. We never heard of them ag'in.'

'Older children or young ones?'

'Both.'

'And you have no idea what happened to them or where they went?'

He shook his head again. 'No, just gone.'

I could read the mayor's face as I looked at him because my thoughts ran in the same direction. The river received all kinds of unwanted items and the watermen regularly hooked young children, their deaths put down to ignorance or disease.

The mayor took a long deep breath. 'How did you escape, Toby?'

'A door were left open one night and I managed to get down the stairs to the back. I broke a winda to the yard and climbed out. Then I clambered up the gate at the back into the fields and then I were out.'

'Only you?'

He nodded. 'None of the others would risk it, see. They were too scared to try.'

'I see. Toby, you have been a brave boy telling me all this, you have given me much to think on.' He scanned the faces in front of him. 'Colonel, Mr Hopgood, Mr Monk and Mr Blake, would you be kind enough to stay seated; would you others forgive my rudeness and go with this gentleman here,' he said, indicating the man waiting in the corner. 'I do not think my rumination will take too long.'

Ned, Kitty, Belle, Alex and Toby, followed the man out and down the corridor. Once the door had closed behind them, the mayor sat back in his chair and gave a long great sigh, as if a bladder slowly deflated.

'In truth, gentlemen, I would rather you had waited until a new mayor had taken up his position. However, I am the one who has had to listen to this litany of debauchery and abuse, so I am the one who has to decide how best to progress,' said Lambert, his face still drawn and pale. He took a large mouthful of his wine and I suspected he never even tasted it. 'That we will act is a foregone conclusion; what is your plan?'

De Veil shifted on his chair. 'My Lord Mayor, I have ordered a number of men to assemble this evening; constables and watchmen, those that I know I can trust.'

'How many?'

'Ten, sir.'

'Not enough,' said Blake, straight away, his hand rubbing the ache in his shoulder. 'Double that at least and there needs to be a few women too. There are children involved and they will need to feel safe.'

The mayor nodded. 'That does sound a little light, Colonel.'

'Also,' added Blake. 'We need a safe place to put the children and we don't know how many we have to deal with. Anyone taken will have to be put under lock and key, so we will need a place for that too.'

'In that case, gentlemen, let me hear your suggestions.'

CHAPTER 21

Ned, Kitty and Little Alex took Belle and Toby back across the river. Young Toby gladly accepted Belle's offer of a home with her. I thought her generous to make the offer and hoped it would work out for both of them. De Veil, Monk, Blake and I made our way to Bow Street where we could finalise the arrangements. The Lord Mayor had agreed to mobilise some of The London Trained Band, the City's militia, to augment De Veil's small force of constables and watchmen. In order to not alarm the general public, the Band would not be wearing their uniforms, instead, each had to wear a red band around their arms for identification. The mayor said he would provide the women, giving us no indication of where he would find them; I just hoped they would be warned about what they might witness. We all had to assemble at Vintners Hall an hour before dusk.

'The Borough Compter will put the fear of God into them,' said De Veil. 'That prison is soul destroying.'

'It's convenient, I'll say that, being on Tooley Street,' said Blake. 'Not too far to take the captives.'

'Do you still think it a good idea to take the children from Joyners Street over to Maid Lane?' asked Monk.

'We have no choice,' I replied. 'The children have to go somewhere and although it is not ideal, it is accommodation.

They will not be at risk once we have removed all the men and workers and replaced them with those trusted to do right.'

'We want to keep them all in the same place as we need to talk to them,' said De Veil. 'Even though their testaments may not lead to anything.'

'Because they are children?' asked Monk.

'Unfortunately, yes,' answered De Veil. 'To be able to prosecute, it would be better to catch these men in the act by trustworthy people, or that one of the men confesses what he knows.'

'We are getting ahead of ourselves,' put in Blake. 'Would it not be best to see what transpires and then act accordingly?'

'It is,' agreed De Veil. 'I just hope that all this does not turn into a waste of time and resources.'

'Have you not been convinced?' I asked.

De Veil turned his head to look at me. 'The Mayor and I are of the same mind, Hopgood. We must, however, temper our expectations.'

I realised that De Veil's nervousness prompted his negativity. I had convinced him yesterday, reinforced again today at Vintners Hall; with everything moving towards a conclusion, the last thing needed now was a lack of enthusiasm.

Blake and Monk exchanged wry smiles.

'I am still not sure why you two gentlemen are here,' snapped De Veil, staring at each in turn.

'I'm sure His Grace knows what he is about, Colonel,' replied Blake. 'You could always ask him yourself.'

I hid the smile that came to my lips just in time as De Veil returned his attention back to me. 'Is there something about this that you have not mentioned to either me or the mayor?' he asked, warily.

I shook my head. 'No, Colonel. This is just simply saving some children from exploitation and abuse.'

'And we are here to help,' added Monk, in a conciliatory tone.

'To give you the benefit of our experience,' added Blake.

And to get hold of any documents before De Veil could get to them, I thought.

Kitty, Ned and Alex arrived at Bow Street and I quickly made my excuses and left, leaving Blake and Monk with De Veil to go over things yet again.

I took a breath of relief as I stepped outside, De Veil's anxiety had started to grate on me and I felt the need to step away to give my mind time to settle. I did not feel guilty leaving Monk and Blake with the colonel, reasoning that they could deal with him better than I, as he would be more on his guard with them, knowing that Newcastle would hear should he prove problematic.

We four took a hackney for a short trip to Jermyn Street where Ned and I could pick up a few items we thought we might need. I felt a little strange doing that as it would be the first time Kitty had seen where I lived. I should have known she would take little notice of my home when we pulled up outside, just a quick curious glance. To Alex, a boy who slept in sheds and doorways, any home was a luxury and mine must have been beyond his dreams, as I saw his face still showing a glazed look of wonder as Ned and I returned to the carriage.

Envisaging a long night ahead of us I ordered the hackney to drop us off in Cheapside, there to eat our fill at a chophouse that I frequented, knowing the excellent standard of the food.

The food went some way in dispelling Little Alex's amazement at my circumstances; boys of that age are forever hungry and destitute boys ten times worse, so his focus changed from my home to the food in front of him, his attention being easily diverted.

We left and walked down Queen Street, some shops now beginning to shut up for the day. Traffic and pedestrians continued to flow as people began to make their way home or to begin their evenings' entertainments.

'You stay close to Ned,' I instructed Alex, my hand upon his shoulder. 'You're there solely to help with the youngsters.'

Alex may have nodded his acceptance but I had little doubt that he would be at the forefront should any trouble develop.

Ned chuckled. 'Not too close, Alex, I must have room to swing; don't want to hit you by mistake.'

'I'm hoping there will not be much need for violence,' I said, as we came towards Thames Street. 'Men of quality may well be indignant if cornered but they rarely attack, knowing that their purses would be deep enough to buy their way out of trouble.'

'You think that will happen?' asked Kitty.

'You know it will,' I replied. 'At least for some of them.'

We turned the corner and then crossed over, avoiding the carts and carriages that filled Thames Street with their noise and bustle. The porter at the gate opened up and allowed us into the courtyard where the men had already assembled, under the gaze of De Veil and Blake.

'Most of us are here now,' said Blake, coming towards me. 'A few watchmen only are still to arrive.'

'What of the women the mayor promised?' I asked, seeing no females present.

'Already here. Monk and the mayor are with them,' he replied, pointing to the door I had gone through earlier. 'Five of them; all work here at the Hall in the kitchen, or as servants to his household.'

'They know what they might confront?'

'Yes, they are prepared, aware they may find things upsetting.'

I nodded. 'Good. As soon as these other men arrive then we can begin.'

We all talked together for a few minutes until the last of the stragglers arrived and then the mayor came out with five mature women, all of whom exuded a no-nonsense attitude. The mayor nodded to me and spoke briefly to De Veil before we divided up into our two separate groups. Monk, Kitty and I would take ten men and three of the women whilst the remainder went with Ned, Blake and De Veil.

Monk and I took our smaller group aside, to explain how we wished to proceed. It did not take long as they had already been apprised of the situation, so we just concentrated on the matter of placing people in their respective positions before and during the raid.

We would use wherries to cross the river, thinking it best not to risk being snarled up on the bridge. The mayor and De Veil assured me there would be transport when we required it later to deal with those taken in the raids. I led our group over to the stairs at Queenhithe where there would be more chance of finding enough boats to carry us across the river. As we walked, I patted my jacket to reassure myself that I still had my pistol and cosh, as well as the long knife. I did not carry my sword as I thought it would be more of a hindrance than help. Kitty, I knew, had a knife hidden in her bodice and I prayed that she would have no need to use it.

As expected, a small crowd had gathered at the stairs, quickly dwindling as boats came in and took people away to their destinations. It only took about twenty minutes before Monk, Kitty and I stepped aboard, along with one of the women. We only had to cross straight to Mason's stairs below Pye Gardens, where the pike pools bred the fish to feed the wealthy and deserving. Our oarsman battled against the tide as it tried to take us downriver; you could see in his grimacing features the effort needed to cross the flow, aiming upriver until we had reached more than halfway, then easing his strokes so that the tide took us casually to our destination. Impressed by his expertise and consideration in tempering his language in the presence of two women, I gave him an extra coin for his trouble.

It took another thirty minutes before everyone came across and we gathered in the street by the gardens. The workers there seemed confused by the sudden appearance of a group of people, if not wary that we planned some mischief. I looked through the railings towards the gardens and I could see a shimmering in the ponds as the fish swam just beneath the surface, occasionally seeing sleek dark darts of muscle and sinew as one broke the surface. A worker tentatively approached us, one of a group of burly men who watched us land at the stairs and now watched us gather together.

'You folk lost?' enquired the man from a distance, the railings between him and us. 'Only Cupers Pleasure Gardens is down that way a bit,' he added, pointing west and upriver. 'Some o' them oarsmen can't be bothered to row down there and tell folk this is the best place to be set down.'

I laughed. 'No, sir, we are not lost, neither are we here to filch your stock of fish. We are just after some entertainment and thought to come here rather than suffer the crush further up.'

'Aye, it gets bad up there,' he agreed. 'P'raps you'd best be on yer way, sir.'

'We will, thank you,' I said, beckoning my group forward.

We turned up Moss Alley, a narrow strip of cobbles covered over by muck and mess, stinking of urine and decay. On Bankside, the soft marshy ground made the buildings subside and tilt, the wooden structures, mainly sheds and storehouses, poised delicately between collapse and survival. Rats proliferated, scampering without a care along the riverbank and onto the wharf, feeding off the detritus strewn around. The alley stank so much that the odour stung the eyes, the concentration of human waste akin to a solid miasma, not helped by the dense smoke from burning fires in hearths and on wasteland.

I felt a little sympathy for the three women as we walked, especially when we left the sheds and storehouses behind and entered the slum housing of the poor. Children played in the squalid surroundings and the local people eyed us with deep suspicion. I noticed the footwear the women wore struggled against the conditions, slipping and sliding, they having to hold each other for support as they tried to find clear footing, the hems of their skirts dragging in the mire and coating them with all manner of unsavoury muck. Gallantly, some of the men offered their assistance, giving their arms and once carrying a lady over a particularly noxious stretch of path.

Eventually, we exited the dire slum and stood on Maid Lane, just along from the skin market. The daylight began to diminish and workers from the various industries began to walk to their homes or to the taverns and alehouses that littered the area.

We had decided on a simple plan. Two men were to go to the rear and guard against anyone trying to escape that way. Two more would guard the front door as soon as we gained entry. Once inside, the hospital would be methodically searched, arresting all adults. The three women and Kitty's main priority would be the children; they would secure them all and make it safe for them.

We had no knowledge of who we would find in the hospital; I just hoped one of the men would be Tewksley, who had some very serious questions to answer.

Monk and I exchanged glances and he gave a little nod, we then set off down the street towards the hospital, so that everyone could walk past and view the property before embarking on the raid later. We would then split up as we had to time the Joyners Street raid to run alongside ours. Whilst waiting, we would watch to see who would come out and who would go in, the intention to apprehend anyone leaving and take them to the Borough Compter for questioning.

I had a feeling the two hours before we could finally act would drag slowly by.

CHAPTER 22

As the gloom of dusk descended into darkness, lights appeared in the windows of a few of the buildings, including two from the upper windows of the hospital, like cats' eyes staring out, a faint flickering as the candles caught puffs of air. A man walked along the street lighting a few of the lamps, the lamps being a legacy of the bear and bull-baiting that once drew the city dwellers across the river for entertainment. People roamed; their toils of the day now finished and the taverns, alehouses and gin-shops all competed for business. A few hopeful jades came out onto the street touting to draw men into their bawdy houses, others would be down at the market looking for custom; the houses here of dubious quality, the girls ostensibly cheap, the sting coming latterly with the high price of the mercury cure.

I stood with Kitty just down and across the street from the hospital, adjacent to a gateway to a coal merchant. We elicited no real interest as people passed by, just curious glances as if we were conducting a transaction. The others lost themselves in the dark shadows but I knew they stood there, waiting and ready.

We had stood for several minutes when the door to the home opened and a male figure emerged. I nudged Kitty, who was looking down the street and then we both saw the figure lit briefly from behind by the light inside before the door closed. The man walked away heading for Deadman's Place. Allowing the man to get ahead of us we began to follow, crossing the street and walking arm in arm at a leisurely pace. I could see two figures detach themselves from an entranceway up ahead, proceeding slowly to allow the man to catch and pass them. Across the road, two more figures began to cross over, angled to intercept the man. I felt a grim smile twitch my mouth as we closed in like predators to the prey.

'A moment of your time, sir,' I called, as we came up behind him.

He half-turned his head and I could see a pinched-faced man of slim build and small stature. He wore a full dark wig topped with a tricorne hat. He briefly looked at me and I saw a guarded look, edging on concern as he turned his head back and increased his pace, walking straight into Monk and a constable who stopped him dead in his tracks.

'What the...?' said the man as Monk took hold of his arm. 'Unhand me, sir,' he continued, trying to shake off the grip. 'I have neither money nor valuables,' he added, now in a panic.

I saw Monk grin. 'I am not after your valuables, sir, just your cooperation, and that we *will* have as I am neither a ding-boy nor a filching-cove. What I do have is the authority of a government man and the gentleman with me is a City Constable.'

The man relaxed a little as he swept his gaze between Monk and the constable. 'I have done no wrong,' he protested. 'I am about my lawful business.'

'That is to be determined, sir,' I said, standing directly

behind him and speaking close to his ear.

The close proximity of my voice startled him and I could see his shoulders stiffen and his head jerk and Monk did not even try to hide his amusement.

'Your name please, sir,' I continued, 'and the reason for your presence in that hospital for children.'

'My...my...my name?' he stammered, wary again.

'Oh yes, your name,' I replied, tapping him on his shoulder with my cosh. 'One way or another we will have it.'

His head jerked again and Monk's grin widened. 'You should answer my friend, sir. He is not very patient if he has to wait too long for a reply.'

I jabbed the cosh into his back for emphasis.

'Th... Th... Thaddeus,' stammered the man. 'Thaddeus Thornton.'

'Well then, Thaddeus,' I said, again jabbing him in the back. 'What were you doing in that hospital?'

'I... I am a tutor,' he answered.

'A tutor? Are you indeed,' said Monk, his humour having now departed. 'And what were you teaching and to whom?'

'Beg your pardon, sir?' said Thornton.

'I mean,' replied Monk. 'Whom did you teach, boys or girls?'

'B... Boys, sir.'

'And what were you teaching these boys, eh, Thaddeus?'

'Their letters. I teach them their letters.'

'So, if I went in there now and asked the boys what Thaddeus Thornton had taught them today, they would say reading and writing — or would they say something else?'

The man Thornton became decidedly more nervous as his

head swung from face to face, his tongue licking his lips and I noticed he began to tremble.

'Buggery and rape are hanging offences, Thaddeus,' said Monk, leaning towards him. 'You may wish to reflect on that.'

Thornton did not deny the accusations.

'You desire me to help his memory, sir?' asked the constable, cracking his knuckles. 'Only just give me the word.'

'I do not think that will be necessary, for the moment at least,' I replied, holding up a warning hand. 'Roger Tewksley, Mr Thornton. Is he inside the hospital just now?'

Thornton hesitated and then nodded in confirmation.

'Anyone else?'

Thornton nodded again. 'Pannod is there too.'

'Lord Pannod?'

Another dejected nod.

'What are they doing there?' I asked, hoping for more confirmation.

'I don't know,'

'You don't?' I said, surprised.

Thornton shook his head. 'I haven't seen them these last few hours.'

'But they are there?'

'Yes.'

'And you do know what they are about, do you not, at other times if not this?' I said, as I realised that Thornton had answered literally, he could not possibly know what Tewksley and Pannod were actually doing at that moment.

'They are teaching those girls to be whores, aren't they?' said Kitty, speaking for the first time.

Thornton turned his head and saw Kitty; he had not realised a woman stood listening to him. 'I... I…'

'Against their will,' continued Kitty. 'Forced to pleasure those men.'

Thornton hung his head and then nodded slightly in agreement as he realised he had either said too much already or alluded to things he should not have.

The two men who had angled their walk across the street to intercept Thornton, stood a little behind me, listening and I beckoned them to come forward. 'Join the constable if you will and conduct Mr Thornton to the safe place. Try not to damage him too much.'

Thornton craned his neck to look at me and I saw his eyes widen in alarm. 'Where are you taking me?'

'Somewhere safe,' answered Monk. 'You may thank us later,' he added, grinning.

Monk handed the arm of Thornton to a militiaman and stood aside. I had not noticed the small tide of people who continually walked past us, one or two of the curious had even stopped a short distance away to watch, no doubt hearing some of what we said too. My suspicion was soon confirmed that they heard as one spat at Thornton as he passed.

Kitty put her arm through mine and then put her head against my shoulder. 'At least we have the confirmation we needed now. That, Richard, is an odious man,' she said, pointing at Thornton.

'Who will likely escape from the serious crime of rape and buggery as the children's evidence may not be deemed reliable, unless, of course, someone decides to turn Kings

Evidence. The most we can hope for is an assault charge with intention to commit.'

'What about the other children's evidence, when you put them all together and they say the same thing, would that not suffice?'

'It can be argued that the children colluded together, it could be children's games. The young cannot answer back, can they?'

The dark of night swallowed up Thornton and his escort, so we turned around and walked back to our place of observation. At least I now knew Tewksley was in residence and I dreaded to think what he and Lord Pannod, our member of the House of Commons, might be doing. Whether any mud would stick to our esteemed member of parliament was another matter.

I checked my watch and found we had less than an hour to wait until our agreed-upon time. I wondered how Ned, Blake and De Veil occupied their time and whether they too had apprehended someone of interest. I pondered too on this trip that Jarmin had insisted I undertake, to this Hawkhurst Gang that seemed to hold the south of England in its thrall — would I discover the murderer there? I harboured a wish that I had already found him, only a few yards away from where I now stood.

The time seemed to drag the closer we got to the appointed hour. Kitty became restless, constantly asking me to look at my watch, hoping that the seconds and the minutes had somehow increased pace as if the world had suddenly become faster. Despite sharing her eagerness to get going, I knew the importance of holding to the agreed time, lest word get back to Joyners Street.

Up until now I had remained calm and composed, even the taking of Thornton had not excited me, yet now, as I checked my watch yet again, I found the beat of my heart increase and felt an energy begin to build. Philip Monk had relinquished his place of observation and came towards us with the constable.

Monk grinned as he came close. 'Thornton has made acquaintance with his new abode and he is not best pleased with the facilities.'

'Is he not?' I replied, feeling a smile come to my face. 'That is most unfortunate. Poor fellow, we must sympathise with his predicament,' I added, keeping as straight a face as I could.

'It must be time now,' said Kitty, a hint of desperation in her voice.

I looked again at my watch and this time I nodded; it lacked just a minute to the hour. 'It is, Kitty. Gather the women and then follow us in.'

Monk turned and then stood in the centre of the street and beckoned with his arm. Straight away shadows moved as men and women came from their various positions, all heading in a single direction.

I rapped on the door hoping that those inside would be oblivious to our presence and we waited a while, impatient, anxious until I heard the noise of a bolt being drawn and then a gap appeared as the door opened. I did not wait for it to be opened fully.

The person behind the door yelped as I forced it open, my shoulder connecting with all my weight behind it. I heard a thump and then a groan and as I came through, I saw a man of middle years moaning as he lay on the floor, blood spilling from his nose.

'Secure him,' I ordered, as the rest flooded into the dim light of the hall. Just two candles on the wall giving illumination.

The men deployed as Monk and I had decided earlier; two to guard the door, four to search the ground floor, Monk and I with two others to search the first floor whilst Kitty and the three women headed to the top. I hoped the two men I had sent to the back of the hospital had managed to scale the gate and now protected the back door.

I ran for the stairs, dark and polished by footsteps over the years, the walls panelled in similar style and I took the steps two at a time as I rushed up, Monk close on my heels. A lantern on the landing of the first floor gave off a little light, the corridor's dimness giving an ambience of uncertainty, perhaps because I understood that things happened down there that had no place in a decent society. I could discern a smell of dampness and human waste, the floorboards creaking as I stepped on the uneven surface. Monk touched my arm and pointed down the corridor where a halo of faint light surrounded a door. I turned my head and looked down the other corridor where I saw two other similar lights. Behind me came the two men who now stood with us, waiting.

'Go,' I said to Monk. 'That side is yours; this is mine.' I grabbed the first man and sent him with Monk.

Monk turned into the corridor with the single light and drew a pistol from his jacket as he walked slowly down, followed by a watchman with his cudgel already in his hand. I thought it a wise precaution, so I reached into my jacket and drew mine, beckoning to the second man up to come with me.

I did not creep silently as behind us the noise of those going up to the next floor countered any argument for stealth. Below, on the ground floor, I could hear screams of protest, an angry shout, sounds of things being broken and tipped over. Ignoring all the noise, I entered the corridor, the militiaman following close behind me and I saw that he too carried a small pistol.

Several doors ran all along its length, three to our left, four to the right, light emitting from the second door on the right and the furthest on the left.

I pointed to the door on the right and nodded at the militiaman who grinned and then reached for the handle, turned it and pushed the door open. I heard a grunting noise accompanied by a pitiful whimpering and bile rose to my throat as the militiaman rushed in, brandishing his pistol and ordering a man to desist. I had no time to witness what was occurring, I just hurried to the last door on my left and without prevaricating, grabbed the handle.

Locked.

I turned the handle again, pushing and hoping but it still would not open. I felt my jaw clench in determination as I stepped back, raised my boot and kicked out, jabbing my foot as hard as I could just where the lock should be. The door creaked and the frame cracked as I pummelled it, eventually, with a splintering of the timber, a final kick caused the door to swing open, crashing against something just behind it. The lone candle guttered as a draught of air breezed towards it, very nearly snuffing it out.

I stepped in.

Just inside to my left stood a large desk, dark of wood, slightly red, a leather desk chair behind it, the candle pushed onto a pricket in the middle of the desk. Ahead a window gazed over the fields at the back of the hospital, adorned with drapery. To the right of the window, a table nestled against the wall, upon it plates of food; bread, cuts of ham, cheese, candied fruit, sugared confection together with bottles of liquid, probably gin, wine and brandy, as well as glasses and plates. Against the right-hand wall stood a bed, the bedclothes ruffled and unkempt, having been hastily evacuated. Next to the bed stood a young girl, swaying unsteadily, glassy-eyed and taken with drink; her straw-coloured hair, long and curly, like waves breaking upon her bare shoulders. She wore no clothing and her age could be no more than seven or eight. Behind her stood a man, hurriedly tying his breeches, his shirt loose adorning his torso, his shoes on the floor in front and he tried to slip his feet into them at the same time as tying his breeches.

'What the devil?' the man exclaimed.

The man looked to be of fifty or so years of age, running to fat, overly large lips, a bulbous nose, small dark eyes with thinning black hair turning grey. Slug-like, he oozed distaste. I could see a wig on a side-table close by him, looking much like a small cat waiting to feed. He saw the pistol in my hand and reached for the girl, pulling her towards him as if a human shield.

'Leave the girl alone,' I ordered. 'Release her.'

The man looked on the verge of panic. 'You are trespassing on my private property, sir. Leave here at once. There are no valuables here; this is just a poor hospital for children.'

'You have the right of it there,' I responded. 'It is indeed a *poor* hospital for children; you abuse them as you will, which is quite apparent from where I am standing.'

'I shall have the weight of the law upon you should you not leave immediately,' he answered, nervously.

Sounds funnelled back from the depths of the building, sounds of protest, angst and umbrage. I could hear slaps, groans and yells of outrage and disgust.

'You said it is your property, sir. Then you are Roger Tewksley, the owner?'

'What is it to you?'

I laughed; I could not help it. 'Listen, Tewksley, your sordid little habits have been found out. You are unmasked as a despoiler of the very young. You are now actually listening to the weight of the law.'

'Who are you, sir?'

'My name is Richard Hopgood.'

I saw him thinking, my name registering in his mind. 'You are not the law, Hopgood; you are just a petty little thief-taker of no consequence to anyone. Oh, yes, I know all about you; visiting my house and threatening my wife.'

'Threatening your wife? Hardly that,' I replied, feeling contempt for the man. I took a step forward, not yet raising my pistol. 'Release the girl, you have damaged her enough.'

'Let me go, Hopgood. You can have her. Allow me to walk out of here and she's yours. I've taught her well, she knows all the tricks, is very compliant; willing too.' He sounded desperate and his offer made me feel nauseous.

'You are disgusting, Tewksley.' I replied, keeping my temper in check. I just wanted to raise my pistol and put a hole in his head. 'Just let the girl go.'

'Richard?' I heard Kitty call out as she hurried down the corridor outside.

'In here,' I called, over my shoulder.

I never took my eye off Tewksley as Kitty entered, her steps, quick at first, slowed suddenly to a stop. 'Who's the slubber-degullion?' she asked, in a tight voice.

'May I introduce Roger Tewksley, Kitty; as vile a specimen of humankind as you would wish to meet.'

Kitty took a sharp intake of breath. 'And he doesn't have the nutmegs to face you on his own.'

'So it would seem,' I replied. I noticed Tewksley put an arm behind him, his hand feeling the panelled wall. He moved a little to his right, the girl still in front of him and felt the wall some more. 'Tell me about Van Hoebeek, Tewksley, why did you—'

As I spoke, I saw an expression of triumph pass across his face.

'Richard,' exclaimed Kitty, suddenly.

The young girl came stumbling towards me as Tewksley pushed her hard in my direction, the outline of a door appearing in the wall. I had no option, I had to put my hand out to stop the girl from crashing into me and momentarily I took my eye off him, just as he stepped back and went through. I raised my eyes again and saw a sneer on his face, just as the door closed with a snap.

I raised my pistol, aimed at where the door had appeared and pulled the trigger, hoping that the ball would have power enough to penetrate. The ear-deafening report reverberated within the confines of the room, the noise setting the girl to scream in panic, even through her inebriated state. I raised the pistol again for the second chamber and then fired again, the advantage of my self-loading weapon, this time to the left of where I shot before.

Kitty rushed to the girl as I stepped around her to go to the wall, to seek the mechanism that opened the door. It took me a few seconds prodding where I saw Tewksley probing until I found the panel that released the catch and the door opened. I took a moment to look at Kitty, who looked up and waved a hand for me to go and so I entered into the cavity beyond.

I stood in a narrow passage, a small window to my right and the light from the candle from the room gave just enough illumination for me to discern that a set of stairs led down a few feet in front of me. I hurriedly descended the stairs, the little light diminishing with every step until it was almost too dark to see. I took a moment for my eyes to adjust and could just about see a short continuation of a passage, ending at a wall. I looked to my left and there, just about waist height, I saw a handle. I turned the handle, pushed and the door opened into the scullery at the back of the building, presumably the one Belle had worked in. I could see the door to the backyard and across the scullery, I saw an opening to another room where lights burned. I quickly stepped across and into the kitchen. Two lanterns gave off the light, perched on a table together with some half-eaten plates of food, jugs and drinking vessels; beyond the table, the hearth gave off a little warmth and light, a large pot hanging from a hook, its contents giving off a little steam. On my left, through an open door, I could hear raised voices, some in anger, some in confusion.

'Has a man just come through from the kitchen?' I yelled, hastening to the door.

A passage led away and a few seconds later a constable appeared at the end, recognised me and replied. 'No, sir, no one.'

'A man just ran down the side-stairs into the scullery; he's disappeared. Come with me,' I added, waving a hand.

'We have taken three women and a man from here in the kitchen, sir,' said the constable. 'They are all currently being apprised of their situation,' he added, as he joined me in the kitchen.

'That is good. Let us hope our two men outside are being vigilant. I want that man especially.'

'Outside, sir?'

'Yes, the two I told to stop anyone leaving by the back door.'

'Ah, er... There might be a problem there, sir.'

'What do you mean?' I asked, feeling a sense of foreboding.

'Er...We let them in, sir. Thought we might need some help here with these people,' he replied, his voice limping to its conclusion.

I closed my eyes and raised my head, fighting not to let my anger come out and explode in this man's face. 'You did what?' I asked, hoping that I had misheard.

'We let them in, sir. Sorry.'

The constable looked at me warily with some trepidation, worried as to what I might do. To avoid any immediate repercussions he called out two names, ordering them to the kitchen and then rushed past me, heading for the scullery and the door to the yard. I turned and followed him as two more men came down the passage, the two who should have been outside and waiting for Tewksley to fall into their arms.

'Blood, sir,' said the constable, pointing to the door handle. 'That weren't there a few moments ago.'

I looked; indeed blood coated the handle and I could see drips of blood on the floor leading to the door to the side stairs. 'He's wounded. One of my shots must have hit him. Quick, he might still be around outside.'

The constable opened the door tentatively, avoiding getting the blood on his hand and we all went through into the dark yard outside.

'Who opened the gate?' I asked, gritting my teeth, seeing a black open maw in front of me.

'I did, sir,' replied a watchman. 'I climbed over and then took the bar out so that Barney, here could get in, too old to climb, he is.'

'You did not think to shut and bar it after?'

'Er... Sorry, sir.'

I took a deep breath, my temper even closer to tipping point now. 'Find some lanterns, one with me and we search the yard. You two, into the fields and search there, turn everything and look under everything; understand?'

Giving a brief description of Tewksley and informing them that he had a gunshot wound, I sent them into the fields as soon as the lanterns appeared. A watchman and I quickly searched the yard, finding nothing.

I stood there, seething with frustration.

CHAPTER 23

I returned to Tewksley's room to find Kitty sitting in a chair, hands clasped tightly as if containing her anger.

'They did what?' she exclaimed, shaking her head and leaning forward. 'I don't believe it!'

'They did and it's true,' I replied, exasperated. 'I nearly lost my temper with them but I still needed their help. They had cleared the kitchen and scullery and as the only way to the kitchen is through the hall, they thought it safe enough to let in the men from outside. They say they checked the door that Tewksely used to get into the scullery, finding it locked, so assumed it to be a storeroom.'

Kitty sighed and slumped back in the chair. 'The one man we really wanted and he's got away.'

I nodded. 'So it would seem; he is wounded so with luck, he may not get too far. They are still searching the fields.'

'You're certain you hit him?'

'Yes.'

I hurried to check the side-stairs that led down to the kitchen, intended, I surmised, for direct access in the olden days when the hospital was a manufactory. I saw blood on the floor and in places all the way down the stairs. Now I knew for certain that I had shot him.'

'Did your firing the pistol not alert them?' she asked.

'No, they thought it not their business as it came from upstairs,' I replied. I took another breath. 'How is the girl?' I asked, looking at the array of drinks and wondering whether to partake myself.

'Recovering upstairs with the women from Vintners Hall. She is not harmed any further and I suppose it's a blessing that she had taken all that drink. She is quite senseless now.'

I gave a grim smile. 'I should check with the watchman and Monk, to find out what they have discovered.'

'The watchman from that room down there?' she asked, pointing.

'Yes.'

A grimace came to her face. 'Philip found Lord Pannod with an undressed girl, Pannod sitting wearing a robe; they had not yet begun anything. The watchman found a judge, with a boy, in the act as it were.'

'A judge? Who?'

'Ravely, I believe. The watchman has seen him at the Old Bailey.'

'Ravely? Good God, he's a hanging judge. Likes nothing more than sending everyone he can to Tyburn.'

Kitty nodded. 'Yes, that one. What are the chances of him visiting Tyburn?'

I pulled a face. 'In truth, little. He will have friends who will save him, or Newcastle might use him; we know that could well be the outcome with influential people.'

'A pity,' she replied sadly. 'The law is hardly equal.'

'You know that as well as I; one law, two ways of justice. How are the children?'

'They are upstairs; the boy found with Ravely is still

suffering.'

'It is always the way; the victim suffers, rarely the perpetrators.'

Monk took the men and women down to the Compter, to see them suitably accommodated, together with most of those who came on the raid as guards. That left just Kitty and I, along with the two men still in the fields and the women upstairs looking after the children. The women told me that most of the children appeared grateful for our intervention, even if a little confused, strangely one or two resented our endeavours on their behalf. From what I gathered, those few had been promised a life of enrichment, comfort and prosperity; I knew how hollow those promises were and like many before them, they would have fallen into a life of depravity, selling their bodies for a few scant shillings leading to an early death. They did not know the reality of their situation at such a young age.

Not to waste time waiting, Kitty and I embarked on the search of the building, looking for anything that may aid us in a prosecution. We began at the top with the children's rooms, and for want of a better word, the nurses' rooms. At the top of the stairs to both left and right a door led into narrow corridors, each side of the building mirrored the other. To the left and right on the corridors there were rooms; the rooms to the back of the building appeared to be sleeping rooms, furnished comfortably with a bed, upholstered chairs, a table and a hearth against the large chimney allowing for heat and to boil pots and kettles. Next to that, we found a room with small cots and a single bucket for nighttime convenience, presumably a room for new arrivals.

The large room to the front had a desk and basic chairs, one leather-covered chair positioned behind the desk, a large chest lined one wall and a cupboard and a table on the other. I looked inside the chest and cupboard, finding all manner of unpleasant things; birches and crops for chastisement, manacles and ropes for restraint, ragged clothes of various sizes and a small number of good quality clothes, these presumably for use when a child needed to be presented. Further down the corridors, we entered the girls' main room, front to back across the building, furnished only with rough cots, at least two to a bed, with thin straw mattresses and thin threadbare blankets. Both boys and girls were gathered in this one room as the boys' room, now empty, was on the other side of the building. To avoid rats and other vermin from interfering with the children, at least the beds had been raised off the floor. There was no hearth for warmth and I suspected that the windows would freeze in the winter.

The children looked warily at me as I looked around, their eyes following my every movement; the women tried to reassure them that I offered no threat, but I could see that few believed.

We checked the boys' room and then moved down to the second floor and counted ten rooms, each furnished as a bedroom with good quality beds, some being tester beds with drapes that hid the occupiers from view. Turkey rugs upon the floors with comfortable chairs and couches; each room had tables and chairs for dining, though only the rooms adjoining the chimneys had hearths. We found books and bibles in each room along with pamphlets and tracts from the more insalubrious publishers, describing and illustrating various forms of sordid encounters. The room where Monk found Lord Pannod gave up a small leather-bound notebook. I could only read it briefly as it made me feel nauseous, the contents describing his exploits, with the names of the girls he abused.

Tewksley's room proved more productive. The desk drawers had intricately designed locks and it took some effort and time to release them, very nearly foiling me. Inside I found ledgers and account books, giving details of the incomings and outgoings of all items needed to run the hospital; comestibles and such like. One book really garnered my interest as it could prove so damning to the names inside that my hands trembled as I turned the pages. Kitty looked over my shoulder and read with me and I heard her gasp, feeling her fingers dig into my arm.

Each page had a name, an amount of money and then incremental payments. A tally of the amount each man had paid into the running of the hospital and presumably for services received. There were ten names: Lord Pannod, Ravely, Frammingham and others were listed, but strangely, not Tewksley.

I put the book on top of the desk and then started to work on the lock for the other drawer. Soon I heard the telltale click of success and drew it open. Another leather-bound book sat within and I admit I gave a shiver as I opened it and read the contents.

The book contained a list of names and ages of children alongside amounts of money and the name of the person who had paid. The ages ranged from five years old to nine and the monetary value from one hundred and forty guineas to three hundred and sixty.

It was a list of children sold.

Most of the children's names on the list were female, counting only three boys. I dare not dwell on the reason why they were bought, because I had to look at things objectively, not emotionally; unfortunately, Kitty could not do that. I looked at her and I could see tears in her eyes, the little beads running down her cheeks, until she wiped them away with the back of her hand.

'This is awful,' she announced simply, with no need to embellish.

I rummaged in the drawer again and at the back I found another book, as I took it out I wondered about the horrors contained in the tome.

Another list of children's names and against these names, the word "absconded" had been written and the dates they had purportedly gone.

I counted forty-three names over the three years the hospital had been in existence.

'This is strange,' I said, pondering the list. 'Young Toby said that it was near to impossible to escape and it had only been with a great deal of luck that he managed to do so, and look, his name is not here,' I added, as I flipped the pages.

Kitty wiped away more tears from her face and tried to compose herself. 'I don't understand, what do you think it means?'

'I think,' I replied, guardedly. 'That these are the names of children who were disposed of. Do you not remember Toby talking about children disappearing?'

Kitty nodded reluctantly. 'Yes, I do.'

'I think this is the record of them. In truth, I don't think they absconded. This is just something that could be shown in defence should someone trace a child back to here; it would not be their fault if a child ran away and was subsequently found floating in the Thames.'

'Oh, Richard, the poor little souls.'

I closed the book not wishing at that moment to read further. I placed all the books and loose sheets of paper on top of the desk and stood up, gathering Kitty into my arms and pulling her close. We stood that way for a long while, both of us lost in our own thoughts. Eventually, we broke apart and I took a last look at the drawers in the desk to make sure I had missed nothing.

'We still have downstairs to search,' I said, without enthusiasm.

'Then we should continue,' replied Kitty, stiffening her backbone.

The kitchen and scullery revealed nothing of interest and neither did the room to the left of the front door. It seemed to be a kind of drawing room, furnished with good quality chairs and tables, rugs for the floor and paintings of views of the river and the countryside. Bureaus and cabinets lining the walls and cupboards contained alcoholic drinks. The backroom where Kitty had originally been taken when she had come searching for her brother was a type of schoolroom filled with functional roughly made benches and tables. At the head of the room, a large desk dominated and next to that, a big slate board used for writing instructions to the class. On the desk, I saw small hand-sized boards for the children to make their letters using small chunks of chalk or soft stone. We gave the room a search, finding nothing here too; thankfully, I felt that we had found enough to damn the adults upstairs and so had to be content with that.

We heard a banging on the front door so we walked back down the corridor to the front lobby where we found that Ned had arrived and behind him, four carts had pulled up packed full of children with the other women from Vintners Hall.

Ned put a grin on his face as he saw me; from his hollow look in his eyes, I could tell that he forced it against his will. 'The kinchins are here, sir, all twenty-three of them. They're confused and scared, though we have tried to tell them that they have nothing to be frightened of.'

I looked past Ned to the carts and saw most of the eyes turned to me. Without doubt they had suffered and still suffered, having been brought back to the place where their ordeals had begun. Looking at the children dismayed me. Dressed in the finest of apparel, they looked like adults in miniature form; silk dresses, hair styled, faces painted and the boys with jackets, breeches and silk stockings. I found it disconcerting to say the least. The women ushered the children off the carts and showed them to the front door.

'Monk is on his way,' said Ned, looking up the street. 'Passed him on my way here.'

A little crowd had gathered outside who watched on with interest at the events occurring; people talked amongst themselves, pointed, gesticulated and no doubt speculated.

'I'll take the poor little things upstairs, Richard,' said Kitty, moving in front of me and smiling broadly at the children, arms open in a welcome. She bent down and took the hands of the first two children, two girls, then turned and guided them inside. The other children followed, taking tentative steps through the door and into the hall.

I had taken a step outside and stood with Ned as the carts emptied, watching the children as they filed in.

'What happened there, Ned?' I asked, as two women guided the last of the children in.

He took a long drawn-out breath. 'We hoped to nab a cully as he came out so that we could squeeze his nutmegs for information, saw two go in but none came out, unfortunately. Then it were the time to go in. So we did. The four bullyboys at the doors put up a bit of a fight, all mean bastards; once they were dealt with it were easy as you like. Everything went pretty smoothly after that. The Mother Abbess and her acolytes put up little resistance, just stood there yelling, they did. Caught ten culls inside, most with their breeches down and being attended to by the children. De Veil found one with a boy and you can guess how he viewed that. All in all, it were a right success but for some reason I can find no joy in it.'

'I can tell that from your brevity, Ned. I'm normally falling to sleep before you have finished your narrative.'

'Aye, well, not this time. Later, when I feel more meself. Left De Veil and Blake going through the place and as I left I heard a shout of triumph, so one of them found something. What about you here, sir?'

'Much the same, Ned. Caught a tutor leaving the place to start with and he told us a little before we went in. We found three men in a compromising situation, one of them being

Tewksley, whom I found. The bad news is that he managed to escape through a secret door. I am certain I shot him as we found blood where he ran down some stairs, fresh blood. The two men who should have been covering the back came into the building, allowing him to get out. They are still in the fields searching. Kitty and I found some incriminating ledgers and such with the names of certain people, thankfully. Oh yes, one of the men was Judge Ravely and the other, Lord Pannod. Both are now enjoying the facilities of the Compter, you'll be glad to hear.'

'Ravely? That old bastard?'

'The watchman caught him with a boy, in the act.'

'Well, well,' he replied, wiping his head with both hands. 'About time something was dished out to *him* for a change.'

Normally after a success I would feel a great sense of satisfaction at what had been achieved. In these circumstances, I just felt disgust at what I had witnessed. Kitty and Ned took little joy from this night's work as well, being subdued, neither of us talking much. Unlike Philip Monk who was full of energy, excitement and anticipation at the apprehending of those men and the bawds, particularly anticipating the information he may discover. I put it down to the exuberance of youth.

Monk took possession of the ledgers and documents and read them briefly with a gleeful look before wrapping them in a cloth and placing them beneath his arm. The time had now come for us to adjourn to the Compter off Tooley Street for a few hours of asking some very pertinent questions. The two men searching for Tewksley returned to inform us that they had been unsuccessful and the man had disappeared into Southwark or beyond. Much as I wished to berate them for their lapse it would not make any difference now, my quarry had gone. I just waved a dismissive hand and they quietly made themselves scarce.

Monk mentioned politely on our walk to the prison that both Ned and Kitty's presence would not be required, so with bad grace on Ned's behalf and a degree of acceptance on Kitty's, the two of them parted company with us at the bridge and headed home. I had given them instructions for how to proceed during my trip to the south coast; their aim, to discover the whereabouts of Tewksley. I suggested visiting hospitals, physicians, apothecaries, barber-surgeons and anyone else they could think of. Kitty had now seen Tewksley so she could identify him and I stressed that Ned had to accompany her at all times.

The Borough Compter in Mill Lane, off Tooley Street mainly housed debtors and those awaiting trial or those newly captured in Southwark to await questioning. The unedifying prison had a squalid reputation and I could not think of a better place to put those we had taken up. The prison, not yet twenty-five years old, had quickly degenerated, probably due to indifference and complacency.

I allowed myself a grim smile at the thought.

CHAPTER 24

The interviews carried on all through the night. I sat in to observe only, not being allowed to participate and so sat at the back of the room, watching and listening. It soon became apparent that those men who had interacted with the young girls in Joyners Street would mostly walk away. They may well spend a few more days in the Compter until the children could be spoken to, which might result in charges, if not, they would have time to reflect and change their ways — they may even suffer the ignominy of having their exploits mentioned in one or two of the newssheets, papers or pamphlets. Lord Pannod spent little time in the Compter, being immediately taken from the prison to Westminster, where no doubt he would dwell on his conduct in the presence of The Duke of Newcastle, or perhaps, Walpole himself, who would use the situation for the benefit of the government.

Judge Ravely's explanation as to his conduct will live with me for the rest of my days.

George Blake conducted the interview.

'You were observed, sir,' said Blake, 'indulging in sodomitical practises with a boy of ten years of age—'

'Not so, sir,' countered the judge, indignantly. 'That is a lie. That man misconstrued the whole situation.'

'Then how would you explain your conduct?' asked Blake,

and I saw his eyes twitch and a slight smile form on his lips as he gave a rub to his shoulder.

'I was instructing the boy in the ways of his manners, how to comport oneself when serving in a household. The boy spilt a jug of water over both my person and himself, such that he had to remove his apparel; my breeches were also affected, so I had to lower them to avoid the dampness. I decided he needed to be punished for his impudence and so I ordered him to bend over the couch so that I could chastise him appropriately.'

'Is that what it is called nowadays?' returned Blake, tongue in cheek.

The judge hesitated for a second or so and then fixed a contemptuous look upon his face. 'The boy needed to be punished,' he said, ignoring Blake's question. 'So I bid him to bend over so that I could beat him on his bare buttocks to remind him to be more careful in his future conduct. When that watchman burst into my room, I was so startled by his intrusion that I stumbled forwards. To my great horror and disgust, I found that my nether regions made contact with the boy's buttocks. Of course, as soon as I recovered from my shock at the intrusion, I removed myself by stepping back. I was mortified, sir, mortified at what had very nearly transpired.'

I saw Blake's face mirroring my own; disbelief, incredulity, humour. A period of telling silence followed. 'Really, sir?' said Blake in the end, in a matter-of-fact sort of way. 'If that is the case, then the boy was most unfortunate to be situated that way.'

'Precisely,' replied the judge. 'A complete accident of

circumstances. So, if you would be kind enough to release me, now you understand what occurred, then I can attend to my business and I will not take this wrongful incarceration any further.'

Blake smiled. 'I think I *do* understand what occurred, sir. Perhaps when the boy is able to sit down again we will have another discussion, until then, you can enjoy the facilities here. We shall remove you from your single cell to a general cell where you can have conversation with like-minded gentlemen, as I don't want you to feel lonely.'

'What?' exclaimed the judge, aghast.

Blake stared at Ravely. 'Don't worry, sir, no one will hear the screams.' He twisted his head around. 'Take him away,' he said to the turnkey.

'Does he actually think we believe him?' I asked, once the protesting judge had been escorted out.

'Who knows with that sort,' replied Blake, sighing heavily. 'They're arrogant enough at the best of times. A day or so in with the felons may make him see otherwise and loosen his tongue. We will wait for the children's testimony and hope we can use that.'

'Who's next then?'

'Thaddeus Thornton; do you want to sit in again?'

I shook my head. 'I have to get to the George. A pity, I would like to see him squirm.'

I found John Fulton waiting in the prison lobby together with a light-haired man named Henry Bram; short and slight of build, Bram looked as if he could have been blown over in a puff of wind. My impression changed when he grasped my hand in welcome, finding he had a grip of steel.

We left the Compter and walked down towards Borough market with dawn heralding the new day's arrival with tinges of flame patterning the sky on the horizon. Fulton wanted to know how things had gone and as we walked, I explained what had occurred and what I had heard.

We carried on down the Borough and arrived at The George, a large galleried inn, serving as a terminus and an embarking point for journeys south to Kent and the environs. We ate a hearty breakfast, with me recounting the interview with Judge Ravely, eliciting an uproarious guffaw of laughter from Fulton, very nearly making him choke on his food. Bram just smiled and shook his head slowly as if nothing would ever surprise him.

I kept looking at Bram trying to work out where he fitted into all this. Fulton's introduction had been brief and lacking in detail, just that Jarmin had decided that he should accompany us. I did not feel wholly comfortable with it and suspected that Fulton knew more than he had said. For the moment I would just have to accept things as they were, receiving no other additional knowledge apart from the fact that I had changed my name; I was now Richard Dunning; Fulton, John Jacobs and Bram, Henry Spinney. All to do with precautions, Bram told me.

Even at that time of the morning, the inn bustled with the comings and goings of the coaches. Soon it became our turn and we took our seats with three other passengers inside whilst four others went above to brave the elements for half the price, eschewing comfort for parsimony.

A florid-faced man in his fifties, rotund of body and

sweating profusely sat opposite me with his diminutive wife, a grey-haired woman appearing meek as a mouse, though I suspected a shrew hid behind the mask as her thin-lipped expression gave the lie to her demeanour. The man loudly announced their reason for travelling; to take the waters at Tunbridge Wells and to visit their son who had recently taken up the position of tutor to the children of a wealthy man of commerce. The other passenger, a sallow young man of few words, did volunteer the information that he was only going as far as Sevenoaks where he resided.

Crushed together like peas in a pod, I thanked providence that my seat abutted the side of the coach where I could at least rest my head, my hat acting as a pillow. Trying to sleep in a coach that hopped, bumped and lurched as the wheels hit potholes, ruts and rocks proved difficult but not impossible. My exhaustion eventually triumphed and I managed to slumber a little even with the jerking of the coach awakening me at regular intervals.

I must have slept more than I thought as suddenly we arrived in Sevenoaks. The driver changed the horses and we lost the sullen young man who left us without a word of farewell. I stayed in the coach and shut my eyes again, thankful that I could doze without being bounced around until being rudely awoken again as the journey continued.

Giving up trying to sleep, I instead stared out of the window, trying hard to ignore the man opposite who pontificated on politics and his adherence to religious doctrine. Bram for some reason took perverse delight in conversing with him, urging the man to make a complete fool of himself, totally unaware that Bram mischievously baited him. Thankfully, we arrived in Tunbridge Wells where the florid-faced man and his mouse of a wife departed the coach and where those of us left could partake of a meal and a drink in the busy inn. We again kept the conversation banal, just talking about everyday things and observing life in general.

A new passenger took the place of the couple and would be accompanying us all the way to Hastings, a pleasant fellow in his latter years embarking on a trip to visit his elderly sister, whom, he said, did not have long in this world.

We passed the night at Keppings Cross, a small village just a few miles from the Sussex border. We stayed in an old house called The Blue Boys, bedding down all together in a warm comfortable room adjacent to what I suppose could be called the taproom, the establishment resembling more of a farmhouse than an inn but it sufficed for our purpose.

After our meal, we three took our leave of the other passengers and took our ale outside, the air being temperate with a light breeze. We sat on a bench where we could view the turnpike.

'You two gentlemen seem to be a little more aware of what we are about than I,' I began as we sat down, illuminated by the lantern outside the house. 'Apart from telling me we are to Hastings to speak to the customs there, I know little else.'

'Unfortunately,' said Fulton. 'There has been little chance to expand, seeing as we have been in constant company since the George.'

Bram nodded agreeing. 'This is really just a simple matter of collecting information. We will take horses at Hastings and then move along the coast. There may be an opportunity for me to take to the sea as part of a patrol but I will only do that if I feel there is a need. Our main task is to discover the source of the contraband and the extent of the escalation.'

'So we are to ask questions?' I asked.

Bram shook his head. 'No, these smugglers are violent criminals. If they hear of someone asking about them then the likelihood is that they will not live long enough to use the answers. Ears and eyes open, Richard, that's what you should remember.'

Two men then came out of the inn and our conversation ceased as they sat down just a few feet away, we three reverting to talking banalities once more. I sighed and took a drink of my ale.

We awoke at dawn, roused from our slumbers by a boy and given a good solid breakfast before boarding the coach. The remainder of the journey should take several hours more, arriving late afternoon. I now felt sufficiently rested and could take more of an interest as we travelled along the road. We broke for lunch at The Seven Stars in Robertsbridge and Bram immediately put me on alert, explaining that the Hawkhurst Gang frequently used the inn. I could remember reading something about this village when I read the files and I found it a sobering realisation of just how far this gang extended its reach.

Bram bid both Fulton and I to remain in the inn, proclaiming quite loudly that he wished to stretch his legs for a few minutes and take a short walk to help his stomach settle from the excellent fare we had just consumed. I shot an enquiring look at Fulton who just very slowly and very slightly shook his head. Bram appeared to be up to something; I could not for the life of me begin to wonder what.

Bram sauntered back, a bland expression on his face, just before we left the inn to board the coach for the final stretch.

Our fellow passengers prevented any discourse regarding Bram's sojourn in the village so again we kept the conversation largely uninteresting, until a few miles down the road when one of the wheels seemed loose.

'Well?' asked Fulton as the three of us stood together, well away from anyone else.

'Difficult to tell,' replied Bram. 'I hoped to spot something tangible.'

'You were looking for smuggling activity?' I asked, perhaps a bit naively.

'Exactly that,' answered Bram, turning to me. 'The evidence I did see could have been either old, or recent; so not that successful.'

'What evidence?' asked Fulton.

'Horse trails, far too many for a village of that size, a fire with the burnt remains of wooden crates and oilskin covers. Time prevented me from looking into the barns and sheds as I had to get back.'

'Not damning evidence, hardly evidence at all,' said Fulton.

Bram gave a small grin. 'No, it's not. Still, my instinct tells me a large consignment came through there.'

'That could be true of most of this region,' said Fulton.

'Indeed,' replied Bram. 'More so now, it would seem and it's vexing His Grace most sorely.'

It then dawned on me; the Duke of Newcastle held great swathes of Sussex as part of his family's lands. There were Pellhams and Holleses dotted everywhere, so this large-scale smuggling must be affecting him on a personal level. I wondered now if the duke had a hand in how interested and helpful Jarmin should be. Everything has happened quickly. So, I thought, who is Henry Bram? I know Fulton from past dealings with him, the same with Blake and Monk but I had never encountered Bram before, nor heard of him. At first, I took him to be another of Jarmin's intelligencers, a man held in higher regard than the rest of us. Bram is in charge and in control of this foray to the south coast undoubtedly. I do not have any concerns as to his abilities, but I do wonder if there is more to Bram than what I actually see.

The driver quickly repaired the wheel and we regained the coach, setting off once more along the lane; you could hardly call it a road, being in such a poor condition despite the attempts to rectify its appalling surface. Rubble had been scattered on some of the stretches and then forced flat with a heavy device, preventing some of the deep rutting that occurred in very soft ground. Our speed of travel had slowed to a crawl and I did wonder whether it would be quicker to walk the final ten miles or so.

The shuddering and rattling continued to shake our bodies and bones as we grabbed, or hung on to, anything attached to the coach for support; admittedly, I cared nothing for those individuals up top travelling on the cheap.

We gritted our teeth and endured the discomfort, eventually arriving, mostly in one piece, into the small coastal town of Hastings, alighting at The Swan in Market Street, thankful that at long last the jolting and juddering had come to an end.

Fulton, Bram and I stood for a few moments stretching our backs and easing our sore and bruised backsides before Bram gave a gratuity and thanked our driver. We then headed inside the inn for a welcome pot of ale.

We secured a small private booth at the rear of the inn and gave our order to the serving boy, then settled back to slake our thirst.

Bram leant forward and beckoned that Fulton and I do the same. 'Remember,' he said quietly, our heads close together, 'to be on your guard. Most people hereabouts are in with the free-traders, whether willingly or not. I'm going to see a gentleman who will help us procure some mounts, just as soon as I finish this,' he said, indicating his pot.

'Who?' I asked, thinking I had been left out of the information circle.

'A Mr Collier, Richard. John Collier.'

'And who is John Collier?' I pressed. Bram sighed and I thought I saw a roll of the eyes, riling my temper a little. 'Look, Bram. You two may know what you are about and how you plan to do what needs to be done. I only knew yesterday that I would be coming on this journey as I have been otherwise engaged these last few days, dealing with a children's brothel and child molesters. Now my patience is wearing thin. My investigation, if you care to remember, showed there might be a situation down here, so do not, I repeat, do not treat me as an inconvenience.'

Bram raised his hand, a placating gesture. 'I apologise, Richard,' he said, seriously. 'I am being remiss. I assumed you had been adequately informed.'

I shook my head. 'I do not know anything other than what you have told me already, Jarmin just said that he would supply two men to look into things with me.'

'Ah,' he replied. 'Then I can understand your annoyance. John Collier is the Surveyor General of the Customs down here; he is also the mayor, incidentally. I have come with John here, because of a report received from one of our men abroad.'

'What kind of report?'

'Last evening something occurred that necessitated my inclusion on this trip. Jarmin spoke to His Grace and became aware of a report not intended for his department. They realised that it could have serious repercussions regarding this investigation; they decided that it might be prudent to allow me to accompany you two to the south coast.'

'What kind of report?' I repeated.

'A report saying that Spain intends to seriously undermine our economy to prevent our prosecution of the war out in the Caribbean; as a result, messages have been sent to intelligencers in France, Spain and Portugal in the hope that what we discover here will be consistent with what is discovered there.'

'I beg your pardon?'

'It is possible, Richard, that *you* may have discovered how they intend to do it.'

CHAPTER 25

I have always regarded John Fulton as a man of brawn, not afraid to use his fists, rather than a man of subtle intelligence; I really should have known better. Newcastle and Jarmin would not employ a simple ruffian just to knock a few heads together.

Bram had left us to visit this man Collier, leaving Fulton and I together. I lit my pipe, stimulating Fulton to beg a gage from the innkeeper, so soon the two of us sat back drinking and smoking, if not contentedly, then certainly in a relaxed state.

'Who is Bram?' I asked, leaning forward, my elbows on the table.

Fulton grinned. 'What Jarmin is to London, so Bram is to the continent,' he replied. 'Look, Richard,' he said, sitting back and shaking his shoulders before leaning forward again. 'I have not been able to explain much to you as we have always had Bram with us or I could not talk freely. There is a good reason why our friend has come along, I assure you. He would not have come if he thought it unnecessary; he has many important situations to deal with other than this.'

'Then why has he not explained himself?'

'Because he wanted to see how you react and act when you do not feel the need to impress. You defer to Jarmin, don't you?'

I nodded. 'Of course; he is why I am here.'

'The thing is, Bram doesn't know you; he only has Jarmin's word. He just wants to see whether you are a leader or one to be led, whether he can trust you or not to do the right thing at the right time. He told me not to tell you his status.'

'You have now,' I said, pointedly.

'Yes,' and he grinned. 'I didn't think it fair and you have already worked out that he leads our little group anyway.'

'No disrespect to you, John but I didn't think it was you and it certainly is not me.'

Fulton gave a wry smile. 'I've never worked with him before. To be honest, I have heard things about him which I cannot reveal, so be content that I do not intend to vex him. He speaks French and Spanish fluently and has a smattering of Portuguese, Greek and Dutch. He is supposedly ruthless if he or his compatriots are compromised. He will not baulk at violence or subterfuge and will protect his colleagues first and foremost.'

'In other words, I should trust him.'

'Implicitly, in my opinion.'

'Very well; I cannot argue with your recommendation. What do you know of his plans?'

Fulton shook his head. 'Nothing. If he has any he has certainly not revealed them to me.'

'Maybe this Collier man will help him formulate something.'

'We should find out soon enough. In the meantime, we may as well indulge in another ale.' He raised his hand to the boy to get attention and then pointed at our empty pots.

With two fresh ales in front of us, we settled back quite comfortably, observing the inn and its customers. The booth allowed us to converse in private and to see a good portion of the inside of the inn. I could see a fair number of men of varying trades, judging by what I could hear of the conversations; talk of politics, talk of commerce, ribald talk. I heard no mention of free-traders, though from what I had gathered from my reading in Jarmin's lair, smuggling happened to be a major trade in this small town.

A good part of an hour had passed before Bram sauntered back into the inn.

'We have mounts,' he announced, sitting down. 'Plus provisions and the goodwill of the surveyor general; mind, that might not be as much help as we would like.'

'Why's that?' asked Fulton, a little bemused.

Bram gave a mirthless grin. 'The officers in this area, or I should say, a large number of the officers in this area are likely to have been given inducements to not be at certain points at certain times, if you catch my meaning.' Fulton and I nodded sagely, we expected as much. 'However, that may not be to our disadvantage.'

'How so?' I asked.

'From what Collier told me there is now a deep fear of the smugglers. The gang's ruthlessness is beginning to erode what little support they previously had, regardless of how the people may profit. When people become scared they tend to seek help. I intend that we are seen as that help.'

'How will we do that?' asked Fulton.

'We will allow rumour to do it for us, John. When we

leave here we will go to the customs house down the road and ask what they know. I would suspect that we will hear very little of substance, apart from being drowned in near misses where they came so close to apprehending the felons. I think that within the hour the news of the presence of three men from London will have left this town and be well on its way down the coast.'

'Does that not just open us up as targets?' I asked, shifting on my seat.

'Possibly,' replied Bram. 'So we must be vigilant. In truth, I don't think our risk is that great. The smugglers would prefer we left ignorant rather than attempt to do us harm and draw the wrath down upon them, especially if someone external is pulling their strings.'

'Like De Griese?' I asked.

'Yes,' answered Bram. 'The gangs will be handsomely paid for their troubles and would not want to jeopardise their income by upsetting their paymasters.'

'And you hope that a rumour will be enough for people to seek us out with information?'

Bram nodded, very slowly, indicating that he did. 'Come, let us set things in motion,' he added, beckoning us to rise from the table and follow him outside.

'This place seems too small to warrant a customs house,' I ventured, as we stepped outside. 'There is no port here as far as I can tell.'

'No, there is not,' replied Bram. 'Just a designated landing place on the beach. The port is at Rye, which encompasses Hastings and comes under its jurisdiction. We came here because I wished to speak to Collier, but we can spread the rumour equally well from here, probably better in fact, as it will have been noted that we have spoken to the Surveyor General.'

A scant few seconds later we stood outside a three-storeyed building, its appearance dirty and somewhat dishevelled, as if a little embarrassed at its countenance. Bram rattled the door and then breezed in with Fulton following whilst I brought up the rear.

The room took up the whole width of the building; to our right, a waist-high counter with shelves behind containing ledgers and other documents; in front of us, a table with rude chairs, quills and ink with blank sheets of paper; a hearth, cold and unlit against the far wall. No one appeared home. Opposite the front door, a passageway led down inside the building and we followed Bram as he stomped down it to a door at the back. Once opened I could see into a small room with battered upholstered chairs, a fire in the hearth giving off a rosy glow and slumped in one of the chairs, his feet upon a small crate, a man snoring contentedly, a jug beside him with an empty cup.

'Good evening, sir,' yelled Bram, kicking the crate away so that the man's feet crashed to the floor. 'Do I see a man of the Customs or are you an interloper?'

'Wh... Wh...?' replied the man, trying and failing to show some dignity as sleepy-eyed he desperately tried to rouse himself from his slumber.

'Attend to your duties, sir,' continued Bram. 'If you lack the wit to notice three men come into the room then how can you have the wit to prevent those wishing to usurp the King's authority by avoiding their rightful dues of revenue.'

'Sir, I... I...' stammered the man, somehow shrugging off the veils of sleep and standing up. He eyed each of us in turn warily. 'I did not know that something was occurring.'

'And neither is it,' replied Bram. 'So far as I know anyway. The immediate problem, as far as I can see it, is that appropriate diligence is somewhat lacking.'

'My apologies, sir. I am yet to begin my patrol. I thought to take a few moments rest now so that I will be more alert later — sir, would you mind explaining who you are?'

'Who are we?' said Bram, placing a stern expression on his face. 'We are from London, sir. Just this short while ago arrived to look into the efficiency of this area, and I have to say, it has not begun well.'

'Not my fault, sir. I shouldn't even be here at this time. I thought to come in early and be ready for later. You'd best speak to Mr Collier, sir, the Surveyor General.'

'I already have,' said Bram, looking around the room. 'He too has received his instructions from His Grace, The Duke of Newcastle, to root out complacency and conspiracy. What do you say to that, sir?'

'I... I...'

'No matter,' said Bram, waving a dismissive hand. 'Bring us your reports, and I mean all of them for this latest year. We will wait in the room next door and be quick about it.'

'They are upstairs, sir. Perhaps you'd prefer to see them there?'

'Very well,' conceded Bram. 'Sort them out and then call us up when you have them ready for examination.'

Bram turned and headed out of the room and down the short passage to the entrance room, Fulton and I following.

A few seconds later I heard the quick tread of a man hurrying up the stairs.

'You were a bit harsh,' I said to Bram, quietly. 'And he will hide any reports he does not want us to see.'

Bram smiled knowingly. 'Of course he will hide things. I want him to feel he has the upper hand and I was harsh because that is how we men from London are perceived: officious, ignorant, superior, easily deceived. I just don't want to ruin his perception of us.'

'He didn't even ask to see our authority or even our names,' said Fulton, chuckling away to himself.

'No, he didn't,' replied Bram. 'Maybe I should remind him.'

We saw just two scant volumes and those hardly worth the effort, containing very little considering how rife free-trading was in this part of the country. Just a few lines scribbled of sightings of strange vessels, the occasional boat in distress, a ship passing on the horizon; even fewer entries of goods seized; just four, discovered on the beach, the owners conspicuous by their absence. All in all, it would seem that the south coast hardly had a problem, that the diligence of the authorities had and was proving its worth in preventing smuggling in the area.

Bram, Fulton and I read the reports straight-faced with the occasional nod and finger-pointing. Bram asked about patrols and the man showed us some barrels of brandy, discovered just a week earlier. The man, a Riding Officer, looked nervous throughout, even though we did not press him and pretended to take him at his word. When we eventually left, we praised him and his fellow officers and Bram apologised for the rude awakening when we first arrived.

Once back outside, we walked up Market Street, politely moving aside to allow other walkers room, above us the gulls cawed and screeched, diving and gliding, looking for scraps of food. All three of us kept our thoughts to ourselves as we walked with no mention of the customs house.

Bram led us up to the top of the street where we came across the Mansion House, the home of John Collier; Mayor, Solicitor, Town Clerk, Surveyor General of the Customs and Politician.

The house, an imposing building of three floors, stood in large gardens with a view of the town and the sea beyond. As we approached the columned front portico, the door opened immediately without even a tap to announce our presence, so I assumed our progress had been noted.

The servant ushered us into a lavishly furnished room at the front of the house containing a large desk, leather covered chairs, wall hangings and paintings plus myriad items of furniture and ornaments. A well-dressed bewigged man in his fifties sat at the desk and rose to his feet as we entered.

'Mr Jacobs and Mr Dunning, sir,' announced Bram, pointing to each of us.

'A pleasure, gentlemen,' replied Collier, giving a polite bow in our direction which we both returned. 'I hope, with all sincerity, that you are successful in your enterprise.'

'That is our aim, sir,' said Bram, moving towards him. 'You have our authorisation?'

'I do indeed, Mr Spinney; just this moment adorned it with my signature. Your mounts are saddled and await you in the stables, as requested by His Grace. Can I be of further service to you?'

'No, sir, you have been helpful enough.' He hesitated a moment. 'Actually, the one thing you could do is mention, on the quiet as it were to your associates, that we three are down from London to look into coastal activities.'

Collier grinned. 'I take your meaning, sir. It will be my pleasure.'

'Then we will trouble you no more,' said Bram. 'And I thank you for your assistance and be assured, I will inform His Grace.'

Collier bowed again and then summoned the servant to show us out and across to the stables where three mounts stood waiting impatiently, held by the stable hands, not looking pleased at their task.

'Mount up, gentlemen,' said Bram, taking hold of the first horse. 'We have maybe an hour or two of daylight left before we need to seek shelter.'

CHAPTER 26

As we set off, the already clouded sky became leaden with the promise of rain and I hoped it did not portend things to come. During the day, I had purposely not thought about Ned and Kitty, although I desperately wished to be with them searching for Tewksley. Being far away in Hastings and unable to influence or communicate with them left me feeling deeply frustrated. I just had to trust their abilities and judgement and hope that when I returned it would be to a successful outcome.

The three of us hunched our shoulders against the threat of the diving gulls as they harried our horses as if to drive us away. Instead of going back down Market Street, we took the other road, turning left towards the church, across the Bourne River to the evidently poorer side of the town where the fishermen, costermongers and labourers lived. Bram led us past the Church of All Saints and then out into the fields and hills, heading towards Fairlight and Pett.

Once we cleared the town, Bram furnished us with more of the information he had gleaned from Collier. 'Rumour has it that the Hawkhurst Gang is recruiting and has been these last few months. We are not talking people so much as boats, carts, horses and equipment. All along the coast there has been a veil of silence and beatings have become commonplace. It is reckoned that we will find it hard to find any inn, tavern, farm or village that has not got an incumbent from the gang, such is their influence.'

We traversed the undulating fields above the cliffs looking out to sea, through wooded areas then back to the open once again. Dark murky clouds scudded across the horizon and being high we could feel the gusting wind. Fishing boats rocked on the waves, far out they looked more like small toys battling against the odds. Without doubt the fishermen risked their lives daily to put food on their families' tables, a hardy breed and I could understand how easily they could take to the illegal trade to supplement, or to provide a main income, to keep them from penury. With the weather turning and the evening coming, the boats headed in, some already beached, some leaving it late, chancing the light.

'What's at this Fairlight?' asked Fulton, as we made steady progress across the cliffs.

'Not much, to be honest,' replied Bram. 'It's a small village just inland, heavily involved in free-trading. I want to get a feel, judge the mood, drop a few hints and we'll move on. We will branch left shortly and come up to the lane leading us directly to the village.'

'You seem to know the area well, Henry,' I said, by way of observation.

'I do, yes,' he replied. 'My father was a tenant on Romney Marsh. Let us say that I am well acquainted with how society works around here.'

'You kept that quiet,' remarked Fulton.

Bram sniffed. 'I'd help haul a cart in the middle of the night full of contraband in my youth and I had a hand with the Owlers taking wool to export illegally; that was rife all around this area, still is really.'

'Owlers?' I asked. 'Who are they?'

'Wool smugglers,' replied Bram. 'They called us that because we would signal with the hoot of an owl. Simple, really,' he said, grinning.

'You made a pretty penny, then,' I said, grinning along with him.

'Hardly,' he replied. 'I admit it did help to put a bit of food on the table. Everyone was into the trade and I came to the attention of Henry Pelham through it, His Grace's brother. He came visiting a manor one day from Laughton, went out riding and came across me and a few others at an old barn. We had just finished stacking the barn full of wool ready to be taken to the coast, with me still inside when he turned up. I hadn't heard the shout as he approached and no one thought to look for me until they were well away. When I came out I felt something strike me on the head and I knew no more until I woke up in a stable, tied hand and foot and with an excruciating headache lancing through my skull. Henry Pelham was a young man then, with a promising career ahead of him; for some reason he took pity on a young lad destined for the scaffold and offered me an education in return for my labour. It did not take much thought and I agreed, discovering a gift for languages and learning that I never knew I had until I began, impressing His Grace when he visited. He obviously saw something in me as I passed from one Pelham to another, rising to the position you see me in today. Now, why have I told you all that?'

Fulton and I looked at each other and we shrugged our

shoulders.

'Because despite my position now, I can empathise with the people here. From what I can gather they are being exploited, and I do not like my people being exploited. I want to know what is behind it all.'

He gave a little kick to his horse and it sprang into a quick trot, angling away from the sea and heading inland. Fulton and I copied his actions and then the three of us raised the pace once more and we hurried over to the hedges bordering a track. We followed the hedgerow until we came to a break and could then access the track of compacted earth, taking us eastward towards the village.

Bram wanted to head first to the Church of St Andrew's, as who better to know the secrets of a small coastal community than the rector, the recipient of all manner of petty squabbles and gossip, of rumour, and of course, fact.

Instead of the dour, intransigent, bombastic individual I expected, a cheerful friendly man of about forty years greeted us as we rode up. Lean of build and of welcoming disposition, he had just come out of the church and watched us approach, so walked to the end of the churchyard to wait by the wall for us to come to a stop.

'Good evening, Rector. I assume you are that esteemed gentleman?' said Bram, touching the brim of his hat.

'Indeed I am, sir,' replied the rector, nodding as if in confirmation to himself. 'May I be of service to you?'

'You may, Rector, if you are willing, that is.'

A puzzled frown grew on his forehead. 'You say willing?'

'Yes.' Bram swung his leg over his horse and stepped onto the ground. Handing the reins to me, he walked over to the gate where the rector stood. 'We three have come from London as there is a rumour that something has, er, changed hereabouts with regards to coastal activities. That change vexes us. You know what I allude to?'

He hesitated slightly before replying. 'I am not sure I do?'

'Maybe we have it wrong, Rector, if that is the case then we can benefit by just having a chance to breathe fresh sea air, to cleanse our souls and invigorate the mind whilst we are here. We may as well take advantage of our brief release from the stresses of the city and take a short trip along the coast to reassure our masters that there is no reason for concern. I will especially mention that the Rector of St Andrew's in Fairlight, a man who would know everything that went on in his parish, knew nothing of any consequence or at least, *said* he knew nothing of any consequence.'

I watched the rector's face as Bram finished his final sentence and noticed a momentary look of unease pass across his features.

'Whom did you say you represent?' asked the rector, concern in his voice.

'I didn't,' replied Bram. 'Though we have just come from The Surveyor General of Hastings, who has been most helpful.'

'Ah, John Collier, you mean. Admirable man, most diligent.'

Bram smiled again. 'We won't bother you any further, Rector. Thank you for your time,' he said, taking back the reins and mounting up. 'Be sure to make enquiries amongst your people, just to be sure there is nothing to be concerned about as one of us may return over the following days to have a further discussion. Now we must be away to Pett to get lodgings for the night. Good evening to you.'

'Er, yes. Good evening,' replied the rector as we began to move away.

I found it easy to follow Bram's strategy; he just sowed a few seeds to see what would develop. No outright accusations and no questions that could be construed as invasive, no probing and no distrust.

'What did you make of the rector?' I asked once we had put a little distance from the church and just before we entered the village.

'In it up to his neck,' replied Bram. 'I wouldn't be surprised if the vaults and crypt are stacked high with contraband, whether he is a willing conspirator or not is another question. He probably hasn't any choice but to be compliant in truth.'

'You think this gentle approach will give us what we need?'

Bram grinned. 'I do, although John here may disagree.'

'Bit too soft for my liking,' said Fulton. 'I've always found a little persuasion can get results quicker, to be honest.'

'It may come to that,' answered Bram. 'Just one of the reasons why you are here.'

'And the reason I'm here?' I asked, wondering what kind of answer I would get.

'Jarmin's decision; I agreed when he explained it.'

I waited a little more for an explanation, giving a little roll of my hand to encourage him to expand.

'An Intelligencer,' he continued, following my prompt. 'Needs to have skills other than a thief-taker. Jarmin thinks you need to develop and enhance the skills you already have to suit his needs. You found out about this intended smuggling monopoly so it would seem reasonable that you follow it through with two other men who have experience.'

'An apprentice?'

'In a way, yes. Our main task here is to discover the source of the goods coming into the country, not so much the smugglers themselves. From what John Collier told me there is discontent amongst the populace so my reasoning is that someone might wish to voice their concerns to a person of perceived authority, namely us. By just softly announcing our presence here rather than going in aggressively, we may draw some people out.'

'If that fails we take other alternatives?'

Bram nodded. 'I'm hoping it won't come to that; it could get very messy.'

His ruse was not unknown to me as I have employed similar tactics in the past, just maybe not on the scale we were doing now. Bram warned us to silence as we entered the village and rode slowly down the centre of the main road. People turned to watch us pass and I could see puzzlement on some faces, hostility on others, even hope on one or two and I thought word from Hastings had already reached the few miles to this village, confirming Bram's prophesy. To enable survival and the need to be one step ahead of the authorities, then speed in communicating was essential in an area soaked in smuggling. The tavern, rough, rude and close to falling down, emptied as customers came out to watch our progression. Bram, Fulton and I gave greetings as we passed, receiving nothing in response except wary glances.

We had ridden a few yards further on when suddenly a loud sharp crack of a noise intruded from behind us as a gun discharged, sending our horses into a panic. Our mounts skittered and jumped as we three fought with the reins and our heels, trying to control the animals whilst behind us I could hear laughter ring out from several voices. Eventually, after a great deal of exertion, we managed to bring the beasts under control. I caught the eye of a woman with a child, the infant crying at the sound of the gun and of the horses' behaviour and she lowered herself to the child's level speaking calming words, at the same time shooting a fierce look in the direction of the gunman before returning her look to me. I saw something in her eye resembling unease and I thought at least one person in this village did not look upon us with scorn and hatred.

CHAPTER 27

From Fairlight, we cut across fields heading north, a scant two miles or so to the village of Pett, where we intended to spend the night.

The inn went quiet the moment we stepped through the door, ears and eyes focused on us through the haze of smoke until a soft murmuring began anew and then talk slowly resumed. The low-roofed rustic house had a beamed ceiling with several wooden posts supporting it. I saw trestles and benches scattered about the stone floor, a fire blazing in the hearth.

We received a cordial if not enthusiastic welcome by the innkeeper who ordered our horses to be seen to and arranged a room to accommodate us for the night.

'You the gennelmen down from Lunnon?' asked the innkeeper, once we had settled everything and took our seats in the taproom.

'We are down from London,' I replied. 'But whether we are the gentlemen you're expecting, I am not so sure.'

'Not expecting any others, sirs. Just heard that some men were down and thought you must be them, seeing as you ain't local.'

'Then word must travel fast around here.'

He chuckled. 'You might say that, sir.'

'What else did you hear?' asked Bram, settling himself down.

The inn was quite full of men drinking and supping from bowls of what looked like a thick broth, all of whom fell silent again as he conversed with us.

'Well, sirs,' he replied, scratching his head absently. 'That you is some kind of officials.'

'I suppose,' said Bram, 'that you are nearly correct; we are just minor ones with little authority. We are here to observe, that is all, the workings of the coast and the ports. Others like us will be garnering similar information so that those we report to will have a full picture of commerce along the coast.'

I heard the murmuring begin again and a few heads turned wearing unpleasant expressions so I held up a hand, now confident that I understood the strategy. 'What my colleague is omitting is that we understand the need for a certain amount of discretion, shall we say.'

Bram nodded along with what I said, and then added. 'Discretion can be guaranteed for *normal* activities,' he said, meaningfully.

'Like or not,' put in Fulton. 'We will find just a bit of fishing, some boat building, some legal imports.'

'Precisely,' said Bram, looking around. 'Though we are not unwilling to hear of anything that may have an adverse effect on the normality of coastal life.'

Bram finished speaking, grinned and looked around, his words and countenance having the effect of returning folk to their private businesses. Heads moved away from giving us attention, speaking to each other in subdued tones; no doubt their conversation centred on us three as we sat there drinking our ales.

The smell of the broth reminded me that I had not eaten for quite a while and when I mentioned the subject, Bram and Fulton agreed. We ordered a portion of the broth and some bread, which arrived promptly. The broth did not skimp on ingredients being full of mutton and vegetables and I was pleasantly surprised to find it quite tasty; the ale, dark and strong, made a good accompaniment and all disappeared quickly.

'I wonder what the wine is like?' ventured Bram with a gleam in his eye. He sat back and wiped his mouth with his sleeve.

'Rough,' said Fulton. 'At least ours would be if we ordered some.'

Bram laughed. 'I suspect that this inn has some fine wines that your friend from Vintners Hall,' he said, turning to me, 'would cherish or supply to the great and the good.'

I could not help grinning. 'Perhaps we should put it to the test,' I said, turning and signalling to the innkeeper. 'We have a yearning for some wine, sir, your best, mind you,' I called to him. 'A couple of bottles should set us up nicely, if you please.'

I watched the man's face for a moment as he digested the request and I could see the dilemma in his features. 'My best? Will set you back four shillings a bottle what with the taxes I had to pay.'

'So be it,' I replied, baulking a little at the cost in a small seaside village on the edge of a marsh, miles from any meaningful civilisation.

He nodded and withdrew, returning a short while later with three small mugs and two jugs of decanted wine.

'I stand corrected,' said Fulton, taking a measure. 'Even I can tell this is the good stuff.'

'French,' opined Bram, after he took a sip.

'Definitely,' I agreed, enjoying my first mouthful. I smacked my lips and took another drink. 'Southern region, I would think.'

'No doubt,' said Bram. 'Seems it has travelled well too; undoubtedly not venturing too far from where it landed.'

I smiled. 'Seven or eight shillings in London, so I would say it is cheap at the price.'

We reduced the two jugs to dregs and droplets in short order. I felt tempted to order more but I refrained, thinking that my funds would diminish quickly, and as I suggested it, I felt compelled to pay.

Fulton sighed with disappointment when it became obvious that I was not going to dig into my purse once more. 'I suppose it's back to the ale now.'

'I would have thought ale more to your liking,' I said, as Bram caught the attention of the pot-boy.

'I would say my purse likes it more,' said Fulton, peering forlornly into his empty mug.

For a small village, the inn seemed to be a popular place as men, and a few women, came in and out as time progressed, with each new customer casting an eye towards our table as if we were an attraction to be viewed.

A boy stacked more logs on the fire as the chill began to permeate the taproom, those nearest the fire felt the benefit straight away, while those furthest away, like us, had to wait for the warmth to tell. A boy went around lighting the cheap tallow candles on tables and even though we were outsiders, and potentially adversarial, an atmosphere of conviviality imbued throughout.

It came to the point where what went into the body had to come out and my bladder told me that the moment had arrived. I stood up, a little unsteadily, surprising myself as I had only had two quarts of ale and two-thirds of a bottle of wine and walked over to the back door where I had seen men come and go.

Light from the window of the inn illuminated the yard, giving just enough light to see. I followed my nose to a wall with a runnel below, emptying into a covered pit where the fluid soaked into the ground, a system requiring little maintenance. I could feel the wind picking up, a strong breeze rustling the nearby trees and bushes. I fumbled with my breeches to extract the requisite part of my anatomy to perform the function required, the pressure becoming intense and I had difficulty in holding back. Just in time out it popped and I gave an involuntary groan as the stream poured out, splashing against the wall and into the runnel. I closed my eyes at the immense relief, finding that relief short-lived as just then a low voice spoke into my ear.

'Don't turn around,' came the order. 'There be a pistol, loaded, primed and cocked pointing at your back. Feel the barrel?'

I nodded. 'Yes,' I murmured, as I felt the pistol dig in. My stream that flowed freely now suddenly turned to a trickle and then petered out into drops.

'Move or try to turn around and I'll pull the trigger.'

'What do you want?' I asked, staring straight at the wall, now suddenly fully sober.

'A friendly word, is all. Maybe something to your benefit, maybe something to mine. Rumour has it that you three are here because you're after the Hawkhurst Gang. Is that right?'

I quickly had a decision to make; keep up the pretence of just being inspectors or reveal a little of the truth. I decided the truth. 'I will say that we hear trade has increased somewhat recently and are a little concerned.'

'Good, that's what I hoped.'

'Meaning?' I asked, perplexed.

'That you and I are on the same side. Most of us don't like what's happening. Too much is coming in an' the gang is getting real nasty with anyone who ain't with them. Most folk are scared and want things to return to normal. We think you have the authority to do something.'

'We may do; why not speak to a magistrate?'

The man sort of laughed. 'Then I'd be dead within the day. You don't know how things work down here. Most of them in authority are paid to look away.'

'What do you want us to do?'

'The three of you might be more use to us as the revenue is in the pay of the gang too. I'll tell you a secret; what you do with it is down to you.'

'What secret?'

'A consignment is coming in, a large one, probably in three night's time. Anyone with a boat big enough has been told to expect the order to put to sea.'

'Where?'

'Off Dunge Ness is what I 'ear.'

'That's east of here?'

'Ay, not far.'

'How will we know when you get the call?'

Only silence pervaded the outside area now and I noticed the pressure against my back was no longer there. Tentatively, I looked around but I could see no one there. Whoever it had been had disappeared as quietly as he had arrived. I let out a sigh of relief and then realised what I still had hold of. I looked down and as I relaxed the flow began anew.

I tucked myself back into my breeches, ruminating that I had been accosted twice in a matter of a few days at a tavern wall, both times coming out unscathed. Thankfully my heart had now stopped pounding and I could breathe easily again. I looked up into the darkness and wondered if the man stood there, watching me still. His accent had not been cultured, a local man, mature and as I thought back to the conversation, I realised he sounded strained, frightened even.

The door to the inn opened, spreading a fan of light into the yard and a man emerged, one hand pressed to the frame for support and I knew I had spent too much time out here. I shrugged my shoulders and headed back, avoiding the man as he staggered to the wall, so inebriated that he did not notice me.

As I sat back down at the table I beckoned Fulton and Bram to come closer. 'Did anyone follow me out?' I asked quietly, our heads close together.

'Not that I saw,' said Bram. 'Why?'

'Because as I relieved myself a man put a pistol against my back, warned me not to look around and then proceeded to tell me that many of the locals are not happy with the

Hawkhurst Gang. They're scared; want us to do something about it. Even went as far as telling me that a large consignment is coming in.'

'When?' said Bram urgently, his eyes brightening.

'Three nights time, apparently. Off Dunge Ness.'

'Did you see who it was?' asked Fulton.

I shook my head. 'He told me not to turn around and as I value my life I was not about to chance it.'

'Then he could be in here watching us.'

'Did anyone come back in while I was outside?' I asked.

Bram shook his head. 'No. So whoever it was isn't here; his friends, on the other hand, might be.' He turned his head to look directly at me. 'The problem with what you just said is that it could be false information. It seems a little fortuitous that the first night we arrive something just falls into our laps.'

'My feeling,' I replied, 'is that he did not dissemble. I do not think it a ruse.'

'Ruse or not, should we just ignore it?' asked Fulton.

'No,' answered Bram. 'I will give it a little thought overnight.'

CHAPTER 28

There appeared to be no tea or coffee to accompany our breakfast so we had to do with just a thin ale to wash down our bread, ham and eggs. I had a restless, wakeful night on a thin itchy straw mattress, tossing and turning, thinking about having a pistol thrust into my back last night. Strangely or not so strangely, I felt it disconcerting and the whole situation kept running around in my head, time and time again. I decided not to mention this to Bram and Fulton, they had both spent the night snoring loudly, unaffected by my discomfiture.

'Winchelsea,' offered Bram when the innkeeper asked after our destination. 'What's the best way?' he asked, chewing the last of his bread.

'Down there aways,' he answered, pointing to the sea. 'Just down there on the levels by the cliff end. A track cuts across the marshes, leads directly to Winchelsea.'

'Thank you, most helpful,' replied Bram, sitting back and belching. 'The track easy to follow?'

'It is if you stay on the track.'

'We have no intention of deviating, I assure you.'

'Then you'll have no problem, sir.'

With that reassurance we collected our belongings, paid our reckoning and left the inn. Our horses appeared to have been adequately looked after and as we mounted up I raised my face to the sky to catch the morning rays. A breeze seemed to be blowing away the clouds and it appeared that a clear sunny day lay ahead.

We headed slowly out of the village, the salt tang of the sea strong in my nostrils. The mile or so down to the shore was bereft of occupation until we came across a few rough cottages close to the levels, timber built, they seemed as if even the gentle breeze we had now would blow them down, or the ingress of the sea would wash them away.

We came to the shingle beach at low tide, the lapping of the sea far away, allowing us to view dark lumps of rock peeking out of the sand looking more like the stumps of trees, though I could not imagine that possible for how could trees grow when submerged by seawater? A little further out I could see the hulk of a wrecked ship, its burnt out remains having been reduced by the ebb and flow of the tides, the power of the waves, especially during storm surges.

We turned left, following the edge of the shore and sure enough after a few hundred yards, I could see a discernible narrow track cut across the marsh. Birds darted or swooped down and away looking for food, the raucous gulls screeching and cawing; not claiming to be an avian expert, I could see curlews, sandpipers, redshanks and even a heron I believe, amongst many others upon the marsh and the seashore.

The grass and reeds of the marsh spread out on both sides and the clumps of greenery appeared solid, giving a lie, as I knew the dangers of thinking that those little islands were traversable. Little runnels appeared now and then coming from inland so I suppose the fresh water mixing with the sea must give the whole a unique environment with the plants, insects and birds conditioned to the habitat.

Bram led us in single file with Fulton behind him and then I brought up the rear. The track meandered as it sought out the firm ground, the sun reflecting off the pools and runnels of water like glinting diamonds. In the distance I could see the town of Winchelsea, not as large as I would have thought as it had once been a major port, now, like a jilted bride, it seemed diminished and sad sitting on its perch, a forgotten island in the marsh.

The track began to rise out of the marsh as we approached a gate in a largely fallen wall, presumably the old town wall now in ruins and making the gate redundant. I could see the remains of a ditch beneath the wall, now partly filled in.

'New Gate,' said Bram as we came towards it.

'It don't look that new to me,' said Fulton, shading his eyes with his hand.

Bram laughed. 'This is actually New Winchelsea, believe it or not. The old one got taken by the sea centuries ago; it use to lie out there,' he said, pointing out to sea over on our right. 'King Edward didn't want to lose the port so he had this town built up here where the river could take the ships. Not now, no port here, just a river and a little fishing. The town is just a shadow of what it once had been.'

As we came through the gate I could see what he meant, the buildings were largely little more than ruins or in serious need of repair. Bram pointed out what little remained of the two hospitals, St Bartholomew's and The Holy Cross to our left. A few lone cottages belched out smoke from their chimneys, showing signs of occupation, amongst the livestock fields and orchards.

We began to ride up a long straight street. 'You will notice,' said Bram. 'That most of the streets and roads here run either straight up or straight across like a grid. Below ground there is an extensive network of tunnels where contraband is stored; even here where the buildings appear derelict there will be tunnels beneath.'

'You been in them?' asked Fulton.

Bram nodded. 'Once, many years ago. I don't suppose much has changed.'

'You said we are not stopping here,' I remarked, looking around the town.

'No, just thought you might be interested,' he replied, turning his head to look at me.

'I am, though what use it will be, I do not know.'

'Knowledge is valuable, regardless of whether it is relevant today or tomorrow. What you find out now may be useful at a later date.'

'True enough,' I answered.

Bram grinned. 'Indulge me, Richard. I'm in my home county and I'm fond of it, especially this part of Sussex and Kent.'

I returned the grin. 'Then do not let me stop you from talking about it.'

'Unfortunately, there are people about now, otherwise I would,' he said, as we reached the inhabited part of town.

The townsfolk watched our progress suspiciously as they went about their business, most of the glares being hostile while some appeared indifferent. I could see the church over to my right, St Thomas's, named for the martyr Becket or so

Bram informed me, standing out like a sentinel over the town, dwarfing the buildings around it.

I do not believe I have ever been the recipient of so much distrust and loathing as I have since arriving on this coast. It seemed as if the very air crackled with it, just simply from riding through a town or village; it was visceral, tangible and I felt very uncomfortable.

'I think they've worked out who we are,' said Fulton, quietly, leaning towards me.

I nodded; I could already tell that from the animosity. Word had already reached this town, like Pett, the evening before, one reason why Bram decided not to spend any time here. Everyone already knew our purpose.

We just followed the wide street up and thankfully, it led to another gate called Pipewell, or Ferry Gate as some called it, informed Bram. With daggers being hypothetically thrust into our backs, we passed through and then negotiated the track down the cliff towards the river Brede, where once, Bram said, there was the port until many years ago when it silted up. I cannot say I did not breathe a sigh of relief as we paid the toll to cross the bridge, then headed over the marsh towards Rye, taking us away from the suspicious people of Winchelsea.

'I will leave the two of you when we get to Rye,' announced Bram, as we rode on the path.

Fulton and I exchanged glances. 'What do you intend doing?' I asked.

Bram took a moment to think or to ponder his decision. 'I mean to take the customs boat,' he said in the end. 'The duke has told me that if what is suspected is true then he has made an arrangement to give our smugglers a surprise; that is, if his messenger arrived in time.'

'What kind of surprise?' asked Fulton.

Bram waved the question away. 'Maybe it's best not to know.'

'I disagree,' I said. 'You should not hide your intentions from us, regardless of whether you deem it a risk. The three of us are here for a purpose, and I do mean the three of us.'

Fulton caught my eye and gave a slight nod.

Bram saw us, read the unspoken words and blew out his cheeks. 'Very well. His Grace and the Admiralty sent a messenger ahead to get the port at Portsmouth to make ready two ships, a frigate and a brig actually. They are to be diverted from going to the Caribbean for a short while. They will sail under my instructions.'

'You intend to catch the supply vessel?'

'And blow it out of the water. Yes, that is the intention.'

'This all to do with what I discovered in London?'

'Yes and no,' replied Bram. 'The report we received and your discovery of the smuggling monopoly, have both played its part. His Grace, Jarmin and I discussed it at length and we thought it would be prudent to be prepared. If nothing else, the ships would be diverted to patrol for a while. What you were told means that if I am quick we can catch the supply vessel, knowing exactly where it will be.'

'You think the man told me the truth in Pett?' I asked.

'I do and the more I've thought about it, the more probable it becomes.'

'Forgive my ignorance, but if, as you said, this supply ship is coming from Spain and is sanctioned by the government, then would it not have an escort?'

Bram nodded. 'Hence the two vessels. A frigate and a brig should be enough. The Spanish would not risk a ship of the line for a smuggling enterprise.'

'And if it does not come from Spain?'

'Then we still blow it out of the water,' replied Bram, with a grin.

'So what of us?' asked Fulton.

'Eyes and ears, John. We'll take rooms at The George Inn. Be warned that the Mermaid and the Bell are the main haunts of the Hawkhurst Gang; that is not to say all the other inns and taverns are free from them, just mind how you go and be wary. I think it prudent that one of you stays in Rye and the other visits Lydd and Romney and the coast along there.'

'To do what?' I asked. 'I am meant to be learning your craft, am I not?'

'Honing your skills,' replied Bram. 'I think a little autonomy will sharpen them a little. You are to continue doing what we have already done, dropping hints that you are willing to listen and hope that someone will approach. Winchelsea was an exception as I did not want to stop there due to lack of time; I need to get to Rye and the customs boat. If someone wants to talk then they will find you, if you are in the area.

Rye like Winchelsea sat on ground rising up out of the marsh. The remnants of a wall still surrounded it, with parts either having fallen down or been demolished. We crossed the bridge of the Tillingham River and then rode up towards the town, entering through the old gate in the wall on the northwestern side into the narrow confines of its streets and alleyways.

Once again I noticed the suspicion in the eyes of the people as soon as they caught sight of us and I felt a tingle of uncertainty run up my spine. I wondered if Bram and Fulton felt the same but I chose not to enquire in case they thought me weak.

Bram seemed to know the town so Fulton and I just followed as we passed shops and taverns all intermingled with the houses. The streets were narrower here than those of Winchelsea with the buildings appearing to loom large over us. The arrangement of the streets differed from Winchelsea too, appearing random, just a street where a street needed to be, a town that grew according to its needs.

We entered Longer Street and rode down, the horses' shoes rattling and clacking on the cobbles, passing carts and drays, their wheels clattering and bumping, the curious and suspicious stares following us. Ahead of me, I could see the church and beyond that a castle. A little further down the street we came to The George Inn on our right and Bram led us around a corner into a street where a few yards down we came to the entrance to the yard. A young lad came out of the stables alerted by the noise of our arrival and we tipped the lad a shilling to take care of our horses. We then went inside the inn to seek a room for a few nights.

The low-ceilinged drab-looking taproom had seen better days; the stale smell of tobacco lingered, the walls stained brown, the floor covered in stains of ale and the remnants of food. Three customers lounged at a table drinking out of tankards, their pipes adding to the smell. The innkeeper bid us a welcome and Bram secured a room as the three drinkers looked on with interest as our conversation turned to our presence in the town.

'You gentlemen have business here in Rye?' asked the innkeeper, trying to make it sound like a casual enquiry, wiping his hands with a cloth.

Bram nodded. 'We have indeed, sir. We are making a study of maritime trade for our masters in London, just the legal trade,' he added, with a wink and a grin.

'Oh,' replied the keeper, indifferently. 'There's not so much of that nowadays, shouldn't take too long.'

'That is what we hope,' answered Bram. 'Unless we find things awry.'

'Got enough revenue men here so that shouldn't be a problem.'

'We will see soon enough,' said Fulton, looking around and settling his eyes on the three men. 'If something comes to our attention then we're duty-bound to look into it.'

The three, brazen in their scrutiny, did not even look away as Fulton gazed at them.

'Something out of the ordinary way of things,' I added, stoking the fire.

'Exactly,' said Bram. 'Now, would you show us our room, we are busy men and have to start straight away. As you show us you can tell me where to find the customs house.'

The room on the second floor could have been of a better standard. Four beds with feather mattresses, a dresser and a chest. The windows had shutters inside to keep out the light. It had not been dusted and I could see the webs of spiders in the corners and adjacent to the furniture. The floor had a large threadbare rug in the middle, the wooden floor surrounding it polished. I hoped the mattresses did not harbour too much life.

The innkeeper took his leave, not venturing a comment on our less-than-enthusiastic observations of the room.

Fulton immediately slumped down on a bed near the window whilst I took the one directly opposite. Placing my bag to the side, I tried it for comfort. Surprisingly it did not sag and it suited me well.

'No time to rest,' said Bram, looking at the two of us in turn. 'We are to the customs house; I wish to be at sea as soon as possible.'

Fulton and I both sighed but being aware of Bram's urgency we reluctantly climbed back up to our feet. We had received the instructions to find the customs house from our host, just west of the Church of St Mary, not far from the inn.

We locked the door and made our way downstairs, back out onto the streets of Rye.

CHAPTER 29

We entered the customs house opposite the church. After the sunlight, it took a few moments for my eyes to adjust to the lack of light. The entrance room appeared dismal, having an oppressive feel, seemingly emanating from the three individuals in residence, all of whom looked up as if we had caught them in some nefarious activity. Two sat at a table rolling dice, the other at another table studying sheets of paper and writing into a ledger.

'Good day, gentlemen,' said Bram, instilling a tone of authority into the greeting.

Immediately the ledger closed and the quill put down, the man flipped over the sheets of paper and placed a hand protectively on top. 'Sir?' questioned the man as the other two palmed the dice and sat up straight in their chairs.

Fulton and I took a step forward so that we flanked Bram, both of us putting on a stern countenance.

'My name is Henry Spinney. This is Mr Jacobs and Mr Dunning,' said Bram, indicating both of us in turn. 'We are come from London, from the Southern Department in Westminster to look into affairs pertaining to this area. Who is senior here?'

'Er… That'll be me, sir,' replied the man with the ledger.

'And you are?'

'Tide Surveyor, Vincent Bloom.'

Bram nodded, smiled and then reached into his jacket. 'This is my authority,' he said, presenting the document to Bloom.

Bloom took it from his hand and read it several times, looking up between each reading before handing it back. 'How may we assist you, sir?'

'Your cruiser's in port?'

'Er... Sir?'

'I asked if your cruiser is in port.'

'Oh, er... Yes, sir, it is.'

'Good. We sail immediately.'

'Sir?'

Bram flashed a tight grin. 'I am not in the habit of repeatedly repeating myself, Mr Bloom. We sail. Immediately. The crew is mustered I take it?'

Bloom nodded, albeit reluctantly and then cast his eyes to his two juniors, who returned puzzled expressions. 'Saving that we are not due a patrol, sir,' he said quietly. 'And they are reprovisioning.'

'Then let us hope the bulk of the work is done as you *are* putting to sea now, Mr Bloom,' said Bram, rubbing his hands together, a little glee in his voice.

'Then perhaps you can tell me the purpose and area?

'All in good time. Whilst you take me to the vessel, Mr Jacobs will cast his eyes over your reports. I trust he will find everything in order?'

'Yes, sir,' he replied, the nerves showing as he spoke the words.

Fulton stayed behind with one of the dice players whilst

the rest of us made our way down to the harbour and the vessel lying there at anchor. Bloom and the other officer, George Tindall, attempted to engage us in conversation, to ascertain the reason for the haste and to discover what we knew or thought we knew as we walked. I took my lead from Bram in being reticent with my replies, having the effect of making both Bloom and Tindall more nervous.

'The cruiser,' Bloom explained, in answer to my question. 'Is a Sloop, one hundred tons and has a crew of twenty-four. She mounts eight guns and is painted black for night work.'

She did seem a smart looking vessel and the crew, some with their red waistcoats and dark blue trousers and jackets, others wearing aprons to protect their clothes, looked competent. I watched as they rowed stores and equipment out to the Sloop, using rope and pulleys to hoist it all aboard.

'Is she fast?' I asked, trying not to show too much ignorance.

'Very,' replied Bloom, with a certain amount of pride.

Bram pulled me to the side allowing Bloom and Tindall to break the news to the crew that their inactivity had come to an end.

'Remember, Richard. Not a word as to where I am going or to what purpose. I'll wait until we are out of harbour and then inform the crew where we go. That way there is no chance of any word getting back here.'

I nodded, hearing the instruction for a second time.

I suppose the crew expected to spend most of the day at leisure once they had resupplied the sloop, Bloom's announcement that the plans had changed made them become surly, though not ill-disciplined.

Bram and I stayed on the quay while Bloom and the chief mate, Tindall harried the crew to finish replenishing stores. It took a little over an hour before the vessel was ready to depart and then the boat came to pick up Bram. He climbed up the side of the sloop and stepped aboard; turning, he raised a hand as the crew made ready to leave. I watched, as did those on the quay and those in fishing boats as the vessel left harbour. I got the impression that the revenue's hasty departure had garnered a great deal of interest and did not doubt that word would soon go around town.

I walked back up to the customs house to find Fulton sitting at the table with a hand of cards in his fist, a few pennies in a stack and the other customs man looking thoughtful. Fulton sat impassive as both players laid down the cards and then he grinned, gave me a wink and then scooped up the pennies, putting them quickly into his purse.

'Henry gone now?' asked Fulton, leaning back in his chair.

'Yes, with Bloom and Tindall.'

'Mr Prentice and me have been getting on well, haven't we, Mr Prentice.'

'Indeed, Mr Jacobs; however, my purse is now somewhat lighter than earlier.'

'Beginners luck, sir. Now, me and Mr Dunning will leave you to your work; remember that during our stay here, one of us will be a frequent visitor.'

'I'll look forward to that,' replied Prentice, not entirely enthusiastically.

Fulton grinned, got up and walked over to join me. 'Good day, Mr Prentice,' he said, over his shoulder.

Once outside, Fulton and I walked silently as several

people took notice of us, some coming close hoping to pick up our conversation as anything overheard would surely be quickly passed around. Our steps inevitably took us back to the George, hunger and a decided thirst urged us on so a few short minutes later we entered the taproom and ordered an ale and a fish pie each, the fish locally caught and, the innkeeper assured us, freshly landed.

'Anything amiss with the reports?' I asked, slaking my thirst.

'Nothing,' he replied, then flashed me a grin. 'Didn't expect to find anything; it's what ain't written down which would garner an interest; a bit like Hastings, if you ask me.'

I nodded and took another pull at my ale.

'I've been thinking, Richard,' began Fulton, in a quiet voice.

I dipped my head for him to continue.

'I think that you should be the one to stay here in Rye.' He sat back a little, defensively.

'I agree,' I answered, having mulled the situation over myself and had come to the same conclusion. 'It makes sense, John. Besides, I've had enough of being bounced around on a saddle, I much prefer to use my legs.'

'Me too,' he replied. 'But I have more experience in this kind of work,' he added, reluctantly.

I could not argue with what he claimed, my conclusion came to me because I thought I would be able to pick up more information staying in one place. Last evening proved that an undercurrent of discontent ran amongst the local populace. I just believed I would be able to tease a little more from the people; I knew Fulton possessed a plethora of skills,

I also knew that subtlety would not be top of that list. He could be brash and forceful at times and I could see a situation develop where he might well find himself resorting to rough tactics. I may be doing him a disfavour thinking that, but I had not quite rid myself of the impression that I first had of him, that of a bit of a bullyboy. It has worked out the best way, for whatever reasons.

Our meal arrived and we both set to it with enthusiasm. The inn began to fill up as the working day drew to a close and we had now got used to the eyes always being drawn in our direction; as yet no one had said anything that could be construed as contentious. I watched two men and a woman come in, glance in our direction then stop suddenly. They conversed quietly then turned about quickly and walked straight back out.

'We're as popular here as a fox in a henhouse,' opined Fulton, observing too.

'Who are the foxes and who are the hens?' I replied, wondering at the answer myself.

When we finished our meal I sat back and drained my pot, my stomach felt full and I wished to walk a little. I shook my head as Fulton pointed at me for another ale. 'No, John, I am full to bursting so will take to my legs for a bit. You carry on; I will see you back here later.'

I rose from the table and headed for the door. I wanted to get a little feel for the town as well as walk off the meal. I headed back down Longer Street, taking my time and peering in at the shops and merchants. Cloth seemed to be the main trade, whether for shipment abroad or for home consumption, I did not know. I passed a couple of alehouses doing scant business from what I could see. The people mainly avoided me, even though I made sure my face had a benevolent appearance and gave friendly greetings to those I passed; one or two even replied in kind and I took that to be an indication that not all the folk in Rye distrusted me. I noticed the Bell on my right, one of the Inns Bram had warned us not to frequent, looking, from the outside at least, like any other inn. I continued to walk and followed the street around to my left near the wall and continued until I came to Middle Street, where I would find the other inn Bram warned me about; The Mermaid. I admit to being curious to see this establishment, having read about it in the files in Westminster and listening to Bram's warning.

I walked up the cobbled hill, slick with mud and muck and came to the inn on my left, the dirty-brown grim facade matching the dishevelled state of the cobbled road upon which it resided. The inn sat amongst tired-looking shops and houses with some detritus littering the street. I could have been in London had it not been for the clean fresh air coming in with the sea breezes.

Curiosity got the better of me and despite Bram's warning, I decided to venture a look inside.

I stepped through the door into a heady mix of smoke and ale, tables and benches scattered amongst the small open rooms. I walked through to the counter at the back where a fire blazed in a large long hearth. Several customers lounged, drinking ale and talking. Yet again my intrusion elicited the normal response of everyone looking up to view the newcomer, the noise of chatter diminishing for a few seconds and then starting up again as if my presence meant little. I saw a spare table and took my seat, signalling to the innkeeper at the counter to bring me an ale. I took my pipe and pouch of tobacco and eased a good few strands into the chamber then lit it with a taper left by the wall candle for just that purpose.

'Staying in Rye long?' asked the innkeeper, placing a tankard on the table.

I shook my head; I had begun to lose count of how many times I had been asked that question. 'In truth, I do not envisage more than a day or two.'

He seemed pleased with my response. 'Wise that, sir, a man in your line of work.'

'My line of work?'

'We all know you're with the Customs, sir. Inspector or some such, they say.'

'Is that a problem?' I asked, taking a drink of the ale.

'Not to me; your money is as good as the next man's.'

'That is good to know,' I replied, not sure if I could rely on that assumption. If this inn is the centre of the smuggling trade in Rye, then surely my presence would be more of a hindrance to that enterprise. 'I wondered if I would receive a different sort of welcome, I mean, with everyone knowing my business?'

The innkeeper barked a laugh. 'You ain't the first and you won't be the last, no doubt there.'

A woman came in carrying a basket of cheese and he broke off our conversation and walked over to her, soon relieving her of her burden and taking it behind the counter and through a door.

The woman looked around the inn, smiling and greeting

some of the customers. I had a pang of disappointment that I should not be similarly blessed by such a striking looking lady. She wore a light green linen bed-gown with a cream-coloured petticoat, a handkerchief, trimmed with lace, covered her chest. A cap and a straw hat adorned her head, trimmed with small flowers; a tall lady, just a few inches shorter than me. She waited patiently, standing at the counter then turned when she heard a laugh. She smiled at the small group and then turned her gaze in my direction and our eyes met. I smiled and nodded.

She held her head to the side for a moment as if in judgement, weighing me up. She returned my smile, so I obviously passed the assessment, then walked the few steps over to me. I stood up, removed my hat then bowed my head; when I raised my head again I saw a few errant tresses of dark chestnut hair come adrift from her cap. She had dark-brown liquid eyes, her complexion smooth and sun-kissed. I guessed her age as similar to mine.

'Good evening, sir,' she said, that smile still on her lips.

'Good evening to you too, my lady,' I replied, and our eyes met.

Something, and I do not know what, passed between us in those few brief seconds, then the innkeeper returned from out back and broke the spell that held us.

'Here you are,' he said, handing over some coins. 'The money from last time included.'

The lady nodded, put the money into her purse, blessed me again with a smile, then turned and walked out of the inn.

'Who was that?' I asked, sitting back down.

The innkeeper grinned. 'That's Ellen. She sells me the

cheese from her cousin. A widow must make ends meet somehow.'

'A widow?'

'Ay, sad thing that were.'

Before I could ask more, he turned and went to collect the empty tankards, pots and glasses.

Ellen, I mused as I took another drink. I wondered about her story and whether it would be a useful one to know.

CHAPTER 30

'Remember to check the customs house for messages,' said Fulton, climbing up onto the horse. 'Or to leave one there for Bram or me, if needs be. Two or three days and I should be back,' he added, twitching the reins.

I nodded; I decided not to remind him that we had already been over that a few times. Like Bram, he wished to reinforce the points. 'Good fortune to you, John,' I said, letting go of the bridle and stepping back.

He gave me a grin and then rode out of the yard and into the street, pleased, I suspected, as I, to be independent for a day or so.

Fulton had found nothing amiss with the reports last evening, even so, I decided to keep the pretence up, to pay another visit to the customs house and go through the reports again. It would give me the opportunity to question the officer to find out what he could tell me or what he would not be prepared to tell me.

My mind turned briefly back to London and to Kitty and Ned, still wondering how they were faring. Being here on the coast and miles away I knew I should not dwell on their labours, I could do nothing and the longer I stayed away the more frustrating it became. Jarmin had put me in this position and though I could understand his reasoning, I certainly did not appreciate it.

The day became cloudy but the wind, coming from the south, had a warm taint so I hoped that as the morning progressed a fine day would ensue. A few people walked and chatted on the corners carrying baskets and sacks, staring at me as I made the short walk to the customs house.

Prentice looked up from his seat at the desk as I came through the door, his face devoid of expression, like a mask.

'Any messages?' I asked, walking further into the office and taking a seat at the table without invitation.

'No, sir,' he replied, looking back down at a newssheet.

'Anything expected today?' I enquired.

He shook his head. 'No, sir,' he answered, continuing to read.

I got the impression that he did not welcome my presence, so I drummed my fingers on the table, staring at the back of his head, letting the tension in the silence grow a little. 'Then what are your duties today, Mr Prentice?'

He sighed. 'Just to be here, sir. Might be some riding officers coming in to report.'

'You have no intelligence to act upon? No searches to conduct?'

'No, sir.'

I chewed a wasp for a few seconds. 'In that case, Mr Prentice, you will oblige by assisting me in going through the reports once again.'

'Sir? I did that yesterday with Mr Jacobs.'

'But not with me, so for the want of nothing else to do, we will do it again.'

Something had changed overnight. Fulton and Prentice, if

not the best of friends, enjoyed a game of cards together and Prentice, if not exactly garrulous, did engage in conversation; not today, it would seem. Could it be that he had come to the conclusion that he best be obtuse with us or had someone spoken a few words into his ear?

The next three hours passed interminably, devoid of any interest and I received only the merest of necessary cooperation. Prentice grunted occasionally as I checked reports, manifests, import and export dues, lists of contraband seized and where they sent it. I did note that a fair proportion had been listed as damaged and destroyed, meaning that the goods would have been found alternative homes before destruction of the smaller portion had taken place. I could have spent a week or more going through it all but in truth, I just went through the motions and boredom soon took hold. I promised myself I would stop by midday at the latest, besides, the taciturn Prentice had won and I did not want to waste any more of my time in his company.

'I think that will do, Mr Prentice,' I said, closing the ledger. 'You have been most helpful,' I added, lying through my teeth.

Prentice's shoulders relaxed, judging that my departure might well be imminent. 'Very good, sir.'

'One more thing before I go. You say you have heard no word of anything over and above the ordinary, no intelligence, no whispers of undue activity?'

He shook his head. 'No, sir.'

'So,' I flashed a grin. 'Put the word out, keep your ears open regarding anything that could be construed as abnormal. I am happy to speak to anyone, Mr Prentice, if they are concerned. Do you get my meaning?'

'Of course, sir. I will do what you say.'

I gave a short grunt and nodded. 'Good; in that case I will leave you to the rest of your duties.'

Blinking against the glare as I stepped outside, the sun having made a welcome appearance, I stood for a few moments wondering what to do. I decided to walk down to the harbour, where if nothing else, I could watch the sea and view the boats coming in or going out.

Several vessels lined the jetties; fishing boats, smacks and small trading boats unloading cargo and I thought Prentice should be in attendance, checking on what they carried. Fishermen mended nets, repaired worn equipment and generally talked to one another. Flocks of seabirds made their presence felt, diving at the baskets of fish being carried to storehouses from those boats just in.

I found a perch with my back to a rock and sat down, immersing myself in the activity so different from the life I led in London. I found it relaxing with the gentle warm breeze on my face and the smell of the sea in my nostrils, so much so that I felt a great tiredness wash over me and I realised I had hardly stopped over the last few days. I seemed to be always thinking, acting or reacting, my mind sorting out and processing events and I felt my eyes closing and the daily toil of the harbour appeared to drift into the far distance, the noise became muffled as if my ears had been stuffed with wool. My head became full of vivid images of ships at sea, of smugglers and their cargo, of murderers and thieves, of a river with its waters glistening like polished silver, of children crying, lost in the swirls of the river as it took them deep beneath its surface, their faces reflecting the horror they felt. Both Kitty and Ned came, their faces ashen, concerned, searching for something or seeing something and I could not discern what it could be. They could not see or hear me as I stood directing them, pointing, gesticulating and I could not overcome the frustration I felt. Kitty suddenly began walking through a field of tulips, brushing their flower heads with her hands, a scowl on her face until she met a man, a faceless man and then she smiled and disappeared into the flowers. The flowers changed into the sea with high waves, flicks of spume, a ship battling the elements, wallowing in the troughs and cresting the tips, being thrown hither and thither until suddenly a gigantic wave engulfed it and the ship vanished from sight. Immediately the ocean settled, calm again, the wind dropping and it became still as a pond. I heard a voice, turned around frantically, searching, unable to determine from where it came, knowing that they called me. Now the trees of a forest came rushing towards me, pinching out the light, pressing against me. I could still hear the call, now immobile, static, my legs routed into the earth and I felt I would suffocate unless I could escape. The voice became more distinct...

'Sir, are you well?'

My fuddled mind took a moment to clear, then my eyes sprang open, slowly focusing and I saw Ellen looking down at me, a worried look upon her face. 'Yes, yes,' I stammered. 'I just fell asleep. Thank you for your concern,' I replied, sitting back up straight.

'I thought for a moment you were going to topple, you leant so far over.' She gave me a bright and wide-mouthed smile, her dark eyes sparkling as the light touched them.

'Then I thank you for waking me,' I replied, climbing to my feet, my initial grogginess evaporating as I looked at her. She wore a scarlet cloak over the same clothes as yesterday. 'I did not mean to fall asleep; it came suddenly upon me as I rested here.'

She had a small basket cradled in her arms containing a few fish, their bodies moist and iridescent. 'You are most welcome, sir,' she replied. 'Now you are out of danger I will leave you to your business.'

'I think my business here is done now, I will make my way back into town.'

'As will I,' she said, still looking at me.

'Then if I am not intruding, may I walk with you?' I said, thinking quickly, not wishing our encounter to end so soon.

She inclined her head. 'If we are going the same way I see no reason why not, are we to be introduced?'

'Ah, Richard Dunning,' I replied, giving a little bow of my head.

'Eleanor Norbury,' she answered, adjusting the basket.

I smiled. 'Then, Mrs Norbury, may I help you with your basket?' I said, reaching out with my hands.

'No, it's no trouble. I'm used to it.'

I pulled my hands back, a little abashed. 'You are involved with the fishing?' I probed, seeking to elicit a little personal information.

'In a way. My husband part-owned a boat.'

'A fisherman?'

She shook her head. 'No, though he was lost in a storm two years ago when he ventured out to sea. We had a shop that sold linen.'

'Then how did he become lost?' I asked, a little confused.

'He wanted to go out with his co-owner and didn't return, fell overboard and the sea took him.'

'I am sorry; it must be hard for you. Do you have children?'

'I feel I have overcome it now, thank you anyway. Yes, I have one child; he's sixteen so more of a man really.'

'He helps in the shop?'

'No, he's apprenticed to my brother-in-law, my sister's husband, in Hastings; a Cooper. I sold the shop as he had no wish to return here and take up the trade.'

'Then I wish him well.'

She smiled again. 'Thank you; and you? I hear you're an inspector with the customs.'

'Hear?' I said, returning her smile.

'Your presence has been noted and talked about, you know.'

I laughed. 'You do not surprise me there; yes, that is correct, for the moment at least. I do other work too and that takes up much of my time.'

'Intriguing, you must tell me more.'

'It is all very boring, Mrs Norbury, I assure you.'

'Something tells me you are far from boring, Mr Dunning.'

I laughed softly. 'Appearances can be deceptive. Tell me, would you not have your reputation damaged being seen talking to me?'

'I do not care what others think, so they can think what they will. I always treat as I find, Mr Dunning and folk around here know that.'

'I sense that you are a woman of independence and you relish that.'

She gave a small, contented smile. 'I am and I do. I loved my husband and loved being with him, since his loss I have become accustomed to making my own choices. The income from the sale of our old shop and the part-ownership of the boat gives me a sense of freedom that many married women do not enjoy. I also help my cousin sell his cheese as he has a farm nearby. Do you have a wife, Mr Dunning?'

I shook my head. 'No, though I admit I do not lack for women's company.'

She giggled. 'You sound a bit of a rake, sir.'

I laughed. 'No, just an unmarried man who enjoys life.'

'Then we are alike in some ways.'

'So it would seem,' I replied, catching her eye.

We walked up the hill and entered the town adjacent to the castle. 'What is that?' I asked, nodding towards the edifice.

'Rye's castle,' she said. 'It's the prison now, some still call it Ypres Tower; to most of us it's just the Castle.'

I gave her a little smile; I knew that we would shortly part company and I felt a little sad for that. All the way up from the harbour the women we passed gave her a knowing look as if sharing a secret and the men looked warily, perhaps even jealously at me, a stranger taking liberties, an interloper, which I suppose I was in a way.

'How long are you staying in Rye, Mr Dunning?'

'A few days I believe. I am with my two colleagues as you are no doubt aware. When we have done what we need to do then we will return to London.'

We seemed to slow our walk as we got close to the church, neither of us making that conscious decision.

'Do you live close by here?' I enquired, as we continued.

'Off Watchbell Street,' she answered, indicating with her head. 'Just down that way, a small cottage which suits me well now I am on my own. The same house my parents had before they died. I will allow you to walk me to my door, if you wish it.'

'Then it will be my pleasure to do so.'

We carried on and I knew I wore a smile. As we passed the church I saw three men appear from a side road and approach, deep in discussion so they did not notice us. I felt a shudder run up my spine and I stopped and turned so that I faced her, my back to the three men.

'Please,' I said. 'Do not move. Do you see those three men, do you know them?'

She looked at me quizzically for a moment and a frown came on her forehead. 'I know two of them,' she answered, quietly. 'Arthur Grey and Thomas Kingshill, and they will bring ruin to this town. The third I believe is a Portuguese trader, a frequent visitor. What is it about them?'

The three walked past on the other side of the narrow street, all with their heads together and fully engaged in their conversation; thankfully, they still had not paid us any heed. I kept my eye on them as they moved further away until they turned down the hill we had just come up and then they disappeared from view, heading to the harbour. A few minutes earlier and we would have met them as we came up.

'The Hawkhurst Gang,' I said. 'Which one is Grey and which Kingshill?' I asked.

'The well-dressed man in the black jacket is Arthur Grey, the man in the green, Kingshill. You look a little ashen, Mr Dunning. What's wrong?'

'Nothing, Mrs Norbury,' and I gave her a reassuring smile. 'Nothing at all.'

But there *was* something wrong; why, I asked myself, was De Griese here in Rye?

CHAPTER 31

'Nothing, Mr Dunning, are you sure?'

We stared at one another and I could virtually see her mind as what I said, and had already said, churned within it. We stood so close that the basket of fish pressed against my midriff, our eyes locked together. A few moments passed before she broke the gaze and looked away as a passer-by enquired as to her welfare.

'No, it's alright, Eliza. This gentleman has just saved my supper from tipping onto the street.' She smiled at the woman as I stepped back and turned to face the other way. I nodded at Eliza and touched my hat giving a very slight bow of the head.

'You sure?' replied Eliza, suspiciously.

'Oh yes,' said Ellen. 'I'd be the first to call if anything was amiss, you know that.'

'True,' agreed Eliza. 'You ain't one fer holding back.'

I took a few steps forward and Ellen joined me; again we walked side-by-side.

'If my suspicion is correct, Mr Dunning, then it would be well if we conversed at length.' I turned my head to look at her. 'Most of the town,' she continued. 'Are not wholly in favour of what has been occurring over these past months. If you are here to look into these things then you would not find the people too opposed.'

I nodded. 'Then we must talk, Mrs Norbury,' I replied.

'We must,' she agreed. 'You come to my house tonight when it's dark. We will speak no more so just walk with me. I will stop by a little track that runs down beside the cottages. Walk down there until you come to another track on the right that leads behind them. Third gate down on the right is my home. I will leave a lantern on at the window to guide you.'

'Will it not be risky for you?' I asked.

'We all have to take risks sometimes, Mr Dunning.'

We walked up Watchbell Street not talking, just keeping step with each other. Two other women stood talking outside a house and Ellen nodded to them as we passed, a one-horse cart clattered along and the driver held up a friendly hand. Ellen acknowledged the few other folk we passed but I kept my silence as requested until we turned off the street into a narrow lane, lined with small stone cottages. A few yards down she stopped, right by an alley that ran down the side.

'Thank you, Mr Dunning,' she said. 'For helping me home. Good day to you,' she finished and without looking or speaking again, she walked to her door.

I did not linger, immediately turning away and beginning to walk, just briefly looking over my shoulder to see her enter through the door.

The rest of the afternoon passed interminably, every hour seemed to last a day. I walked the streets of the small town to familiarise myself with it. I followed the wall, discovering side-streets and alleyways. I peered into shop windows, I sat and pondered. I did not engage in conversation with anyone.

Following my short talk with Ellen, I now believe that the distrust and antipathy I detected earlier may have been misconstrued and that instead, I thought I saw a little hope in some of the people's eyes as I made my way around. I soon became bored just walking aimlessly so I repaired to the inn just down from the yard entrance to the George, The Red Lion, where I filled my empty stomach with some mutton chops, washed down with a decent bottle of claret. I spent an hour or so there, mostly keeping to my own company, apart from the occasional word to the friendly innkeeper. We engaged in short bursts of conversation, arousing my suspicion as to his motive because he kept returning to the subject of my being in Rye. Eventually, having fielded the questions put to me, I left, with the innkeeper as ignorant of my purpose as when I arrived. I returned to the George and my room where I stretched out on the bed and tried to think clearly; what was De Griese doing in Rye? My thoughts galloped like a prime racehorse from De Griese to Ellen and back until I finally drifted off to sleep.

I awoke as the last rays of the sun slunk away; in the darkness, I fumbled with the flint, eventually managing to strike a spark so that I could light the candle. I sat back on the bed with my head resting against the wall and checked the time with my pocket watch and thought it too early. I waited another half hour until I could wait no longer then snuffed out the candle and proceeded downstairs, quietly and with stealth, as I did not wish for anyone to see me leave.

Keeping to the back streets and alleyways, those I had walked earlier, I made my way, seeking out the shadows where I could and stepping back into the dark places when anyone came within view. I took my time getting to Ellen's as I had no wish to be seen near her home and thus possibly compromise her standing in the community. Fortunately, I only took evasive action twice to avoid people before turning into Ellen's narrow street. The track she had indicated led into darkness black as pitch and I carefully walked into it with my hand on the wall to give me a sense of progression. I soon came to the gap of the alleyway and thankfully the sky lightened somewhat as a cloud moved to reveal the moon. I counted the gates as I touched them and hesitated a little at the third. I took a deep breath and then pushed the gate open, revealing the promised lamp in the window bathing the yard in a weak light. I crossed the yard silently, avoiding knocking into the bathtub, washing bucket and various odds and ends to the backdoor where a dilemma surfaced; should I knock and possibly alert a neighbour, or just open the door and walk in? I chose the latter, turning the knob and pushing the door open. I took a tentative step into a small scullery.

'Mrs Norbury?' My voice soft, barely above a whisper. 'It is Richard Dunning.'

The door in front of me opened and Ellen rushed through, one hand against her throat as if in shock. 'Mr Dunning,' she said, as if expecting someone else. 'You've come.'

'I thought that was the intention, Mrs Norbury; if you have changed your mind or I am intruding, then I will leave straight away.'

She shook her head, brushed past me and closed the door. 'No… No, it's just… I wondered if you had changed *your* mind.'

I shook my head and held my hands out briefly. 'No, as you can see. I am sorry if I startled you.'

She gave me a weak smile and I noticed the corners of her eyes crease a little, a genuine smile then. 'In truth, you did a little. I had been waiting by the door for you and just stepped through to stir the pot. I know it's not late, but…'

'You thought I would come as soon as it got dark?'

She nodded. 'I did; you're here now, and I'm most grateful.'

'I am the one who should be grateful,' I replied, thinking it an odd statement for her to make.

'Are you hungry?' she asked, changing the subject and speaking as if we were old friends. 'Only I've made enough for two, just in case.'

It would have been churlish of me to decline so I smiled and nodded and she then smiled again.

'Come through, Mr Dunning, please.'

She turned and headed through the door to the front room; a small room with a small hearth, a pot balanced on a small stand. A snug room, clean with two comfortable chairs either side of the fire, a linen-covered plate and a pricket with the candle aflame sat upon a table with three stools below, a dresser contained her cooking equipment as well as plates and jugs. Shelves on the walls had ornaments and trinkets and the wooden floor had a small rug for comfort. The window and door had a cloth covering for privacy and for keeping out the draughts.

She indicated for me to sit and as I did so I realised that I still wore my hat; apologising, I hastily removed it. 'My manners seemed to have gone adrift,' I said, by way of explanation. 'I apologise again.'

'Accepted,' she replied as if it did not matter. She knelt by the fire and stirred the pot, releasing an enticing smell; fish definitely, mixed with other aromas that rose tantalising in the steam. 'Just a pottage,' she explained, turning her head. 'I hope it will be to your liking.'

'I am certain it will be,' I said, sniffing and smiling.

She took a cloth and used it to take the pot's handle and lift it, placing it on a stand next to the fire, then stood up and walked over to the dresser, took down two bowls and returned. She ladled the pottage into the bowls then took them to the table. She then took two glasses from the dresser then leant down and produced a bottle of wine, opened it and placed it on the table.

'Come, Mr Dunning, sit you down and enjoy,' she said, pointing to the bowl nearest me.

'My name is Richard,' I said, taking a stool. 'Please feel free to use it.'

'And you must call me Ellen,' she replied, smiling.

She wore a plain blue gown, lined with lace. her hair bare and pinned up into a tight knot at the back. She smiled again, sat down and urged me with her hand to eat. I took up a spoon and tasted the first mouthful and I do not know what herbs she used but it was delicious. She took the linen cover off the plate to reveal fresh bread and we both continued eating. I remarked upon the good quality of the wine.

'This is a smugglers' town, Richard,' she said, with a slight chuckle. 'One thing we do not lack for is good wine.'

'Ah, now that brings us to the reason I am here,' I replied, raising my glass to her.

'It does,' she said, somewhat sadly.

A few moments of silence passed before I broke the peace and disturbed the spell that seemed to have been placed on us. 'You said the town is not best pleased with what is happening at the moment with the gang of smugglers; why is that?'

She sighed and put down her spoon. 'People have become frightened. Arthur Grey and the gang are nothing more than violent criminals, forcing folk to their will. No one has a choice now; you aid the gang or suffer the consequences. The amount of tea, wine, brandy, tobacco and the rest has become like a flood. There is so much coming in that it makes people unnerved, even though we all profit from it, be it money or contraband.'

'The customs men hereabouts know this?'

She nodded. 'Let us say that arrangements have been made. Their purses are not empty and every now and then a few barrels or bales are deposited for them to "find" to prove that they are diligent in their work.'

'So why this flood of contraband now?' I asked.

She shook her head. 'I don't know. Only a few months ago things were normal; boats would go over to the French coast and come back with their cargo, yes regularly, but the quantity now is like nothing before. Now the boats go out and meet a ship and load out there,' she said, pointing towards the sea. 'Maybe two a month, sometimes more.'

'That would need a lot of boats.'

She nodded. 'Every boat along the coast. Before, you had small gangs of smugglers doing independent runs; now Arthur Grey has changed all that. He controls everything.'

'How has he done that?'

'Money and violence; what else?'

'Are you caught up in this?'

'We all are to a certain degree, Richard,' she replied, her eyes downcast.

'These ships, Ellen, do you know where they come from?'

She raised her head. 'The men say that they have heard Spanish voices coming from the ship. Does that answer your question?'

I sighed; Bram was right. 'It does, London expected as much. What's your role in this?'

She gave me a wry grin. 'Thankfully, not very much. Sometimes I hold the lantern to guide the boats in. I have no cellar so I cannot store the goods so the lantern is all I can do, and that not always. I am yet to discover if I'm needed for the next shipment.'

'When is that due to happen?'

'Tomorrow night. Richard, you cannot stop it, you know.'

I nodded. 'I know; I don't intend to stop it. I am thinking of following the goods to London.' Her mouth opened in surprise. 'I wish to know where they go.'

She studied me for a few moments then slowly closed her mouth. 'You are not a customs inspector, Richard, are you?

I gave a slight smile. 'I have already said that I do other work too, haven't I?'

She nodded. 'Yes, but that could mean anything.'

I decided that I could not continue with the lie about me and my name so I took a deep breath then began. 'Ellen, my name is Richard Hopgood, not Dunning. My business in London is in investigating crimes. Some call me a thief-taker and occasionally the authorities seek me out to undertake work for them. The third man we saw, the Portuguese trader, his name is De Griese and he is a suspect in a crime I am currently investigating. I didn't expect to see him here.'

'What kind of crime?'

'A murder, which may or may not involve smuggling, hence why I am here.'

'And your name?' she asked, narrowing her eyes.

I held out my hands in apology. 'Not of my doing. The men I am with decided I had to use the false name. In truth, it is well I did.'

'Why?'

'If De Griese finds out I am here then I am not sure what he will do.'

'He is a danger to you?'

'Only if he knows I'm here.'

She stared at me for several seconds and I wondered whether I should get up and leave. I had just shattered the burgeoning trust that had begun to grow between us and my heart sank at the thought that she would hate me for it.

'What else have you not told me?'

I shook my head. 'Just the name and I cannot sit here in all conscience and lie to you. I'm sorry,' I stood up and began to leave.

'Richard, please stay,' she said, surprising me by standing up and reaching out an arm. 'You didn't have to tell me that, I would have not known otherwise. I thank you for putting your trust in me. What of your colleagues.'

'De Griese does not know them, so they are safe.'

'They are thief-takers too?'

'No, they are officials from the Government and I have been sent to accompany them.'

'The Government, not the Customs?' I saw her steady herself with her hands on the table. 'To look into smuggling?'

I nodded. 'I cannot tell you any more than that we are interested in the excess smuggling. We all know the trade will happen despite what is done to stop it; it is just that it has now reached a level that is detrimental to the country. This influx of contraband has to be stopped.'

'So that things can return to normal?'

I nodded. 'Yes, hopefully.'

She took a deep breath and then walked over to the fire, removed the stand and added a log, poking it into position. 'Pack horses will take most of it away as soon as it's landed,' she said, looking at the fire. 'The rest will be hidden and taken later. I know some of the route for the first few miles; if you really want to follow, then I can help you.' She then turned her head towards me and gave a sad smile.

'Really? You would do that for me, despite my lying about my name?'

'You have told me the truth about your name, you didn't have to— Ow!' she exclaimed as a spark flew out from the settling log and caught her hand.

She moved back onto her heels and put the burned finger between her lips to take the heat away. I moved towards the fire and knelt next to her. 'Let me see,' I said, taking her hand and turning it over, seeing a small red mark developing on the side of her finger. 'You should survive this,' I remarked, furrowing my brow in mock concern.

She gave a small laugh and then smiled. 'I hope so; I'm yet

to help you.'

'I am forgiven?'

'You have done nothing to forgive. You have not deceived me, only told me things that could do you harm. You trust me and I thank you for it.'

I still had hold of her hand and I felt an increase in pressure from her fingers, returning it with mine. We looked at each other, our heads mere inches apart and said nothing for a moment until without conscious thought we closed the gap, our lips meeting in a soft gentle kiss.

We broke apart, slowly, reluctantly and then our eyes locked together, not speaking, as we had no need for words. Her eyes sparkled from the light of the fire, a vibrancy, an expectation as though something within her had come alive. My gaze lowered to her mouth, soft, sensuous, her lips glistening from her moist tongue, then her mouth widened in a smile and she released my hand and snaked both arms about my neck. Still kneeling we turned and pressed our bodies together, my hands around her waist and we kissed again, this time with more urgency, more hunger, more desire.

Panting slightly with the need to take a breath, our lips relinquished full contact and I could feel her warm exhalation against my mouth. We stayed that way for a few moments and then she sat back a little, reached up to her hair and removed the pins that held it in place. She then shook her head to allow the tresses to fall down her back and at that moment she seemed the most alluring woman I had ever met.

I smiled and as I pulled her towards me again, she placed her two hands upon my chest. 'Richard, I want you to know something,' she said, lowering her eyes.

'What is that?'

'I may not be the woman you expect. I have only ever known one man; my husband. I want this more than anything but I don't want to disappoint you.'

I shook my head. 'You won't disappoint me; there is no danger of that. We will do only what you wish to do or nothing at all. I assure you, I will not press you. I can only say that you honour me.'

She shook her head and I saw that smile again. 'I wish all of you, Richard. You will be gone from here in a day or so; maybe I will never see you again. For the time we do have, I want to know you and I want you to know me.'

I cupped her cheek with my hand and gently stroked my thumb against her. 'Are you sure?'

She nodded and then stood up, took my hand to raise me to my feet then turned and walked, leading me to the door and into the scullery. She unlatched a door just inside, revealing a staircase rising steeply up. She picked up the lantern and then took me upstairs, the steps nigh vertical like a ladder. At the top, I could see a small bed in the corner and the room had a divider made of canvas and netting. She took me behind the canvas where I could see a larger bed. A table with a mirror and a small chest the only furniture. She put the lantern on the table and turned hesitantly to me. I took a step forward and enfolded her into my arms, kissing once more, our passion rising.

I fumbled with her ties and hooks until she began to giggle and I too began to laugh.

'I'll do it, I'm used to undressing on my own,' she said,

lightly biting her bottom lip.

We stepped back a little and both began removing our clothing, the lantern shining a golden glow over our expectant bodies. She stepped out of her dress leaving her as nature intended. My eyes took in her full breasts, her delicate waist, her rounded hips and her long slim legs and she looked beautiful. We came together again, skin against skin and I luxuriated in the warm, soft, sensuous contact as we both began to touch each other.

We fell into bed like two innocents discovering the joys of love for the first time. Before long, I knew every inch of her by touch, by caress and with my lips and she came to know me. When we finally joined, we did not hurry, we took our time, the moment too precious to rush, allowing the intensity to grow until neither of us could wait any longer.

We lay quietly in each other's arms, our limbs entwined, our sweat mingling, our breathing coming in soft pants of satisfaction. We held each other tightly, both of us lost in the pleasure and our own thoughts.

'Can we do that again?' she asked, her breath hot on my chest.

CHAPTER 32

The night in Ellen's bed passed far too quickly. We dozed, we drank wine, we talked and between, we took our pleasure. The lantern had long burned out when the first flicker of light of dawn seeped through the window like a silvery blanket, nudging my senses to wakefulness. We lay in close contact, our arms around each other, her head against my shoulder, my cheek against her head. I moved a little and saw strands of hair covering her face; I raised my hand and drew the errant hair away, tucking it behind her ear. She snuggled closer and gave a soft sigh. I stroked her cheek and her beautiful eyes came open, her mouth twitching into a smile.

'Good morning,' I said, softly.

She kissed my chest. 'Yes, it is,' she said, her voice muffled.

'I must go,' I replied, with a heavy reluctant sigh. 'Your neighbours.'

'No, you must stay. My neighbours can go to the devil,' she replied, clinging to me tighter.

'What of your reputation?'

'What of it?'

'People will talk.'

'Let them. They will talk anyway, Richard. It will make no difference if I bed a company of dragoons or stay a celibate widow.'

I laughed. 'A whole company?'

She laughed too. 'Maybe half of one.'

I kissed the top of her head. 'After last night, I think you could take on a regiment.'

She giggled. 'That was then; I think If I have to take on a regiment then I had better get a little more practice in,' she said. 'This morning, I mean,' she added, suggestively.

I left Ellen's cottage in mid-morning, leaving the same way as I arrived, hoping for her sake that I would be unobserved. If I did not need to check for messages and to see whether Fulton had returned early from his journey along the coast, I think I might well have stayed for the day. I promised Ellen that I would return later in the afternoon, hoping that the respite would allow me to restore my depleted energy.

Prentice hardly stirred as I walked into the customs house. He looked up for a moment and then continued his perusal of the newssheet.

'Anything for me, Mr Prentice?' I asked, taking a seat.

He shook his head. 'Nothing, sir. Nothing at all,' he said, without glancing up.

'A pity,' I replied. 'I had hoped for something. Tell me, yesterday I observed Arthur Grey and Thomas Kingshill in the town and they were with another man, a Portuguese I believe; do you know them?'

He looked up this time. 'Everyone knows Grey and Kingshill, sir, and yes, we know what they are about. However, knowing is one thing, catching is another.'

'That is true; what about this Portuguese?'

He hesitated a little before answering. 'I believe you are referring to a Mr Da Silva. A merchant trader from what I understand.'

'What does he trade in?'

He shrugged. 'Never had cause to know. Don't bring anything here.'

'Then why is he in Rye?'

'Wouldn't know; you'd better ask him.'

'But you know who he is.'

'Small town, Rye, sir,' he said, by way of explanation.

I felt Prentice knew a lot more than he was prepared to say, certainly making it clear that he would not expand the conversation; unless I resorted to threats or violence then I would have to remain ignorant. At least I knew that De Griese or Da Silva was here in Rye and that smuggling lay at the heart of it. If this run tonight still went ahead, then I knew that De Griese would be a prominent force in it.

Convinced now that Prentice took bribes from the Hawkhurst Gang to look the other way at times, I sat and viewed him as I would any other felon. Taking money in office as a Customs Man was anathema to proper order and compliance. How could the man conduct himself properly to execute his duties? The citizens of Rye, especially those who comply with the law, must feel betrayed. I could well understand Ellen's assertion that trust had long ago disappeared with those in authority; the officials so lacked numbers, how could they hope to keep control of the illegal trade? I suppose that many customs men decided it easier and safer to receive a little extra money for turning their eyes away.

I realised I had contradictory thoughts, despite that, they did not dispel the fundamental belief that there is no excuse for a man employed by a government department to accept payment for ignoring a crime by those perpetrating that crime.

I left the customs house before my thoughts turned vocal; I did not have the authority to confront the man, I must leave that to someone else. Whether they would or not, is another matter.

Keeping a wary eye open in case I stumbled upon De Griese, I made my way to the George where I could see if Fulton had returned or had left a message. I could also refresh myself and I hoped that a bath would be available, if not I would make do with a towel and a bowl of hot water.

With no sign of Fulton, or of messages, I sat in the taproom with a pot of ale and a light lunch waiting for the water to heat. Much to my surprise a bath was indeed possible. A few customers sat eating and drinking and after giving and receiving a polite greeting they left me alone. I finished the last of the bread and pulled out my pipe, relaxing in my seat as I drew in the smoke. The door opened and in walked two men wearing workaday clothes, each of them armed, one with a musket slung over his shoulder, the other wearing a pistol in his belt, both exuding an air of confidence.

The newcomers cast their eyes around the taproom, their gaze momentarily resting on me before they walked purposefully over to the counter. I turned my head to watch, just briefly seeing the innkeeper's eyes widen in alarm before he took a step back as if to give himself room for an escape.

The two men leant over the counter with one man

grabbing hold of the innkeeper's jacket to pull him closer. Whatever they said to him did not sit well with the man, he just blustered a response, which seemed to satisfy the men as I saw them nod. I resumed studying my pot and pipe, averting my gaze, hoping that I might be ignored.

The few customers, sitting in their little groups, huddled closer together with their heads down, as if for protection. The two men began to walk slowly around, visiting each group in turn, speaking quietly so I could not hear the conversations; from the language of the bodies involved, the stiff backs, the frowns, the twitching eyes, the hesitant replies, I could tell that threats had been made.

The two men, having spoken to all others in the inn began to move towards the door, then one laughed and cocked his head in my direction putting a hand out to halt his colleague's progress. They turned, straightened their backs, and then moved towards me.

I avoided eye contact to begin with, then the musket barrel banged down hard onto the table with the angry end pointing towards me. I noticed that he had not cocked the weapon. I looked up, my gaze going from one to the other and then I nonchalantly raised my pot to take a drink, my heartbeat increasing and thumping in my chest. I said not a word. The men exchanged glances and I saw that the one with the pistol appeared more wary than the other, his face twitching as he swallowed saliva. He then licked his lips and pulled his battered felt hat lower over his eyes as if to hide his appearance.

'We've 'eard about you,' said the musket man, his unshaven face taking on a sneer. 'A Customs Man, it's said.

That true?'

I raised my eyebrows and put the pipe to my lips then nodded.

'We like customs men in this town; at least those who like us. You like us?'

I took a draw but found the pipe had gone out so I took the taper on the table, set it to the candle, then to my pipe and blew out a large cloud of smoke, regarding each man again in turn.

'Don't say much, do you?' ventured musket man. 'We're trying to be friendly.'

'Is that right?' I replied. 'With a musket pointing at me?'

'Got t'put it somewhere, ain't I,' he said, laughing at his own weak joke.

Pistol man tapped his colleague on the arm and gestured with his head.

'Just so you know; you be friendly to us and we'll be *really* friendly to you,' said musket man, raising the weapon and putting it back on his shoulder. 'Pays to be friendly around here, it does,' he added, nodding to himself. 'You understand?'

'I think I do,' I replied, taking another draw on my pipe.

The two men waited another second or so then turned around and walked slowly out, giving the other customers a look that could have been a warning to comply with whatever they had said.

Once the door closed the innkeeper relinquished his place of safety behind the counter and came over to me, concern apparent in the furrowed lines of his brow. 'Accept my apologies for that intrusion, sir. It was not of my making.'

I held up my hand for him to desist from apologising further. 'It is of no matter; unfortunately, the gentlemen failed to introduce themselves.'

'Ah, they… er…'

'What was it about?' I asked, pretending I did not know that they came to call for assistance for the run that night.

'Um… You'd best not know, sir. Safer that way.'

I nodded. 'I think I have worked out whom they were anyway and it is of little consequence. Do not concern yourself on my behalf. Tell me, is my water ready?'

The innkeeper seemed to relax. 'Yes, sir. I'll show you where it is.'

He took me out into the yard to a small building adjoining the inn and showed me the facilities; a wooden barrel-shaped thing that could accommodate a person. Steps allowed entry and I could see the steam already rising from within. Most people did not bathe as several learned men deemed it unhealthy, but I liked to be clean and so am used to regular immersion into water and it has not harmed me yet.

I slid the bolt on the door once the innkeeper had retreated, divested myself of my apparel and stepped in. Finding a small seat to sit upon, I sat down, letting the hot water engulf my body and taking long slow breaths, allowing my heart to return to normal. I am not ashamed to admit that the confrontation with the two men unnerved me somewhat; that they could brazenly walk into an inn, armed, knowing that they would not be challenged, said to me that there was something seriously wrong in the town.

I put all my thoughts aside, untied my hair and dunked my head. For a few extra pennies, lye soap had been provided, thankfully, not the fragrant kind like Mary made at home — she added lavender and other flowers.

I dried myself with the cloth and then dressed, feeling a lot better having rid myself of the grime of the last few days. I slid the bolt and opened the door to find a girl waiting with a pile of washing. I raised my eyes in question and she blushed.

'No need to waste the warm water, sir,' she answered, gathering the pile and hurrying through.

I found myself smiling as I walked up to my room.

Fulton had not appeared and I felt relieved that I would not have to change my plans. I put on a clean shirt and repacked my bag, leaving it upon the bed for quick retrieval later and then left, heading back to Ellen's where I hoped to spend the next few hours.

As I walked, I detected a nervous feel to the town. People now scurried, hunching their shoulders, moving quickly, sharp turns of the head looking into alleys before passing. The exchanges I witnessed appeared subdued, careful of not being overheard. I put it down to the Hawkhurst Gang and the illegal run later that night.

I made my way to the back of Ellen's cottage and entered the gate; quickly traversing the yard to the thankfully unlocked door into the scullery.

I entered the front room to find her standing looking out of the window, her hands clasped together, nervously wringing them. She turned her head as I came in and immediately began to relax.

'Is there a problem?' I asked, closing the door behind me.

'They were here, the gang, I mean. They left just a few minutes ago. I was so worried you might have come across them.'

I shook my head. 'No, not here anyway.'

'What do you mean, not here?'

'Two of them came to the George; do not be concerned,' I said, holding up a hand. 'They didn't disturb me. What did they want with you?'

'I'm to keep a lantern alight, atop the Strand as a beacon to the incoming boats; another will be at the castle and one between the two.'

'Then the run is still on?'

She nodded. 'Yes, tonight. I have to do it, Richard. I cannot refuse as I have to live here.'

'I know, you cannot give them any reason to distrust you. You must hold the lantern. Is it just you or will you have company?'

'Just me, others will be down by the harbour.'

I took a step towards her and wrapped my arms around her, kissing her forehead. She clung tightly to me, her face pressed against my shoulder. 'That might not be such a bad thing; I can watch with you.'

'Someone might well come to check on me.'

'Then I will hide; it will be dark and surely there will be somewhere?'

I felt her head move. 'Yes, something will hide you; I just hoped I would be free from it tonight.'

'But you're not, so we will have to make the most of the time we have left.'

'Yes, that is what I said last night, isn't it?'

She raised her head to look at me and I smiled. 'You did, and you were right,' I said.

Her worried look departed and she took on the confident countenance of yesterday, as if a candle had suddenly come alight. She pulled my head down to hers and we kissed long and passionately until we broke apart, then without saying a word, we headed upstairs to her soft warm bed.

CHAPTER 33

Ellen warned me to expect a sudden banging on the door to summon her to duty and when it came I hastened into the scullery and pushed the door closed, leaving a little gap; the angle of my viewing did not allow sight of the front door but I could hear well enough.

She opened the door. 'Take these,' said a voice and I heard a clatter. 'You have a flint?'

'Yes,' replied Ellen. 'Don't worry, I know what to do,' she added, sounding a little exasperated.

'I know you do, Ellen. You've done it afor. Just keep checking, lives depend on it.'

The door closed and I heard her take a breath. 'He's gone, Richard.'

I opened the door and stepped through to see her holding a small sack.

'Lantern and candles,' she explained, holding the sack up. 'It's shuttered so will only shine in the direction you choose.'

'And you are one of the three to designate Rye Harbour?'

'The furthest right, thankfully, or left if you view from the sea.'

'When must you go?'

'Now, Richard.'

She put the sack on the table and then clasped me tightly,

both of us pressing together in the hope of retaining the feeling and the closeness.

'This will not be—' I began.

'No, don't say it. Don't give a promise you may not be able to keep, Richard. I would prefer to live with a memory rather than live in hope. I must go. You know where I will be, just be careful.'

'Do not worry, no one will see me.'

She donned a man's heavy winter coat, once belonging to her dead husband, then let me out the back door. I heard the bolt sliding back and it sounded like a farewell. She would go to the front door to join the other people who had tasks to perform to aid the smugglers; the lantern holders, the landsmen, those to unload, those to hide the goods. Up and down the coast, many people would be doing the same and the customs men would be nowhere to be seen, having been paid off to be discreet.

It had gone midnight when I made my way out through the back gate and into the alley. I waited a while where the alley connected with the little street, the sky giving little light as the moon stayed hidden behind the clouds. I bided my time until all became quiet and still and then I judged it safe to emerge.

I diligently followed Ellen's directions, keeping to the darkest parts and hoping I would not come across the people going about this nefarious business. A barking dog intruded into the silence, cut off with a yelp and a whine as someone took exception to the noise. I hurried up Watchbell Street to a little dirt lane that led behind the cottages towards the Strand. I kept my hand on my pistol in readiness as the still of the night leant an ominous air to the surroundings. I felt nervous, more for Ellen than myself, resolving not to approach her should there be any threat of discovery.

I exited the lane and turned right, walking through the scrub and the grass. The sea lay to my left beyond the small ridge and a breeze rustled the foliage, hiding my footsteps and bringing the salt tang from the sea more intensely to my nostrils. I crept along being careful where I placed my feet and then I angled in towards the sea and lowered myself onto my haunches, looking out into the darkness to where the town wall came to an abrupt halt. A few stars now appeared through a break in the clouds, just a brief shining before they quickly disappeared again. I looked along the ridge towards the harbour, hoping to see the outline of Ellen or even a glimmer of light from her lantern. At first I could see nothing, then a few yards away I noticed a shadow move and become elongated, the form of a person starting to appear against the slightly paler sky. I drew a breath, thankful that I had judged correctly and then stood up, taking a tentative step forward. Something jangled in my mind and I stopped moving for a moment and looked intently; the figure I could see did not match the form of Ellen, being too rounded, resembling a ball. I waited another moment and then my apprehension became a certainty as the figure began to sing a song; the voice, low of volume, sang out of tune, discordant, grating; more importantly, it was male.

I stepped back carefully and then retraced my route, giving the male form as wide a berth as possible; something had not gone to plan, so if Ellen was not here, then where was she?

Keeping to the darkest areas, I crept along, past the lane

where I emerged and then continued, hoping that Ellen had just changed position and now took the middle of the three lights.

It did not take me long to come across a silhouetted figure just about discernible against the night sky. I moved quietly and kept low, resting on one knee as I tried to make out the shape of the person. The more I studied, the less likely I thought it to be Ellen. I hoped a sound might come, a spoken word that would help me decide. I reached down, gathered up some pebbles and threw them away from me.

The head whipped around at the noise. 'Who's there?' came the voice, guarded, a hint of concern and immediately I relaxed.

'Don't worry, it is me,' I said softly, scrambling across the ground towards her. 'What happened, I nearly walked up to a man?'

'Shush,' she said, indicating with her hand for me to keep low. 'Lawrence Beauman decided he wanted to stay close to his house so they swapped me,' she explained, quietly. 'Here, Richard,' she added, pointing to a spot just in front of her. 'There is a small ledge below me; you won't be seen.'

I came level with her and she sunk down and held out her hand. I took it and peered over the edge. I could not see a thing.

'Just there, a few feet down,' she said, softly.

Holding onto her hand I sat down and swung my legs over, sliding tentatively into the unknown until my feet encountered a firm footing about four feet below the edge.

She sat herself down as I stood and her head was just a few inches above mine so I reached up, drew her face down and kissed her.

'Thankfully you did not do that to Lawrence,' she said, smiling.

'No, that would have been embarrassing,' I replied, returning the smile. 'I am sure the experience would not be so sweet either.'

I gazed around looking for the lantern and then I noticed a few feet further on a small beam of light illuminating the scrub on the edge; out to sea, that little light would shine like a star, the shutter hiding the light from anywhere but directly in front of it. 'How long must you wait?' I asked, turning my gaze to the sea.

'Until all the boats are home. A signal from below will tell me when the last has returned.'

'That could be some while then.'

'Sometimes it takes until dawn.'

As the time passed the temperature dropped and I rued the fact that I wore just my jacket and not my riding cloak as well. Ellen did not notice the cool of the night, being wrapped snugly in her coat. Although tempted to talk to pass the time, we refrained as we both knew the dangers of complacency; it would not take much for our voices to rise as we conversed, possibly alerting someone to my presence. We could at least touch hands, a small intimacy to give us solace in the vigil.

After an hour or so Ellen's head moved sharply to her left and she peered into the dark, then her neck straightened. 'Someone's coming, Richard. Stay low and don't move.'

I crouched down on my haunches and took a slow breath, hoping that I would not cough or move, giving away my presence. A few moments later I heard footsteps approach and then a man sniffed loudly, followed by a hawking sound and then a spit to remove the gob of phlegm.

'Still aglow, Ellen?'

'It is, Paulie, no need to fret.'

I imagined a nod of acceptance.

'Night's getting cooler, my girl; if yer getting a mite cold I know a way to warm you up,' he said, chuckling to himself.

'Do you, Paulie? Reckon your Tilly might have something to say to that,' Ellen replied, and I could hear the irritation in her voice.

He chuckled again. 'You don't say nuffink, then I won't neither.'

'Ah, but I would, Paulie, as well you know.'

'Yeah, more's the pity. Ah, well, a man can live in hope.'

'You going to be hoping for a long, long time in that case.'

'You know how to spoil a man's dreams, you do, Ellen,' he replied, followed by a long slow sigh.

Ellen gave a little laugh. 'Now, be off with you, Paulie, stay much longer and I might give in to your manly ways.'

'If only, Ellen,' he said, and then I heard him walking slowly away.

'He's gone for now,' said Ellen, a few moments later. 'He'll be walking back this way shortly, so stay down.'

'He won't engage in conversation with this Lawrence?' I asked, quietly.

'No, not with him. They can't stand the sight of each other.'

True enough, a few minutes later I heard the returning footsteps as Paulie came back. When he got level with Ellen he called out again. 'You sure you're not needing a warming?' he said, this time from a little further away.

'Sure as eggs is eggs, Paulie,' Ellen replied. 'I have other ways to keep warm.'

'A good-looking woman like you needs a— What's that out there?' he said, cutting himself off.

I turned my head to look out to sea and then I could see flashes of light over to the left and then shortly after a rumble of thunder, or what I first took to be thunder.

'My god,' exclaimed Paulie. 'That's gunfire, that is.'

'What?' replied Ellen.

'Gunfire,' said Paulie. 'Out there, where our boats are. Shit, this ain't gonna be a good night.'

I heard him running away, his expletives left behind in the air, the sound diminishing the further he moved along the ridge.

'Do you think that really is gunfire, Richard?' she asked, anxiously.

'Your friend Paulie thinks so and he must know more than I do.'

'Then the men out there are in danger. Is this to do with you and your colleagues?' she asked, pointedly.

'I am not sure. Probably. All I know is that one of us went out in the customs vessel. It may well have something to do with it.'

I heard her take a breath in; I could practically feel her anxiety for her townsfolk.

We watched the sparks of light and listened as the noise rolled in until quite suddenly, it stopped. The silence and the absence of flashes from the vista in front of us made me feel very uncomfortable.

'It's stopped,' she said, looking keenly into the distance.

'So it would appear,' I replied, looking too.

'Will our boats be safe, do you think?'

'I hope so. They are quick and manoeuvrable I imagine. They would have got out of the way when it all began.'

'I do hope you're right, Richard. Most don't want to be there.'

'I know; if it is my colleague then he will only be after the ship and escort, not the running boats.'

'He has that much authority?'

'No, not him, the note he carries does, however.'

She studied me in silence for a few moments as if thinking about my replies. 'I'm not sure about your world, Richard. It seems a little dangerous.'

I gave a low chuckle, more ironic than anything else. 'It is not boring, I will grant you that.'

'Maybe I should come to London, to find out.'

'Maybe you should,' I replied.

She did not say anything for a moment. 'Thank you,' she said, in the end.

'For what?'

'For not hesitating in replying. I don't think I will come to London. I don't think I would like it much and besides, I think I might complicate your life if I did. Maybe you'll come back to Rye?'

'Would I be welcomed?'

'By me, yes. I hope you will come back,' she said, looking at me. 'Let us say no more on it. Whether you come or not, it will be down to you. I'll always be here in Rye, Richard.'

I cast my eyes to the sea again, thinking; if she did come to London then some changes would be sure to happen and I did not know if I was ready for them, not yet anyway. We needed to know each other better for that. Perhaps I deluded myself; this time, this short time might be all we will have, a temporary infatuation for both of us, fading over time when absence occurs. I also had to think of Kitty and one or two others whom I call upon. No, Ellen is correct that her coming to London would complicate my life even more than it was already. A widow from a small seaside town would find life hard and bewildering in the London that I knew — should I even think that would be an issue? I reached up and took her hand, squeezing it gently before bringing it to my lips. I wondered if I would ever find that out?

We did not say any more on the subject, we just both stared out to sea. Paulie did not return and the only thing to break the stillness was when Ellen had to change the candle in the lantern.

Two more hours must have passed until Ellen suddenly sat up straighter and peered down towards the harbour where a series of flashing lights came to her notice.

'They are all home, Richard. All the boats from Rye have returned.'

'What now then?' I asked.

'I'll take you back to my house and then I'll go to find out what happened.'

She snubbed the candle in the lantern as I climbed up from the ledge.

'Let me go first,' she said. 'Give it a few minutes and then follow; I'll unlock the back door.'

Dawn had still to come so with little chance of me being discovered I hastened off the ridge and made my way through the silent streets.

We kissed briefly when I arrived and then she quickly left once more, hurrying to find out what had occurred, leaving me in her small room to wait until her return.

I had much to think upon.

CHAPTER 34

'What happened?' I asked once she had closed the door behind her.

She stared at me for a moment, her breathing quick and concern written upon her face. 'Arthur Grey is apoplectic with rage. The ship carrying the contraband has been sunk. The escort ship managed to get away after being badly mauled. Only five boats came back fully loaded and the rest were lucky to survive. Grey is looking for someone to blame and he is aware that three officials have come to Rye and that one went out in the customs boat and is yet to return. He also knows that one rode out of Rye and that one still remains. You, Richard.'

I held my hands up, palms outwards, 'Do not concern yourself, Ellen. There is nothing he can do.'

'You don't know Grey,' she said, the worry still etched on her face.

I took a few steps towards her and wrapped my arms around her. 'I know his type,' I replied, dismissing her concern. 'He might find he needs me more than he thinks.' I spoke the truth with my reply because we only came here to look into the excess of smuggling, not the normal activities which Grey would undoubtedly wish to continue. 'Any harm to me or my colleagues and then without doubt he will wear a hempen rope. Leave us alone and he may be allowed to carry on as before.'

'Carry on?'

'Yes, if not him then someone else will. Grey's activities are known and if he learns to temper certain aspects of his trade he might be allowed to continue.'

'The devil you know, you mean?'

I nodded. 'Yes, so you see, he has more to lose should he want harm to me. Now, when are they moving the contraband to London?'

She looked at me for a while as if I had grown a second head. 'You still intend to follow?'

I grinned. 'Of course, I have to.'

She wriggled out of my arms and turned around, leaning her back against me, staring at the wall. I had my hands on her waist, my chin and cheek resting against the back of her head.

'Not this day,' she said in the end. 'They move at night and there is little darkness left tonight.'

'Makes sense,' I replied.

'I'll find out later for you,' she said, a reluctant tone to her voice. She yawned and pressed her hands against mine. 'Once I've had a little sleep.'

We did sleep, both of us, until late in the morning. We lay together for a while, not talking, our bodies snug against each other, relishing the intimacy and the slow, languid joining on waking.

She gave a reluctant sigh, slipped out of bed and then began to dress, my eyes watching her as I tried to fix the vision in my mind.

'I won't be long,' she said. 'Stay here. I'll find out what you need to know.'

I reached forward and caught her arm. 'Do not endanger yourself,' I said. 'Don't probe; if the information is not forthcoming, then leave it.'

'Don't worry, Richard.' She smiled and bent down to kiss me. 'It will be common knowledge about town by now.'

I lay back in bed feeling somewhat inadequate in allowing Ellen to discover what I should be discovering myself. I knew the sense of it, realised that she would find out more than I would; in London, I would not hesitate in asking Kitty to do the same thing, so why should I feel the reluctance here?

I decided not to ponder on the question because of where it might lead and to what it might reveal, perhaps I already knew that Ellen had touched a part of me that had hitherto remained dormant. Why this, now? Could it be that I am in a strange town with people I had never met and this is a novelty, something new, something different? I realised all of a sudden that I *was* pondering upon things and it made me feel exposed, nervous, out of control.

Wresting my thoughts away from Ellen, I turned instead to London and my business there. I still felt frustrated that I knew nothing of what Kitty and Ned were doing, whether they had tracked down Tewksley or not. Perhaps something had happened to them whilst I was here, spending my time in bed with a woman I had never met before, who had kindled something within me; and here I was again, pondering, my attention span regarding Kitty and Ned inexcusably short.

Thankfully, I drifted off to sleep, avoiding a fleeting

resolution that came upon me in that moment where thoughts turned to dreams and reality became surreal.

A noise woke me from my slumber, a click and then a rattle and I struggled for a moment to get through the layers of sleep and then realised the precarious nature of my situation, my pistol being in my jacket over the other side of the room. Footsteps came from the stairs and I slid out of bed, naked, the floorboards creaking as I put my weight upon them.

'Richard, it's me,' said Ellen.

She must have heard the noise I made and I began to relax, chiding myself for falling asleep and not taking precautions should someone else appear. She came around the canvas screen to see me standing still naked with the pistol in my hand, feeling vulnerable.

She took one look at me, gave a start of shock and then laughed, her hand going to her mouth to stifle her amusement. 'Oh, Richard. You look so funny.'

I tried to picture myself through her eyes; my pistol raised, my hand covering my manhood, my hair dishevelled, a grimace on my face and I could not help laughing too.

'I apologise for my appearance,' I said, lowering the pistol and removing my hand. 'I am undone.'

'Undone you may be but it is a beautiful sight and one I will always cherish.'

I put the pistol down and we briefly hugged.

'I found out what you need to know,' she said, looking me in the eye. 'Tonight. Packhorses are to leave along with twenty men to protect them.'

'Then we still have a few hours together,' I replied, touching her face with my fingers.

'Maybe,' she replied, turning her head away. 'Richard, there is something else; your friend has returned, he's at the inn.'

'John?'

'If that is his name. He returned this morning.'

'How do you know this?'

She grinned. 'If you want to know something, you go to the gossip. I did not ask about your friend, that information came as a bonus, freely given. I only asked if she knew what had happened during the night and her mouth didn't stop working from then on.'

'I must go and see him.'

She nodded. 'I thought you'd say that. You will return after?' she asked, a little hopefully.

I nodded. 'Yes, if you will receive me.'

'Just don't bring your friend, Richard,' she said, smiling coyly.

'No, no need to worry on that count.'

She leant forward and kissed my cheek. 'You had better get dressed first unless you want to walk through town like that.'

I found Fulton nursing a pot in the taproom of the inn, an empty bowl next to him. He looked up as I entered and I could see the relief in his features, his frown of consternation immediately easing. He waved his hand to me, and after greeting the innkeeper, I went over and sat next to him, both our backs against the wall.

'The innkeeper says he's hardly seen you these last two nights,' said Fulton, once I had a pot in front of me. 'I've been sitting here wondering whether I should turn the town upside down.'

'You would not have found me,' I replied, smiling. 'Thank you for your concern anyway.'

'Judging by your demeanour, your accommodation was far from unpleasant.'

'You could say that, John.' I quickly changed the subject. 'Last night I saw a firefight out at sea, heard that several boats returned empty of cargo and have now heard that the goods that *were* landed will leave tonight. Does any of that pique your interest?'

We kept our voices low with no danger of being overheard.

'Much of that I already know. Henry must have enjoyed himself, I reckon. I watched the battle too.'

'Where were you?'

'On the beach near Lydd and a finer sight I couldn't wish to see.'

'Undoubtedly one with a resolution. The merchant vessel has been sunk, the escort damaged.'

Fulton turned his head slightly to me. 'Really? You know that?'

I nodded. 'I do, it's not Grub Street news. Just five of Rye's boats returned laden, the rest were empty.'

Fulton grinned. 'Then Henry'll think he's a right whipster for pulling that off.'

'He will. What about you, did you learn anything of use?'

He gave a wry grunt. 'Less than you, that's for sure. I

know they're all scared of the Gang; one or two people went to open their mouths, then clamped them shut before telling me anything. The only way I knew about the run was from what you were already told at Pett. I just sat on the beach near some boats and hoped. Sure enough, they went out and I knew it was on.'

I took a drink and then looked around and it seemed everyone wanted to avoid my eye. 'This Hawkhurst Gang are grievously distressed at the failure. Word is that they are looking for someone to blame. Grey was apoplectic with rage and we were in his line of sight; that was after the boats returned so maybe he has calmed down by now. There's one more thing I have not told you; De Griese is here. I saw him talking to Grey and Kingshill; he's in this up to his neck.'

'Well, well,' said Fulton. 'Somehow that don't surprise me. He still here?'

I shrugged. 'I don't know; he is posing as a Portuguese merchant. Been here before, several times.'

'What'll he do now?'

'Return to London, probably. Whether with the packhorses or not, I do not know. I would think he would want to stay close to them.'

He gave a slow nod. 'Then we should too.'

'That is what I intended, even if you had not returned. They move at night mostly and the contraband will be guarded by twenty armed men. I am assuming that more will join them from along the coast. Other boats must have returned loaded.'

'I didn't see any at Lydd but that don't signify.'

'Either way, if we follow from here we should discover

where they store it for London.'

'I'll leave a note for Henry; he'll have to make his own way back.'

'What if he goes straight to London?'

'I reckon he'll come back with the customs boat.'

'Should one of us wait for him?'

He shook his head. 'No, he wouldn't expect us to.'

I finished my drink and made to move. 'I have something I need to do, John. I will be back later.'

He grinned. 'A fond farewell?'

'Something like that,' I said, walking away.

Ellen stood up to greet me as I came through the door. She put her arms around my neck as I held her and we pressed close together, looking at each other. After a few moments she broke the gaze, turning her head to rest it on my shoulder. 'I don't regret anything, Richard,' she murmured. 'Not a thing.'

'My regret is that I cannot stay longer, Ellen.'

'I would want you to stay too,' she moved her head from my shoulder to look at me. 'I knew you would be going and you must. We can't stop time.'

'More's the pity,' I replied.

She gave me a sad smile. 'You want to know the route, don't you?'

I nodded and could see the distress in her eyes.

'You will be careful?' she asked, placing her fingers on my face.

'Always,' I said.

She sighed. 'They will go across Romney marsh,

northwards to Appledore using tracks not roads where they will meet up with others at a farm. They then go to Hawkhurst where Grey has a house. More will join them there. I don't know where they will go from there. Richard, there may be two hundred men in all.'

Two hundred? I felt a shiver run up my spine. 'No matter,' I said, keeping the concern from my voice. 'A group that large will be easier to follow.'

As she opened her mouth to say something else I quickly took the opportunity to kiss her, shutting off any protest or warning. The number of men she mentioned needed to convey the contraband did indeed worry me; I would have to discuss the risk with Fulton later but it would make no difference. We would just have to keep our wits about us.

'When are you leaving?' she asked, once I took the pressure off her lips.

'Two hours,' I replied. 'Can you think of some way we can pass the time?'

She did and straight away we headed upstairs.

CHAPTER 35

The rough road, firm and deeply rutted, twisted and turned following the edge of the marsh, weaving between the contours and keeping to the higher ground. I could see reed beds to my right, clumps of vegetation behind the hedgerows and could smell salt and decay in equal measures. We had to take care with our horses so as not to stumble and break a leg. In places, rivulets crossed it, trickling away into the marsh.

As soon as I returned from Ellen's, Fulton and I took our leave of the inn, giving the innkeeper instructions to return Henry's horse to Hastings, should he not return within the next few days.

I wanted to leave Rye, I felt I had to and quickly for if I stayed any longer, I would inevitably be drawn back to the small cottage just off Watchbell Street and to the comforts of a woman who had touched me deeply.

It only took two days from that first eye contact in the Mermaid Inn to the feeling that now ran through me; like grief, a severing of hearts, an emotion I had never felt before.

Those last two hours had been intense, full of passion, desire, want, a need. Our parting, bittersweet and something that I found hard to accomplish. She even contrived to be at the gate as we left town, smiling and wearing her scarlet cloak. I saw her face and I thought I saw a tear in her eye. I smiled back and wanted to raise a hand in farewell, hesitated and then before I knew it, she had turned and stepped away.

What a frail heart I must have to be stricken so.

'You're lagging behind,' said Fulton, bringing his horse to a stop and then turning in the saddle. 'We must press on, get to this Appledore before darkman's.'

'Sorry, I was lost in thought.' I replied, coming to my senses.

He chuckled. 'Bet you were. Take my advice; love 'em and move on to the next one. Once one gets their claws in you, you won't know yer arse from yer elbow.'

'Thank you, John. I'll bear that in mind.'

'You do that, Richard. Now, let's get going,' he said, turning back and giving a heel to the horse.

We planned to travel along the edge of the marsh to Appledore, once a thriving port from what Ellen had told me; now the land had taken over and the ships had long gone. From there we hoped to pick up the smugglers' trail; all those men and horses must make a significant imprint on the tracks and byways, horse dung if nothing else. Ellen said south of the village, so the smugglers would have to cross the road we travelled on. It should be easy tomorrow to retrace our steps until we found a heap of manure and then follow. Fulton felt confident in his abilities in the countryside, me less so. If all else failed, at least we could go straight to Hawkhurst and pick up the trail there.

We continued along the road, down the dips and over the ridges; beyond the hedgerow I could see in the distance a large earth rampart running from west to east, bisecting the marsh. I had no idea what it was there for; it just looked imposing, as if protecting something. We passed a few cottages of habitation, the occasional farm in the distance to the west, eventually coming to the outskirts of a town sitting on a higher point of the land, Appledore, and my first impression was of a community in decline.

The street leading through the small town was lined with buildings from an earlier age; timber framed in the main with many in need of repair, the few stone houses seemingly dirty and neglected. The populace appeared wary of two men on horseback as we slowly rode through, searching for the inn and accommodation for the night. I tried to see evidence of a port once being here, but perhaps I looked in the wrong place.

We found the inn after a sullen individual had vaguely pointed us in the general direction, discovering a dirty dishevelled-looking building with small dark and grimy windows — inside appeared much the same. The stable boy, with a few coins in his purse, became efficient and helpful and promised to take good care of our mounts.

The innkeeper grunted acquiescence to our enquiry of beds for the night and showed us upstairs to a communal room with several straw mattresses scattered about. There appeared to be no other occupants so we chose the cleanest ones and hoped that the fleas and lice would at least be merciful. The meal would be better suited for the pigs, the ale weak and insipid, the bread stale and gritty; I did not envisage rushing back to the place.

Being careful with our words, we spoke little, just offering the innkeeper the information that we intended going to

Whitstable where we hoped to secure an investment for a client. We did not dally in the taproom, finding the fare and the company poor; already my stomach had begun to complain and I envisaged a turbulent time on the morrow with my bowels.

We rose early following a night of scratching and itching, my prophecy of discomfort immediately coming true as both John and I voided our meal of the night before. The offering of breakfast we refused, instead just paying for our bed and leaving as quickly as we could.

The road out of Appledore wended northeast, the ground rough with ruts. We had to stop, dismount and find a place to squat by the side of the road several times, making progress slow.

'Your gripes any better?' I asked as Fulton finished his latest episode.

'For the moment, yes. I don't hold out any hope for much longer.'

'Me too. I wonder what we ate?'

'Or drunk. That were a foul brew.'

I nodded my agreement from my saddle hoping my discomfort would ease forthwith; I could not believe I had anything else left to void.

Despite our predicament, we carried on as planned, albeit a little slower than we hoped. Turning off the road to the west, a mile or so above Appledore, we entered into a wooded area and then headed back, aiming to skirt the town, hopefully unseen. Our bowels did their best to thwart us as we negotiated the several hundred yards of woodland and then entered the open fields bordered by hedgerows. We could see no one working the land so hurried across, then kept to the hedge line working south. We could see the roofs of some houses in the distance which must be Appledore and carried on for a mile or so, coming across a track heading west. Fulton grinned when we found a gap, as there on the track we found a large quantity of horse muck, fresh and all but steaming.

'You think this is them?' I asked as Fulton checked the muck.

'Must be,' he replied. 'Recently shat, in my opinion.'

I looked along the track wondering how far ahead of us they were. 'We cannot get complacent. They may have stragglers or rear guards.'

'Certain to,' he said, climbing back onto his horse. 'Which is why we will keep off the track as much as we can.'

My stomach had started to settle down and I felt confident that my need to evacuate had subsided and hoped Fulton was the same. Neither of us broached the subject, I suspect because we did not wish to tempt fate. I certainly did not.

Our problem materialised straight away. The open farmland. I could see copses of trees here and there, hedgerows, barns and an isolated farmstead. I admit I had not thought it through when I decided to follow, with or without Fulton.

John could see my consternation.

'We have to look to the other side of the track too,' he said. 'If you are right and they travel at night then they'll have to have a place to bed down during the day; farms, manors, villages. We do not want to stumble upon them.'

'Then how?' I asked, now a little confused and probably

showing my naivety.

'The evidence is on the track; muck, hoof-prints, boot-prints. We go wide and then return, look at the ground and see if anything has passed. If not, we work our way back until we find something. We don't follow as such; we try to anticipate.'

We twice cut back to the track and found signs of a large group passing. The third time, we found the ground clear. We had just taken a wide route to avoid a village so dismounted and walked our horses back along the side of the track until we came to a copse on the outskirts of the village.

'Wait here,' ordered Fulton, handing me the reins of his horse.

As he disappeared from view I found a comfortable spot and sat down against the trunk of a tree. I felt hungry now that my discomfort had settled and I looked around for some of nature's bounty, anything to relieve the pangs in my belly and spied a bush of blackberries just a few yards away. I stood up, hobbled our mounts and sauntered over. I ate several handfuls, conscious that too much might start the gripes again. I resisted the urge to continue and returned to my resting place, my back once more against the tree trunk, waiting for Fulton to return.

It took a lot of effort to resist the urge to slumber even when a slight chill came with the air. I could do nothing, so I just had to wait, fighting to keep my eyes open and my wits about me.

An hour or so passed and I began to get a little concerned. I stood up and paced a bit, keeping my eyes searching, spying some workers in the distance attending to the fields.

Eventually, I saw some movement ahead and Fulton came from beyond a rise in the landscape, walking quickly and keeping low.

'They're there,' he announced when he came within a few feet of me. He slumped down against my tree and grinned. 'Something to eat?' he asked, bringing a chunk of bread out from the folds of his jacket. 'Got some eggs too,' he added, producing four eggs. 'Don't mind 'em raw, do you?'

'Not in the least,' I said, taking a bite of the bread and chewing. 'Where did you get this?'

'Filched it. Someone left the door open.'

I looked at him for a moment. 'Careless of them,' I replied, thinking that he took a bit of a risk. 'What now?' I asked, swallowing.

'We keep ahead of them, I reckon,' he said. 'Find a likely spot down the track and then wait for 'em to pass in the night. They don't pass then we return and find the way they went. Should be easy enough.'

We kept the track in view as it meandered across the countryside but I would not have said I found it easy. I did find it stressful, far worse than following someone in London where you could disappear into the crowds or dip into an alley to avoid detection; out in the countryside, those options did not exist. I felt exposed, vulnerable. We slept when we could; hiding close to where we believed the smugglers would pass, always wary of being discovered. When we came to the place in Hawkhurst that Ellen had told me about, Seacox House, my nerves really began to jangle.

We were almost found out.

Grey's house, still under construction, sat in its own

grounds. The main part of the house seemed largely completed and occupied, with a few elements remaining part-built. Other groups now joined the smugglers, presumably from other parts of the coast. As I looked upon the gathering from our place of concealment within the grounds of the house, I had to marvel at the organisation and planning that had gone into the enterprise. If Bram and the Navy had not intervened then the numbers would have been far greater, the contraband for London on a massive scale, swamping the legal goods imported.

Ellen had said that there could be upwards of two hundred men gathering; she was wrong. There were far more than that, perhaps three hundred with the packhorses weighed down by their loads. That many men and some women too, with the addition of alcohol became a hard-to-control mob. Discipline had departed and the men and women, fuelled with drink, became raucous, many of them spreading out into the grounds to find privacy.

Four people approached us from the house, swaying unsteadily as they walked, drinking straight from bottles. We crouched behind our large shrub and watched as the two men dragged two women down onto the grass. The men discarded their bottles then dropped their breeches while the two women hitched up their skirts. One man fell forward onto a woman and just lay there, unmoving — and then I heard a snore. The other two began to rut, just a few feet from us, in broad daylight.

We dare not move.

Getting as low as we could we watched as two of them at least attempted some sort of congress, the effects of alcohol allowing the man just a few short movements of the hips before he stopped altogether. Both women now had immobile men snoring on top and they pushed and whacked and swore at each man as they tried thrusting them aside. Eventually, the women succeeded, rolling the men over onto their backs and I cast an eye at Fulton who just grinned and winked. I did notice that he had managed to pull out his pistol. The men continued to snore loudly, oblivious to their lack of performance. One woman kicked out at her man, then both went through the clothing of the men, stealing anything of value before heading back to the house, presumably to find someone more able to do the deed.

Fulton nudged me and we crept away from the sleeping men, not chancing our luck by risking another encounter. Somehow we managed to contain our mirth, keeping it in until we reached the horses and then we let out the laugh that was desperate to come out.

'Gives us men a bad name,' Fulton opined, regaining his composure. 'That was a pitiful display.'

'One might have found the target but the other did not even start,' I replied, taking a breath.

'Reckon he battered away at nothing and didn't even notice. Pitiful, falling asleep like that.'

Needless to say that our conversation remained bawdy as we dissected what we had witnessed and I admit that it helped relieve the tension that had been building.

We rode north, giving Seacox House a wide berth, looking for a track that we thought they might take. We found three about a mile away. We settled down close to the middle one as the day began to turn to dusk. We had bought bread and cheese from a village a good distance from Seacox, water we could gather from streams. We could not risk a fire, even during the day, as the smoke would be seen from miles away.

Soon after night had come we heard the men and horses, not from the track we expected but the furthest west. Their drink-fuelled day resulted in a raucous discordant night as angry retorts and shouts came wafting with the air.

Three more days passed before we came to the outskirts of London. The smugglers stayed at another village and then a Manor House, assuming the owner had a vested interest in the enterprise. The last night they stayed at a derelict house, long since gone to ruin. The day after that turned into the day that Fulton and I looked forward to.

CHAPTER 36

The farm seemed derelict, from a distance at least. From our position we had difficulty in assessing the layout accurately; we would need to get closer, perhaps risking discovery.

I thought a little ironically that we began in marshland and now, at the end of the journey, we were in marshland again.

Fulton had ridden ahead to get a better indication of our position, leaving me to keep watch on the farm. From where I stood, I could only see one lane leading to it where occasionally two men would appear, looking up and down the road and then they would disappear again. A man and a woman walked past pulling a cart, possibly local going about their business. They did not take an interest in the farm, just walked straight past without even a look.

I did not have to wait long for Fulton's return. Within half an hour he came back, bringing news I could hardly credit.

'River's just over there,' he said, pointing ahead of us. 'That way,' he added, indicating a little to the east, 'are the Spring Gardens in Vauxhall. We're not far from the village of Stockwell.'

I stared at him in disbelief for a few seconds. 'That close?'

He nodded. 'We are. I could practically spit to London from here.'

I had a suspicion we were getting close. When we entered the marshland a feeling ran up my spine. If it wasn't for the trees and bushes ahead obscuring the view, I would see St Paul's. I had been no further west than the pleasure gardens before, though I had heard of Stockwell.

'We need to find out what is going on over there,' I said, indicating with my hand.

Fulton nodded. 'We do.' he replied, a grim expression on his face.

We hobbled the horses where they could graze, then made our way through the scrub and over the track, hoping to come to the rear of the farm. We crouched low in a stoop as we walked, keeping to the hedge line and avoiding the boggy ground. Fallen branches and dead twigs lay everywhere and it took some concentration to avoid treading on them, possibly alerting those in the farm to the presence of intruders. Slowly we worked our path until we had arrived at the back where high scrub bushes blocked our view. Wild animal paths led into the scrub, small tunnels of opportunity and Fulton and I needed no other encouragement to explore them.

Fulton took the one just ahead of us whilst I moved down a little to another one a few yards away. I lowered myself and then proceeded on hands and knees and then after only a few feet I had to go down onto my belly, crawling and scrabbling into the gap. Another few feet and I could poke my head out of the scrub giving me a good view of the farm. I looked to my right and saw Fulton in a similar position; he turned his head and grinned at me.

We could see the farmyard crammed with horses, most of them still laden; the ones that had been divested of their loads were led to the left of the yard where they would wait. Men carried the contraband into myriad sheds and barns and judging by the amount of goods going in, they must have cellars or underground storage.

Ahead, the single-storey farmhouse took up the left-hand side and fronted onto the yard. The roof tiles seemed in reasonable repair with the rest of it looking tired.

I could recognise Thomas Kingshill but I could not see Arthur Grey. Kingshill seemed to be the man directing the men, indicating where he wanted the goods to go. Occasionally he would turn and consult someone else, hidden from my view — would that be Grey?

After watching for a while, Fulton threw a pebble to attract my attention, he had seen enough and he indicated with his head for us to withdraw. I began to scramble back and then took a last look at the farmyard and I froze for a moment. The man that Kingshill had been talking to stepped into view and with him, another — De Griese and Tom Jaggers. I stared as they talked, cursing inwardly, then another man came to speak to them, Martijn Thyssen.

'That lot will take some shifting,' said Fulton, as we emerged from the scrub. 'We'll need to organise something.'

'A raid?'

'Reckon so. Jarmin will decide what to do. You alright, Richard,' he said, seeing my perplexed expression.

'Yes,' I answered. 'Just a bit surprised. De Griese and Jaggers is there along with Martijn Thyssen, the overseer from Van Hoebeek's. He hasn't wasted any time in falling in with the smugglers.'

'Your murdered man?'

'Yes, however, I'll think on it. We had better get back to London, and quickly,' I said.

As always when I return to London after some time away, the first thing that strikes me is the rank smell emanating from the city and the river. The second is the noise and the density of the populace, the sheer numbers thronging the streets, living and working cheek by jowl with carriages and carts, drays and hackneys. If a space appeared then someone or something would fill it.

To me it was home and I loved the bustle and the life, then I tried to look at it through Ellen's eyes, would she feel the same as I? Unlikely, I doubt if she would feel comfortable within London's embrace. She would yearn for the peace and relative quiet of a seaside town where she had room to breathe.

We entered Southwark, urging our mounts on through the busy streets then crossed over the bridge, joining the crowd and slowing our progress. Once across, we then headed straight for Westminster to make our report.

Leaving our horses at the stables designated for use by the officers of The Duke of Newcastle we entered the basement to be met by both Henry Bram and Jarmin, as if they expected our arrival.

'Richard, Fulton,' greeted Jarmin. 'What news?' he asked, without preamble.

'Can we get something to eat and drink first?' asked Fulton, his stomach rumbling.

'You should have thought of that before you got here,' replied Jarmin, sending out for victuals none-the-less.

Bram sat there looking especially pleased with himself; after destroying the vessel, I suppose he had the right to appear a little smug.

'How did you get here so quick?' I asked, as I settled in a chair.

'Later,' said Jarmin, holding up a hand. 'First you can apprise me of your efforts.'

Fulton and I looked at each other and I nodded for him to begin, and he did where we parted company with Bram.

He kept the report relatively short and succinct; I knew Jarmin required just simple facts, clear and concise with no embellishments. When Fulton had finished I added my experiences and observations in Rye, giving scant details of how Ellen had assisted me.

'This woman, Richard. I assume you embarked on a relationship?'

'I should think he did, if it was the one I saw when we were leaving Rye,' said Fulton, winking.

'Er…' I stammered, in reality confirming the fact.

'Then I hope you haven't left her with reason to compromise you.'

'On the contrary,' I answered. 'She would be the one to suffer should my position become known.'

He nodded. 'Quite probably. Even so, I hope you left on good terms; she might be useful at some point in the future. Now, let us return to this farm. You saw both De Griese and Jaggers there, you say.'

I nodded. 'Yes, and a Martijn Thyssen; I know *he* does not mean that much to you but he does to me, the Overseer at my murdered Dutchman's warehouse.' Jarmin raised an eyebrow then beckoned me to continue. 'De Griese and Jaggers appeared to be the ones organising the contraband. Most of the men and packhorses came from the coast so I would assume they will return within a day or so.'

'They were armed?'

Fulton nodded this time. 'Yes, they are taking no chances.'

'Then we must assume that those they leave behind will also be armed.'

Fulton and I agreed.

'Then I need to see this farm.'

Food and drink arrived and being ravenous, having not eaten properly since Rye, I ate my fill as Bram related events from his point of view.

'True to His Grace's word, two vessels were at my disposal. A frigate and a brig, both ready to sail at a moment's notice,' he said, leaning back, relaxed in his chair. 'The crew of the revenue's sloop had no idea that they would be detained. Bloom and Tindall protested at the imposition but I could not have them running around. I suspected that the officers believed the crew would end up on a King's ship; as far as I know, that did not happen. Bloom and Tindall came with me; I wanted them to be complicit, so we boarded the frigate to have conference with both captains. Both of them related the risks involved in a nighttime attack, arguing that it would be better to stand off until dawn and then make a move. I impressed upon them the importance of the operation and eventually, with a little persuasion, they agreed. We set sail immediately, the tide and winds fortunately in our favour.

'Both ships were in position as night came and then it was

only a matter of time before we could press the attack. The captain reiterated the dangers and the possibility of failure but I insisted and left him to determine how best to achieve what I wished.

'And achieve he did, far beyond my expectation. The two vessels, our targets, that is, both showed lights, giving us the advantage as we were cloaked in darkness, excepting for the occasional flash of light to keep our ships apart. The brig bore down on the merchant ship and caught it totally unaware, firing a broadside into its timbers. The other, a smaller ship than ours, twenty-eight guns, our captain informed me, stood off a little then attempted to flee, receiving a fine broadside from us and I saw a mast fall as a result. It returned a desultory fire and then continued to try to escape and then a second broadside from us did even more damage. I thought it better for that ship to return damaged to port, with its tail between its legs, so it could report its abject failure. We only suffered one casualty, a seaman with splinter wounds. Our captain wanted to press the advantage and continue to attack but my argument won the day.'

'What of survivors from the merchant ship?' I asked.

'There were a few,' conceded Bram. 'Five were picked up by the brig. All five of them Spaniards,' he added, grinning.

'All that loss of life,' I replied. 'Was it worth it, in reality?'

'I think so,' interjected Jarmin. 'They knew the risks they were taking.'

'All the same; how many made up the crew?'

'Forty-four, from what the survivors said.'

'And just five to live to tell the tale.' I shook my head sadly. 'I did not realise as I watched it unfold from afar.'

'How did you get back to London so quickly?' asked Fulton, possibly to change the nature of the conversation after he saw my face.

'I spoke to the survivors as soon as we returned to Portsmouth and then knowing it was not worth returning to Rye caught the mail coach to London. I left the sloop to return home with a warning in Bloom's ear.'

'Think they'll heed it?' asked Fulton.

'They'd better,' said Bram. 'Or I'll hear of it otherwise.'

I wondered on that. Keeping quiet when involved in the destruction of a ship would be difficult. No doubt they would discuss it amongst themselves and as to the crew, they would have been told on the return voyage. I felt certain one of them would mention it at some point, there were too many to keep that to themselves. Family, friends, a few drinks in the tavern and it would all come out.

'What has De Veil been doing?' I asked, changing the subject. 'His inspections?'

Jarmin grinned. 'Our august magistrate and Inspector of Imports and Exports has been turning the port upside down. He's sent clerks and inspectors into its very heart, delving into the paperwork and causing mayhem. I dare say he will continue for several days more and I don't envy him collating all that results from it. His Grace is most impressed, even knowing that it may be a fruitless exercise as far as this smuggling is concerned. De Veil may unearth some interesting things so we will wait for his findings.'

'What of this farm?' asked Fulton. 'What are you thinking?'

'I'm thinking that you will take me there.'

'And me?' I asked, wondering what my role would be.

'There is no need for both of you to come; besides, I believe you may have another business to attend to.'

'Tewksley?'

'So I understand. Monk found out he had been treated by a drunken ship's surgeon out in Limehouse, it is believed that you will find your friends there at the moment.'

I gave a long slow sigh. Limehouse?

CHAPTER 37

I alighted at Narrow Street where elegant and substantial houses had and were being built for the wealthy, many of whom had business interests in the area. The smell and smoke from the limekilns further up the river seemed less intrusive here, though no resident could escape its influence entirely. The street was busy with traffic coming and going, a few pedestrians walked about and I joined them, preferring to walk to where Jarmin said I would find Kitty and Ned.

Leaving Narrow Street I walked past the long lane where the workers made the ships' ropes, the open countryside just to my left behind the sheds and warehouses; another few steps took me into Fore Street, which ran alongside Limekiln Dock. The kilns, situated on the further side of the dock, burned the lime to produce mortar for the building trade. All around me industry flourished; shipyards and boat-builders, docks for unloading coal and lime and within the streets, chandlers, carpenters, metalworkers and all other trades allied to seafaring. Sailors from all around the world sought passage home having arrived crewing ships from distant lands. It was a melting pot of races and creeds, all seeking employment from the docks, warehouses and the shipyards, to earn the money to either pay the fare or to work the passage. The accents, the languages, the dialects, all mingled to one great cacophony of noise. The food too, an eclectic mix from all over the world, eateries from Africa, the Mediterranean, the East and beyond; spices and flavours that tantalised the palate when added to plain London ingredients. I had sampled the fare on my infrequent visits to the area.

Warehouses lined Fore Street and from the information given by Jarmin, I should find Ned, Kitty and Monk, a little further down where the dock came to a point at Limehouse Causeway. Myriad establishments served ale and gin, to sailors mostly and their doxies and jades.

I must have walked up and down six or seven times and had not had sight of any of them so began to think that my time would be better spent elsewhere, perhaps even to go home to sleep, when instead of finding them, they found me.

'Thought it was you,' said Monk, as if I had seen him just a few minutes ago. 'Kitty saw you earlier, then you just disappeared when I came to find you.'

He came up from behind, drawing level before speaking. We both stopped walking, eliciting a few oaths from a man close behind who just avoided colliding with us.

'I'd lost hope of finding you,' I said, looking at him. 'Jarmin told me to look for a ship's chandler.'

He grinned. 'Come with me, I'll show you where we are,' he said, turning around. 'Were you successful in Rye?' he asked, over his shoulder.

'We were,' I replied, falling into step with him. 'I'll tell you more when we are all together.'

'That's good. Kitty has been concerned.'

Ah, perhaps I will not tell everything that occurred and would hope for Fulton's discretion.

We walked back a few dozen yards until we came to an alley running down the side of a shop, unnamed with no merchandise in the window, explaining how I did not see it. On closer inspection, it did sell charts, maps, sextons, chronometers and such like to people who already knew it to be there. Monk guided me down to the door at the back which led up a flight of stairs to the first floor where I found Kitty looking out of the window, studying the street. The small room had just a table and stools, two upholstered chairs and a chest, with just plain wooden unpolished floorboards.

'Richard,' exclaimed Kitty, rushing towards me and flinging her arms around my shoulders.

I smiled and gripped her waist, feeling her against me. 'Anyone would have thought I had been away for weeks,' I said, after we kissed a welcome.

'It's just good to see you back in one piece.'

'For me too, I hope you didn't worry, I was in little danger. Tell me, why are you here?'

'Tewksley,' said Monk. 'We reckon he's gone to ground hereabouts.'

'How so?'

'A gentleman caught in the Joyners Street brothel wished to negotiate to save his reputation. Tewksley has various properties and one of them is just over there,' said Monk, pointing to the other side of the street and along a little. 'That warehouse is empty at the moment but someone is sleeping there. I went in yesterday to take a look.'

'He wasn't there last night?'

'No,' said Monk, shaking his head.

'Then he could have moved on?'

'Unlikely. Whoever it is has bedding, food, drink, money and there were bandages. Ned and I found a ship's surgeon, a drunk looking for work; he took the ball from Tewksley's shoulder. This surgeon is in a lodging house a few streets away. I don't think Tewksley will go far; he might need to see him again.'

I nodded. 'How come you to be here?'

Monk grinned. 'Let us say that the Chandler is what you might call indebted to Jarmin.'

'For what?'

Monk shrugged his shoulders. 'You don't ask that sort of question. Jarmin has quite the network.'

'I see,' I replied, wondering what the man downstairs had done. 'We wait then. Where's Ned?'

Monk nodded to my first statement then said. 'Ned is around the back of the warehouse, along the dock. There is another entrance there. We change places every couple of hours.'

'So, Richard,' began Kitty. 'What of you?'

I grinned. 'As Jarmin was informed. The Hawkhurst Gang were smuggling with the Spanish…'

I then gave the details of what we discovered and how we resolved it with the destruction of the merchant ship by the Navy, ending with the farm near Stockwell. Needless to say, I did not mention Ellen or my involvement with her. Kitty was not the jealous type and knew about my other liaisons, even so, I will keep this one quiet.

I turned back to Monk. 'Philip, why are you here? Do not get me wrong, I am not complaining, it's just that I would have thought Jarmin would have given you something else.'

He gave a rueful smile. 'I want to see this resolved. I asked and Jarmin allowed me to continue. After what I witnessed and learned of Tewksley's activities, I want nothing more than to see him pay for it.'

I dipped my head, understanding his feelings. 'Thank you, anyway.'

Monk exchanged places with Ned and when he came up I related my story again, for his benefit as Kitty gazed out of the window.

'I'd liked to have seen that,' he said, referring to the attack on the ships. 'All them guns spitting out their venom; mind, I wouldn't like to be on the receiving end of it.'

'No more would I,' I replied. 'All those men, dead; and for what?'

We lapsed into silence. I for one contemplated on the fragility of life, how quickly it could be snuffed out. All those men; alive one moment, dead the next. Their women and children would probably not yet be aware that they had now become widows and orphans, their men never to cross their thresholds again. The scale of the deaths disturbed me, the many dying in one incident that did not need to happen.

'You must be tired, Richard,' said Kitty, studying my face. 'Why don't you sleep?'

'Maybe I will for a while. I admit I am a bit sleepy.' In truth, I felt exhausted. Since Rye, I had only slept in short bursts which sustained me at the time; now, sitting in safety, I could feel the tiredness sweep over me, my eyes heavy with fatigue and as if Kitty had given me permission, I allowed my eyes to close.

When I awoke night had come, the room in darkness and I felt disorientated for a few moments. Kitty had woken me; she knelt with her hand on my arm, gripping it gently. Ned had replaced Monk on the dock and I could see Monk's silhouette against the window, fixed in place.

'What time is it?' I asked, yawning.

'About nine,' replied Kitty.

'Nine? I have slept too long.' I made to get up.

'Don't worry. Philip thinks Tewksley has come,' she said, pushing my arm down.

I slumped back and stared at her.

'I just saw a flicker of light in a window. Unlikely to be a reflection,' said Monk, from his vantage point.

'Then Ned must have seen him enter, if you did not.'

'It's possible I missed him. It's busy down there and the lack of light.'

'It matters not,' I replied, easing forward and standing up, alert once again. 'You know your job better than I. If you think he's there then I am not about to argue.'

'We'll know shortly; I can see Ned coming across the street.'

The three of us turned expectantly as Ned came through the door.

'Someone's there,' he said, breathlessly. 'It could be just a drunk looking for a place to rest his head, staggering all over the place, he was; definitely the worse fer something.'

'Drunk?' My heart sank a little. 'I cannot see Tewksley as a drunkard.'

'Mebbee it ain't him but it's someone,' replied Ned. 'I didn't take much notice of him at first, then he sort of fell through the door. I waited for a few minutes to see if he came out again but he didn't.'

'Then we had best find out who he is,' I said.

'You go with Ned, Richard,' said Monk. 'Kitty can stay here and I'll go through the front.'

'No I won't,' protested Kitty, a determination in her tone. 'I'll come with you, Philip, whether you like it or not.'

He had little time to argue and I knew Monk would only lose anyway. Maybe he still had a little to learn about women and Kitty in particular.

'We have lanterns?' I asked, checking my jacket for my pistol.

'Yes,' said Monk. 'Two small ones. Over there,' he added, pointing to a sack on the floor.

We lit the lanterns, shuttered like those Ellen had used and ran down the stairs. As soon as we came out of the alley, Ned and I ran across the street as Monk and Kitty went down it. The evening economy had begun with those out carousing visiting the alehouses and taverns, while jades sought custom and we threaded our way between it all, hands pawing us as we passed; some of them beggars, other jades. Ned led, as I had no idea of where we had to go, so I followed as we dipped down a dark and odious alley until we came onto the dock. I looked left and right and saw a line of warehouses set back from the edge of the dock; the acrid stench of the lime kilns more prominent here as if the river itself drew the foul odour. Some warehouses still worked, with lights shining from within aiding the workers as they hurried to finish their tasks. The side of the dock, littered with detritus, could easily catch someone unaware, pitching them over the edge and into the water.

Ned led me to the door of the disused warehouse, a dark and dank wooden construct with big double doors, a small wicket door set within them. It was locked, so he handed me the lantern and delved into his jacket. Producing the implement he searched for, he set to work. A few scrapes later I heard a click and the door swung open.

Inside loomed a cavern-like space, smelling musty and damp. I shone the light into the dark and saw the remnants of what used to be kept there; split sacks, piles of small rocks and powder, broken wooden implements, rusty tools, everything in decay and obviously forgotten. And the rats, always there were rats.

A similar light to mine appeared opposite and I knew that Monk and Kitty had gained entry. We walked towards each other, careful of our footing amongst the rubbish and the scampering rodents, until the stairs came into view. The four of us stood looking up and then Monk nodded and pointed.

Monk led the way, taking the treads carefully, conscious of keeping any noise to the minimum, despite the creaks and groans coming from the wooden steps. In single file we climbed the stairs, stepping into an open space at the top. I could see a winching contraption above a trapdoor, presumably to draw heavy items from the ground floor up to here. I could see doors at the back of the building and Monk beckoned us forward, angling over to the one he suspected contained Tewksley.

I drew my pistol, handed the lantern to Kitty and gave her a supportive grin. She looked a little anxious as we hesitated outside the door, as I suspected we all did in that moment, waiting to find out what lay beyond.

Monk and I exchanged glances and then he reached forward, grasping the door's handle. My heart began to race in expectation and I took a deep breath as the door began to swing open.

A pale light shone through the gap as Monk levelled his pistol and took a step inside. I followed just behind and as I cleared the door, I could see a man cowering in the corner, his back against the joining of the walls, wrapped in a blanket.

Tewksley.

Even in the dim light I could see the state of him; pale, shivering, his breathing rapid, beads of sweat upon his brow. He looked at me through hooded eyes, a vacant look as if our presence had not yet registered in his mind. He had one hand outside the blanket and it trembled as it gripped a pistol. A sweet sickly odour of decay emanated from him.

'Roger Tewksley,' I said, to get his attention. 'We have been searching for you.'

His eyes took on a focus and his head lifted a little, rolling on his neck. He cackled then, a harsh grating noise of indifference. 'And now your quest is over,' he replied, sniffing and coughing. 'Though what good it will do you, I don't know.' A statement, not a question.

'He's ill,' said Kitty, taking a step forward.

Ned put an arm out to prevent her moving towards the man. 'No closer,' he warned. 'He's still capable.'

'Of what?' asked Tewksley, turning his head languidly to look at Ned. He cackled again. 'She's hardly what I look for.'

I heard Kitty suck in a breath of disgust where moments ago she had a little sympathy.

'You need a doctor, Tewksley. We will make sure you are treated for what ails you,' I said.

'Doctor?' he answered. 'Doctor? Seeing a doctor got me into this state, that and the ball you put into me, Hopgood. That dirty drunken man shoving his filthy fingers, his rust-riven knives, into my shoulder. Did you know it's agony in its purest form?'

'So I hear,' I replied.

'Five guineas it cost. For what, eh? Sitting in my own filth as the wound festers. If it was my arm it could be cut off, the canker taken away. This is what you've made of me, Hopgood. I hope you are satisfied.'

'You made this yourself,' said Monk, answering for me. 'I've read all the ledgers, all the books, the notes. It's all there, what you've been up to. All those children, their lives ruined before they could begin.'

'Ruined? I prepared them. Showed them what their future would entail. Hardly ruin, it was education.'

I found my head shaking slowly at the absurdity of his reply. 'You delude yourself if that is what you think. It was plain abuse of innocents to satisfy your, and others' perverted inclinations.'

'Willing they were,' he replied, without remorse. 'There was no abuse.'

I found myself shaking my head, knowing that answering back would be a waste of time. His warped mind could not see the truth of what he had done. 'What of Pieter van Hoebeek, Tewksley?' I asked instead.

Tewksley's breathing began to get more ragged as if the effort of speaking was getting too much. 'What of him?' he asked, a sly grin coming to his lips.

'Why did you kill him? We know you argued with him outside your house.'

He did not reply for a few moments, just stared at me. 'He loved my wife, you know. Infatuated with her. Kept trying to get her to leave me, go back to him. The irony is that he didn't know her. You think I did everything myself?' He shook his head a little. 'Has my wife bedded you yet, Hopgood? No?' he asked, watching my face for a reaction. 'She will, like she has bedded half of London: men, women, boys, girls. All of them, everyone is an opportunity for her. She persuaded me to open those places, helped me, encouraged me and participated actively on occasions when one took her fancy. Van Hoebeek knew nothing of that, and he accused *me* of being depraved and deviant!'

'Which you are,' spat Kitty.

He cackled again, triggering a hacking cough. The sweat began to pour off his forehead and the shivering became worse. The hand holding the pistol jerked as a tremor ran through him and he looked up at me as the coughing eased.

'Did I kill Van Hoebeek, Hopgood? Did I tell him about my wife? I think there are some things you will never know...'

His hand moved again, this time raising the pistol. Before I could move, he placed the barrel in his mouth, angled upwards towards his head, his eyes lucid and clear as they met mine.

He pulled the trigger.

The firing pan flared as the hammer came down, lighting the powder in the barrel, exploding in an ear-deafening roar, accelerating the ball at maximum velocity down the barrel until it met the soft flesh of his mouth. Tewksley's head jerked as the back of his head exploded in blood, brains, skin, bone and hair, splattering the walls behind him as if a pot of paint had been thrown. The lifeless body toppled to the side, the noise still reverberating, the blood and matter dripping down the walls. The pistol, now no longer being held, dropped to the floor.

Behind me, I heard Kitty gagging, Ned retching and Monk taking a long calming breath. I felt bile rise to my throat and fought to keep the contents of my stomach from coming up. Ned could not contain himself as I heard him then vomit. The sickly-sweet smell of blood became noticeable, mixing in with the odour of Tewksley's contagion and Ned's expulsion, making the air heavy and nauseous.

Monk recovered the quickest. He removed the pistol and then quickly searched the body; just a purse with a few coins and a pouch of tobacco. We then left the room hurriedly, none of us wanting to prolong our stay.

We stood for a good few minutes outside the door regaining our composure, each of us looking at the others, hardly speaking.

Ned wiped his mouth with his sleeve and took a breath. 'That went well,' he said, somewhat ironically.

Monk barked a laugh, forcing the humour.

We moved downstairs to the front door where the noise of the gunshot had drawn a crowd. As we came out I looked at the curious assembly.

'Is there a Constable or Watchman hereabouts?' I asked, searching the faces.

Several members of the crowd laughed.

'A Constable? Here?' came a scathing reply and then a laugh. 'Sod all chance of that, my bene cove.'

If we left now there would just be a naked body to find later, the opportunists would take everything, probably even his teeth. I could not allow that to happen, despite what I thought of the man. 'Ned, go to St Anne's church and find the rector. Get him to organise the removal of the body. You go with him, Kitty. It will take your mind off what we just witnessed.'

Monk and I secured the warehouse and it took a bit of effort and a few threats to stop the people from forcing their way in to satisfy their curiosity.

We sat just inside with the door locked and waited. Slowly, with nothing to see, the crowd dispersed, bored at standing around when they could be doing things of far more interest.

An hour or more passed before Ned and Kitty returned with the rector, a cart and two more men. Word soon spread that something was about to happen and the people began to gather again; the curious and the inquisitive all speculating, newly immersed in the entertainment.

Ushering the rector and his men inside I closed the door. Ned had explained the circumstances so I had no need to embellish what had already been said, so Monk and Ned guided the rector and the men upstairs to remove the body.

'Are you alright?' I asked Kitty, as we waited at the door, my arm around her shoulders.

She nodded. 'I'm better now, Richard,' she said, giving me a sad smile. 'This mob outside, I never imagined being on the receiving end. They just want a glimpse of the body.'

'Then they will be disappointed. Tewksley will be

wrapped.'

A few minutes later I could hear the bumps as the men dragged the body down the stairs then put it into the waiting cart.

'Thank you, Rector,' I said, as they made ready to leave.

'Not a pretty sight, Mr Hopgood. The man deserved his demise by what I've been told.'

'And more, Rector. I will inform the authorities; no doubt a coroner will attend at some point.'

He nodded and then I opened the door to see a sea of faces, all craning their necks to get a better view.

'We should sell tickets for this,' suggested Ned. 'Make a bloody fortune, we would.'

CHAPTER 38

To say I welcomed the ale would have been an understatement; I just desired to sit and relax for a few moments, ordering my thoughts, getting things in perspective.

We arrived a little late at the White Hart and the four of us sat nursing our drinks at a table, amongst those who had lately been entertained at the theatre, all the booths already taken. It had already been decided that Ned and I would rest our heads next door in Kitty's lodging. Monk would take a hackney to Westminster to report and catch up on proceedings there.

Ned studied his ale intensely and thoughtfully. 'Never seen the like of that; the way the head just exploded. I'm sorry I disgraced myself, sir,' he said, once he had found his voice.

'No matter,' I replied. 'I nearly joined you.'

'And me,' admitted Kitty.

We three turned to look at Monk who just shrugged. 'Seen similar before; you tend to get used to it after a while,' he said, not unsympathetically.

We lapsed into silence again, contemplating. I could still see the back of Tewksely's head as it blew apart as if time had slowed down, hear the report of the pistol as the noise echoed, smell the stench that even now seemed ingrained into my nostrils. I took a large swallow of my ale. 'It still has not resolved the issue of who killed Van Hoebeek,' I said. 'He admitted nothing, denied nothing.'

'Except for what he did to those children,' said Kitty. 'He seemed proud of it.'

'He knew that festering wound would kill him before justice came calling. He must have hated his wife to implicate her so, so why not admit to murder?' I said, trying to reason it out.

I had neglected the murder over the last few days. The Hawkhurst Gang, Ellen, both had taken over my mind and left Van Hoebeek a poor third. I resolved now to put that right and finally solve the mystery of who killed the Dutchman.

'He was playing with you, sir,' opined Ned. 'He knew what he were going to do, kill himself, I mean. He just wanted to make it difficult for you.'

'Perhaps,' I answered, still thinking it through.

Who would gain the most? I thought. Who would stand to profit, or in Tewksley's case, would have profited? I felt certain I had already met the killer, had interaction with them. Could I dismiss Tewksley now that he was dead?

'Time for me to go,' said Monk, draining his pot and standing up.

Kitty stood up too. 'Thank you, Philip,' she said, moving towards him. She placed a hand on his arm and I saw him smile. 'For all you've done,' she added, kissing him lightly on the cheek.

'Just another day's work,' he replied, nodding at Ned and I. 'Tomorrow then, Richard,' he added. 'Jarmin will be expecting you.'

'Are you and Philip, er…?' I asked, once he had gone.

Kitty shook her head. 'He's nice, but no. Not like that couple there,' she said, indicating a woman who stroked a man's arm.

'You just did that to Philip.'

'Not in the same way. Those two will be in bed together within the hour.'

Despite my tiredness, something made my mind jerk, niggling at me, something I should take notice of. When I tried to bring it to conscious thought it stayed elusive, just a fingertip away. Perhaps tomorrow it would occur to me.

'One more, I think,' I said, studying my empty pot.

'And then bed,' replied Kitty, stroking my arm and giving me a wink.

I saw Ned fumble in his jacket. 'Oh, sir. I forgot. This came for you when you were away.'

He handed me a note, sealed. I opened it and read that Cornelia Visser invites me to call on her — insisting I call upon her, with the promise that my pleasure would be at the forefront of her mind. I screwed it up and stuffed it into the pocket of my jacket.

We finished our drinks and made our way to Kitty's where Ned made himself comfortable on the sofa whilst Kitty and I adjourned to the bedroom.

I quickly undressed and fell straight into bed, my eyes heavy but not so heavy that I could not watch Kitty disrobe by the flickering light of the single candle. A Venus undoubtedly with her tiny waist, her soft rounded buttocks, her tapering legs. She raised her arms to untie her hair and I gazed at her sculptured neck and shoulders, sensual, especially when she let her silky hair cascade down her back, caressing her skin. She turned, pulled back the blanket and climbed in, kissing me before turning so that we snuggled together like two spoons in a drawer.

She settled against me. 'You're not too tired then,' she said, provocatively moving her hips.

Plainly, I was not.

I arrived at Westminster to find Jarmin leaning over the table, studying a hand-drawn map, another to his side. Fulton and Monk occupied themselves by cleaning pistols. Bram and George Blake sat in chairs, watching Jarmin.

'Ah, Richard,' said Jarmin, looking up from the map. 'A shame that your man Tewksley blew his brains out.'

'A shame? I would put it on another level. A deviant who should have faced his peers and suffered the consequences. He died far too quickly for proper justice.'

'And you still haven't found your murderer. Do you think it was him?'

I shrugged my shoulders. 'I wish I knew for certain.'

He gave a slow nod of the head. 'You may still find him; it could be De Griese or Jaggers. Now, to change the subject. Look at this and see if it matches your memory.'

He had already dismissed Tewksley and my Dutchman but Jarmin worked that way; he just concentrated on what was important to him. I walked over, nodded to Bram and Blake, and viewed a rough map of the farm.

I nodded. 'From what I remember, it seems accurate; you've added some details that I did not see.'

'Good; Henry, Fulton and I went late yesterday. We managed to get various viewpoints before it got too dark. Most of the horses and men had left so I think that the rest would have gone by now. Hopefully, there will be only a small number left for us to deal with.'

'Just the six of us?' I asked, thinking we may be a little light.

Jarmin shook his head. 'No, there should be forty of us. Others are waiting by the river. Militia, the Trained Band again, just wearing their red bands about their arms. They seemed good men and worked well the other night.'

'How do we proceed, then?' The more men we had, the more comfortable I felt.

Jarmin grinned. 'We will split into four groups. I will lead one here,' he said, pointing to the main track leading into the farm. 'I envisage a couple of guards at least, seeing that they have just received a consignment. Bram will take one here,' he added, pointing to the field opposite the entrance. Monk and Fulton will take another here,' he said, pointing to a small copse to the north. 'Blake and you will go here,' he said, pointing to the south, close to where Fulton and I had been. 'Fortunately, there is cover all around the farm, good for them regarding seclusion but good for us too. Each of us to deploy men at the rear of the barns to prevent escape, preferably armed with pistols. The farm is in Stockwell Common, just south of the village.' He pulled the other map over. 'Here,' he said, dabbing his finger. 'This is Loughborough House; apparently a school for young gentlemen; judging by some of the young gentlemen I know they must teach gambling and whoring as part of the curriculum. This is the village of Cold Harbour, the road here goes up to the house. We will assemble here in Camberwell Lane and then divide. There are lanes and tracks to allow us through the wet ground so we should be able to approach the farm without too much trouble. If we came from the north, we would be seen as the ground is fairly open. It will be just a short walk for us as we will disembark at Vauxhall, near Nine Elms. We will assemble first and then go to the designated positions to await my move into the farm. You will have no doubt when that occurs, I assure you. If you need to fire weapons, then make sure you hit them and not us. Does that seem easy enough?'

I nodded. 'It does. I'll be guided by George as you undoubtedly have been through this with him several times. Why do we not use horses and carriages?'

'Too much noise,' replied Jarmin. 'Too much of a chance to be seen. This way will be better. Don't worry, once we have taken the farm we will have transport; that has already been arranged.'

'When do we go?'

'No time like the present,' he said, folding the maps. 'Boats are already waiting.'

Just off Parliament Stairs by Timber Wharf, several wherries waited, ignoring the few people waiting to cross who signalled with rising impatience at the assembled flotilla. Many of the Militia had already arrived and had gathered just down from the stairs. As I arrived, the last of the stragglers turned up.

The river looked angry, the grey waters whipped into a

rolling sequence of waves by the wind. The overcast sky, the clouds lined by dark streaks, appeared threatening, looking like it could rain at any moment.

Jarmin began to divide the men into groups. The Militia had been given just scant details and it would be down to the group leaders to acquaint them properly when we alighted on the south side of the river.

Blake and I gathered our ten men and took two wherries, each with a pair of oarsmen. Aware that something was occurring, but not exactly what, our rowers asked their probing questions. Fortunately, little response came from the militiamen, as in truth, they knew little of the task ahead of them. The choppy waters rolled, rocked and bounced the boat, making it seem unstable. Hands grasped anything, the gunwale, the seat, or the nearest man, to get a feeling of safety. Our oarsmen grinned at the men's discomfiture, comfortable with their knowledge and experience with the water; I got the impression that they manoeuvred the vessel for the maximum discomfort.

Slightly nauseous, we stepped off at the stairs. I waited for Bake with the rest of our group and then walked up towards Spring Gardens to gather in the tree-covered ground adjacent to it. Blake explained to the group what we had to do and received a mixed response, judging by the expressions on their faces. I could sympathise a little as most of London took advantage of the cheap prices and to hear that they would now put a stop to a large amount of contraband did not sit easily on their minds. I assured them that the trade would still continue, regardless of how many of the crew we would take into custody. That seemed to appease them and we left before they had a chance to think further on it.

I felt a frisson of anticipation as I took that first step along the road. Blake had a rudimentary map and he guided us along the trackways and lanes crossing the marsh, over the fields and through copses. The few people we saw must have wondered at the reason for the appearance of all these men.

It took an hour or so to reach Camberwell Lane and then we just had to wait until we all assembled, only for us to divide up again and make our way to the farm.

'Are you ready for this?' asked Blake, rubbing his shoulder as we set off across a field.

'I am,' I replied, walking beside him. 'I just hope that who I want to be there, is there.'

'This De Griese?'

'And Jaggers. Both of whom I consider to be dangerous.'

'Likely to be armed?'

'Of a certainty.'

'Should make things interesting then,' he replied. He turned his head to the man behind. 'Come on, hurry up.'

The soggy ground made walking heavy and difficult with mud and muck clinging to our boots as if wading through a sea of molasses. Eventually, we gained the further side of the field and found it a lot drier and it gave us a chance to rid our boots of the weight of mud that clung to them.

As we closed on our objective, I bid the men to keep quiet and to make ready whatever weapon they carried. Blake and I led the men forward, through a gap in the hedge and we eased along, keeping low with the hedge to our right.

I could see the scrub of bushes where Fulton and I had watched the farm just ahead; Jarmin had placed us a little further down, where the scrub divided to allow ingress and egress into the field.

I felt an increase in my nerves now, a heightened sense of anticipation. I breathed quicker and I had to make an effort to slow it down. I looked at the men around me; some licked their lips as if all moisture had departed, others repeatedly touched their swords, knives and cudgels. Four had pistols and I hoped they would not discharge them accidentally.

Blake waved the men down and put his finger to his lips to indicate silence, then he rubbed his shoulder and beckoned me forward into the scrub where we could look at the farm.

We lay on our bellies and studied the view. Straight ahead was the farmhouse, so we had a limited view of the yard, seeing just the right-hand side of it. I could see no contraband stacked, waiting to be stored.

Jarmin appeared to be correct as the men from the coast and their packhorses had gone. The farm had become a calm enclave with little activity. I saw one man amble across to a barn on the right, lift the latch and enter, leaving the door ajar. Apart from that movement, everything else seemed still.

Blake whispered in my ear. 'Ready?' he asked.

I nodded, feeling the sweat on my hand as I held my pistol. I took a deep breath, waiting for Jarmin to make his announcement. Time slowed down and I began to feel more nervous, my mouth becoming dry. I raised myself into a crouch, feeling my knees creak, poised to sprint into the yard.

Minutes passed and I began to wonder if something had happened, maybe Jarmin had got lost so I turned my head to Blake and mouthed the question. He just grinned and held up a hand to wait.

Suddenly, I heard the report of a gunshot, quickly followed by another coming from the right-hand side, where the entrance to the farm met the lane, shattering the peace and tranquillity. The man I saw entering the barn rapidly exited and looked bemusedly around before giving a shout of alarm and running across the yard, disappearing from view.

'Now,' yelled Blake, perhaps a bit too close to my ear for comfort.

I leapt up, my ear still ringing and from behind I could hear the men following. In their excitement, they raised their voices as if in battle, whooping and yelling, the sound intending to give themselves confidence in the upcoming encounter or to issue a warning announcing that a great horde descended.

A man came running into the yard as if he had the very devil on his heels and then Jarmin and his men appeared, brandishing their weapons, a fierce expression on their faces. One of Jarmin's men stopped, raised his pistol, took aim and fired, just missing the running smuggler who managed to get into a barn unscathed. Two of my men went to the rear of the farmhouse to prevent anyone leaving whilst the rest of us came to the side of the house. Opposite me I saw Fulton and Monk running in between two barns, their men fanning out to each side, all looking wary. Bram came from my left, unhurriedly, calmly, as if for a Sunday stroll, the men behind him, ambling at the same sedate pace.

The whole of the farm complex should now be secure with men at the rear, armed and ready for any escapees.

Blake jabbed a finger at the first three men to take control of the old barn immediately to our right where the man had exited and I watched as they eased tentatively towards it, expecting the worst. My attention moved towards the noise of men yelling, then another gunshot echoed across the yard and I ducked, not knowing from where it came. I felt my heart banging in my chest, my mouth dry, my nerves jangling as across the yard I saw two men emerge from another barn, both with pistols. They took a quick look at what confronted them then hastily withdrew, back to shelter, slamming the door as Fulton shouted an instruction to his men and a small group ran towards the door with Monk. A shouted command to come out received no reply so two pistols were discharged, the balls travelling into the depths of the barn, splintering the wood as they passed through. Blake grabbed my arm, diverting my attention and ushered me to the front of the farmhouse, the intention to swarm in and catch anyone there.

Bram deployed his men to search the two buildings close by whilst he stood nonchalantly at the side of the yard, his eyes missing nothing, taking everything in.

Blake and I quickly looked at each other before approaching the door, the five men close behind. We each stood to the side and I reached out, pushed at the door and it began to swing inwards. A blast of gunshot came from within, peppering the door, splintering the timber and we all ducked in reflex.

'Are you alright?' yelled Jarmin, just a few yards away.

Blake turned. 'We are,' he replied. 'No damage.'

Apart from the door, I thought wryly.

Blake beckoned the two men behind who had pistols. 'We are going to push the door again and fire blindly; are you ready?'

The two nodded, albeit hesitantly.

'Here,' I said to one. 'Stand behind me.' The other went behind Blake.

'Ready?' asked Blake as he nodded to me.

I hardly felt ready as I swallowed nervously, hesitated a second then, pushed the remains of the door open and all four of us aimed into the gap and pulled our triggers.

The noise of four pistols being discharged in close proximity and virtually together deafened my ears and I could feel a pressure as if they would explode. They still hurt moments later as Blake took a chance and peered in.

'Got him,' said Blake, his voice seeming a little muffled.

Behind me in the yard, I heard shouts of triumph and I turned to look, seeing Monk emerging from his barn with two men, both now disarmed and pleading for their lives.

I returned my attention to the inside of the farmhouse and as I stepped in I could see a man lying sprawled on the floor, groaning, a musket fallen beside him. He appeared to be in the process of reloading as one of our shots hit him, blood ran in ribbons from his chest. We stood in a large room; an oak table with four stools, two ripped upholstered chairs, a dresser stacked with cooking equipment, a hearth with pots for boiling; the bare floor, dusty, dirty and splintered. A home for a family, who would have eaten, drank and talked, but many a year had passed since those times.

Blake kicked the musket aside and the two men reloaded their pistols as I looked at the only other door inside the room. I still had two more shots, the advantage of a repeater. The house had an ominous feel, my nerves on edge, waiting because I expected another shot to come from the other room.

The man continued to moan and writhe on the floor.

'Where are the rest,' demanded Blake, giving him a nudge with his boot.

'Help me,' he responded weakly.

'Not yet,' replied Blake. 'Not until you answer.'

The man moved his head and looked at the inner door.

'Through there?' Blake asked.

The man gave a slight nod, his loyalty disappearing rapidly with his injury.

'How many?'

'Two,' he said, the effort causing him to cough, releasing a flow of blood from the corner of his mouth, his eyes screwing up in pain.

I stepped tentatively forwards, to the side, away from directly in front of the door, the wall against my shoulder. I reached for the latch, raised it and then pushed, turning quickly, pressing my back against the wall, waiting and expecting gunshots from within.

Nothing happened.

Blake pulled one man forward. 'Keep an eye on this one,' he ordered, pointing to the shot man. 'If he gives trouble then finish him off.'

'Don't think he's capable of that, looks near dead to me,' he replied, pointing a sword to the chest.

I eased to the door, took a breath and holding my pistol out straight, risked a look into the other room; fortune favoured me again as no shots came my way. Crates, bales, packages and bottles filled the room, stacked and layered, some split open, empty bottles scattered but no men to threaten me.

A trapdoor broke the contour of the floor; if the injured man told the truth, then this would be how they had got out. Blake stood at my shoulder giving a thoughtful murmur.

'What do you think?' I asked, keeping my eye on the trapdoor. Outside I heard the discharge of more weapons, our heads turning briefly in that direction.

'Not our concern,' said Blake, snapping his head back. 'I'm thinking,' he continued, gazing at the trapdoor, his hand going unknowingly to his shoulder. 'That like it or not, we have to go down there.'

I gave a rueful grin knowing that he was correct and in truth, I did not look forward to it.

'Stand back,' said Blake, leaning forward and grabbing the rope handle.

He pulled up quickly and the opening appeared, the door flying back on its hinges and crashing against the floor.

I could see wooden steps leading down into the cellar, a weak illumination coming from below; a lantern. We stood for a moment listening for sounds denoting occupation; a sniff, a cough, a scraping of a foot. Hearing nothing, Blake took the initiative and began to walk down, peering low and taking his time, step by step. He took the last step and then crouched, pistol out before him, sweeping the cellar.

'No one here,' he said, quietly.

I hastened down the steps to join him, the four men left behind, waiting. The cellar spread out before me, like the room above, stacked with contraband. As I thought, a lantern glowed from a shelf giving just enough light to see. Ahead, on the far side, I could see another opening, this one in darkness.

A tunnel.

Blake looked up. 'One of you go to Jarmin and tell him what we are about. There is a tunnel here leading somewhere; we will explore it.'

To me, the tunnel did not look safe. Wooden struts supported the roof and sides from the ingress of earth, weak-looking struts at that. Water dripped making the floor damp; whoever had dug this through marshland had taken a great risk. In the mud on the floor, I could see footprints and two parallel tracks as if something had been dragged along — a sled maybe.

'You three. Follow behind us,' said Blake, to the three men who now warily descended the steps from the trapdoor.

Somehow, I led the way, though I did not think Blake contrived it, after all, he had braved the trapdoor and cellar. I had to bend my head and crouch to enter the low opening and I took half a step into the darkness, looking intently, wary. I sensed movement behind me and then I had a lantern thrust into my hand. I eased forward, pistol in one hand, lantern in the other, step by tentative step. As I moved forward my senses heightened, listening for sounds, expecting the worst. I swallowed nervously, not relishing walking into the unknown but determined to live through it. Another few steps and still nothing happened and now the light from the lantern showed an opening ahead. I approached to within a few feet and then stopped, hesitant to go further forward. Blake nudged me from behind and I turned my head slightly to say something then thought better of it. I took a breath and stepped through the opening.

Another cellar, more contraband and no light other than

the lantern I held — more to the point, no gunshots either.

I looked up, hearing footsteps above and then indistinct voices arguing. Blake and I exchanged glances and then he pointed to the steps leading up to another trapdoor, this one large to accommodate the lowering of bigger quantities of goods, I presumed.

The crack of a gun being discharged came from upstairs and I ducked in reflex.

'Over here, sir,' said one of the men, quietly. 'Another tunnel.'

Blake hurried over and looked inside. 'Bring the lantern over, Richard.'

Mindful of what was going on above, I rushed over, holding the lantern out.

'Blocked,' observed Blake. 'The roof has fallen in.'

'Recent?' I asked, looking in.

He shook his head. 'I don't think so; could have been like this for a while.'

Another shot and we all crouched down, our faces looking up.

'We can't sit here,' said Blake. 'It's either go back or go up.'

Instinctively, I thought to go back, the safer option. We had no knowledge of how things stood up there, nor how many men. It seemed suicidal to me to venture into something unknown. I opened my mouth to voice my opinion when I heard hurried footsteps clatter onto the trapdoor. A moment later the decision was taken out of our hands as the trapdoor lifted.

Light flooded in, then the crashing of the door as it

slammed against the floor. A figure appeared in the aperture holding a musket, a man with black-grey hair, wide-eyed and burly. Blake and I stared for a moment then brought our pistols up together.

I saw the momentary shock on the face of the man and then the features turned to hatred. He brought the musket up just as we aimed and fired together; the cracks of the pistols reverberated, the noxious smell of gunpowder infused the air and both balls hit him full in the chest, flinging him backwards and out of sight, the musket clattering where it dropped.

'One down,' said Blake, a fierce grin on his face. He began to reload straight away.

I signalled the three men behind me. 'Get out of sight,' I ordered.

They quickly scattered, needing no further encouragement, into the bales and crates around the floor, seeking cover, self-preservation foremost in their minds and I could not blame them.

I heard a movement above and then another shot, this one coming from outside the building, then a crack as a ball hit a wall and I imagined stone splinters flying.

Blake calmly continued loading as I aimed into the gap, my finger poised on the trigger, ready should anyone appear.

Footsteps patterned the floor above and then they stopped. A few seconds of peace followed until a disembodied voice broke the silence.

'We seem to be at an impasse, gentlemen,' said a man, almost conversationally. 'You come up and we'll shoot you.'

I could not place the accent. Blake finished loading and

shrugged when I looked at him.

'But you cannot come down or go outside, otherwise *you* will be shot,' I replied, keeping my voice calm, despite my jangling nerves. 'Lay down your weapons and you will be treated fairly, I assure you,' I continued.

The man gave a harsh humourless laugh. 'Really, you expect me to believe that?'

'You have no choice,' I replied, staring up.

'There is always a choice,' said the man. 'I just have to pick the right one.'

'He's playing with us,' said Blake, quietly. 'It's giving him time to think.'

I heard Jarmin's voice, shouting from outside, echoing my instructions for the men to lay down their weapons and to leave the building.

I heard a quiet, urgent, fraught discussion. I could discern at least three different voices, maybe more, all trapped with no hope of escape. The men moved away from the trapdoor so I could not listen to what they discussed.

Sporadic shots resumed from outside when Jarmin received no reply, just random shots in hope, probably unaimed.

'Very well,' said the voice, now closer to the trapdoor. 'We will put down our weapons. You may come up.'

'I don't believe him,' said Blake, quietly.

'Nor do I,' I replied. 'Why not just shout to Jarmin?'

'Exactly. He's up to something.'

'But what?'

'I don't know. I suppose there's only one way to find out.'

I nodded, not relishing putting my head through the

trapdoor; my heart pounded in my chest at the prospect, my mouth still without moisture.

'Stand where I can see you,' ordered Blake.

I heard some shuffling and four men came into view.

'Show me your hands,' said Blake, taking the first step.

Pistol out in front of him, Blake climbed up.

I recognised two of the men. De Griese and Jaggers stood with their hands visible as I came through the opening, De Griese's eyebrows rising a little in mild curiosity. Jaggers on the other hand showed stark hostility.

'Come up,' I said to the three men below.

We stood in a large barn, the back wall made of stone blocks, the rest, of timber. A high roof with supports and a level reached by a ladder along three of the sides. Contraband lay in piles and stacks, and I could smell alcohol and tobacco, spices too.

Blake manoeuvred towards the door, giving the four men a wide berth, whilst I kept my pistol raised and pointing at each in turn, ready to pull the trigger.

The three militiamen came up and spread apart, the two with pistols aiming warily as they took up a position to the left of me, the third carrying a large-bladed knife, moved to my right.

Outside, a hubbub of shouts and curses filled the yard, rising in intensity. Blake had reached the door and with one hand tried to lift the inside locking bar. He called out to Jarmin and then swore when he got no reply.

De Griese kept his eyes on me, smiling as though he knew something that I did not. His gaze swept momentarily over to Blake and then returned to me. 'This is all very inconvenient,

Mr Hopgood; how did you find us?'

I sniffed. 'I have been following you since Rye.'

'Rye, you were there?'

I nodded. 'You even walked past me once.'

'Did I? Well, well, that is a surprise. You should have made yourself known, we could have had a nice little conversation,' he said, still with that irksome smile on his face.

'I am not so sure I would have enjoyed that,' I replied. 'I did not relish the company you kept.'

He chuckled. 'I take it then that you were one of the customs men down from London, the architect of the ship's destruction. All those lives lost down to you?'

I shook my head. 'No, not me. You and Grey, maybe.'

'Oh no, not me. You fired the guns. Grey was really put out about that, he wanted to tear the town apart looking for this last customs man until I persuaded him the folly of doing that. You have me to thank for being here today, you know. He planned to bury you alive, after beating you senseless first, of course.'

I felt a shiver run down my spine at the thought, knowing that Grey would not hesitate to do something like that. Ellen had told me how ruthless that gang could be. 'Then I thank you,' I replied, with a slight bow of my head.

Another chuckle came from his throat. 'Had I known it was you, then maybe I would not have been so persuasive.'

'That I do believe. However, it is too late now, De Griese; you missed your opportunity.'

'I did indeed, and now look at us. You have me at your mercy and here am I, compliant, without threat and cooperative.'

Jaggers emitted a snarling noise as his face screwed up in anger.

'Tom is most unhappy, Mr Hopgood. I apologise for his countenance. Though, considering the circumstances, I'm sure you understand.' He took a glance to his side. 'Tom, you must show a little more respect, after all, we agreed with this action of ours.' He turned back to me and I saw his hands and shoulders give a slight shrug.

I still did not trust De Griese and Jaggers; they were being too accepting of the situation. I knew we needed to get the door open to let Jarmin and the other men in. The noise outside began to abate and I shot Blake a look. 'George?'

'Stuck,' he replied, struggling to lift the bar with one hand. He grunted, putting a little more effort into it and the bar finally moved up. He opened his mouth to yell to Jarmin again and then what I was afraid would happen, did.

'Now,' shouted De Griese.

Jaggers and the other two men leapt forward, shouting and yelling. I still had my eyes on Blake so did not react quick enough to pull the trigger; I had diverted my attention, too slow as Jaggers crashed into me. I felt the breath knocked out of me as my back slammed onto the floor with the weight of the big man on top. Spittle splattered my face, the hot rancid breath just inches away as I felt a blow to my ribs, a knee pressing between my legs in an attempt to grind my nutmegs. A hand gripped my wrist of my pistol hand, preventing me from turning it. I swung a punch and connected with the side of his face and he grunted. I managed to move my leg and forced it up between his to reciprocate though I could get little force behind it. I could hear activity of a like nature to my side as the others fought. Blake yelled to De Griese to stand still, though it hardly registered in my mind being somewhat preoccupied. I gritted my teeth and stared into two hate-filled eyes then felt a hand move to grip my neck, ready to squeeze the life out of me. I writhed, determined to get him off balance. I had one hand free so I reached up and grabbed a fistful of hair and yanked violently, receiving a satisfying scream of pain as the hair parted company with his head. The pressure on my throat relaxed a little, so did the grip on my wrist and so I increased my writhing and managed to find the strength to push and twist him over so that he was half on his back. My pistol hand came free and I did not think twice as I pressed it into his torso and pulled the trigger. The noise reverberated inside the barn, the ball slicing through his insides to turn it to mush. Jaggers jerked through the initial pain and force of the ball and I heard a sharp guttural exhalation. His mouth twisted and grimaced, then his eyes became panicked and his back arched as he tried to suck in a breath. I took in a great lungful of air and climbed to my knees, looking down as Jaggers grabbed my arm, a look of abject fear now on his face. I could hear the noises of the others and l saw the knife-wielding militiaman thrust the cold steel blade into the side of one of the smugglers. Jaggers managed a gasp and as I looked, I saw his eyes cloud over as his life left him, the hand holding my arm flopping to the floor.

The stabbed smuggler cried out in pain and raised himself half upright just as Blake aimed and fired, the ball thumping into the man's back and he keeled over, collapsing onto the militiaman beneath him. The other smuggler threw a last punch as he caught sight of his now-dead friend and then scrambled to his feet, rushing to the trapdoor, intending to disappear into the void and the cellar below. The militiaman he fought quickly brought his pistol up and fired. The man let out a cry of pain and frustration just as reached the trapdoor, his momentum carrying him through and flinging him down the steps and I could hear the thumping as he bounced all the way to the floor of the cellar. De Griese had not moved until then but now he did. With three weapons now discharged he had only one to contend with and he rushed forward, pulling a pistol from the back of his breeches. He grabbed me as I still knelt and tried to catch my breath, dragging me to my feet, the pressure of the cold stark barrel now pressed into my neck.

'Hold,' ordered De Griese to the militiaman, the one on the floor with the loaded pistol. 'You have a habit of getting in the way, Mr Hopgood,' he said, jabbing the barrel into my neck.

I heard moaning and groaning coming from the cellar, then a cry of pain followed by a deep sigh petering out into silence. Jaggers and the other shot man just lay there, dead. Muskets and pistols fired from outside, the wooden door splintering as the balls came through. Blake ducked protectively, gave a grunt and doubled up as a ball slammed into him.

I looked on aghast; Blake had been shot, again; this time from his own side.

De Griese grabbed hold of my jacket and laughed, the pistol still in my neck.

'How fortunate,' he said, into my ear. 'It would appear luck is on my side after all.'

The militiaman with the still loaded pistol aimed it at De Griese, the barrel shaking and I knew the aim would be well off, a frightened man, not knowing what to do. I saw his gaze waver, a glance, quickly returning it in my direction. I wondered how quickly I could move, whether I could push the barrel away from my neck before it fired.

'Luck has just taken a walk,' said a voice behind. 'Lower the weapon. Gently now.'

I heard and felt an exhalation of breath on my face as if of resignation. The barrel withdrew and I felt the grip on my jacket relax. The weapon fell to the floor and I spun around.

Bram stood there, grinning, a pistol now against De Griese's neck. 'Thought I'd come through the tunnel, see what you and Blake were up to. Good job I did, eh?'

'What happened to the man down there?' I asked, looking at the trapdoor.

'Dead, if you mean the one at the bottom of the steps. Stuck my knife into him. Thought it might be prudent, under the circumstances.'

Blake groaned, grunted and twisted in pain, his shoulder temporarily forgotten.

'Bind this one,' ordered Bram to the nearest militiaman, giving De Griese a little shake. 'And make sure it's nice and tight, if you please.'

CHAPTER 39

Blake should thank the god of fortune. The ball that came through the barn door hit a thicker strut of wood so that it was largely spent as it hit him in the back. I lifted up his jacket and shirt to examine the wound and found the ball had not penetrated, no blood, just a livid bruise and a bit of swelling. He would certainly suffer pain and discomfort for the next few days until the bruise disappeared. Maybe he should keep the ball as a souvenir.

'I can't believe I've been shot again,' exclaimed Blake, as I helped him to rest against the barn wall.

'Just a bruise,' I replied, seeing the irony. 'No major damage done.'

Jarmin stood at the barn entrance with Fulton and several other men. He viewed the carnage with a practised eye.

Blake gave a sharp, shrill utterance of pain as I let him down, drawing Jarmin's attention.

'Is he alright?' he asked, looking at the pale face.

'He will be,' I said. 'One of you shot him; thankfully the ball did not penetrate.'

'One of us?' said Jarmin, surprised. 'Perhaps I should order more practice.'

I grinned and somehow Blake barked a laugh.

Jarmin strode across the floor to study the newly bound

De Griese; to the bodies littering the barn, he hardly gave a glance. 'Who is this, then,' he asked.

'De Griese,' I said, standing up and walking over. 'That's the name he has been using; whether that *is* his name, I do not know.'

Jarmin glanced at Bram who gave an almost imperceptible shake of the head.

'Well, Mr De Griese,' said Jarmin. 'It seems as if your little enterprise has come to an end. You and I must have a friendly discussion, very soon. I trust you will be talkative.'

De Griese smiled and I had the impression that he truly thought the prospect amusing.

I looked down at the body lying at my feet. Jaggers, one of my prime suspects for the murder of Van Hoebeek, lay dead. That made two so far and I now felt the frustration of my impetuous nature, self-preservation being wholly in my mind as I shot Jaggers just a few minutes ago. I only had De Griese left to question, maybe the only opportunity to find out the how and the why. I still had the feeling that smuggling and the Dutchman's death were connected in some way. I had to find the truth of it for my own peace of mind, if nothing else.

De Griese stood flanked by the armed men, seemingly relaxed, his demeanour quietly confident.

'Mr De Griese,' I said, facing him. 'Why did you murder Pieter Van Hoebeek?'

He smirked. 'Van Hoebeek, why would I kill him? A merchant, I believe.'

'You know of him, then?'

'Of him, Mr Hopgood. The man who knew him lies there,' he added, his head indicating Jaggers.

'In that case, did Jaggers follow your orders to eliminate a problem?'

'He was not a problem, Mr Hopgood. Not to me, anyway.'

'Then he was a problem to someone?'

'Obviously someone wished him dead; otherwise he would still be alive.' He still had the smirk on his face, enjoying himself.

'You wished me dead on London Bridge.'

'Ah, yes, that is true. I should have slid a knife between your ribs instead, but it seemed a good opportunity with the cart coming just then.'

'You're callous, De Griese.'

'Practical, Mr Hopgood.'

'What do you wish to happen to these men outside?' asked Fulton, coming into the barn.

Jarmin turned his head to look at him. 'Secure them and then send Monk to bring the transport. There must be a horse here somewhere.'

Fulton nodded then looked at me. 'Nice to see you're still here, Richard. Where's George?'

'Over here,' replied Blake, a catch of pain in his voice. 'I've been shot again, probably by you.'

Fulton looked surprised. 'Me?'

'Someone shot him from outside,' I said. 'Don't be concerned, the ball was spent when it hit him.'

'Bugger me, better pack the powder better next time.'

'Jarmin has already intimated something similar,' I said, finding a grin on my lips.

'Ah, never mind, George. We all have to learn by our mistakes.'

I turned back to De Griese. 'Van Hoebeek was in your way, wasn't he? A merchant who would not bow to your pressure. You wanted him out of the way to exploit his business.'

'Did I?'

'I think you did.'

'Then you think wrong. I've already told you he was not a problem — to me.'

We stared at each other, him confident, me not believing a word he said.

Jarmin stepped forward. 'That will do for now, Richard. I'll allow you time with him later, when I have finished with him.'

I nodded acceptance then turned away.

'Take him outside,' Jarmin ordered to the men flanking De Griese. 'Put him with the others.'

I took a deep breath, then sighed.

'Frustrating, isn't it?' said Jarmin, once De Griese had left the barn. 'He knows more than he's saying, that is for certain. I will keep your problem in mind when I have words later.'

'Thank you,' I replied, a little dismayed.

Jarmin turned to Bram who had found a crate and sat, resting his legs. 'I have a feeling, Henry. You've been quiet and you have that look on your face.'

'Our friend there, De Griese. That is not his name.'

'You know this for certain? What is it then?'

Bram smiled. 'His name is, and I will see if I can get it right, Juan Francisco de Guzmen Robles. An aide, or he was, to the Spanish Ambassador in France. Ostensibly a translator, he had other duties too, shall we say. As you know, I spent a little time there,' he said, enigmatically.

Jarmin shot me a look. 'We will not dwell on that, Henry. You know him, which is enough for me.'

'He does not know you?' I asked, wondering how that could not be so.

Bram shook his head. 'I believe he does not. He was just a lowly aid then, though he has excellent language skills.'

Jarmin forced a cough, indicating that I should desist from enquiring further.

Fulton helped Blake to his feet, his injury making standing difficult. Then he walked slowly, as if a bent old man, weighed down after years of toil.

Outside, I took a breath of air and surveyed the collection, albeit small, of smugglers. All now bound, some seven of them, including De Griese, sitting in the yard surrounded by the militia who preened themselves following the success. The felons looked dejected, their heads bowed, all except for De Griese who sat with the smirk still on his face.

Fulton went to speak with Monk to send him on his way for the transport. Within minutes Monk had found a horse and hurried out of the yard. I felt at a loose end and so strolled around, looking into the barns and sheds, amazed at the amount of contraband contained within them. Jarmin began to organise the militia; the farm would need guarding until all the contraband was removed. I began to wonder how much of it would be lost into purses and pockets, for the temptation would be too great not to take the opportunity, especially at night.

Fulton sat on the edge of a trough to take his ease, so I joined him. 'What will happen to them?' I asked, nodding towards the prisoners.

He grinned. 'Like as not they'll be decorating Tyburn tree soon enough; can't see any judge letting 'em off lightly, not with this amount of stuff. Reckon His Grace will demand the fullest of penalties and let's face it, a judge will not go against him.'

The sigh left my body almost involuntarily. The aftermath of the raid had left me with a strange deflated feeling. I stretched out my legs and looked again at the sullen prisoners, still hunched over, probably aware of the fate destined to be theirs; Jaggers and the three dead men may be the lucky ones.

A militiaman began to bate the prisoners, calling them bottle-headed clunches, codsheads, by-blows, stall-whimpers and every insult he could think of. Most ignored the tirade but a couple did look up and one spat on the mud and then sneered.

My mind continued to work, sifting, filtering tiny bits of information that lay dormant at the back of my head and I desperately tried to bring it out as I stared at the prisoners.

And then things began to become ordered, shining a light in the direction I needed to travel. I felt a frisson of excitement and I wanted to slap myself on the head for being so blind, ignorant and narrow-minded. The answer to who killed Pieter van Hoebeek came at me in a rush. I needed but one thing to confirm it all.

I stood up abruptly and walked over to Jarmin. 'Do you still need me?' I asked, interrupting his conversation with Bram.

He shook his head. 'Not if you have somewhere to go.'

'I do,' I replied, feeling the smile come to my lips. 'Tell me, the ledgers from the brothel and hospital, where are they?'

'With His Grace. He intends to make use of them.'

'Ah, no matter. I'll leave now; I have something to do and it cannot wait any longer.'

I hurried back to Vauxhall to take a wherry which should prove quicker than borrowing a horse and taking the bridge, as always when I am in a hurry, that edifice seemed to conspire against me and I did not want to take the risk.

Fortunately, I did not have to wait long for a boat and I hardly even noticed the swell of the river as the wherryman plied his oars. I kept going over the facts, ordering them anew until the boat pulled up at the jetty and I nodded to myself, more certain than ever.

The hackney conveyed me home where I hoped Ned would be, and sober, thinking I might need his assistance. I also needed to check on something in my study.

I need not have worried as Mary had him suitably employed waxing the upstairs floors; needless to say, my appearance pleased him no end.

'That woman has no mercy, sir,' he said, looking towards the kitchen. 'Ever since I got here this morning it's been Ned do this, Ned do that; I haven't stopped.'

'Well, you have now,' I replied, mildly amused at his protest. 'We will pick up Kitty on our way,' I added, as Mary appeared. I could see she wanted to say something so I stalled her with my upraised hand. 'No time, Mary.'

Ned flashed her a grin as we went through the door.

As we progressed, I apprised him of events at Stockwell, Jaggers demise and De Griese's arrest and the revelation that he is a Spanish Intelligencer probably working for the state to undermine our country's ability to fund the war.

Kitty, Ned informed me, intended to be in Covent Garden at her stall, so I waited in Henrietta Street with the hackney while he went in to collect her. Several minutes passed and I began to suspect she had gone somewhere else and we would have to proceed without her when the two of them came hurrying around the corner.

She climbed in and the light in her eyes clearly showed her excitement and anticipation. 'I've left the stall with Alex. Ned just told me, I just hope you're right, Richard,' she said, settling down next to me and grabbing my hand tightly.

'We will know soon enough,' I replied, as we set off again.

The journey seemed to take forever and again, for her benefit, I related events at Stockwell. Unlike Ned, her concern centred on any danger I might have encountered rather than that the smuggling gang had been discovered.

Eventually, despite the traffic, we arrived at our destination, alighting just down the street so as not to signal our arrival.

'Give me fifteen minutes. If I'm not out by then do what you can to gain entry, even if it means forcing the door. You have that pistol loaded?' I asked Ned.

He grinned and nodded. 'Of course, sir. Fifteen minutes it is, unless we hear to the contrary.'

I began to walk and then Kitty grabbed my arm. 'Take care, Richard. Be careful,' she said, giving me a wan smile.

Taking a deep breath, I knocked upon the door, feeling confident that I had come to the correct conclusion. I just hoped that nothing would go wrong.

The door opened; the servant looked down disdainfully at me, waiting for me to announce myself, to enquire.

'I wish to see the lady of the house. My name is Richard Hopgood,' I said, outwardly relaxed. I gave a smile, impressing him not one bit.

'I will see if she is at leisure to see you, sir. One moment, if you please,' he said, before closing the door and leaving me outside.

Looking down the street, I could see Ned and Kitty gazing towards me, both of their faces serious and determined and I admit I felt reassured by their close presence. I gave them a brief nod, then returned my attention to the door, waiting for it to open.

I stepped back, looked up, adjusted my jacket and then my hat. I took a breath and then pursed my lips and finally, I heard the faint sound of footsteps coming from inside. The door opened and the servant allowed me into the hall.

I had fifteen minutes.

The servant walked ahead of me, up the stairs and into the drawing room.

'The lady will be with you shortly, sir,' he said, stepping back and closing the door.

I walked over to the window and looked out before turning and moving towards the hearth, a small fire glowing in the grate. I tapped my foot and controlled my breathing until the door opened silently and she came in, gliding across the floor, a seductive expression on her face.

'Mr Hopgood, a pleasure to see you,' she said, smiling.

'Miss Visser,' I replied, giving a slight bow of my head.

She wore a green silk gown, very low cut with her breasts

struggling to stay constrained within the fabric. Looking intently at me, she teased the locks of her long hair with her hand, her tongue caressing her lips, slowly, moistening them in preparation. 'I knew you could not keep away for long,' she said, coming towards me and placing a hand upon my chest. 'Now you are here we shall have to amuse ourselves, shall we not?' she said, her top teeth placed coyly on her lip, a slight smile appearing.

She did not know about her husband's death, I surmised, looking at her. I *hoped* she did not know about her husband's death.

'Miss Visser, I think you may have misconstrued my presence here.'

'Really? I summoned you, you have come. Are you not flesh and blood, Mr Hopgood, Richard? You are a man and I saw your desire in those eyes of yours.'

'You are not unattractive, Miss Visser,' I conceded. 'Were it not for Pieter van Hoebeek, I may have been more susceptible to your undoubted charms.'

I saw a hard look cross her eyes for just a moment. 'Pieter, what do you mean?'

'You killed him, Miss Visser. You put that knife into his chest.'

She turned away sharply. 'Me? Preposterous. I did no such thing. A footpad, a thief must have done it.'

'No, it was you,' I countered.

She took a breath and then twisted her head around to look at me. All her seductive expressions had gone; she now showed a hard face, fierce, angry, vicious even. 'I am appalled by your accusation, sir.'

'No accusation. You killed Pieter.'

'He was a friend.'

'He may well have been once, Miss Visser. But you wanted him gone.'

She shook her head, vehemently. In denial, frustration, guilt?

'You lied about seeing him recently, you met him at his warehouse. This last time, he unlocked the door for you and waited, came towards you as you entered, met you in the middle of the floor, I should imagine. You took the knife you had hidden and stabbed him. The angle of the wound meant that it came from a person short in stature, like yourself; an upright thrust. You did that. He staggered back, shocked at what you had done. He bled to death as you just turned around and walked out. No remorse?'

'No,' she replied, denying. 'Why would I do that?'

'Did Martijn ask you to do it?'

'Martijn?'

'Martijn Thyssen, your current lover, or one of them.'

She opened her mouth, her lips moving, her voice mute, just staring at me.

'I saw you at Pieter's funeral. I saw how you approached Martijn, how you touched him. You did not touch him in the manner of a casual acquaintance; I saw an intimate touch, a lover's touch.'

She took a hesitant step back and her legs met the chair; she sat, her hands bunched into tight fists.

'I think there are two strands to all this. Pieter did not want to know about the smuggling with Jaggers, spurning that offer and staying with Janssen. Martijn heard about it and spoke to you. You tried to persuade him and so did Martijn, all to no avail. You and Martijn came up with the idea of removing Pieter because of the money to be made from the illegal contraband.

'Around the same time, Pieter had the argument in the street with your husband, learning about a darker side of you. I do not think he believed it and so confronted you. You denied it, of course, but it would not go away, it lay there at the back of his mind and he kept bringing it up. So another reason to remove Pieter. You killed him, was Martijn too weak to do it for you?'

She looked at me, wide-eyed in shock.

'Oh, yes, I know about your dark side. You sent me the note, the same hand as that found on Pieter. "I Will come" you had written, matching the script of the one you sent to me, nearly the same words. "You will come." I thought when I saw the ledgers that the writing seemed familiar. Your husband told me the truth before he blew his brains out.'

'What?' she exclaimed.

'Your husband is dead. I shot him. The wound festered and when we found him last night he denounced you as a depraved whore, before putting his pistol into his mouth and pulling the trigger. He hated you, you know.'

'No!'

'You wrote in the ledgers in Maid Lane, did you not? The proof that you were complicit in the hospital and sampling the wares.

'You had already begun the next stage by getting Martijn to court Femke. She would do what you said as you knew how to manipulate her, how to blackmail her if necessary, her sapphism being her weakness. Martijn would marry Femke and take control of the merchants. What happens next? With Pieter now out of the way, Martijn would have easy access to the money. What further plans have you made?'

She had her head in her hands now, sobbing. 'No,' she wailed, denying it. 'Martijn,' she screamed.

I heard a door slamming and as I reached into my jacket for my pistol the door was wrenched open and Martijn Thyssen stood there, breathing hard, a pistol in his hand.

'He knows it all,' cried Cornelia Visser. 'Everything.'

Thyssen stared at me, his face full of fury. 'You're wrong, Cornelia. Not knows — knew.'

I saw his finger tremble on the trigger.

'Do not, Martijn,' I said, displaying the calm I did not feel. 'You won't live long enough to regret it.'

He pulled the trigger.

I saw the hammer slam down and heard it strike the pan and I felt my bowels twitch. Somehow, I managed to keep control, holding my breath, expecting to feel pain. Instead, there came nothing; the thing had misfired.

All the moisture had gone from my mouth, my breathing would not begin and I knew that if it had not been for fortune then I would be on the floor, bleeding my lifeblood away. Somehow, I managed to take a breath and as I did so, I brought up and levelled my pistol, the sweat on my hand making my grip precarious but I would not allow it to slip. I took half a second to close my eyes and send up a prayer of thanks to whatever deity intervened just as I heard a gunshot from downstairs and then a door being kicked in, feet shortly after pounding up the stairs, Ned yelling, Kitty shouting.

Thyssen turned as they came onto the landing then he stepped inside, waving the useless pistol in their direction. Cornelia Visser fixed her gaze on Thyssen.

Ned warily looked at the weapon in Thyssen's hand.

'It's not working,' I informed him, amazed that I could speak. 'A misfire.'

Thyssen's face showed consternation; he could not understand how things had gone so catastrophically wrong. He gazed at the weapon and then threw it against the wall; a final act of indignation, regret and anger that their endeavours had been discovered.

Kitty eased past Ned and rushed over to me, avoiding blocking my aim. 'Are you hurt, Richard,' she asked, touching my arm, concern in the tone. 'You could have been killed.'

'But I wasn't, Kitty. I am fine. Truly I am.' I replied, as calmly as I could as I patted her arm with my free hand. I had no wish to show her how close I had become to soiling my breeches.

Cornelia Visser now just stared at me, tangible evil emanating from her, no doubt blaming me for her misfortune.

What she had planned to do next, I had no idea. Perhaps Femke would be the next to die, and then to get her hands on the merchant's, would it have been her lover, Martijn? Who would know with such a mind, warped as hers must be?

It was strange that none of the servants had come to the aid of their mistress.

EPILOGUE

Femke van Hoebeek put a hand to her breast as the other flailed behind, seeking the arm of her chair. Eventually, she found it and guided herself slowly down into a sitting position. Her face, which only moments ago appeared fresh and rosy, now appeared pale, her eyes wide and her mouth slack. She stared at me in disbelief, her world turned upside down.

I had come straight from the magistrate's court following Cornelia Visser and Martijn Thyssen's remand to Newgate to await trial. The two of them had spent the night in the watch-house and when I collected them first thing in the morning both had suffered, being dishevelled from sharing the room with drunkards, whores and rogues. I had no sympathy whatsoever.

'I cannot believe it,' she said, shaking her head after I had told all I knew. 'Cornelia is my oldest friend, my…'

'I know,' I replied. 'I know of your relationship with her and I know that she urged you to accept Thyssen as a husband. She has kept her warped mind hidden from you. Unfortunately, you are as much a victim as your brother. Sometimes you just cannot know what is in the heart of those closest to you.'

'So what am I to do?' she asked, her hand screwed up in a

fist, gripping the empty air.

'That is something you must decide,' I said, not unsympathetically. 'I suggest you speak to someone you can trust; Ruud Janssen maybe. He may well be able to offer assistance to keep your business going.'

I saw her hand relax a little. 'Ruud? Yes, yes, I will send him a note.' She looked at me again. 'Ruud has also proposed marriage, Mr Hopgood. Perhaps I may accept.'

'You will do what you think is best. Whatever you decide, I suggest you take your time to think through everything; what you want and what you can give.'

She nodded. 'Yes, you are right, Mr Hopgood. This revelation has been such a shock to me. I cannot think clearly at the moment.'

I took a few steps to the door. 'I will send an account to you of my expenses shortly. I will leave you now to reconcile what I have told you. You wish me to call a servant for you?'

'No,' she replied, now looking forlornly into her lap. 'Perhaps I need some time on my own.'

I left her, feeling sympathy for her as I thought her hard nature was a front to protect her from the travails of life, to protect her vulnerability. Maybe Janssen is already aware of who she is and will make adjustment. Their marriage would not be the first of that kind. I could only hope that should it go ahead she would find some happiness in it, as would he.'

Sometimes I wonder whether Jarmin ever slept or even if he had a life outside of the department. I arrived at Westminster to find him at his desk, scribbling away.

'Reports for His Grace,' he said, as I sat down. 'A never-ending task. Did you make a successful conclusion after you left yesterday?'

'I did,' I said, leaning back in the chair. 'Cornelia Visser murdered Pieter van Hoebeek. Martijn Thyssen assisted her. This Thyssen is also involved with De Griese, or Robles as Bram called him. I had them up at the magistrates this morning for the murder and they will enjoy a little time in Newgate to await trial. What will happen now with De Griese?'

'Congratulations for catching your murderer, Richard. I must say, your investigation opened up a box full of serpents.' He lay his quill down and rubbed his face with his hand. 'De Griese will be kept in isolation for a time. He will likely end up returning to Spain in exchange for certain people whom we wish to be returned here — not before we get what we can from him. He's a clever fellow, I'll give him that.'

'And the rest?'

He laughed. 'The rest? Well, those four, er… young gentlemen; Cannard, Sommerville, Balton and Ransom will be rounded up today. I have no doubt that they will not be pleased with their immediate futures; their accommodation has already been arranged. Newgate, as it happens, so they may well share a room with your murderers. Whether they knew what they were getting into or not, we will discover later. I have ordered that they are to receive no privileges when they take up their accommodation.'

'I am sure they will enjoy that,' I replied, seeing the squalor in my mind and how they might appreciate it.

'The men at Stockwell will no doubt feel the rope about their necks; they have no excuse, just pure greed. At least we have put a stop to it now. The market will not be swamped with smuggled goods and the economy will have a chance to generate money for the war effort. The seized goods will be taken to a warehouse to be sold off at market prices and the estimate of what is there will please His Grace no end.'

'And the Hawkhurst Gang?'

'Will carry on as before. The revenue will deal with them as and when they can. I am not entirely happy with that but my hands are tied. Bram, I believe, explained that on your way to Rye.'

I nodded. 'He did; I still do not rightly know why they should continue.'

'You and me both, Richard; the powers that be dictate what we do and do not do. I suspect they are partial to a little piece of contraband every now and again themselves.'

I had no other option other than to accept that. The Hawkhurst Gang are violent criminals and will continue to be so, albeit not on the same scale — until when exactly? I felt my head shaking as I thought of Ellen and her townspeople in thrall to the smugglers. I was not naive; I realised that the trade would continue with or without Arthur Grey, it just seemed to me a missed opportunity to do something about them.

'What of Maid Lane and Joyners Street?' I asked, hoping to hear some good news regarding all that.

'Ah… I have been avoiding speaking to you about that. You may be a little disappointed.'

'How so?'

'Well...'

'What?' exclaimed Kitty, as I repeated what Jarmin had told me.

We sat in the White Hart in our normal booth at the rear of the tavern. Kitty, Ned, Little Alex and I. We drank our ale and nibbled on some bread and cheese as I went over the events of the day, leaving the unsavoury item until last.

'One case of keeping a disorderly house, resulting in a fine. One case of buggery and one of assault with intent to commit buggery; no other charges relating to the Joyners Street brothel. They will go to the Old Bailey as it could result in Tyburn if they are found guilty. The girls all stated that they were over the age of ten and it cannot be proven otherwise. For them, they had food, a bed and received a little money now and again with some of the customers even giving them gifts. Do not forget that for them, to entertain men, was normal and they are too young to know how they have been exploited. The charges of buggery and intent have come about because they were caught in the act and the men do not have the influence to negotiate. The other men do have the influence, it is sad to say, so they will not trouble the courts further, the magistrate dismissing those cases as insufficient evidence.

'Most of the men listed in the ledgers have been taken into custody and the hospital in Maid Lane will be closed down. The magistrate did believe Toby and Belle, deferring the case of Thornton and two more to the Old Bailey again. Most of the children there are too young to give evidence so much of the abuse there will largely go unpunished. Judge Ravely, caught with a boy, will go unpunished, apart from being forced to resign; Lord Pannod will not face charges either, the

Mayor being particularly livid on those accounts. One of the ten men running Maid Lane has taken his life, following receipt of a warning; the solicitor, McCreedy. There is a caveat to all this; His Grace, the Duke of Newcastle has the ledgers and the notes from both places with the names of all those connected to them. He will be using that to his advantage, in the coming weeks and months and probably years, should they not get prosecuted.'

'That is awful,' said Kitty. 'What has happened to those children?'

'Well, some, the youngest, have been sent to homes across the city. Most, the older ones, have been sent into the streets, old enough to look after themselves. I think we know how that will end.'

Kitty looked down and shook her head forlornly. 'It's unfair; those poor mites.'

'There's little justice for the young,' said Ned, putting down his pot. 'Whores and villains will be the end result.'

'Nuffing wrong wiv being a villain,' piped up Alex. 'Wot do you think I were doing before all this?'

'No doubt destined for Tyburn,' said Ned, reaching over and ruffling his hair.

'But we finished what we set out to do,' I said, gazing at them. 'We found a murderer and we put an end to a children's brothel and the hospital that supplied it. We uncovered a plot to ruin London by using smuggled contraband, ran,' and I leant forward to keep my voice low, 'by a Spanish intelligencer. We should really be congratulating ourselves, not staring into our pots as if the world had ended.'

Kitty put her arm through mine and pressed close, her

head upon my shoulder. 'That is true, we should be; I would if it wasn't for the children, I can't help feeling sad for them. They are tainted by all that happened to them, their innocence taken; their lives may even be ruined by what they suffered.'

'And tainted and ruined will be the men involved. Newssheets and Gazettes will print names from the trials; if some do not suffer from the law then they will suffer in other ways.'

'I suppose so, though it doesn't go far enough for my liking.'

'I agree with you; we can only do what we can do, it is now up to the law, for what it is worth.'

Kitty sighed, then sat forward to take a drink. 'Sometimes, I don't like this city.'

'But other times you do,' I replied, also taking a drink. 'We just have to be hopeful that things change, for the better, in the years to come.'

'Some hope,' said Ned, with a derisory sniff.

'In the meantime, we just get on with things,' I said, giving a wry grin.

Ned drained his pot and thumped it down on the table. 'Does "getting on with things," mean that we should have another ale?'

This time I sighed, slowly shook my head, then waved my hand for the pot-girl to come over.

Later, I might have time to think on the last few days, what they have done to me, on the things that happened and the feelings I discovered. Feeling Kitty pressing against me brought me back to reality and I knew I should be thankful, even if I did leave a little bit of me behind in a small seaside town on the Sussex coast.

end

If you enjoyed this novel, then please consider leaving a review or a rating.
I would very much appreciate it.

A Small Matter of Importance is a work of fiction. It is set in London in 1741 with some of the characters within the novel being real people. I have made assumptions about the characters of those people according to my research. The Devil's Tavern, Wapping, is now The Prospect of Whitby, a pub well worth a visit. I apologise for any mistakes or errors, which are entirely my own.

In order to write this historical novel, I have poured over numerous books and used many online resources. The following is a list of the main resources I used.

Locating London's Past- John Rocque's 1746 online map of London.
Blackguardiana: or a dictionary of rogues-HathiTrust digital library.
The Gentleman's Magazine v11 1741- HathiTrust digital library.
The Chronicles of Newgate by Arthur Griffiths (Project Gutenberg)
The Old Bailey online
British History online
Smugglers' Britain - Smuggling.co.uk
The Smugglers by Charles G Harper – Gutenberg.org
London in the Eighteenth Century by Jerry White
London, the Biography by Peter Ackroyd
Georgian London, into the streets by Lucy Inglis
Various essays of Rictor Norton

The National Archives, online
Hastings Independent Press, online
Rye, westsussex.gov - online

ABOUT THE AUTHOR

Clive Ridgway spent many years as a paramedic, until deciding that there must be another way of earning a living. Can be regularly found shooting arrows at his local archery club. He lives in Bedfordshire in the UK with his wife, son, and dogs.

Please visit my website
www.cliveridgway.com

Printed in Great Britain
by Amazon